Alpha Tribe

Book Two of the Fahr Trilogy

T.K. Boomer

Alpha Tribe

ISBN 978-0-9951667-3-8

Dedication

During the writing of this book, I had three author friends pass away, each one younger than I. This is for Kevin Quast, Robin Young and Debra Fieguth and for the words they left unwritten.

Author's Notes

"Alpha Tribe" is the second book in **The Fahr Trilogy**, the sequel to 2016's "Planet Song". The books share a single narrative line and should be read in order. I have reduced the price of "Planet Song" for this reason.

The following appendices are in the back of the book.

Appendix A This is a short summary of "Planet Song", first book in "The Fahr Trilogy".

Appendix B This contains a brief explanation of all things "Fahr" including a description.

Appendix C. This is an alphabetical list of all the significant characters in The Fahr Trilogy.

T.K. Boomer

Act Six: The Aftermath

Silence

Andreas fell, secured to the co-pilot's chair and fingers rammed into both ears. The aircraft disintegrated around him, but the pain in his ears was so intense that focusing on anything else was impossible. He closed his eyes.

Eardrums screamed. Pulsed. Screamed again. Pounded.

His eyes flew open in time to watch himself hit the water. The chair took most of the impact, but he had no air in his lungs. Bubbles, some huge and others as minute as sparks of light, raced by in the opposite direction. The cold rasped every inch of his skin, sending a huge shock wave straight to his empty lungs. His hand found the clasp on the seat belt. He swam for the surface and gasped for air when he found it.

Around him the pieces of the aircraft sank. Given the carnage, it made no sense he survived. His inner ears pulsed with pain. He could hear nothing, and if he didn't get out of the ocean soon, hypothermia would make his survival redundant.

He looked up. Metal blades, like those of a giant lens aperture, retracted the opening of the alien ship. Behind these blades the water was visible and concave, some unseen force pulling on it from deep within the ship. Not a single drop fell. He shivered. The blades made slow and steady progress toward closing the hole, now down to about eighty percent of its original size. Once this was closed what would the ship do? Leave? And if it left, how would it leave? Just fly away, going to another destination on the planet or return to space? The latter scenario would require enough thrust to escape the Earth's gravity. He did not want to be anywhere in the vicinity if that happened.

An island sat in the ocean a few hundred yards away. Shelter? Hypothermia sapped at his energy and stiffened his limbs, but he kicked toward it, hoping to get there before the cold got him.

Andreas staggered onto the island's pebbly beach, shivering uncontrollably. The swim had been surreal, no sound of splashing water, gull cries or even his own labored breathing. Just a constant pulsing pain in his ears. Now even this had stopped. Complete isola-tion. Behind him the alien ship, a giant piece of burnt toast, hovered over the water. He could no longer see the remains of the B-25 or any sign of its crew members. Where were Jeff, Reb or the Major? In his panic, he'd forgotten them, as if he hadn't just spent the most traumatic three hours of his life in their company.

A dozen harbor seal pups eyed him. He could see them calling out. Andreas had never heard a seal pup call, wondering what it would sound like and what would happen to them if the Fahr ship were to launch? He looked up and down the beach in case any of the others had made the same swim, shook his head and climbed the sandy hill toward the island's interior.

He discovered a miniature temperate rain forest, dense and hard going. Andreas longed to hear the bird song he knew would be there but heard nothing, not even the crunch of his own footfalls. Instead he noticed how everything smelled, the loamy mossy odor of the forest floor, pine needles, guano, kelp, and salt spray. When he fought his way through the forest to the island's other side, he found a steep cliff face. He scrambled part way down to the entrance of a large cave. The floor had a collection of driftwood and large clam shells. *Perfect*.

The cave was elevated enough to make it unlikely the drift-wood had washed in during high tide. He bent down and took a pinch of soot from the floor—the faint remains of a hearth. The shells were intact, harvested at low tide. *Some other castaway,* he thought. *Eventually rescued,* he hoped. It occurred to Andreas that he wouldn't hear or see the launch, so unless it generated seismic activity that felt different from the waves pounding against the cliff face, he wouldn't know. And would he recognize the event even if he felt it? He looked at his watch and shook it before remembering electronics no longer worked. He would wait until dawn.

One chunk of driftwood sat in the center of the cave, larger than the others and with a sofa-like appearance, perhaps placed there as furniture. The surface was like an irregular park bench, hard and unyielding but comfortable enough long as one didn't attempt sleep. Andreas didn't think he would be doing that.

He scratched his stubbly chin and ran fingers through ragged hair. He'd done a quick hack job with a pair of scissors in a public washroom off the Coquihalla Highway. Rather than looking like an aging hippy, he now took on the appearance of an ancient punk rocker. It wasn't much of a disguise, but Jeff hadn't recognized him so that was good. His clothes had dried, and he'd stopped shivering, but there was still the cold northern night to come. *A silent night,* he thought, remembering the old hymn. He sang the original German lyrics, hoping to hear the reverberations off the cave walls, but it was, indeed, a silent night.

Lift Off

Kale lay on the floor of the Zodiac. The aliens could only see him if they were looking from above, but it wasn't as if he could hide. The boat was bright yellow against a blue green sea. Perhaps they would see the boat and not realize it had an occupant. He breathed deeply hoping to gain control and stop shaking. After a few minutes, he calmed enough to study the dome above him. The support structures appeared web-like as if some giant spider had spun them and filled in the spaces between with sprayed-on gray insulation. A cloud-like presence that glowed an ambient yellowish color, shimmered below the dome with no obvious source. Half a dozen gulls, in panicked flight, flew in and out of the fog, their cries and wing flutters echoing off the dome. The birds had been sucked into an alien ship along with several cubic miles of Pacific Ocean and like him, were not the intended targets. *The humpbacks. It had to be the humpbacks. Why else would the aliens collect so much water?*

One gull wore the brown plumage of a younger bird. Kale sat up higher to get a better view; hiding was pointless anyway. As he watched, the bird tired and looked for a solid place to rest. It landed on a humpback, but the animal submerged. The young gull took to the air again, this time heading for the edge of the dome. It tried to set down on something pillow-like attached to the wall. A ring of these objects stretched all along the water line. After several attempts to find footing the bird took to the air again, this time deciding to settle on the water.

The arch of the dome wasn't 180 degrees like the ocean horizon, more like 100 degrees. Whatever this enclosure was, it contained more seawater than air, an aquatic habitat for the humpbacks and other creatures sucked into the massive alien ship. The air was still, which explained the gulls constant flapping. No thermals to ride on. By now all the birds were resting on the water's surface.

He noticed one of the Zodiac's lost paddles drifting within arm's reach of the boat. He grabbed it. A weapon and a means of propulsion. Time to investigate the ring of objects at the water line. Time to find a way out.

At first Kale thought they were stromatolites, like the ones he'd seen while vacationing at Shark's Bay on the coast of Western Australia. As he drew closer, he realized these structures were much too big to be stromatolites and were mostly submerged. These were large sponges. He reached out to one. His finger sank in as if he were touching the sponge equivalent of quick sand. No wonder the young gull could not find footing.

He paddled along the ring of sponges. There were minor variations in each one but also uniformity in size. These were cultured, put in place. No gaps between them, no obvious exit at least not along the water line. If there was a way out it was at the bottom of an enclosure deep enough for humpback whales and well beyond his free diving skills. He would not get out that way.

Kale turned his attention back to the sponges. *What was their purpose?* He reached out, poking one again. The sponge stiffened, becoming more resistant to his finger. The next sponge reacted the same way.

The Zodiac vibrated. He looked down. The surrounding water was agitated, as if caught in a downpour, but there was no rain. The ship trumped out a deep roar. Gulls took flight and whales submerged. The air seemed to lack oxygen, his deepest breaths gasping for nothing. His heart pounded.

The sponges pushed into the side of the Zodiac. More sprang from the water around the boat and pressed into it. Kale fell back, landing on his backside in the center of the boat. Beneath him the middle of the Zodiac's soft floor folded, trapping Kale in a clam-like embrace. He resisted with all the strength his weakened arm would allow, but he was immobilized at the boat's center. A quick look around told him the whales were suffering the same fate, secured and held in place at the water line by giant sponges. The roar increased, and he felt movement like being in giant elevator. His breath came back. He screamed.

Honi

Everything happened at once. The first thing Honi noticed was the death of her computer; it fizzled like frying bacon, but then so did she. Honi fizzled or at least tingled at the same time as the computer shut down. Gone also were the motorized functions of her wheelchair, her respirator, the lighting in the house. After a few moments, Honi realized she could no longer hear the quiet hummings of the air conditioning unit or refrigerator. She now breathed in tiny little gasps.

Her father, Peni, was frantic. He had done due diligence by making sure they had an oxygen tank in case her respirator failed, but this too had an electronic component to it, a gauge to control the flow of the gas. It had met the same fate as her wheelchair, respirator, and computer. He had to get the gauge off the tank, but it was attached by a powerful sealant. So far it was resisting his efforts to remove it with a pair of pliers.

"Hand me the crescent wrench," he said to Noelani, Honi's mother.

Noelani passed him the larger tool. "Go easy," she said. "You don't want to create a spark. It is oxygen, you know."

"Honi can't breathe," Peni sputtered.

"She can breathe, just not well. Take your time. It's better you don't damage the tank."

Honi looked at her mother. Noelani wore her usual loose floral dress and was passive by nature, a person who reacted rather than acted. Her reactions were good ones though, thought out and reasonable. She was a calming influence in any situation.

Her father's balding head glistened as he adjusted the wrench. He gave it a little tug and heard a slight hiss.

"OK, now turn off the main valve before you go any further," her mother said.

"I know what I'm doing," Peni said, turning the valve.

The oxygen mask was attached to the gauge and designed to work in sync with it. Her father removed the hose, a thin clear tube like those used in aquarium setups. The gauge's nozzle was smaller than the one from the tank. He stared at it. Noelani reached out, took the mask out of his hand, and rammed the end of a pen into the tube. This action widened the end of it. She handed it back to her husband.

"There, try that," she said.

Peni fit the hose over the tank's valve. It held tight. He put the mask over Honi's mouth and turned the valve in tiny increments.

Honi's breathing slowed, and she felt the light-headedness pass. It wasn't the first time she'd had to do without her respirator, and she had learned to calm herself as best she could when the option of taking deep breaths was not available. Her father, however, always overreacted.

"We'll have to go to Big Island Medical and get another tank," he said to Honi's mother.

"It's a long walk," Noelani said.

Peni nodded. "Still..."

"I wish I knew what was going on," her mother said.

"My chair doesn't work, or my computer or the respirator. We have no electricity, can't use our cell phones, and the car won't start." Honi looked thoughtful. "You guys are old enough to remember the Starfish Prime nuclear test, right?"

Noelani laughed. "That was several years before I was born! Your dad might remember though."

Peni shrugged. "I was four years old. You don't remember much when you're that young."

Honi took a shallower breath, reminding herself that she was now on pure oxygen. "They set off this nuclear atmospheric test blast a thousand miles away from here, and from that distance, it knocked out about three hundred Hawaiian street lamps. Some electronic pulse or something burned out the circuitry."

"So?"

"Well, at the time those street lamps were high tech. They contained modern style circuit boards, and that's what made them vulnerable. Now everything has a circuit board."

"You think this was an atomic bomb?"

"Nothing works, Dad."

"Well, we won't find out anything if we stay here, that's for sure. And we will need more oxygen. Maybe two tanks to be safe. Who knows how long this will last."

"How are you going to carry two tanks?" Noelani said.

"I'll take the wheelbarrow."

"You're going to push the wheelbarrow all the way into town?"

"You have a better idea?"

"No. But, if you're going, stop by the hospital. They have a backup generator, I think. See if they have room. We can't keep Honi here if there's no electricity."

"Jesus, Mom, I hate that place!"

Noelani laid her hand on Honi's shoulder. "I know," she said.

Command Centre

President Maria Alatorre ran her fingers through her short curly hair, took a deep breath and exhaled. She couldn't see anything but the vaguest outlines of the men in front of her as they walked in darkness. She wasn't even sure she was seeing so much as hearing and feeling them. They stayed close in a tight little cadre around her, smelling like they all used the same aftershave. *Secret service issue?* she wondered. Odd the things one thinks about when stressed. Her left foot slipped, and Maria silently cursed the stilettos she was wearing.

"What the hell is happening with the lights down here?" she demanded of the secret service agent walking in front of her.

"Nothing is working, Madam President," the man replied.

"Nothing? Not even the emergency lighting systems?"

"If it has a circuit board of any type it's not working, Madam President. That includes the emergency lighting systems, landlines, flashlights, cell phones, anything using a battery. On the next level, we will have candles and propane lamps."

"If you have propane lamps on the next level, then send someone to fetch one," Gerald Garneau said. Alatorre could hear the impatience in her chief of staff's voice.

"They're still looking for the propane, sir."

8

"Looking for it?"

"Yes, Sir. By candlelight, sir."

"They're searching for flammable gas using an open flame?"

"The gas will be in a tank, sir."

Alatorre shook her head.

"Then get us some candles," Garneau said.

"We're almost there, sir. Just around the corner."

"What corner?"

"Here, sir."

The secret service agent came to an abrupt stop right in front of Alatorre. She stumbled into him and fell.

"Madam President! Are you all right?"

There was a quick flash and Alatorre found herself staring up at a lighted match. "I'm fine," she said while getting to her feet. "I don't suppose you could have brought that little item out earlier?"

"I'm sorry, Madam President. I'd forgotten I had them until just now."

Alatorre looked at Garneau and shook her head. Her feeling of security, always transient at the best of times, took a serious hit.

The agent dropped the match and lit another. He held it up as he walked around the corner. The others followed. Alatorre listened to the footsteps behind her, now echoing in the wider hallway. She'd almost forgotten about the other agents in their party—they'd been so quiet. Another match dropped and another lit. Ahead of her Alatorre could just make out the outlines of a large door. The agent walked up to it and knocked. A security window slid open, and the agent held up the match to illuminate Alatorre's face. The door opened to the Presidential Emergency Operation Center. *This is what passes for security under these circumstances,* Alatorre thought. She was not reassured.

Inside the room, Coleman lamps were giving a soft wavering illumination. There were multiple large black slabs on two of the four walls. Dead computer monitors. Input devices of various types littered the large table in the center of the room, every bit as inert as the monitors. Around these swarmed frustrated technicians in civilian and military garb. Soldiers, armed with semi-automatic rifles, stood alert against the two empty walls.

"I guess this is what passes for a command center," Garneau said.

"I guess," Alatorre said. People were now just realizing who had just entered the space. It was by far the least grand entrance she had ever made as President. A three-star general walked toward her from the other side of the room.

"Who is this?" she whispered to Garneau.

"General Comry. He's in charge of this…"

"General Comry," she said and extended her hand.

"Madam President," he said, taking her hand. "I'm so glad you're safe." He gestured to the room. "I'm sorry, we're dealing with some technical difficulties…"

"I suspect the entire planet is dealing with the same technical difficulties, General."

Comry seemed surprised at this. "Oh? Have you heard from other governments, Madam President?"

"No, and I doubt you have either. Am I correct?"

He nodded. "Communications was the first thing to go. Then the power, then the electronics…"

"Does anything work down here?"

The General shook his head. "It can't be an electromagnetic pulse," he said. "We're far too deep for EMP penetration. How would it get through?"

Alatorre studied him. "Consider the source, General. We have no idea what we're dealing with here. If it's not an EMP, then it certainly acts like one or at least like an advanced version of one."

"So, you think it's…"

"Far too many things have happened to make me think otherwise. And as strange an explanation as it may seem, I think it's also the most obvious. We were told to unite, we didn't, that huge ship appears out of nowhere, and now this."

"Then I think we should…"

"Do what, General? Attack them? It will be damn difficult to coordinate a response if we can't talk to each other."

"We don't know the extent of the damage This could be a localized phenomenon."

"It could be, but I doubt it. If they knocked out Washington, they'd only be taking out a small pocket of global resistance. Whatever their agenda, they wanted to deal with a united planet. Without global leadership, they would have to deal with the disparate elements. They've come, so it's obvious they felt this was an option. My guess is this is a planetary shut down. Moscow, Beijing, London, Paris, Jerusalem, Rome, Ottawa, Berlin... I'm sure they're all in total chaos at the moment, all in their various bunkers just as helpless as we are. This gives rise to the obvious question." Alatorre waved at the room. "What is the likelihood of any of this becoming functional soon?"

General Comry took a moment to answer. "I can't answer that, Madam President, but I know this is a secure location for the government. We need to keep you safe."

"But the reason you need to keep me safe is so governance continues. If this equipment isn't functional, there will be no governance from this location. We're dead in here."

"We must keep you safe..."

"The point is, General Comry, we have to come up with new ways of doing things and we have to do it quickly. If I'm right about the extent of the problem, millions of desperate people will soon depend on us. Let's start by moving the command center topside. We're going to need natural sunlight to see what we're doing."

"But security..."

Alatorre reached out and slapped the holster riding on the General's hip. "That gun is mechanical is it not? No circuits?"

"Yes..."

"And these fine soldiers providing the security here. What about their weapons?"

"Well, all right but..."

"I know there's a risk, General, but we can't govern from down here. We'd be doing it blind. I trust you to keep me safe, but we must go topside. Set up the best security perimeter around the White House you can, and we'll start from there."

Missing

Landing a Fahr military cruiser on Planet Song while releasing the ballast water required focus. As the cruiser hovered over the collection site, Chief Navigational Officer Baronth was bothered by the computer records of the event, a small glitch in the graph that shouldn't be there. Something, besides the water, had also been ejected, or perhaps launched would be a better word. Its trajectory had taken it well away from the ship.

"Commander Agastin," he said into the com system. "I think we have a problem."

"Not with the collection, I hope," came the reply.

"No Commander, that has gone well. We have nineteen singers in the containment area, and the aperture is ninety percent closed. But, during the descent, something launched from the ship. I was too busy with the ballast release at the time to notice it, but it's visible on the charts."

Silence. "Thryke," Agastin said. "Vice Commander Thryke report."

Nothing.

"Vice Commander Thryke report!"

Again nothing.

"He's launched the Xburner, that archaic atmospheric fighter craft he had in the ship's hold," Agastin said. "Vice Commander Teracia!" he shouted into the com system.

***

With no signals to monitor, Communications Officer Teracia had been swimming the hallways in a daze. Homines had been dealt a devastating blow and she could not stop it. Her ballow concaved against her forehead to the darkest gray the physiology allowed. It would be eighty years before Occeane and Derath would hear of this and another sixty before she would hear from them. She was on her own with no one to talk her out of the gray.

"Vice Commander Teracia!" the com system barked. She stared at it, trying to pull out of the gray to respond. "Vice Commander Teracia!" it said again. Agastin's voice. They hadn't yet left the planet and already she was being restored? This pushed the gray aside. What had Thryke done?

"Teracia here," she said not yet willing to use her restored title.

"Thryke has launched the Xburner," Agastin said.

"The Xburner, Commander? Are you sure?"

"Baronth detected a launch during the decent. Thryke used the ballast release as a kind camouflage. He's out there somewhere. Can we find him?"

Teracia thought for a minute. Any Fahr vehicle built within the last forty or fifty generations would be connected to the tracking network, but the Xburner dated from before that time.

"It wouldn't have a beacon. Too old," she said. "We'll have to feed its specifics into the system and do a scan. But it will only work if it's flying. If it's on the ground, we won't pick it up."

"Do it," Agastin said.

"Yes, Commander. And Commander?"

"What?"

"Did you call me Vice Commander Teracia?"

"I told you your position would be restored. Do it now." The com connection went dead.

Teracia swam back to the Communications Room. She waved a clasper at the panel.

"Ready," the panel said.

"This is Vice Commander Teracia. Is the Xburner still on the ship?"

"No."

"Bring up the specifics of the Xburner flyer, feed those into the tracking system and do an atmospheric scan," she told it.

"Search is negative," came the reply.

Thryke has either landed the Xburner or it had been destroyed. *What could Homines have that could engage an Xburner?* she wondered. Planet Song's defenses were compromised. It was more likely Thryke had landed the Xburner. *Why?* It didn't matter. They had to find him.

She hit the com button. "This is Vice Commander Teracia," she said. "Connect me to Commander Agastin and Chief Navigational Officer Baronth."

"We have less than fifteen minutes to launch sequence," Baronth said. "We won't have the energy to get off the planet if we search for him."

"Then we leave him," Agastin said.

Teracia reddened. "But if the Homines find either him or the Xburner, the push factor would be..."

"The damage is done," Agastin said. "Continue with the launch sequence, Chief Navigational Officer."

Teracia found a wall sponge and allowed it to pull her in. She felt the gray return.

Looting

It took only about forty-five minutes for the lab to become a hub of unease. The Internet went down, then came the brown out and the crash. What they heard was more of a boom, two cars colliding in an intersection a block away and several stories below them. Only lower frequencies traveled that far.

Peter Howard wore a lab coat over suit pants, dress shirt, and a tie, overdressed for lab work. He was in charge and felt he needed to look the part. Howard was a few months shy of forty and had served in Afghanistan to earn his shot at a college education. He tried to maintain a military fitness level, but the demands of his new position cut into gym time, and now there was a certain gumminess about his body.

He joined the techies and grad students at the window and watched the chaotic street scene unfold below them. Most of the damage involved cars. Two had collided and were in flames, another had hit a woman, and there were several fender benders. All remaining vehicles had stalled and now blocked the road in front of the building. Nothing mechanical was moving except for student bicycles and a single florist's push cart. Students milled around the street, glancing upward.

"Are they looking at us?" one of the grad students asked.

"Probably looking for the aliens," said another. They had all seen the feed of the black object passing in front of the moon earlier that day.

Peter Howard tapped Jeffries on the shoulder.

Jeffries looked at him, his slim slouchy posture straightening, the blond Jesus on a cross falling beneath his shirt.

"Go down there and see if you can find out what's going on," Peter said.

"Yes... Sir."

Peter caught the gap between the words. Jeffries was not used to using the word 'sir' when addressing someone of color. A few years earlier, when the death of Freddie Grey was in the news, Jeffries had pointed out three of the six officers charged in the incident were black. Then they put Peter Howard in charge of the research. The promotion had taken the researchers by surprise, himself included. He'd worked hard for it, but he couldn't get over the feeling he should have worked harder. No one should conclude that John Hopkins School of Medicine had pulled an affirmative action move. But Peter was sure some of them, Jeffries included, had come to that conclusion anyway.

"I'll have to use the stairs, Dr. Howard," Jeffries said. No gap this time.

15

Peter nodded then took out his cell phone and looked at it again. "Anybody got a working phone?" he asked.

Thirty minutes later the injured woman was still in the middle of the road attended by several people. The fact that they hadn't moved her told Peter they suspected a spinal injury and were reluctant to transport her without the proper equipment. By now most of the students and faculty from the surrounding buildings had made their way on to the street. Some were walking home, but most were just standing around. Jeffries had yet to return, and there was no sign of an ambulance. Peter hadn't heard a car engine since the brown out.

"Can we leave, Dr. Howard?"

Peter looked away from the street and back into the laboratory. Bethany, one of the technicians, already had a bag over her shoulder and jacket over her arm. Without power, there wasn't much any of them could do. He looked over the anxious faces in the room.

"Yes, you can all go," he said. "Just make sure everything you're working on is put away before you leave. And I'm assuming whatever this is will have been dealt with by morning, so I'll see you then." Peter wasn't sure he believed this.

They were all gone within two minutes, projects left as they were. Peter Howard wandered through the lab, unplugging expensive equipment in case of a power surge and refrigerating samples. The refrigerators weren't working but were still cooler than the room. He left them plugged in, hoping the power would come on during the night and save some of the work. Satisfied, he grabbed his attaché case, tried and failed to engage the electronic security system, shrugged his shoulders, locked the laboratory door with his key, and made his way to the stairs. These were in the interior of the building and pitch black. He used the handrail to feel his way down the stairs to ground level.

No one manned the security desk in the front lobby. He slipped behind the counter and glanced up at the monitors. *Dead.* He looked at his wrist watch and realized, for the first time, this too was not working. *Even my watch has stopped,* he thought. *What is this? What could do this?* He pushed his way through the door to the street. He looked up not sure what he expected to see from the ground level that hadn't been visible from his lab. No aliens anyway.

The double-glazed windows in the lab kept the street smells from him, but at ground level they assaulted him. Smoke filled the space, a combination of wood, plastic, rubber and oil. Yet apart from the two vehicles smoldering in the intersection he could not find the source. There were other smells too: drywall dust, food, urine, vomit. Afghanistan. The same spooked faces. He shuddered at the memory, checked his watch again, shook his head and then studied the posted bus schedule.

"Anything go by?" he asked a smoking gray-bearded black man dressed in groundskeepers' fatigues.

"Where the hell have you been for the past hour?" the man replied.

Peter pointed up. "Top floor."

"Anything working up there?"

Peter shook his head.

"My riding mower just stopped, dead as a doornail," the man said. He pointed to the downed pedestrian on the street and then at an approaching gurney about a block away. "That poor woman's been lying there for almost an hour. They couldn't even call an ambulance 'cause nobody's got a working cell. They finally sent a runner to the hospital. It's what somebody should have done forty-five minutes ago, but I guess if you're so used to doing things another way..." He made a broad gesture to the street. "Even if they could have called an ambulance, how the hell is it going to get down this street with all these stalled cars? This is so fuckin' weird. It's like the aliens pushed us into another dimension or something."

"So, no buses?"

The man shook his head. "I'm guessing your quickest way home is those two legs you're standing on."

"I live in Randallstown," Peter said laughing. "A four-hour walk. How about you?"

"Waiting for my squeeze. She's 'posed to meet me here. We were goin' out for a bite and some brews. But she didn't tell me what she'd be doing beforehand, only that we should meet here. Now I don't know where to look for her and my cell's not working. So, I'm going to hang around, in case she shows."

"Well, good luck with that," Peter said. He looked down the street in the direction he would be walking. There were no obstacles to pedestrian traffic he could see. People congregated around the doors to every building, anxiety etched on their faces. He opened the attaché case, pulled out the shoulder strap, put it over his head, adjusted it, and started the trek. At least Sonya and Tracy would be together in a predicable place. His wife worked as a secretary at Tracy's school only a few blocks from their home. His daughter hated that.

Johns Hopkins University had the charm of a nineteenth century campus with a liberal mix of newer buildings. Walking through them now was like walking down a long open-air corridor, one in which the sounds and the smells were contained, an auditory and olfactory ambiance. He'd already been confronted with the mix of odors, but now he was drawn to the sounds. There were voices, people laughing, people weeping, angry, excited, frightened people; any emotion he could think of was there. Missing was the sound of vehicles and electrical machines, the white noises of a modern city. The absence unsettled him as if this had contained the more extreme emotions and now those had been set free. He tried not to look at people as he walked, but they were looking at him. He picked up his pace. Sonya and Tracy were waiting.

Every intersection was a scene of carnage. At one he had to pick his way through smoldering wreckage to reach the other side. At another two men had fallen to their deaths from a construction crane, their bodies lying beneath a blue ground tarp. The further he got from John Hopkins, the worse it got. Now buildings were on fire and firefighters without rigs were doing their best to control them. The cops were everywhere now, on foot with a few riding bicycles.

Orleans Street was now seeing a steady stream of pedestrians, almost everyone had a visible injury. He walked against the flow. One man was bleeding from a head wound, had his hand in a sling and was limping. Peter walked over and offered his arm.

The man scowled at him. "Get away from me," he growled.

Peter stepped back.

A cop was watching the interaction and stopped him. "You injured?" he asked.

"No, but my home is in that direction," Peter said, pointing down Orleans Street away from the hospital.

"Then find another way. We're trying to keep this road free for those who need to get to the hospital."

Peter stared at him. This was a wide road. He wouldn't be in the way. He could tell the officer he was a researcher at the John Hopkins Medical School and a former Special Forces medic, but if he did, it might delay his return to Sonya and Tracy. The cop waved him down a side street.

Peter couldn't remember the exact layout of this part of town, mainly upscale conversions of heritage buildings, most dating from the turn of the previous century. It was trendy and inhabited by white professionals perched in lofts above the storefronts. He'd been in the area a few times with moneyed research supporters, wining and dining them in the finer restaurants. Sonya had talked of moving there if he got the promotion, but it was well out of Peter's comfort zone.

It was now early evening and would have been still bright if not for the heavy cumulonimbus clouds overhead. He heard a few cracks of thunder through the human white noise. Home was still at least two hours away and rain was coming. Then he noticed them, roaming packs of men and women: blacks, working class whites, and a few Latinos. As he drew closer to one of these, he realized they were casing the storefronts, and they had crowbars and hammers.

He looked around for a way out and when he didn't find one, got past them as quickly as he could. If they started something he would be implicated just by being in the area. The cops wouldn't care if he carried an attaché case and dressed in a suit. He jogged.

Then he heard a window crash and the nearest pack gave a triumphal shout and charged into the shop. On cue other groups further down the street did the same thing. As he ran past they emerged with televisions, computers, clothing, jewelry, cell phones, anything of value. Wild cries of elation accompanied the looting, and as Howard ran past them, he caught glimpses of the area's residents watching from their second-floor lofts.

He picked up the pace. The further he ran, the more looting he saw. Now it seemed like everyone on the street was involved. Where were the cops? Garbage cans were set ablaze and revelers danced around, spraying each other with shaken cans of looted beer. The ground became slick and then the rain started. Peter's brogues were new, the soles smooth leather. He went down hard.

The fall knocked the wind out of him and attempting to catch his breath pierced his left side with pain. He lay there for a moment trying to catch his breath, each attempt screaming at him. His right hand flexed, and Peter realized he was no longer holding the attaché case. He struggled to his feet, gasping and holding his side.

"Nice dive," said a spiky blond man with a five-day beard wearing a Mötley Crüe T-shirt and pair of cargo shorts. He held and examined Howard's attaché case.

Peter reached for it, but the man stepped away.

"Now where, I'm wondering, did a guy like you get the money for something this nice? And look at that suit. Sure as hell didn't come from Walmart, now did it?"

Peter said nothing as others gathered around the man with the case.

"That look like a Walmart suit to you, Niko?" the man asked one of his friends. This man was much larger, a fried chicken kind of man.

"Looks like a stolen suit to me. And the fancy shoes? That's a dead giveaway."

20

"I'm a professor at John Hopkins," Howard wheezed.

"A professor?" said the first man. "Well, maybe you stole this stuff from a professor. You're a long way from John Hopkins."

"The attaché case has research papers in it," said Howard.

"So, you're admitting stealing it from a professor?" The others laughed.

"That is a serious crime," Niko said.

"And no cops about," said the first man.

"And we don't have the keys to the jail." Niko looked at Howard with mock compassion. "Maybe we should just turn him loose?"

"Yeah, maybe. But we can't let him keep all this stolen loot. I say, at the very least, we should try and get this stuff back to its rightful owner."

"Sounds like a plan."

The first man studied Peter. "Now we're going to give you a choice, here. Either you can remove those fancy clothes yourself and hand them over to us or we're going to remove them, and that might go a tad rougher."

"It's pouring rain," Peter said trying to ignore the pain on his left side.

The man shrugged.

Howard studied the faces of the men and women surrounding him. They would do this if he didn't. He removed his suit jacket, handed it to the first man, winced and gestured to Niko. "I know his name—what's yours?" he gasped.

"Why should I tell you?" the spiky blond head said.

Peter applied pressure to his side. It seemed to help. "I suspect you'll want to be lauded by our local constabulary for your brave actions. Be hard for them to do that if they don't know your names. I'd be happy to tell them for you."

Niko grinned. "Lauded by our local constabulary!" He laughed. "Maybe he is a professor, Tommy!"

"Shut the fuck up, Niko."

"Hey, you told him my name."

Tommy turned to Peter. "Get the rest of it off, now!"

Peter took off his dripping shoes and rain-soaked pants, suit vest, shirt, and tie. He handed these to Tommy and was left standing in boxer shorts, socks, and an undershirt. He gestured to them. "I bought these at Walmart."

Tommy nodded. "So, I see," He pulled Peter's wallet out of the pants pocket, thumbed through the contents, and pulled out a business card. "Dr. Peter Howard, medical geneticist," he read. "He really is a professor!"

"I told you," Peter wheezed.

Niko leered at him. "Run, professor boy, run!"

Howard ran. His ribs screamed.

The street where he lived was calm, most people inside because of the rain. He staggered up the front steps and banged on the locked door. Sonya peered out the window and then pulled him inside.

"Peter! What happened to you!?!"

He gasped holding his side. "Looters, rioters, the city's imploding. Fill the backpacks." He sucked in a slow breath.

"You're hurt!"

Peter shook his head. "It doesn't matter. We've got to go. Things will get much worse. We have to get out of the city, away from people."

"Away from people?"

"Away from hysteria," Peter said.

White House

The White House's East room normally had little furniture. Now it was full of desks, cubicle dividers, filing cabinets, and half-century-old Underwood desk typewriters. Alatorre had ordered the golden curtains be pulled back, allowing for as much natural light as possible. It was bright during the day, and she had sunglasses stashed in her office drawer.

She put on the sunglasses and spun her chair to look out the window behind her. The trees had been pruned back, giving her an unobstructed view of the south lawn. They had emptied the place, apart from security personnel and soldiers. The entire area between 15th and 19th Streets, Constitution Avenue, and H Street south had been cordoned off and the public evicted. Now they had machine gun nests in place and were in process of finishing a vast ten-foot-high fence of razor wire to enclose the entire area. Soon she would have to look through this to see anything beyond the White House grounds.

What she would see then would be a variation on what she saw now: vast accumulations of Americans expecting the government to take care of them. Food was a major problem. Within a day all non-perishable items had vanished from store shelves in the greater capital region, most of it looted. Everything in refrigerators had spoiled and there was no gas or electricity for cooking. All the barbecue charcoal disappeared from local stores and became an expensive black-market item as was firewood of any kind. They'd been feeding people by trucking in food the government itself had looted from the surrounding communities using vehicles old enough to not require any form of electronic circuitry to start the ignitions.

She grimaced and watched in the distance another of the few functional military trucks bringing a fresh load of razor wire. The transport appeared as if through a fog, smoke still rising from the smoldering fires. Two jumbo jets had dropped from the sky over DC and set a tenth of the city on fire. There were no operational fire trucks and no water in the hydrants, but a storm had blown in and kept the flames from spreading. Alatorre knew there had been thousands of such jets in the skies over America when the aliens attacked. So far there had been a few hundred reports of downed aircraft and the resulting fires, but there were many parts of the country she had not heard from. The trucks came to a stop just inside the perimeter. There had been more of these vehicles at the beginning of the attack, but a number had been hijacked by right-wing militias. The cargoes and the soldiers guarding them had all disappeared.

Gerald Garneau appeared at her side. "We should stop this," he said. "Those trucks should bring in food, not razor wire."

"To delay the inevitable?"

"We have to do more."

Alatorre sighed. "I think you need to accept reality here. Unless we can find some miraculous way to restore our entire infrastructure we will lose people, a lot of people."

"So, razor wire is a better option?"

"It will give us time to think. To work things through. When the barrier is finished, we can send for more food, but it will have to come from further away and it'll be a temporary fix." She paused and stared out again at the throngs of people beyond the razor wire. "Frankly, I'm surprised we've kept them at bay this long."

"They're smart enough to know what machine gun nests mean, but they're also smart enough to know the trucks are now bringing in razor wire. The fuse has been lit. The only question is how long it will burn."

"Long enough to get the razor wire in place?" Alatorre sighed. "Did you get over to Carnegie yesterday?"

"Yes. They're estimating three months' minimum to get the most rudimentary manufacturing processes underway. Chips and circuit boards are the biggest problem. They're at the core of most manufacturing processes including the manufacture of chips and circuit boards."

"So, we need the chips and circuit boards to make them, but we don't have them?"

"Exactly. What they're suggesting is we round up consumer electronic devices in the hopes we can scrounge working bits and see if we can adapt them to the manufacturing process. Part of the problem is anything in stores has been looted. I guess the thieves were thinking the power grid would only be out temporarily and that, somehow, the TVs and computers in the stores were not fried by the

24

Fahr. They've stolen a bunch of useless electronics but won't know it until the electricity comes back on."

"What do they say about electricity? Water?"

"Well, the electrical grid will require a massive rebuild. All the East Coast nuclear facilities are off line. Retrofitting them with analogue diesel generators for the cooling pumps allowed us to avoid meltdowns, but everything about them requires electronic control. I don't know the technologies behind these, but they're telling me it will be quicker and safer to go back to coal generation, at least on the East Coast. That will take time. It's several years away, but there will be bits and pieces happening before then, depending on how we prioritize. In the short term, we can power essential stuff through diesel generators, for localized applications at least. Without a lot of vehicular traffic, we should have plenty of fuel. The grid itself, the transmission lines and all the rest, will take as long as the building of new coal-fired plants."

"And water?"

"Collect rain water and boil the rest. The treatment facilities are all off line. They need electricity like everything else."

"Is there anything that doesn't require electricity?"

"Not much."

"I think we're about to find out just how resourceful the American people are and how many city folks can do farm labor. Without all that powered machinery, we're going to need a lot of muscle."

Garneau gave her a grim look. "Muscles need energy," he said.

She nodded. "And the Fahr are gone?"

"We don't have a lot of information. The few accounts we've received have their ship landing in the ocean off the West Coast of Canada and then leaving a few hours later, without generating the blast one would normally associate with trying to escape the planet's gravity. That may mean it hasn't left the planet, but it hasn't been seen since. Hiding an object of that size anywhere on the Earth would be difficult. Until we hear otherwise, we should assume they've left the planet, however they managed to do that."

Alatorre nodded. "And we still have no idea why they came?"

"They landed in the Pacific Ocean, not on land. So, whatever they came for seems to be connected to the ocean. I'm guessing it has something to do with whales."

"Whales?"

Garneau pursed his lips. "It's flimsy logic, I admit. But I can't stop thinking about the song they used. It's a song about the killing of whales and then when they land, they land in the Pacific Ocean."

Alatorre brightened. "International waters! No one country has control over those animals, which means any negotiation about them would have to be international. They would need to talk to a global government or authority. They wanted us to unite, and we didn't. That made negotiation impossible so, if they wanted whales, they'd have to disarm the entire planet to take them. That they have done."

"But what is it about whales that would be that valuable?" Garneau asked.

"I have no idea, and we may never know. At the moment, we have other priorities."

Garneau nodded. "The survivalists were correct."

"Yes, but not for the reasons they thought. I guess we'll find out how effective their preparations were, and how quickly they can organize."

Board

Greyling knew he would not survive this downing, not physically. He survived the previous six cycles due to extraordinary measures. When a suitable replacement had not been found, he had gone on as Song Corp's CEO, hyped up on stimulants and painkillers that pushed him well beyond the normal life expectancy. Now the Board had approved his choice of Wrasse. The Minister of Pets was in for a rude awakening when he returned to Centrix, an event three hundred years in the future. Lord Greyling would wait for him though not in a state that Wrasse would be expecting.

Wrasse was a strange choice for the CEO of Song Corp, if for no other reason than his flamboyant persona. The CEOs of Song Corp were constrained and controlled individuals, fahr that radiated contained power. But Wrasse was quite a capable of wielding power—as Minister of Pets he had shown this on numerous occasions—but he also had a playful side and a sexual orientation that would take the public a while to adjust to. Still, Greyling saw him as the best choice, but it had taken a long time to convince the board.

Had this been a normal downing Greyling would have drifted into insensibility by now, his mind barely conscious when the menders came for him, the thought processes so slowed he would have been mentally inert. The downing put him into stasis until his worn-out body could be rebuilt. But the transformation was not an act of physiological rebuilding, and it required him to be alert.

The menders who came for him had an arrangement with Song Corp. There was a fine line between giving one unlimited access to virgin song and expecting the receiver to be in control. The discipline necessary was a rare commodity and perspective menders were watched for centuries before being offered the opportunity. When they were, most chose to be repeaters, extending their occupations into their next millennium to enjoy the perks.

"Lord Greyling, it is time," the first of the menders said as they entered his mansion.

Greyling nodded. He disliked honorifics, but it was pointless to protest. Once the transformation was complete, he would forever be a lord, anyway.

The menders had a ceremonial gurney, one to carry him upright. By now most of the Centrix population knew he was entering his last downing, and they would wait along the route to say their good byes. Such were the ways of celebrity death. The menders strapped him in.

"Remember, Sir, they won't be expecting you to be lucid."

"I can loll with the best of them," Greyling said, extending his tentacles and allowing them to free float. As they pushed him through the door, he did the same with his tongue. This would be his most undignified journey, but he took solace in the absence of recorders. With national heroes, the last swims were never recorded. It wouldn't do to have archives showing such fahr in the worst light. It was bad enough the image of him in this state would permanently be on the PDMs of every fahr in attendance, but at least those were private memories not intended for public consumption.

Greyling closed his eyes, much easier than trying to keep them open but unfocused and vacant. The multi-voiced drone started, common fahr expressing their appreciation for him. He knew this would go on until they reached the stasis chambers, a good forty minutes away. He tried to relax.

The most annoying bit was the state of his tongue once they had reached the stasis chambers. All the lolling had left it strained and dehydrated, a fact he put down to the higher salt content in the water outside his mouth.

The menders were undoing the straps on the gurney. "We've prepared a meal," one of them said.

"A meal?"

"The first part of the process will take several days," the mender replied. "The most efficient way we have to capture the material is for you to download the occupations one at a time. Then we will transfer each one from your cerebral cortex. It makes for a more accurate reproduction of the synapses. You'll have no energy for this if you haven't eaten."

"And I thought I'd already had my last meal," Greyling said.

"Well, Sir, in a sense you have. What we've prepared for you will optimize the process, but it's not tasty."

Greyling's gills flattened. "Well, get on with it then. I want to be out of this tired body."

Expansion. Song Corp's biggest secret, a database driven by an ancient but efficient supercooled quantum computer. Within it Greyling had cast off the limitations of the biological brain and now had perfect recall of every memory from all of his occupations without downloading. Even as he drew on them, he could feel new connections between the parts of his segmented memory. His seventeenth occupation, when he had been a song chaser under Song Corp's previous CEO, now made connections with his forty-ninth occupation when he had overseen corporate security. Before the transformation those two occupations could never have occupied his biological brain at the same time.

Without a physical body, Greyling found he lacked a sense of corporeal time. It was so bad he had no idea how long it had taken him to reach this conclusion. All he knew was he had been busy re-experiencing memories, establishing connections, and creating synapses, or whatever the quantum equivalent of those were. Then a second realization hit him; he was not connected to anything outside of his own mind, or if he was, he had yet to discover the connection. He had spent so long exploring his own expanded mind that, before now, this had not even occurred to him.

"You've arrived," a voice spoke into him.

The voice was that of the previous CEO of Song Corp. "Lord Spargill," Greyling said. He had thought fleetingly about Spargill and the others, but the experience of the expansion had over-whelmed him.

"You've only been alone for a few weeks," Spargill said. "I know it seemed longer, but the quantum engine of this technology allows the capture of your full intellectual expansion to happen with incredible speed. In effect, it allows you to create all the connections your mind requires at two to the sixteenth factor, capturing and connecting the disparate aspects of one hundred millennium worth of memories in a few weeks. You don't realize how fast it's happening because you're inside it, and you have no external reference points."

"But you knew I was going through this?"

"Experience has taught us the first few weeks of transition are overwhelming, and the only mind that can establish those connections is your own. We would be in your way. One of the universals, however, is the time it took each of us to question elapsed time and external connectivity. Once you've done this, you're ready for the rest of us."

"And the business of Song Corp," Greyling said, becoming aware of the hundreds of ex-CEO consciousnesses that were also stored on Song Corp's massive database.

"Welcome to the Board."

"And what is on the agenda today?" Greyling asked.

"The same thing is on the agenda every day—the maximization of profit."

If Greyling could have looked at himself in a reflector, he would have. He knew, of course, that after death he would continue seeking that for which he had dedicated one-hundred millennium of corporeal existence, but he also wanted a break. It seemed he would not get one. He would spend eternity seeking economic expansion, or at least he would do that until someone found the server and destroyed it. *Welcome to corporate hell.*

Fort Irwin

Fort Irwin was only a six mile walk from the Goldstone Deep Space Communications Complex, except that six miles was a walk in the Mojave Desert during the midday heat, and Trent had forgotten his Tilley hat. Again. Six miles was long enough to give one hell of a sunburn. He grabbed a linen towel from the bathroom, soaked it, smacked it on his head, and let the water drip down his back as he walked out the door clutching a plastic bottle of water.

Billy pulled up beside him, shifting his weight between two sandals reclaimed from old tires. The left one squeaked, so every second stride it punctuated the conversation like a whimpering puppy. "That thing left one hell of a vapor trail," he said looking skyward.

"Yeah, it did," Trent said. There was a wide swath of dissipating vapor and smoke stretching south to north, horizon to horizon. "I wonder where it landed."

Three squeaks. "San Francisco... Seattle, maybe? What else is up there?"

Trent shrugged. He pointed down the road at smoke accumulating in the skies above Fort Irwin. "Looks like stuff caught fire. If that was an EMP then there's probably more damage."

Two squeaks. "I read somewhere EMPs wouldn't affect smaller electronic devices. Something about there being a certain minimal length to the wires."

Four more squeaks. "I don't suppose you've thought of lubricating that?" Trent said, pointing to the sandal.

Billy stomped his foot hard, then tested it. Nothing. "There you go."

"Thanks," Trent said. "Everyone's cell phones are dead, not just not receiving signals, dead as in fried. The only person who has a working watch is Fatima, and hers is an ancient Bulova windup. No electronics. This sure looks like an electromagnetic pulse to me. And, just before everything was fried, the satellites went missing. Gone. All of them. And just before that we see their spaceship, or whatever it was, eclipsing the moon over Australia thanks to that feed from the ABC. Think about it. If you wanted to cause total chaos on this planet before you attacked it, what would be the best way to do it?"

They walked on in silence.

"I'm not sure this is an attack," Billy said.

"How could it not be? You read the last message. *Talking is better than war.*"

"Yeah, but we're walking the road between one of the most advanced communication centers on the planet and a military training base. If this was an attack, this is one place that would see action, if for no other reason than Goldstone's capabilities. And, given the speed at which everything else has happened, we'd expect to see it quickly. But instead all we've got is no electricity, a bunch of stalled vehicles, fried electronic devices, and this weird silence."

Trent stopped and listened. Normally one would hear cars, trucks, aircraft, lots of man-made stuff. Now desert winds, insects, birds, and the sound of their own footsteps predominated. "Calm before the storm," he said and walked again. "Besides, if they've fried the electronics and the electrical grid, it would be like rendering Goldstone useless. Where's the threat? And almost everything in Irwin's military arsenal has circuit boards."

"Well, we'll soon see I guess," Billy said. "All that military grade hardware is supposed to be protected against EMPs."

"Against any known source of EMPs you mean." Trent gestured to the sky. "They've already shown us technologies far beyond what we can do. Who knows what they've got at their disposal? It might not be EMPs at all. It might be some other thing that acts like an EMP. You saw the Humvees in the parking lot, military grade hardware and it's not working. We don't know what we're dealing with."

"Well, they're not attacking." Billy said. "Not at the moment."

"Not here, anyway. But then Irwin is an army training facility. It's all ground forces. This conflict is likely to be in the air, at least initially."

Billy nodded. His left sandal squeaked again. He stomped it hard. "I don't like our chances of finding an older operational vehicle," he said. "It would have to be mid-eighties or earlier. I can't remember when they started using circuit boards in vehicle ignitions and engines. Besides the base will requisition any such vehicle for its own use."

"Diane just wants us to try. Having a vehicle will make things easier."

"You know what would still work, though?"

"What?"

"Bicycles. No electronic parts."

"Oh, Jesus!" Trent said looking down the road. A dozen soldiers jogged, their rifles trained on them.

"Hands on your head!" the sergeant shouted.

"We're Goldstone!" Trent shouted back.

"I don't give a damn if you're Winnie the Pooh. Hands on your head!"

Trent and Billy complied. The sergeant reached out and fingered the NASA lanyards hanging around their necks. The man was uber fit, and his cap had the crossed pistols insignia of the military police.

"You folks realize we're in a state of war?" the sergeant said, grinning at the linen towel covering Trent's head.

"Are we? With whom?" Trent asked.

"Well, that's just it, isn't it?" the sergeant said. "We don't know, so under the circumstances, anyone could be the enemy. What we do know is the entire grid is gone. And all the electronics on the base are all fried. A pure act of aggression if there ever was one."

"It's the same at Goldstone," Trent said. "We've been sent to find a working vehicle."

The sergeant laughed. "You wouldn't find much that's working in Fort Irwin," he said. "Even if we let you try. As it is, we've been ordered to bring in anyone who doesn't belong on the base."

The room they put Trent into was not a holding cell. It had bare dark green walls, two straight-backed chairs, and a table. On the table sat a glass of tepid water. The room had a single window, large enough to allow in a lot of sunshine and still accommodate an air conditioner. He knew this because the mounting brackets for the device were still in place, but the air conditioner itself had been removed. Instead the window was open, an easy squeeze through for his skinny body. Outside he saw a courtyard with a few picnic tables. Around these sat a half dozen robust soldiers smoking and playing cards. *Maybe later.*

The door creaked, and he looked back into the room. A late middle-aged man in khaki dress entered carrying a clip board. The man had two stars pinned to the collar of his shirt, a major general and likely the base commander. Trent stood up, reading the general's name tag as he did so.

"You can sit, Mr. Proctor," the General Rice said.

33

"Thank you, sir."

"My apologies for the security procedures, but we're cut off here. I have no idea what's going on in the outside world. None of our communication devices or vehicles are working. And we're fighting half a dozen serious fires with hand axes and buckets of water. Under the circumstances, I felt I had to take maximum precautions."

"I understand, sir."

"So, I'm going to assume, for the time being, that you are what your lanyard says you are, an employee of NASA."

"I am, sir. Where is my colleague?"

"He's in another room like this one down the hall. I'll be talking with him when I finish with you."

Trent nodded. Standard TV police procedure.

"I'll start this interview by asking you what happened at Goldstone."

"Well, first we lost contact with the satellites..."

"The satellites? Which satellites?"

"It appeared to be all the ones connected to our system, sir. But everything happened so quickly we didn't have time to check. Within a minute or two we lost everything else. We're as dead out there as you are here."

Rice shook his head. "We've yet to find a single piece of functional electronic equipment on this base. Watches, cell phones, children's toys, car or truck ignitions, radios, door buzzers... We even have things in Faraday boxes that don't work."

Trent said nothing.

"I saw it crossing the sky, burning and generating clouds at the same time. You're the space expert. What the hell was I looking at?"

"I don't think any of us knows, sir."

"Speculate."

Trent pursed his lips and looked at the General. "You've been following the news?"

"The stuff about the flashing moons, the hijacking of NASA's radio signals to play that hippy song from the seventies, the supposed communication with some aliens who wanted us to unite under a single world leader... I tried to ignore it. The earlier part of my career was spent at Edwards Airforce Base. I've had my fill of little green men."

"Well, when the song first appeared on the Pioneer 10 frequency... Do you remember?"

"Vaguely," Rice said.

"It went on for about three months. We assumed the source was terrestrial, but we couldn't find it. Then it stopped. We hadn't heard a thing on that frequency for ten years. Pioneer 10 is too far away, and its batteries are long dead. We stopped monitoring the frequency because, even when all the recent stuff was happening, there was nothing there. Until this morning. I did this random check and found a message, one sent twenty days earlier. It said, 'Unite. We are coming. Talking is better than war.'"

General Rice went white. "Twenty days ago?"

Trent nodded. "About the time the flashing moon disappeared. We would have found it earlier but there was so much other stuff going on, with all the press conferences and trying to re-establish control over all the missions, downloading the missing data... Monitoring the Pioneer 10 frequency was not a priority."

"Did you tell anyone about this?"

Trent shook is his head. "We had no chance. The satellites went down almost as soon as we found it, and with them all our communications. You're the first person outside of Goldstone to know about it."

Rice shook his head. "And I have the same problem—no way of communicating."

"Are there any vintage cars or motorcycles on the base, anything that doesn't have a circuit board that's crucial to its operation?"

The General nodded. "We have a few old Harleys and a half dozen muscle cars from the sixties and seventies. There are a few older military trucks as well, but they're not operational. We have

35

the mechanics working on them, of course. I've already dispatched the Harleys to some of the nearby bases. They won't know about your message, of course."

"There's another thing about that message. We don't think it came from whoever or whatever is in charge on that ship. The few official communications between the aliens and the Security Council came through the Institut de Radioastronomie Millimétrique in Grenoble. This message came on the Pioneer 10 frequency and only happened once. That may mean the message was not official."

"Someone or something was trying to warn us? Too little, too late I'd say." He studied Trent. "I doubt if you NASA folks are much of a security risk, so I'm going to let you and your colleague go. But I can't give you a vehicle. It's only a six mile walk to the base, anyway. I suspect we're all going to be doing a lot more walking."

"What about bicycles? Can you lend us bicycles?"

General Rice grinned and shook his head. "Goldstone is only a six-mile walk. We're going to need all the mobility we can get. Tell you what I will do though..." He walked over to the closet, opened it and removed a baseball cap. "Try this on."

Hospital

The building had a backup generator and one old enough to work with a simple pull on the cord. With several stiff pulls, it sputtered and coughed on old fuel. Lights came on but little else.

Peni sat on the chair beside her bed, exhausted. "I never should have gotten rid of your old chair," he said.

Honi nodded. Her father had pushed her in the heavy and quite dead motorized wheelchair eight miles to the hospital, while trying to balance the oxygen bottle in her lap. When they arrived, the staff only gave her more oxygen, this time through the nose. The hospital respirators were all fried, just like the one on her chair.

They propped her up in an emergency room hospital bed, Honi's useless arms inert by her side and moved on to more serious cases.

She could see some of these cases as they wheeled them past her. Half were burn victims, a third of Kona in flames and the fire-fighting equipment useless.

Now people came from further up and down the coast, brought in by ancient vehicles driven by the cousins. Old was gold.

"What are they going to do for food?" her father wondered aloud.

Honi hadn't thought about food since everything had crashed.

"Are you hungry?" he asked.

"Maybe a little," she said.

"I'll see what I can find."

Her father stood up and was soon out of her field of view. A few minutes later he returned with a banana and a large container of juice. "Kitchen's down, and the vending machines don't work." He held up the juice. "They said you should drink this because it will go bad anyway. No refrigeration."

"I can't do that, Dad," Honi whispered.

"Why not?"

"Check the bag. I think all that bumping around on the way here loosened the seal and it's probably full."

Peni blushed. "Oh Jesus, honey, I'm sorry!" He stood up. "They must have some here. I'll ask a nurse."

"They're busy."

Her father rushed off again.

Honi sighed. She knew she couldn't eat. There were too many competing stenches. Like burnt flesh. She'd never smelled that before, but she knew what it was. She knew it the instant the poor blackened man was wheeled past her. And then there was vomit, the smell in the air and the taste in the back of her throat. And decaying vegetable matter. It was an odor she didn't normally associate with hospitals, but it was there, like the compost pile in the back of their garden. And the hated bleachy citrusy smell of disinfectant, a single scent that could pull her back into all that was terrifying. She had lived in this hospital for nine months following the accident that broke her spine, not knowing whether she would live or die. But beneath it all was the smell of urine, her own. She would have known sooner that there was a problem if not for the masking by other odors.

Her father had never changed the bag. It was a mother/daughter thing or done by the nurse attendant on one of her twice-weekly-give-the-parents-a-break visits. Now he stood at the bottom of her bed holding a urine bag kit and looking helpless.

"You'll have to walk me through this," he said with his high-pitched stressed out laugh.

"So, you found a nurse?"

"They're all busy. I found the medical supply room though."

Honi studied the kit in her father's hands. "You'll also need a clean white towel and sterile gloves. Those won't be in the kit but are probably in the same supply room. And wash your hands with disinfectant soap. There's some in every hospital bathroom."

Her father scurried away. With him no longer at the foot of her bed, she again had a clearer view of the carnage coming through the emergency room doors. It was getting worse. They were now lying people on blankets on the floor. The doctors and nurses were rushing around, telling the family members and friends how to care for the injured. Those already treated were trying to help those arriving. It was chaos, but chaos with compassion.

She would soon be excluded, and she knew it. A stressed medical system would not have the resources to deal with someone in her condition. It was only a matter of time.

Her mind went back to a project some of her cousins were working on, a carved double-hulled canoe, a re-creation of the ocean crossing vessels of their ancient ancestors. The cousins had already made short trial crossings between the various islands of the Hawaiian archipelago. They had been talking about Tahiti, a journey crossing over 2,500 miles of open ocean. It was a trip she dreamed of going on. Honi wondered why she was thinking about it now in these circumstances, with her useless limbs splaying out across a hospital bed amidst such carnage. She was doomed, and she knew it, but fantasy in its various forms had been her dwelling place since the accident. Nothing had really changed.

In the end, they realized Honi's health was in more danger at the hospital than at home. Peni abandoned her now useless high-tech chair and borrowed a lighter hospital wheelchair for the push home. He jerry-rigged straps to hold two oxygen tanks in an upright position on either side of the chair.

"Dad, I want the nose plugs out," Honi said when they were half way home.

"Out? But your breathing..."

"I'll survive. I didn't pass out this time, did I?"

"You were barely conscious. You need oxygen."

"But there's a limited supply. I will have to breathe without it. You know that. And I didn't pass out. That's the thing. So, if I can build on that and figure out a way of breathing that forces me to use more of my lungs, if I can do that before the supply runs out, then maybe we can get through this."

"How are you going to do that?"

"I'm going to visualize about gaining more control over my lungs."

"Visualize?"

"Neuroplasticity."

Her father stopped pushing the wheelchair, walked in front of it, and squatted in front of Honi, meeting her gaze. "That's brain stuff. It has nothing to do with the spinal cord."

"It's all part of the same system," she said.

Peni shook his head.

"It is, Dad. It is, damn it! I can do this!"

His lower lip quivered, and he bit it. He reached out, removed the plugs, walked behind her, and pushed again. Faster, she realized, as if getting her home would give him more control over the situation. But they would have the same two tanks of oxygen when they got there, and she would still have to breathe on her own.

Diane

They gathered in the shade of the closest array. Without electricity, the buildings were hot and dark. Diane wondered about the soldiers across the parking lot. They had long since abandoned their attempts to start their trucks and Humvees but did not seem willing to move away from them. That put them right out in the desert heat, rotating in and out of the small bits of shade the vehicles offered.

She turned back to her crew. "Is everyone all right?"

"Yes."

"Sure."

"Fine."

"Any news?"

The man who had asked was thumbing a Rubik's Cube, the latest in a series of retro entertainments that had found their way into the lunchroom. And the only one that didn't require a battery.

"Now where would I have gotten that from, Sean?" she asked. "Have you seen me using some kind of secret communications device?"

Sean pointed down the road. "Maybe they know something."

Diane looked. Billy limped. He'd been an idiot to wear those sandals on such a long walk. Trent was sporting a Fort Irwin baseball cap, the one with the rearing horse. That appeared to be all they'd requisitioned from the base. Trent threw up his hands in a gesture of defeat.

"They have two old Harleys and a half dozen seventies muscle cars. Wouldn't even lend us a bicycle. Got this cool hat, though."

"Yeah, well, I guess they have to prioritize, especially if we're fighting a war. Thanks for trying."

"The General wants us all moved to the base," Billy said. "Said we're going to run out of food and water out here."

"So, he's thinking long-term?" Diane asked.

"Their circuit boards are all fried, just like ours. It will not be a quick fix. Even if they get the electrical grid back up quickly, the stuff won't work."

Diane nodded. Everyone was looking to her for leadership, but who could have envisioned this scenario? Her expertise was in the tracking of space missions, not in crisis management. She pulled Trent aside.

"What do you think?" she asked him.

Trent shrugged. "I'd go with the General. He seems reasonable. Just make sure he's got people securing this place."

"Yeah," Diane said. She looked out at the desert. "Fort Irwin may have more food and water than we have, but we'll still be in a desert. If this goes long-term, how will we eat and drink?"

"You're getting ahead of yourself, boss."

"I suppose." She turned to the crowd. "All right, everybody. Here's what we're going to do. I want you all to go back into the building and gather whatever personal items you have in there. We're going to walk to Fort Irwin so cover up, take water, and only carry what you think you can manage over a six-mile walk."

"What are we going to do when we get there?" someone asked.

"They're going to give us shelter, food, and drink. That's all I know at this point." Diane sighed. "And so, it begins," she said to Trent

"And so, what begins?" he asked.

"Whatever this will turn into. I'm not optimistic."

Stowaway

Capturing the Singers, escaping Planet Song's gravity, and parking the ship in an orbit around its moon used ninety percent of the ship's energy. They would need a stellar recharge before taking their precious cargo back to Centrix. At this distance from the star, it would take 6.8 days with the stellar energy capture sails unfurled. Thryke had reassured them, even if Homines had not been disarmed, they still could not strike the ship.

Thryke! Teracia pinked angry. Going back to search for him was out of the question. He and his precious Xburner had to be left behind. Even with his technological superiority, Homines would eventually defeat him, becoming more than pushed. They would be accelerated. Given the speed of their evolution and the accompanying immaturity, this would be fatal. Teracia grayed and sunk back into the sponge, allowing herself the continual gray shimmer of grief. Hers was worse than a failure. War between the two species would have been conducted from a distance. Homines would never have known what they were facing, would never have had physical contact. They would have been defeated without knowing their enemy, but they would have survived, at least a remnant of them. This situation was far worse, especially if they got a hold of Thryke's PDM and learned to decode it. Given the speed of their recent advances, she knew they could do this.

Teracia sank deeper into the sponge.

It was Wrasse who contacted her. "Vice Commander Teracia, we have a problem," he said through the com system.

Wrasse was the last fahr Teracia wanted to talk to now. Agastin had empowered him to act as Song Corp's senior representative on board. He was the enemy, but he was also the fahr she would have to work with during the trip home. Teracia was the only one of the crew who could enter the Singer's environment.

"Minister Wrasse," Teracia said. "What's the problem?"

"It appears we have one of your little bipeds on board."

"I'm sorry, Minister Wrasse, would you repeat that?"

"The collection process sucked one up. It's floating on an inflatable device in the middle of the containment area. The Commander thinks we should just dispose of it, but I argued we should wait until you've talked with it."

Teracia blanched and then pushed herself out of the sponge. "Talk with it? Yes!"

She spent a few hours observing the homine, but during that time, it did little more than watch the Singers when they were at the surface or watch the birds. Once or twice it attempted to scoop fish out of the water, but he was ill-equipped for this and failed. After a while it began licking its lips. Then she realized its thirst. A land-based mammal needed fresh water.

Teracia filled two large containers, entered the containment area from the bottom, and swam up toward the silhouetted boat. There was just enough Planet Song atmosphere in the containers to make them buoyant. She released them on either side of the boat and then made her way back to the bottom of the containment area. There she had stashed another item, a net used to capture injured fish. This item would not float so she would have to give it to the Homine. First contact. She hoped the experience would not be too frightening.

***

Kale wasn't sure how long he had been on the alien ship. His best guess was four days based on variations in the yellowish glow above the water. It had dimmed four times, and Kale thought this might be an attempt to emulate night and day on the Earth. Whatever the case he was now in a state of constant thirst with nothing to drink. At first, he thought he might solve the problem by catching fish. He knew their flesh would contain fresh water but had nothing to catch them with. Attempts to use his bare hands proved futile. Whoever these aliens were, Kale was sure he was not their intended target. The humpbacks had been provided with an environment that made sense for them. He had not.

Dying by thirst was not a pleasant prospect, but in this scenario did a pleasant prospect even exist? He was alone and probably permanently. Nothing about his current situation gave him hope. He kept thinking of Honi and the cousins, doing his best to consolidate his last memories of them. For what purpose, he wondered. Whatever reality awaited him would not include them. He would grieve them, and they would grieve him, neither understanding what had become of the other. Kale leaned his head on the inside of the Zodiac and closed his eyes.

He was dozing when two translucent brownish pillows bobbed to the surface on either side of the Zodiac. He dragged them on board. Each contained a clear liquid. Water? He could think of no other logical reason for their sudden appearance other than someone or something had realized his thirst. They looked disgusting, but he was too thirsty to care. Both pillows had a hollow sausage-like appendage. Drawing on one of these produced a warm and tasteless water, but it was fresh and did the trick. Against his better judgment, Kale drank until he could hold no more.

A sulfurous froth appeared by the side of the boat followed by an inflated green and veined balloon. As it rose through the water, Kale realized to his horror this projected out of a broad scaly forehead. Beneath this were a set of cat-like eyes and a small round mouth flanked by a large set of gill slits. He stopped breathing. What looked like an elephant trunk rose out of the water and dropped something into the boat. Kale didn't see what it was, his eyes locked on the predatory gaze of the creature. Slowly it sank back into the water.

Kale heard rather than felt his heart pounding in his chest. His breathing resumed with one huge gasp. He turned slowly and looked at the item dropped into the boat. It resembled a giant muddy and loosely strung squash racket, a net. *To catch fish,* he realized. *It wants me to survive!* He let out a long, slow breath. *But for what purpose?*

Island

A lot had happened and trying to make sense of it all was not conducive to sleep. Andreas spent most of the night staring out at the water from the mouth of the cave, hoping to notice some change, some visual clue that would tell him the alien ship had left. All he saw was a half-moon on the ocean horizon and a bit of fog.

At dawn, he climbed up the cliff face and back into the forest on top of the island, searching for food and water. He found a few early ripening blackberries that put a nick in his thirst but nothing else. A seal pup seemed like the most logical food choice, but this would mean a fire.

By now his hearing loss had taken on a new normality. He hoped there was nothing in this environment that could endanger him if he didn't hear it coming. Cautious with his movements, Andreas scanned every direction as he moved through the forest. A few more berry bushes presented themselves, again with meager pickings. He made his way down toward the beach. The alien ship was gone. Had it taken off during the night?

The adult seals were still lying on the sand, so he'd have to wait. It wasn't a good idea to get between any mother and her child. He dared not make his presence known until the adults decided everything was safe and left their pups to go feed. He noticed some of the debris from the B-25 had washed up further down the beach. He could check out the wreckage while waiting for the adult seals to make their way into the ocean.

Most of this was bits and pieces of shattered fuselage, but there was also a single tire, still inflated but ripped from its original housing. How had he ever survived that crash? Nothing he found had any food value, and he had no idea if the crew had packed anything edible. He wouldn't know what to look for. Andreas continued down the beach.

The shore narrowed, and he came upon large stones. He'd seen similar rocks, erratics, dropped by retreating glaciers on the Canadian plains and wondered if these were the same, He couldn't remember for sure, but he thought the West Coast had been free of glaciers. If so, something else must have put the stones on the beach. Earthquakes maybe? He came around one of them and stopped. There, half buried in the sand, sat the remains of the alien craft Reb had shot down the previous day.

What had looked like a giant house fly from a distance now looked like an inverted punch bowl. It sat in an almost perfect circle in the sand, surrounded by structures that could have been anything from small wings to loading cranes to support legs. There was a retro steam-punk look about them as if the aircraft had come forward in time from Victorian England. But there was nothing steam-punk about the corpse within the punch bowl.

Andreas caught himself. He was too close. If this thing was giving off any kind of alien germs he needed to back off, but he couldn't help himself. He crept closer, trying not to breathe. Holes where Reb's rounds had pierced the punch bowl were now evident, but they had shattered nothing. Each had passed straight through, so whatever this material was, it wasn't glass or hardened plastic. The rounds had gone into the... He couldn't think what to call it. What looked like a deflated red balloon grew out of its huge forehead, a wide fat rooster comb of a thing. Beneath that was a yellow eye, and further down the face a small round mouth half full of water with a large set of gill slits trailing away from it. Whatever this was, it was aquatic. A single fin protruding from the water confirmed this. *Attacked by a fish.*

He would have to tell someone, but who and how? Andreas sat down on the sand and stared out to sea, numb, half expecting a Wilson volleyball to appear on the beach beside him. He'd had more life-changing experiences in the past two days than in his entire life. Every one of them was screaming for his attention, but he would have to prioritize. *Food and water. Food and water.* Everything else could wait.

46

He looked up, and as he did, he felt the first pricks of rain against his skin. He smiled and stuck out his tongue. A few drops trickled in, but he knew any rain accumulating on the beach would be undrinkable. Too much salt. The forest was a better bet. A strong wind came up and with it, heavier rain. Instant storm. It was odd being in the middle of this and hearing nothing. The near horizontal rain was soon smacking his head with enough force to give him a headache. He cursed and began the climb into the interior.

Pools of water accumulated on the forest floor, so he dropped to his knees, cupped his hands, and ladled it into his mouth. It had a piney loamy taste, but he was too thirsty to care. Soon his thirst was quenched, but now he had an unbearable aftertaste no amount of spitting could remove. He grimaced and made his way back to the seals.

In his absence, the adults had gone out to feed.

"How hungry are you?" he asked himself.

"They're too cute and clams are easier," he answered.

He wandered onto the tidal flats and dug out fifty large bivalves in less than half an hour.

"Bring any matches?" he asked himself.

"Nope."

"Know how to start a fire without them?"

"Theoretically." But when he thought about this, it worried him. He knew the basics, but he'd never tried to do it. Matches and cigarette lighters were ever present in his pockets unless they weren't. Like now. Previously there had been no need to start a fire in any other way. Now there was.

He stepped back and addressed the footprints he'd left in the sand. "Go up to the forest, find me some kindling and dry moss. Then come back down here and collect some driftwood." He laughed at the absurdity of it all. It was bad enough he was talking to himself, but he couldn't even hear what he was saying. *Some kind of wishful thinking? Maybe if I talk, I can will myself into hearing again.* He shook his head and wondered if this was PTSD.

The forest floor was still wet from the rain, but he gathered hanging moss, twigs, and grass, and broke off a sapling. He carried these down to the beach and spread the kindling over the warming rocks to dry. The B 25 debris yielded string, and he used it and the sapling to make a loosely strung bow. A flat piece of rock with an indentation on its surface served as a base. He filled the indent with bits of dry moss and the fluff from a gull feather, wrapped the string around a sturdy twig and tried to create a warming friction in the kindling. It was hard work and took far longer than he expected, but eventually a small stream of smoke rose from the moss and feathers. Andreas blew on this until he saw a small orange flame. He fed this with larger pieces of moss twigs, more feathers, and bits of drift-wood. As the fire expanded, he found smooth stones around the beach and used them to build a barrier to enclose it. Some of the stones he pushed right into the flames, flatter ones where the clams could bake. He had attended clam bakes over the years, but it was always someone else doing the baking. It occurred to him that he had no way of cleaning the clams before baking them. The only source of water were the pools in the forest with that god-awful taste. But the alternative was cooking the clams straight out of the ocean complete with salt water, sand, and whatever other contaminants might be present. Eating seal pup meat would probably be safer and tastier. He resigned himself to a bit of nastiness.

The meat had a gamey taste and reminded Andreas of organ meat, with a pinch of fish sauce. He had no spices or butter and could not get the meat to cook evenly. The chunks of flesh continually slid off the makeshift spit and into the fire. He had to drag the seal pup through the sand. Soon his mouth was full of grit. Still, he ate as much as he could.

Once finished, he sat down on the sand and tried to take stock of the situation. He was the only survivor of the B 25. Andreas knew he should feel something for Jeff, Reb, and the Major, but he knew little about them, not even their family names. He was in a state of shock, but there was still the ever-present problem with what to do about the alien. It had to take precedence, so he pushed away the thoughts of the other three again. He had to get a message to the mainland. Andreas looked at the fire. *How did one make smoke signals?*

Somewhere in the deep recesses of his memory, he recalled something about green spruce branches giving off heavy smoke when burned. There were plenty of those in the forest. It was time to find out if this was a true or false memory.

By the time he was finished, his hands were sticky with sap and raw. He dragged about two dozen branches down to the beach and fed them into the fire. These did generate smoke, and he waved at this with one of the larger branches. This created strange rippling shapes that ascended into the sky above the island. Andreas had no idea if smoke ripples would communicate anything, assuming someone saw them, but kept it up until he tired. He paused only long enough to watch the seal pup's mother find its discarded carcass. The beast didn't look in his direction.

Ottawa

Pierce O' Malley, the recently elected Canadian Prime Minister, was both a populist and a pragmatist. His early morning routine involved free weights and a spin bike, and his tailored suits gift-wrapped his body for public consumption. His blond hair was a few snips short of a mullet, a jockish hairstyle that on anyone else would have looked dated and foolish. On O'Malley it had a goofy charm that women loved, and men envied. That took care of the populist side of things; his knowledge of how shallow this was made him a pragmatist. He had no idea what caused the destruction of the nation's electronic and communications infrastructure, what had rendered most forms of transportation inoperable, or why any of this had happened, alien spaceships notwithstanding. But he knew one thing: with the country as large as Canada, communications had to be restored quickly. Canada Post with its antiquated expertise in the delivery of snail mail was a major part of the solution. And so, his first act in response to the crisis was to sign an executive order requisitioning working vehicles and putting those at the disposal of the "posties".

Haida

Charlie sat in the stern of the boat, his bicycle-gloved hand wrapped around the throttle of the old Johnson. His father, George, sat in the bow and stared at the island they were approaching. This speck of land was nothing more than a nesting site for seabirds with a small beach favored by harbor seals. He passed by it many times on fishing trips. Now smoke appeared to be coming from the other side of the island.

"What makes you think those are smoke signals anyway?" Charlie said. "They don't look like smoke signals to me."

"Two things," said George. "First is where it's coming from. The smoke's rising from that island. How often do fires get start-ed over there? And the second thing is they kind of pulsate, like someone was waving a blanket or something at the smoke. Maybe trying to attract attention? With all the strange shit that's been hap-pening the last few days, it could be somebody that lost power and got stranded."

Charlie looked back at the Johnson. "It's amazing this old piece of shit still runs," he said.

"Those old Johnsons never die. That's from your grandfather's time. It's never let us down, not ever. 'Course it vibrates a bit."

Charlie smiled at his father and said nothing. There was a reason he was wearing his cycling gloves. You couldn't hold on to the throttle for more than fifteen minutes without your hand going numb, the main reason they didn't use it much. Now it was the only outboard they had that would start. *But, damn, the thing was loud!* Everything had been since yesterday.

He was nineteen, wore his hair gelled and spiked with a purplish bandanna across his brow. Everything else was denim. His father had named him after Charlie Edenshaw, the Haida sculptor, hoping that it would instill some pride in his ancestry. But Charlie just wanted to get out, to try his luck as a DJ in the big wide world. He'd worked hard in school though, getting good university-entrance-type grades, while most of the less-motivated kids floundered. It was a back-up plan in case the music didn't work out. From Charlie's point of view, returning to Haida Gwaii after he'd made his escape was out of the question. It was a hard attitude for his father, a Haida elder, to swallow.

Charlie took the cable connected to the oscillator output, found the other end of it, and pushed that into the filter section on the old analog synth. Then everything went dark. Brown outs were a common enough problem on Haida Gwaii but real annoying. He looked at his hand, at least as much of it he could see in the darkened room. It felt like ants were dancing on his skin. He noticed a certain crispiness in the air as if he was wearing studio grade headphones and had cranked up the volume on the microphone preamp, so it was capturing the tiniest of sounds. The volume increase made little sense. All his DJ equipment was dead from the brown out. He could see nothing operational. Odd.

He'd spent the money for high-grade surge protectors. Brownouts and surges could ruin sensitive equipment. The tingling on his arm subsided but the odd crispiness in the air remained. He opened the door and walked out into the street. Most of his Haida cousins, who had been inside, were now out.

The neighbor three doors down stood on his front porch talking to his wife, who as far as Charlie could see, was still inside their house. They were a good fifty yards away, yet he heard every word.

"Bring out your cell," he said. "Mine's dead."

"All right," she said.

Charlie watched her emerge from the door carrying the phone. He saw her thumb it a couple times and heard the clicks.

"Mine too," she said. "It's not even showing the low battery icon."

Charlie dug out his own cell from a pocket and looked at it. Same thing. Dead.

"Shit," the neighbor said. Charlie could tell from the man's tone the word had been spoken softly, at near whisper level, yet he heard it as if the man were standing right beside him. He noticed other things, the buzzing of insects and his own heartbeat, a distinct liquidly throb.

"So, what do you think is causing this?" Charlie said, tapping his ear.

His father gave him his wise old Indian look, the one he put on for tourists. "A lot of things aren't working right now, so there's a lot less stuff making noise. You're just hearing what you didn't notice before. Like when we're out in the bush."

"I didn't hear insects crawling around under the ground when we're in the bush, and I didn't hear people whispering from half a block away."

George shrugged. "You're just noticing stuff you didn't notice before, that's all."

They were approaching the cliff face side of the island. Charlie could see a cave entrance about half way up the face. "I wonder if anyone's ever checked that out?" he said, pointing to it.

George shrugged. "We can explore it later, but right now we should find what's causing that smoke. Take her around to the right."

Charlie pulled the boat around the island's point. They both gasped.

"What the hell is that?" George said.

Charlie looked at the partially submerged dome, and then at the large fish-like creature within it. "I don't know," he said, barely audible over the sputtering Johnson. There were also mechanical arms or projections of some sort coming out of the water at regular intervals around the dome, an attempt at a mechanical octopus. But it was the creature within the dome that got his attention. He'd lived on or near the ocean his whole life and never seen anything like it.

"Maybe this has something to do with that huge black thing," his father said.

Charlie stared at it, his mouth open and beads of sweat forming below his bandanna. They'd all seen the Australian news coverage of the black thing passing in front of the moon. Charlie was the only person in town who took it seriously. Then it flew right over the northern tip of Haida Gwaii and scared the shit out of everyone.

"We'd better find the source of the smoke," George said. "If it's people, then maybe they can tell us what this is."

Charlie forced himself to look away from the creature.

A large rock blocked their view of the rest of the beach, but soon as the boat was around it they saw him, a tall white guy sitting beside a smoky fire. As the boat steered toward him, they pushed through some floating wreckage, of what Charlie couldn't tell but suspected was an aircraft of some sort. The man didn't seem to notice them and was looking off in the opposite direction. Given the racket the old Johnson was making, this was odd. The man turned and saw them and began frantic waving.

Charlie steered the boat into shore, slowing down until the bow struck the sand on the beach before pulling up the Johnson. The two of them got out, pulled up the engine and dragged the boat further up the sand.

"Saw your smoke," George said to the man standing by the fire. He gestured to the floating rubble. "What the hell happened here?"

The man looked at them, frustrated. He was scruffy in a homeless kind of way, like a grunge rocker who hadn't taken a bath in a month. He made funny little waving gestures to both of his ears.

"The plane I was on was shot down by some kind of sound weapon when we engaged that alien ship," he said in a German accent. "It damaged my hearing. If you want to talk, you'll have to write on the sand, unless you have something else to write on."

"You attacked that alien ship?" Charlie looked again at the rubble on the beach. The man handed him a stick and gestured to the sand.

"He just told you he's deaf, and that his hearing is damaged. That means he can talk but he can't hear you," George said.

"OK, OK, Dad, I get it," Charlie said. He wondered at the irony of it. This man had lost his hearing due to an alien encounter while his own hearing seemed to change at roughly the same time. Maybe the two things were connected. He scribbled his question in the sand.

"Yes, we attacked it," the man said, shaking their hands. "My name is Andreas, and I think I'm the only survivor. Three others were on our plane, but I've seen no trace of them since our plane went down. We shot down a small one, but when we tried to engage the bigger ship, it made this incredible noise and shook the plane apart. And deafened me—I can't can hear anything. It's a miracle I survived the fall into the ocean and swam to this island."

George nodded. "George," he wrote, pointing to himself. "Charlie," he wrote, pointing to his son.

"That thing down the beach? Is that an alien?" Charlie wrote.

"I think so. We need to call somebody as soon as possible," Andreas said.

"Call who?" Charlie wrote.

"The government, I guess. The police. Someone in authority."

"Hard to call anyone. No phones. No Internet. No power. Nothing," George wrote.

"Then we'll have to find someone," Andreas said. "You guys from Haida Gwaii?"

George nodded. "Massett," he wrote.

"Got a police presence there?"

"RCMP," Charlie wrote.

"Can you get us there?" Andreas said.

Charlie smiled and gave Andreas a thumbs up and gestured to the boat.

They all pushed the boat back out into the waves and climbed in.

A few yards offshore Charlie pulled on the Johnson cord a few times and it roared back to life. Andreas cupped his hand to one ear and grinned. "I can hear that. It's faint, but it's there."

Constable Fisk was six feet, six inches tall and had a whisk of mowed blond hair. He had a small jagged scar on his left nostril. One of his favorite stories was about some dude tearing out the piercing during a fight. Charlie also knew Fisk had had large tattoos removed from his arms before applying to the force. The procedure had left large pinky patches above the elbows, and the local gossip was Fisk had drawn perpetual "aboriginal" duty because of his shady past. They all loved him though. He never played favorites and would always take folks home if they were impaired, a free ride in the back of his squad car unless, of course, they'd done something worse. That didn't happen often in Massett.

They found Fisk doing paperwork in the small detachment office. The constable smiled at Charlie as he and Andreas entered. George had gone off to deal with other matters.

"Hey, Charlie," he said giving one of those arm-wrestling handshakes. "Who's your friend?"

"This is Andreas," Charlie said.

Charlie could see Fisk giving Andreas the once over, not impressed with what he was seeing. Still Fisk shook the German's hand. "Andreas?" he said.

"He can't hear you," Charlie said. "The aliens made him deaf."

"Aliens?"

"So, if you want to talk to him you have to write it down. He can talk, though."

"You been into the THC, Charlie?" Fisk asked. He never called pot pot.

"No. Dad and I saw some smoke signals coming from one of those small islands to the west, and we went to investigate. We thought with all the strange shit that's been going on, maybe someone got stranded. Anyway, that's when we found Andreas and a dead alien."

Fisk gave Charlie one of his tolerant looks, then looked at Andreas and pulled out a pad of paper.

"He telling the truth?" Fisk wrote.

"I didn't hear what he said, so I don't know," Andreas said. "But we're here to report a downed alien craft on the other side of that island. There's an alien corpse in it. How it got there is a long story, but we thought the authorities should know about this. Alien microbes infecting us and all that."

"So, this is legit?" Fisk asked Charlie.

"Yeah, it is," Charlie said. "I saw it myself before we found Andreas. You probably need to go see it."

Fisk grabbed his coat. "I'm assuming you've got a working boat?"

"We're going to see it," Charlie wrote on the pad and handed it to Andreas.

"Is that a good idea?" Andreas asked. "Without experts or something? Because if that thing is dangerous, if it constitutes a biological hazard, then you'll be exposing yourself."

Charlie looked at Fisk.

Fisk nodded and wrote. "Understand my position here... You've just told me there's a dead alien in some kind of vehicle, which I'm assuming is also alien. If it wasn't for all the strange shit that's gone down the past few days, this wouldn't have a pinch of credibility. There's still the possibility this is just some kind of hysteria and I need to know whether or not it is before I can bring in anybody. Besides it's not as if I can just make a call."

Andreas nodded. "How's communication, anyway? Can you talk to the mainland?"

"Only by sending someone over in a boat," Fisk wrote. "Nothing that requires electricity, even battery-powered, is working. Here or there."

"Any chance I could get something to eat and maybe a change of clothes before we do this?" he asked. "It's been a rough three days."

Fisk shook his head and pointed to the wharf.

They met George on the way. The old man's pockets bulged with granola and candy bars, and he carried a six pack of warm Pepsi. "After you described drinking pond water and eating a seal pup, I figured you might want something else to cleanse your pallet."

"You ate a seal pup?" Fisk said.

Andreas didn't understand what either man had said, but he gratefully took the food from George.

"Yeah, he did," Charlie answered for Andreas. "He was in survival mode when we found him. Not a hell of a lot else to eat on those islands."

Fisk gave Andreas a sideways look but said nothing.

"So, what's the plan?" George asked.

"Going to go check out the alien," Charlie said.

"Make sure the fuel tank is topped up. We burned at least half a tank this morning," George said.

"You're not coming?" Fisk asked.

"She rides low in the water with four people in it. Charlie can get you there."

Fisk nodded, pulled out his notebook, and described the situation to Andreas. "I'll want your story too. All of it," he wrote.

***

Jonathan Fisk thought he'd seen it all in his forty-one years, most of it already forgotten. But he would not forget this. He'd taken the old Canon TX camera, the one in storage at the station since long before his time, and the black and white film that still sat in little yellow boxes in the fridge. The film had expired years before but had been refrigerated until three days ago, so Fisk hoped it would still take an image. The detachment's digital camera met the same fate as everything else electronic in the village, so if he wanted to take photographs, the old mechanical camera was his only choice. No meter though, because that too needed a battery. He would have to guess at the exposure. Fisk wondered, as he brought the strange creature into focus from yet another angle, if anyone on the mainland would have the equipment to develop the film even if it was good. *Not my problem,* he thought.

But the preservation of the scene was his problem, at least for the time being. At high tide the alien craft was partially submerged, and they were one West Coast storm away from losing it altogether. It could be washed out to sea. He took the last of the film cartridges out of the camera and dropped them into a plastic bag.

"Think you can get this to Rupert?" he said to Charlie.

"You want me to take it?"

"Look, I'm improvising at the moment. Nothing is normal about what going on, and the stress level in this community is going up. It will continue to go that way until things get normalized, and who knows when that will happen. I can't leave at this point and I think you know that. I'm trusting you to get this over to Rupert."

"In that old boat?" Charlie said.

"Got another one?"

"That's like eight to ten hours, and those waters aren't safe for a small craft."

"It's the only way we can do it. None of the float planes are flying. The authorities need to see this. It's important."

"My arm will be a scrambled egg before I get there," Charlie said.

"So, switch arms. It's not like you need precision steering to get across that water."

Charlie nodded.

"I'll write it up. You take them across. OK?"

"Yeah, sure."

***

Andreas stood at a distance, watching as Fisk and Charlie decided what to do. He'd been careful not to be in any of the photographs and was glad his disability meant he had been excluded from much of the discussion. Were he not on the run, he'd want to be front and center on this, but under the circumstances, that was unwise. The small bit of fame he would receive as an Eco-terrorist paled compared to this. Bad timing. Ironic but true. What he needed to do first was take stock of this new reality, and to do that he'd need to get off this island.

"Charlie will take the film across to Rupert," Fisk wrote to him.

"In this boat?"

Fisk nodded.

Andreas turned to Charlie. "Do you want some company?"

Charlie shrugged.

"I need to get back to my family," Andreas said. "They've had no word for three days and are probably worried sick."

Charlie nodded a reluctant acceptance.

"Charlie knows the risks out there," Fisk wrote. "You don't. Life vests are mandatory."

"I had to swim across a mile of open ocean to get to that island, and that was after a plane crash. I survived. I doubt if the risks compare to that."

"Still, the vests are mandatory," Fisk said, and Andreas heard him.

Communication

Teracia's biggest problem was that she alone could go into the containment area. The whales were not yet singing but when they did, the result would be fatal to any fahr caught within the area. Personal filters might protect other fahr from death, but the resulting impairment would render them useless for any task. She was on her own.

The computers could not yet synthesize Homines speech. Her own vocal apparatus, a combination of mouth, tongue and diaphragm, generated nothing but squeaks and drones in atmospheric conditions. There was only one way she could communicate with the Homine: written language. To do that, she would have to improvise a writing surface, one that would work in atmospheric conditions. The technicians had provided for a wide variety of contingencies, but this was not one of them. She set them to work on a solution. In the meantime, she improvised by scratching words on a turtle shell and held them out of the water for the Homine to read. Her first question caught it off guard.

"Can you sing?" she wrote.

The creature looked at her and made a series of incomprehensible noises, nothing even remotely close to song, though there were non-musical pitch changes. She would have to provide it with writing tools. The terminal would have to be two-way. More work for the technicians. She tried again.

"Shake head or nod," she wrote. "Can you sing?"

The creature looked at her again and then nodded.

"Good," she wrote.

***

Kale concluded that the creature must have been a fahr. That was how the aliens had identified themselves in their interactions with the Security Council. It also appeared he was in no immediate danger. This fahr was helping him to survive, but he was growing tired of a diet of tepid water and raw fish. He wondered how it was affecting his health.

But there was the whole issue of its first question to him. Not "How are you?" or "What is your name?" or "Who is your leader?" or "How did you get on board?" No. It wanted to know if he could sing. Sing? Why was that important? Would he have to entertain them to survive? It was odd, but he knew, from now on, everything would be. Keeping his sanity depended on his ability to adapt.

Survivalists

It had to be the oddest rendition of Reveille ever played at a military establishment. Or perhaps "renditions" was the better word, plural in the sense that old Robby Saunders never played it the same way twice. Bebop Reveille he called it. The way Dizzy would have played it, he said. A modernized version of "The 'Boogie Woogie Bugle Boy'," he said. Jake Punster had no idea what he was talking about. Sometimes old Robby would vamp on the tune for as long as ten minutes. It was impossible to sleep through that, and that was the point. Robby got everyone up. Love him or hate him, you were awake before old Robby finished his solo.

Jake was always awake long before old Robby started to blow. They were tent mates, and old Robby had no concept of how to drag himself out of his cot without making a racket. Usually he fell out, and when he did, he moaned and cursed God, an unchristian thing to do. Old Robby would then repent down on his knees before his cot, loudly asking for forgiveness. You could no more sleep through that than you could sleep through his trumpet playing.

Jake Punster didn't care. He was a morning person anyway, and just as old Robby had his instrument, Jake had a Winchester

Model 70 he'd inherited from his father. Every morning he cleaned and polished the rifle before he got dressed. He hadn't always been good with guns. Until a few months back he couldn't hit much of anything.

Then came the Ted Nugent incident. That's how he liked to think of it, anyway. He was at a shooting range firing at paper targets with "Cat Scratch Fever" cranked up to ten on his iPod when he gets zapped by a pair of wireless headphones. How the hell does that happen? But it did, and when it did he lost the headphones and the iPod, so hot they were smoking. He was so pissed he fired the rest of the rounds in rapid succession, and every shot hit the target. Every shot. Now he could hit something the size of a silver dollar at a hundred yards even if it was moving. Ground squirrels were easy. There wasn't much left of one if he hit it, and he usually did.

He put the gun down, got dressed in his usual Ted Nugent tee and jeans, picked the gun up again and held the barrel of it up to his face. With the other hand, he held a mirror. His sergeant had told him mirrors were a vanity item, and they should be used only as signaling devices and not for personal grooming. But Jake couldn't help himself. He liked the way his beard had grown in since the aliens attacked. It covered most of his acne and made him look much older than his eighteen years. And tougher. He liked the tougher part. He'd rolled up the sleeves on his T-shirt to show off the snake tattoos coiling his arms. The urbies wouldn't mess with him if they knew what was good for them, their own bloody fault for being unprepared.

They had a group of urbies tied together in the center of the camp. The men would be given a chance. If they could handle a gun, tie basic knots, demonstrate wood lore, and had a decent amount of Bible knowledge, they might be allowed to stay. The women? Well, they'd have to repopulate once the urbies had all starved to death. Jake liked that idea. They'd all be like the Mormons with several wives apiece.

Abe Thompson was walking around the urbies, inspecting them. The commander had a Crocodile Dundee hat covered in fishing lures and always had smokes, not roll-your-owns like everyone else, but looted ones. Jake had found some once going through an old farm house and turned them over. Thompson had given him one of his gap-toothed smiles and smoked all six packs in three days. Jake wished he'd kept at least one pack for himself.

The commander stopped in front of one urbie, a black man in a tattered jogging suit. "And what were you before all this happened?" he asked.

"A geneticist, sir." the man said.

"A geneticist?"

"A scientist. I worked in a lab at John Hopkins studying the human genome."

"In case you hadn't noticed we've got no laboratories here," Thompson said. "Got any other skills?"

The geneticist thought for a moment. "I'm a competent gardener," he said.

"A gardener? So, what you're saying is you want to do women's work?"

The geneticist opened his mouth as if to speak and then shut it.

"See, we keep things simple here. People have roles and they fill them. The women do the gardening here. They also teach, do housekeeping, child minding, and cooking. We, on the other hand," he gestured to the well-armed group of men standing behind him, "we do the hunting, scavenging, camp building, preaching, and if need be, the killing. So, if you're going to join up with us you'll need those kinds of skills. Got any of them?"

The geneticist hesitated. "I've done quite a bit of camping," he said.

"Camping? What kind of camping?"

"Well, we had a tent trailer we pulled behind our..."

"A tent trailer?" All the men laughed.

"I was also a combat medic," the geneticist said.

63

Thompson looked at him and then at his men. "With the Special Operations Forces?"

"Yes, sir. In Afghanistan, sir. For two years, sir."

"And then you got out, got a free veteran's education, became a scientist and a gardener, and pulled a tent trailer?"

"I used a Humvee, sir."

The men collapsed in laughter. Thompson grinned. "Well, at least you got a sense of humor. You being a scientist doesn't interest us much, but if you've been a combat medic, we can use that. You know if you don't have those skills we're going to find out damn quickly."

"I'm a little out of practice, sir. It's been twelve years."

"You'll get plenty of practice with us. You got family?"

The geneticist gestured to the women and children. "My wife and daughter are over there."

Thompson turned to Jake. "Find them a tent," he said and turned back to the geneticist. "What's your name?"

"Peter Howard, sir. Dr. Peter Howard."

Thompson studied him. "I don't care that you're a black man, Howard, or that you've got an education. But some here will, so do yourself a favor and forget you were ever a professor."

Peter Howard's daughter, Tracy, was a cute little brown thing, but she didn't have much meat. Jake figured she was thirteen, maybe fourteen so she'd grow into that. He liked his women slim, anyway. Not that he'd had much experience. In high school most of the girls had been turned off by his interest in guns and the paramilitary. Every photo he posted on Snapchat showed a pimply-faced kid with a rifle.

He led the Howards to one of the older army surplus tents, a patched and ragged affair that had gone unclaimed for a reason. Water pooled on the floor whenever it rained. In the field, it would have held eight soldiers, so it had more than enough room for a small family.

Howard's wife sighed to her husband once Jake had ushered them through the tent flaps.

"We'll make it work, Sonya," he told her and raised a finger to his lips to shush her.

"I'm hungry," Tracy said.

Jake handed them three lanyards, all with a picture of a very white Jesus enclosed in clear plastic. He gestured to his left. "There's a mess tent down the way," he said, smiling at Tracy. "Wear these and you'll get fed."

Sonya was staring at the empty cots along the tent's wall. "Bedding?" she asked.

"I'll ask around," Jake said. "Maybe somebody's got some to spare." He turned to Tracy and gave her his warmest smile. "We'll see you later," he said exiting the tent.

Canoe

The breaths were longer than before, and if she remained calm, she was fine. Honi was not sure whether this was a case of training her brain to get by on less oxygen or controlling more of her lungs. It didn't matter. She could breathe. If she could keep herself on an even keel and didn't allow herself to become excited, she could breathe. But things were ramping up, and she felt herself getting lightheaded.

The cousins had come to the house for the three of them.

Her father was standing in the middle of the room, arms folded across his chest and shaking his head. "She won't survive. You know she won't survive," he told them.

"None of you will survive if you stay here," Ka Pua said as she matched Peni's folded arms. "Even the bloody Mormons are running out of food."

Kale had once confided in Honi he thought Ka Pua was cute. *Cute and formidable,* Honi thought with a grin.

"We can eat fish," Peni said.

"There aren't enough working boats. You'll never survive."

In her addled state Honi began to think about milk, cold milk splashing down her throat. For the past week they'd been eating papaya, a few vegetables, bananas, macadamia nuts, pineapple, and fish. That morning Noelani had fed her daughter watery oatmeal sweetened with cane sugar. A Mormon elder had dropped off the supplies with a copy of the Book of Mormon a few days earlier. The young elder had called it a treat. Honi remembered the incident with a little gaspy giggle as she imagined chowing down on the holy book. Her father looked at her.

"You see, get her excited and…"

Honi found a deeper breath. "Dad!"

"You'll never survive."

"We'll never survive," she whispered, "Which is worse?"

"You won't be able to move, to use your chair. They'll have to strap you in."

"California, Dad. I want to see California. And I want to sail on the Israel." She hummed "Somewhere Over the Rainbow" and giggled.

Her father was silent.

Honi frowned. "What else have I got to look forward to?" she whispered. "I want to learn how to read the stars, and the sun and the moon and the waves. I want to be a wayfinder."

"Like Nainoa Thompson," said Ka Pua nodding. "Or Mao Piailug."

Peni sighed. "What do you think?" he asked Noelani.

Mother looked at daughter. "I'm getting awfully tired of papaya," she said with a grin, but Honi could see resignation behind the cheeriness.

The cousins had named the double hulled canoe the Israel Kamakawiwoʻole after the late native Hawaiian singer. The name was so long it stretched over half the length of each hull. The boat's frame was a golden brown and hand carved out of large dacha logs imported from Fiji. To Honi everything about the vessel glowed. They'd fixed her chair and bed dead center on the lower deck with her sole remaining oxygen tank close by in case she needed it. It put her right in the middle of the action.

They were now about half a mile offshore; the main mast had been raised and the wayfinders were in the final stages of planning their trip to California. Unlike Tahiti, California was a big target, but it was also one not usually chosen. Most long voyages for such canoes were to other Polynesian islands. After much discussion, they had decided to reduce the target size to San Diego, America's closest port at 2500 miles. But such an uncommon destination also meant they could not go by traditional routes. Reading the sea and sky had to be done differently, so even though the canoe had been launched and they were on their way, much remained to be worked out.

Honi listened to their chatter until she tired and nodded off. The most difficult thing about her improved breathing was it had not yet become autonomic. Taking deeper breaths was something she did purposefully while awake. When she slept, sometimes she would wake and find herself struggling to breathe. She suspected that during dreaming her unconscious mind reverted her breathing to how she had been before. But once she was awake, regaining control was easy. It sometimes made for a restless sleep, but things were improving.

This time it was not her breathing that woke Honi. It felt like one of the cousins had thrown a bucket of water over her, but it wasn't a cousin. A giant humpback had breached right in front of the Israel, soaking her and the cousins. A wild whoop of delight came from the crew. Then more animals did the same, breeching in a circle around the craft. Soon the entire crew was baptized, and the boat was rocking back and forth on the wake created by the animals. Then the whales stopped, floating to the surface and surrounding the boat. They were so close Honi could smell their rancid blowhole breath and hear their sucking inhalations. She thought back to

67

Uncle Mikala's funeral. There were more humpbacks now than there were at the ceremony. Somehow, they knew of the importance of these events. She wished Kale was here to see this. Any lingering doubts about the intelligence of these great beasts would be gone.

Then they disappeared beneath the waves. She thought of Kale, stranded somewhere in Alaska.

Charlie

Andreas wasn't much of a companion. The German sat in the bow of the boat and stared out at the water, giving only the smallest grin when a pod of orcas broke the surface near the craft.

With his hands on the vibrating throttle, Charlie couldn't write messages, couldn't communicate, at least not in the sense of asking questions. He assumed Andreas would retell his story, regaling him with more details about the alien encounter, but Andreas seemed preoccupied. The German waited until they were within sight of Prince Rupert before he said anything.

It was brief and to the point. Andreas repeated the basics of the crew's encounter with the alien spaceship, their shooting down of the smaller craft, and their eventual destruction at the hands to the spaceship's sonic weapon. He restated his belief the smaller craft they had shot down was the one they found on the beach, complete with the dead alien.

Charlie had lots of questions but no way to ask. When they got to the dock Andreas jumped out of the boat and told Charlie he'd need a washroom fast. The German left Charlie to tie up and secure the craft. Charlie did and searched for more than an hour before realizing the German was gone.

The RCMP detachment was in a red and blue building about half a mile from the port. Charlie walked through the door and set the bag of film on the counter top.

"What's this?" The woman at the counter asked him. She was matronly, had big dyed-blond hair that looked like she'd slept on it, and a cheap polyester green pant suit.

"It's a present from Constable Fisk in Masset," Charlie said. "He asked me to bring it over to you guys."

The woman spilled the contents of the bag onto the counter top.

"Thirty-five-millimeter film?" she said.

"Yeah, well none of the digital cameras in Masset are working just now," Charlie said. "We had to use an old thirty-five mill camera."

"These for some ongoing case?"

Charlie steeled himself. "I guess that will depend on what cases you have opened now," he said.

The woman glared at him. "I don't have time, none of us have time, to fart around here. You see any constables in the station now? Most of them are going twenty-four seven dealing with the issues caused by that thing," she said waving at the air. "So just tell me straight what this is about."

"It's about that thing. We found a crashed alien aircraft of some sort on one of the small islands off the northwest coast of Haida Gwaii. It's got a dead alien in it. These are pictures of it."

"What?"

"A dead alien. The photos are of a dead alien and the spaceship it was in. Constable Fisk took them himself and I was with him when he did it. Here are his notes," Charlie said, fishing the papers out of his jacket.

The woman read them. "You're not kidding, are you?"

"Develop the film," Charlie said.

"How the hell are we going to do that? It's been years since the last time we used a darkroom. I'm not even sure one still exists in this town. And if it does, it'll need electricity."

"Got working generators?" Charlie asked.

69

"A few," the woman admitted.

"Then I'd prioritize this. I just made a five-and-half hour trip across the water in a small boat to bring you this. I was asked to do that by Constable Fisk. This is real and because it's real, it's important."

"You come alone?"

"No," Charlie admitted.

"So, who came with you?"

Charlie gestured toward the papers. "The guy Fisk talks about in his notes. Andreas is his name. He has a German accent. I think he's a pilot or something."

"So, where is he?"

"I don't know. When we pulled into the dock, he said he was going to the can, and then he didn't come back. I tried to find him but..." He shrugged. "That was about two hours ago."

She looked at him. "So. You arrive here with undeveloped pictures of a dead alien shot on thirty-five-millimeter film. The guy who's supposed to have shot the thing down comes with you, but he takes a powder as soon as you get over here. Is that correct?"

"I don't know where he went," Charlie said. "Or why."

The women sighed. "Have a seat," she said. "What's your name?"

"Charlie."

"Last name?"

"Dayaang."

"Isn't there a Haida chief with that name?"

"He's my uncle."

"OK, Charlie. My name's Vera Pollock It's not my place to make a judgment call here—though Lord knows we're short of staff and that's happening anyway—but one of the constables should be back soon. I'm thinking you won't be heading back to Masset tonight. You got a place to stay?"

"I have relatives here, but they don't know I'm in town." Charlie shrugged. "It's not like I can call them. I'll wander over there after I meet with the constable and see if they're around. If not, I might need to do something. You offering?"

"Let me know if you need a place, and I'll see what I can do."

Charlie read his way through an entire issue of Sports Illustrated before the constable returned. He wore the standard cop utility belt that included everything he might need, including a pistol.

"You waiting to see me?" the constable said. He was short for a cop, a little flabby at the waist and thick through the legs. Charlie could hear the resignation in the question.

"For a while, yeah," Charlie said.

Vera pushed forward the bag containing the film. "Fisk sent him over with photos of a dead alien," she said.

"What?"

"Yeah, exactly," Vera said, passing Fisk's notes over to him.

The constable read the paper, eyebrows raising as he did so. He looked in the bag. "This is old undeveloped film. What are we supposed to do with this?"

"Jesus, Frank, I don't know. Find some place to get it developed, I guess."

"Doesn't that require power?"

"Vera said you guys had access to generators," Charlie said. "That thing is rotting on the shore off that island right now. Scientists are going want to see it before there's nothing left."

Constable Frank looked at him. "You've seen this thing?"

"I was there when Constable Fisk took the pictures. I'm even in some of them. It's real. Probably came from that black thing," he said gesturing to the sky.

"Jesus," said Frank. "If this is legit then it has to go much further up the chain. I say we forward the negatives to them and let them worry about it. There's a couple of old float planes they've now got working. Let's get this to Vancouver."

"One thing, though," Charlie said. "I'd like to be a part of this when it happens. I found it."

"Not my call, kid," Frank said.

"It's on our territory," Charlie said.

"Yeah, well, it's still not my call."

"The German guy Fisk talked about in his notes?" Vera said.

Frank looked her. "What about him?"

"Came over with Charlie in the boat and then vanished."

"Vanished?"

"Yeah, a bit odd that. You'd think he'd want to stick around and tell his story."

Constable Frank looked at Charlie. Charlie shrugged. "I can't explain it," he said. "He left me in the boat. His business, I guess. But I know what I saw. The alien is real. Fisk thinks it's real too and you've got photos. The negatives at least, and it's not as if you can Photoshop those."

Frank smacked his palm against the counter top. "I've got an entire detachment dealing with hysteria, drunks, and looting. It's not like I've got the resources to deal with..." He read through Fisk's notes again. He looked at Charlie. "The guy who came over with you. He's a pilot?"

"Well, he never said he was. Not to me, anyway. But I think he said something like that to Fisk. I wasn't paying that much attention."

"You said his name was Andreas? Get a last name?"

Charlie shook his head. "He's got a German accent."

"And he takes a powder as soon as he gets to the mainland? I'm thinking he doesn't want involvement with law enforcement."

"He told his story to Fisk," Charlie said.

"Yeah, but Masset's pretty isolated at the moment. Worse than here. Probably didn't see Fisk as much of a threat. German accent, eh? Maybe he's here illegally."

"Just before all this stuff happened," Vera said. "You know when everything was still connected? There was this report out of somewhere in Northern B.C. I can't remember which town about an explosion..."

"The Twin Otter blowing up on a runway? A timed explosion? That was Fort Nelson, I think. I can't remember the details. But I know they couldn't find the pilot, but they were looking for a German immigrant, Maybe..."

"You think this is the guy?" Vera laughed. "I suppose it could be but, I mean, why would he go to Masset?"

"Yeah, then there's that."

"He was in the World War II bomber that flew out of the Abbotsford Airshow," Charlie said. "I think he said he was just a passenger. They chased that thing, and it led them to Haida Gwaii. The rest just happened, I guess."

"And he'd have to get from Fort Nelson to Abbotsford. That's like driving the length and width of B.C. Two day's drive. Doesn't get my vote."

Frank grinned at her. "Your vote doesn't count," he said.

She stuck out her tongue at him. "You don't work in a place for twenty-five years without getting a feel for it, you know."

"Anyway, I still think we have to find him. The powers that be will want to question him." He turned to Charlie. "You think you could describe him?"

"Well, he's wearing my clothes. He's got a faded black hoodie with totem poles on the back. A pair of Levi's. A pair of old Doc Martens. It all fits him pretty good."

"So, he's about your size?"

"Yeah, except his arms are longer. The sleeves only come to above the wrist."

"Hair color?"

"Brown, graying a bit. Scruffy beard. See, I only have an electric razor and..."

"Can I deputize you?" Frank asked.

"Deputize?"

"Well, not really, but I will need your help rounding up the other constables, so we can make this a priority. I'll point you in the right direction and give you a note for each of them. If you do that, then I'll recommend that you accompany whoever comes to investigate this. No promises but I'll do my best."

"Sure," Charlie said.

Frank turned to Vera. "Hold the fort. I'm going to go down to the dock and see what I can do about engaging one of those ancient float planes. God, I hope this is legit, otherwise I could be looking at early retirement."

Andreas

Rain. That's what Prince Rupert was known for, and that's what it gave him. Andreas stood by the side of the Yellowhead Highway with his thumb out. The damn thing was wrinkled. He'd never had that happen before, at least not outside of a bathtub or a swimming pool. Every part of him dripped. Anyone who gave him a ride would be inviting Noah's flood into their back seat. He needn't have worried. One old clunker passed by every fifteen minutes or so, each one full of passengers and none interested in adding to their load. But he could hear them, the Doppler effect of each car as it approached and passed by. The sound was still distant and muddy, but it was there.

A 1978 Ford Thunderbird blowing gray smoke from the exhaust slowed, loaded with six burly men passing beers around.

"Where are you going?" the one in the front passenger seat shouted and Andreas heard him. It was faint, but it was there.

"Vancouver," he shouted back.

The car erupted in guffaws. "It's about a three-month walk," the man said. "You should try the coast. Much more direct. Trouble is, you'll have to swim!" More laughter as the car drove off.

"I think I am swimming," Andreas responded under his breath to the receding vehicle. He'd heard the laughter and every word the man had said. His ears were healing. The horizon showed, at best, he had an hour left of sunlight. Rain light? He grimaced, turned, and started the squishy walk back into town. *They're going to get me anyway.*

The first person he met was an RCMP constable on a bicycle, most of it covered by a huge rain cape.

"You, Andreas?" the cop asked flashing a little sign with "Andreas?" printed on it.

"Take me to your leader," Andreas said, "but only if he has dry clothes and a fireplace."

The cop grinned. "Welcome to Rupert."

"You know what I miss most about not having hydro?" Vera said trying to wring out Andreas's sodden clothes.

"A dryer?" Frank said.

"Exactly," she said placing the jeans Andreas had borrowed from Charlie on a drying rack. The three of them were in Vera's front room. She had the biggest fireplace in town.

Andreas sat on a stool wrapped in a Hudson's Bay blanket and shivering. He took a hot chocolate from Frank and nodded his thanks.

"So, I guess we'd better get started. We can't tape this session, so Vera will take notes."

Andreas told his story, starting at connecting with Jeff on line and the invitation to join the crew of the B-25 in Abbotsford, and how the alien encounter played out after they took off. He said nothing about his previous life. Constable Frank asked some questions, but Andreas was careful not to give him any more information than he'd given Fisk. Frank pulled his chair around, so he was facing Andreas and studied him.

"I have a few questions," he said. "Let me know if you're having trouble hearing me."

"My hearing is coming back," said Andreas. "It's not all the way back yet, but it's getting there. I'll let you know if you should repeat something."

"Good. So, my first question is why you felt it necessary to leave Charlie in the boat and try to hitchhike out of town?"

"I'm guessing you have some theories about that," Andreas said.

"I don't," Frank said. "It doesn't make a lot of sense, because if you were trying to avoid the police, why'd you talk to Constable Fisk?"

Andreas shrugged. "Someone needed to know about what happened. I figured if I told him, I'd have done my duty. He could take it from there. And I'm not trying to avoid the police. I'm just trying to get home."

"Home?"

"Yes."

"Where is home?"

"Edmonton," Andreas said. This was true, technically. He owned a small condo that he used when visiting the Alberta capital.

"But the constable said you were trying to get to Vancouver?"

"My truck is parked at the Abbotsford Airport. I thought I'd collect that first."

"Truck?"

"An F-150," Andreas said. Shit! Too much information!

"An F-150? Interesting." Frank studied him long and hard. "You didn't perhaps purchase it in Fort Nelson?"

Andreas blanched and attempted to meet Frank's gaze. "Fort Nelson? Why would I go to northern B.C. to buy a truck?"

"So, you know where Fort Nelson is? Most people don't."

"Of course, I know," Andreas said. "I'm a bush pilot. We often fly in and out of there."

"In a Twin Otter?" Frank asked.

Andreas said nothing.

"Someone landed a Twin Otter in Fort Nelson about a day before the aliens attacked. A few hours later a bomb went off in that plane, destroying it, and damaging other aircraft. Now I'm out here in Prince Rupert, so I'm not paying too much attention to the details. It wasn't my problem. I didn't get the name, for instance, of the person they were looking for. But one thing I do remember is some guy came forward a few hours after the news broke and said he'd sold his F-150 to some German guy in a bar. He said the fellow he'd sold it to paid him extra just to delay the transfer of registration. A few hours later an old RCMP buddy of mine—same graduating class—drops me an email and tells me he's in shit because he failed to check the insurance and registration of a guy he pulls over for speeding and let's off with a warning. That's a violation of procedures, but he does write down the plate number. Turns out the plates were stolen."

"And you think that's me?" Andreas asked.

"The guy he pulled over had a German accent. So, they're putting two and two together, and they figure this is the guy who bought the truck in Nelson. Our entire communication system is down so I don't have access to any information now, but it seems there are a few too many coincidences here."

Andreas looked away. "Martyrdom," he whispered.

"I'm sorry?" Frank said.

"It's an odd concept don't you think? The idea one individual can sacrifice his life for the common good. Jesus did it if you buy the Gospel narrative. The thing is I'm no longer sure condemning oneself to a prolonged time in prison qualifies. Especially in the light of what has happened since. I blew up a plane to protest global warming, to protest the way we were raping our environment and driving all these species to extinction. But then the aliens show up and now, in the light of what's happened, blowing up a plane just seems kind of pathetic. Maybe it always was. I don't know."

Constable Frank stared at him.

Hinton

Constable Frank got the film and Andreas to Vancouver by commandeering one of the few working de Havilland float planes. The officer delivered Andreas to the authorities and sent the film with Charlie to the University of British Columbia. The scientists at the University of British Columbia wasted no time assembling a functioning darkroom and a HAZMAT team. A day later a barge loaded with biological containment equipment, and towed by an old but powerful diesel tug, was on its way to Haida Gwaii.

A day later the recovery team, including Charlie, was on the same de Havilland heading for the crash site. He sat in the front seat with the pilot. "Think you can recognize that island from the air?" the pilot asked Charlie.

"Yeah, sure. It's kind of burned into my memory."

"Good."

The plane flew over the island from the cliff side, made a wide turn and approached from the beach.

"How quick is the drop-off?" the pilot shouted to him once the plane was down.

"Pretty gradual," Charlie answered. He watched as the plane approached the shore. "We should be able to wade in from here."

The pilot cut the engines and everyone behind him talked at once. Dr. Andrew Hilton, an older balding man with a ponytail and a graying goatee, shouted orders. "All right, everyone, put your packs on and carry your boots. We'll make a pile on the beach until we've unloaded everything." Hinton was the head of the Biology Department at UBC and so far, had barely acknowledged Charlie.

Most of the equipment was camping gear. Little of what Charlie saw looked like scientific equipment. "How can I help?" he asked Hinton.

"For now, just help us carry the gear to the shore. You're the other witness?"

"Yeah, me and my Dad."

"I've already had several sessions with the renegade pilot. You and I will have a talk later."

Charlie nodded. "Seems to be mostly camping gear," he said.

"The barge has the equipment for a field lab. Should be here soon," Hinton said. "We do have a couple of HAZMAT suits so a couple of us can do a preliminary evaluation. We'll do that after we set up camp."

Later Hinton took Charlie aside and asked him about his initial alien encounter. The questions centered on Charlie's well-being and that of his father. Soon it became clear Andreas had already filled in most of the more interesting details, and Charlie was being treated as a secondary witness. Charlie had hoped for more but knew Andreas had the better story. The interview was brief. Afterwards Hinton returned to his team, all of whom were doing little more than standing around their equipment and observing the alien through binoculars. Charlie wandered over to the lone female member of the team. She looked Asian but had a Salish orca tattooed on her face

"Hi, I'm Charlie," he said to her.

"Cynthia," she said with a brief forced smile.

"Why aren't we getting closer?" Charlie asked.

"We're taking a risk as it is," she said. "We have a tug on the way pulling a barge with a lot more equipment, including decon showers for the HAZMAT suits. It should be here in a couple of hours."

"So, we wait?"

"We wait. And hope we don't breathe in or encounter anything contaminated. The isolation on this island is a good thing, because if something does go wrong, it'll be easier to confine it. In the meantime, we have no way of disinfecting the suits so putting one on would mean staying in it, at least until the barge gets here."

Charlie thought about this. During his first encounter with the alien, he'd been a lot closer than this. No negative effects far as he could tell.

"Look at this, Dr. Hinton," Cynthia said, handing the professor the binoculars and pointing to a group of seals in the distance. "I've been watching them for over an hour. No signs of distress in those animals. Normal behavior as far as I can see."

Hinton took the binoculars and studied the seals for a few minutes. He pursed his lips. "Well, all that means is the alien microbes, if the seals have been exposed to them at all, are not having a catastrophic effect so far. Not with these animals anyway. But there's a multitude of possible explanations for that. Still it's a good sign." He turned to Charlie. "How close did you get to it?" he asked.

"Five yards maybe," Charlie said.

"And there's been no change in your health since then?"

"Like what?"

"No rashes, diarrhea, joint pain, that kind of thing?"

Charlie shook his head.

"You should all be in isolation," Hinton said. "Would be if the situation was normal. Four of you were directly exposed. You, your dad, Andreas Huber, and Officer Fisk. And that exposure took place three days ago. And many other people have been exposed to the four of you since then, without outward manifestations of infection in anyone. *Yet.*"

"It didn't smell," Charlie said.

"Smell?"

"Sure. Anything of that size that washes up on the shore goes bad pretty quick. Whales, dolphins, sharks... Those can get gross. I didn't smell anything but salt spray and kelp when we were near it."

"We can't detect an odor from this distance," Cynthia said.

Charlie closed his eyes and rotated his head back and forth. When he opened his eyes, his head pointed in the general direction of the alien wreck. He pointed about twenty degrees to the left of it. "Wind's coming from there. We should smell it."

Hinton took a deep breath. "Nothing... At least not from this distance. You're right. Given the size of it, with normal decomposition, we should be able to detect it."

"But we can't, and the insects haven't started in on that thing yet either," Charlie said.

"Insects? How would you know that?" Hinton said.

"They'd make noise. I'd be able to hear them."

"Hear them?"

Charlie shrugged. "I have better hearing than most people."

Hinton studied Charlie. "You can hear insects eating?"

Charlie nodded. "It's kind of a high-pitched crunchy sound, but sometimes it sounds like someone sucking on a straw."

"Really?" Cynthia said.

"It's a little weird, I know, but I bet you when you open it up, you don't find insects. At least not ones feeding on it."

Cynthia and Dr. Hinton looked at each other. Charlie knew he shouldn't have said anything.

Prostallen

"Just one?" Prostallen asked.

"Yes," Teracia said.

"And why is that significant?"

"We left Thryke on Planet Song. Now we have two reasons to return there."

Prostallen said nothing. His tentacles floated in front of him, twitching. He turned to the mender in the room. "Could you please secure these? I can't retract them, and they keep floating in front of my face. I can't carry on a conversation with that going on?"

"It will further restrict your movements and make you more vulnerable to...," the mender said.

"I don't care. I want to see the face of the fahr I'm talking to."

Teracia watched as the mender strapped Prostallen's tentacles to the sides of his body and rotated him to face her. He was now immobile. Because of his poor health, the ex-commander attracted more than his share of parasitic fish, feeding on his diseased scales and fins. Now he would be even more vulnerable.

"You may leave," he said to the mender.

"Are you sure, sir?"

"Vice Commander Teracia can help me if need be. Go."

He waited until the mender had left and then turned to Teracia. "So, what are you suggesting?"

"We have a homine on board this ship in an environment ill-suited to his survival. And we have a member of our own species stranded on a world that is also ill-suited to his survival. And you know as well as I do that should the Homines find the Xburner or Thryke himself, we can abandon the word 'push' to describe what will happen. 'Accelerate' would be a more appropriate word, especially if they get their hands on his PDM."

"Thryke was an idiot, and his actions will probably threaten the planet. Granted. But you cannot seriously be suggesting we now turn this expedition into some kind of Homines rescue mission?"

"Considering what we've already done, we have a moral obligation to..."

"I think you fail to understand something here," Prostallen said. "In a Centrix court of law Thryke's action will be seen, not as a corporate act, but as the action of an individual. And, given the way he did it, no one will hold Song Corp responsible. At the moment, the leadership on board seems quite upset by Thryke's actions, but they will soon understand this as a fortuitous event. A bit of spin will allow them to pin everything on him."

"That is your only concern here? The legal implications for Song Corp?"

"You act as if I or any other representative of Song Corp was responsible for Thryke's actions."

Teracia said nothing but her ballow inflated a deep crimson. "He was on this ship!"

"And he acted in defiance of a direct order, using his military experience to launch the Xburner undetected."

Teracia said nothing. "You need me," she hissed.

Prostallen blanched. "I don't have the level of influence you think. This is Wrasse's game now."

"What are you talking about? Agastin is the Commander of this mission."

"The moment the Singers vocalize the Commander will be lost to them. I think you know that. Wrasse may seem like a fahr of little consequence, but he was chosen to replace Greyling. They wouldn't have done that unless they were sure of his abilities. And, despite his eccentricities, he is good at what he does and at resisting temptation."

"Chosen to replace Greyling?"

"Yes. By the time we get back to Centrix, Wrasse will be the new CEO of Song Corp, perhaps before then."

"Wrasse?"

"Yes."

Teracia blanched. She swam several times back and forth across the room while Prostallen watched.

"Who knew about this?" she said.

"Greyling put him on this ship to test his willingness to do whatever he was called upon to do. As you've already realized Wrasse hates space travel, so for him this was a major test. We have already collected the Singers, so barring some catastrophe on the way back, Wrasse will be CEO."

"You didn't answer my question."

"I knew."

"Only you?"

"Until recently, yes. Agastin knows now. You may have noticed his change in attitude toward Wrasse."

"Who chose Wrasse?"

Prostallen's gills rippled. Several of the fish began picking at him. Teracia waved them away.

"Thank you. Damned annoying things. I can deal with the immobility but being eaten alive is quite another matter."

"They serve an ecological function," Teracia said, quoting the rationale for the inclusion of parasitic organisms on the biosphere.

Prostallen pinked.

"Who chose Wrasse?" she asked again.

"Well, that's the big question, isn't it? Greyling had a hand in the decision, but my understanding is he would have to get the board approval. No one, not even the highest-ranking executives within Song Corp, knows who's on that board. It's the biggest mystery at Song Corp. Has been for generations."

"Perhaps there is no board. Perhaps it's only Greyling."

"Two things work against that idea. First the board has been around for many generations of CEOs, so it's unlikely to have been fabricated by one of them. The second reason is that Greyling has often been upset with board decisions, and when he is he's difficult to be around. He may be the public face of Song Corp, but he's not all-powerful. Few common fahr know this about him, but it's true."

"It doesn't matter. Wrasse will need me. You will need me."

"You're right. I will need you, but I'd be careful using that as leverage with Song Corp. The closer we get to Centrix, the less valuable you will be. As for the homine, I'd take a different tack. Make sure it can sing."

"I've already thought of that."

"And can it?"

"Yes."

"So, you've talked to it?"

"I asked it that one question, yes. I had to bring it fresh water and a net to catch fish. It's in shock, of course."

"Wrasse and Agastin will not turn this ship around. Their mission now is to get the Singers to Centrix. But you might convince them to keep the homine alive, especially if it might be profitable. If it sings that will help. That will at least give it a novelty value and might give you the time to convince Wrasse of its PR potential."

"PR potential?"

Prostallen pinked. "All these years under my mentorship and you still haven't learned the basics. The courts will not hold Song Corp responsible for what happened to Homines, but the public might. If so, Song Corp may want to make a gesture. Returning the homine to Planet Song might seem like a good idea, an attempt to right an unintentional wrong. We might even be convinced to help repair the damage done."

"Six hundred years from now! By then there might not be anything left of Planet Song!"

"Well, Homines might survive. They are resourceful, but your personal options are limited. Keeping your little biped alive seems like your best course of action. And you'll get what you've always wanted, a chance to relate to another sapient species."

"We'd have to keep it alive for six hundred years. That's almost ten times its normal life span."

"At last count, we had three bored genetic engineers on this ship. They came for the taste, but their jobs amount to little more than minor adjustments to the stasis systems. They'd welcome the challenge of extending the homine's lifespan."

Jake

Hoarding was against militia rules. If you had more than you needed, you gave your extras to others who needed them. But some people wouldn't do this if they thought the others were undesirable. Like Blacks or Jews or Democrats.

Jake knew who had extras and what the Howard family needed. Tracy Howard had that big-eyed brown girl smile. It made him forget she was still a year or two off being a woman. He was only eighteen himself. In a few years no one would care about a four-year age difference. So, Jake decided to be helpful and gather the extras himself as if it were he who had the need. No one needed to know who the stuff was actually for.

Several times that night Jake showed up at the Howard tent with various items he had scrounged, and soon they had everything they needed. He helped Peter Howard fix the leaks in the tent roof. His last act, before leaving, was to slip Tracy a package of looted Twizzlers. She beamed at him and he melted.

He knew she'd be watching, hidden in the trees. But Thompson was there too, right beside him, evaluating. Jake fired ten rounds from a prone position, then ten more standing. All hit their mark. Thompson nodded his approval and then looked in Tracy's direction. He smirked and walked off.

Thompson called him in few days later, ten minutes after he had slipped Tracy another package of looted Twizzlers. Jake didn't know if Thompson had seen the exchange, but he expected the worst.

"How's that Winchester?" Thompson asked.

"It's fine, sir. I keep it cleaned and oiled."

"Still picking off ground squirrels?"

"No sir. That would be a waste of ammunition."

"Good. Because you're going to need that gun. We're going to make America great again."

"Sir?"

"The President," Thompson spat out, "has a new ground vehicle. They found some operational Brink's trucks somewhere, and they're using a large one to move her around. It's easy to spot because it never goes anywhere without a military escort. So, if we can take her out, we eliminate a big problem."

"Alatorre?" Jake said, his face draining of color.

Thompson said nothing.

Jake felt his heart rate go up. "I can't hit her in a Brink's truck, sir."

"You shouldn't have too. The local militia is going to disable the truck, so she'll have to leave it. And they're going to do it in as wide-open a space as possible to give you a clear shot." He studied Jake for a moment. "You up for it?"

"Yes, sir!"

"Good. Because you'll be going to Boston. When you get there, you'll be connecting with the New England Militia. They're urban so they don't have the talent we have, no snipers among them. That's why we're sending you. They all wear ball caps. You can identify the leadership by the guys who wear Boston area caps. Got that?"

"Yes, sir."

Thompson studied Jake. "I'm thinking this will remove you from your little temptation. You may have an excellent skill set with firearms, boy, but you are lacking in common sense. Here's hoping you acquire some of that during your time away."

"Yes, sir."

Inert

With the arrival of the tug and barge, the team set to work constructing the field laboratory. Hinton handed Charlie a clipboard and had him checking things as they came off the barge. Soon everything was arranged in neat little piles on the beach.

The equipment included four industrial strength pull start generators, any of which could power his DJ equipment. Charlie shook his head. It was the first time he'd thought of his turntables in a week. Just like that a major priority in his life changed. He no longer cared about remixing, loop triggering, and beat boxing. What mattered was that thing half-submerged on the beach, the one that had just changed the course of human history. What mattered was making sense of it.

Dr. Hinton and Cynthia were struggling into HAZMAT suits.

"Need a third person?" Charlie asked.

Hinton shook his head. "It takes a while to learn how to operate in one of these things. And we don't have proper breathing gear." He held out a mask that looked like the old pictures Charlie had seen of trench soldiers in the First World War. "Our usual masks have electronic components and like almost everything else, they don't work. These are just particle filters. They offer some protection, but they're usually inadequate for this kind of work. So, we're taking a risk going in with just these on. I can't ask you to take the same risk."

"I've already been exposed to it," Charlie said. "Nothing happened."

"Nothing that you know of," Hinton corrected. "I'm sorry, I can't take that risk. You can help us put these on, though."

"I have some First Nations' blood in my family," Cynthia said to Charlie as he helped her don the suit.

"Really?" Charlie said. She looked Asian but did have a Salish orca on her face.

Cynthia nodded. "It goes quite a way back. My great-great-grandfather was one of the original Chinese railroad workers. Back in his day the Chinese workers socialized with the Native communities because they were more accepting. There were many marriages between lonely Chinese men and First Nations women. My great-great-grandmother was one of those."

"Salish?"

"I don't know," she blushed and looked down. "I got the tattoo before I knew. It's kind of a cultural appropriation move, I know. I just liked the design, and it fits with me being a marine biologist. One of my family told me about my great-great-grandmother just a few months ago, but she didn't know much either. I intended to research it but, well... On line ancestry research is no longer an option. Be nice if she was Salish, though." She shrugged.

Charlie nodded. Cynthia was pouty cute. She had shaved the hair on the tattoo side with the remaining gelled black hair pulled straight and stiff away from the orca. As a post doc, she had at least eight years on him. He put a mental tick beside the word hormones and focused on the task at hand.

They took about half an hour to don the suits and check the seals.

"Give them a hand with those decontamination showers," Hinton said to Charlie, gesturing to the work the others were doing. "We'll need them as soon as we get back." With that Dr. Hinton and Cynthia began the slow waddling walk to the alien.

"As far as we can tell," Hinton said, "there's been no degradation at all. It's almost as if the creature was made of plastic."

Charlie smiled. They all had a newfound respect for him because, as he predicted, no insects.

"The morphological structures most resemble those of a fish, as do the cellular structures," Cynthia said, "but they're not decaying. Even when we add agents that should promote decay, it's not happening. The good news is it's not reactive with terrestrial biological material. It's inert. No rotting fish odor. Which means in its current state, it poses no threat to terrestrial life forms. That could change, however, which is why we'll continue wearing the suits."

Now that samples of the alien had been brought back to the field lab, everyone was wearing the suits, Charlie included. It felt like a giant sweaty diaper, but he didn't care. This was where he wanted to be.

"Are we going to move it?" one of the team asked.

"We're working on the logistics," Hinton said. "This is no small beast. It will be the equivalent of moving a beluga whale without the power equipment. And we can't damage it, so getting it out of the sand will be like working on an archaeological dig. It will have to be done with the utmost care. We don't want to miss biological material that may prove important."

"Most archaeologists don't wear HAZMAT suits," Charlie said.

Everyone looked at him.

Lame, Charlie thought. "My uncle has an old tow truck with a winch. Still works," he said. "We could bring it over on the barge, rig up some canvas slings and pulleys, and move it that way."

Hinton looked over at him and nodded.

"I have good marks," Charlie said to Hinton later. "Can I get into your department?"

"University application deadlines were several months ago," the professor said.

"Most of it done on line, right?"

Hinton nodded.

"So, right now they don't know who's registered and who isn't, right?"

The professor laughed. "There's not much functional on the administrative side at UBC. That's true."

"I wrote the SAT," Charlie said.

Hinton raised his eyebrows. "The SAT? You were thinking of going to school in the States?"

Charlie shrugged. "I was just testing myself. Against a bigger pool if you know what I mean. The school in Massett is small. Anyway, I did all right. Good enough to get into most colleges in the States."

"I thought you wanted to be a DJ?"

Did I tell him that? Must have. Shit. "What did you want to be when you were eighteen?"

Hinton smiled. "I wanted to play defense for the Boston Bruins. You see, Bobby Orr had just retired so there was a hole in their lineup."

"So, how did that go?"

"The following year I wound up at the University of Alberta. Played two seasons with the Golden Bears while getting my undergrad degree."

"Yeah? Well, I'll probably DJ a bit, earn some money on the side while doing my studies."

Hinton nodded. "OK, things will be chaotic when I get back, but if your grades are as good as you say, I'll do what I can to get you in."

Agastin

Commander Agastin was wary. He had treated Wrasse, the newly appointed CEO of Song Corp, like an inconsequential minion earlier in the voyage, making his life miserable. Now Wrasse equaled him in stature, at least far as those back on Centrix were concerned, so more care had to be taken. A change in status required a change in attitude, but this was not an easy transition for an ex-chancellor. A 60,000-year-old lifetime of entitlement was not so easy to abandon, and even if he could, such an action could be perceived as weakness.

"Why aren't they singing?" he demanded.

Wrasse's ballow maintained its green, even allowing entitlement gold around the fringes. He reached out and touched Agastin's shoulder, the action of an equal not a subordinate. When Agastin pinked, Wrasse removed his clasper and did a controlled gill ripple. Agastin decided, at that moment, to make no more demands of Song Corp's CEO.

"We're not dealing with vast stretches of ocean on this ship, Commander," Wrasse said. "We already know they sing partially as a way of locating each other over long distances. But on this ship the furthest they can get away from each other is a few miles. It's possible they may not feel the need to sing in such close quarters."

"I have a crew that's expecting taste. I'm expecting taste," Agastin said.

"Even though it's likely to be fatal, Commander?"

"We will filter it."

"Then it will not be taste. Taste is, by definition, unfiltered song."

Agastin went a deeper red. "The point is, Minister Wrasse, they're not singing!"

Wrasse maintained his green. "They are eating though, are they not, Commander Agastin? As you well know stressed animals usually have appetite issues and that appears not to be the case here.

Overall, I'm pleased with the current state of affairs, though I want them to sing as much as you do. And breed, of course. We want them to breed, but these things should happen naturally."

There was a condescending tone in the way Wrasse was talking to him. It took every bit of control he had to avoid inflating red. Agastin changed the subject. "You know about the homine?"

Wrasse's gills rippled. "This voyage has been full of unexpected events."

"What do you think we should do with it?"

"You're asking my advice?"

"You'd rather I not?" Agastin said.

"It will keep the Vice Commander distracted."

"The damage to Planet Song..."

"Teracia is angry enough already. But she's the only fahr who can go into the enclosure. We need her. I say we cooperate with her attempts to keep the biped alive, even bring the stasis engineers into play."

Agastin nodded. "If she thinks she has a chance to save it, she might be more cooperative."

"The degree of her cooperation—the degree to which she serves Song Corp's interests—will determine her fate."

Agastin reminded himself he was no longer Chancellor. "Yes, of course."

"Your Vice Commander has the potential to be a major public relations problem. There are various ways in which we can handle that, but let's begin with leverage shall we? And don't worry, Commander Agastin. I'm not in the slightest bit interested in running this ship. I leave that to you and your able and expendable Vice Commander."

Device

Dr. Hinton liked him. Charlie had no idea why, but he found himself included in everything the professor did. He was part of the team that constructed the massive biosafety cabinet (BSC) needed to contain a creature of that size. He was allowed to observe their initial investigations once they placed the creature in it. It meant hours sweating in a HAZMAT suit, but he didn't care.

"This bit here is odd," Cynthia said, extending a gloved hand into the cabinet and pointing a scalpel at the almond-shaped patch below the creature's neck.

"How so?" Hinton asked.

"It's not consistent with the surrounding area. There appear to be minute differences in texture between it and the surrounding scales."

Charlie studied the patch. She was right, the patch had a smoother surface, not as rough as the scales around it.

Hinton's brow creased, and he frowned. "Do a light drag over the surface and that of the scales surrounding it," he said.

Cynthia let the scalpel lightly touch down on the patch, moving it back and forth from it to the scales surrounding the patch. Charlie saw the minute bounce each time the barrier was crossed.

"It's not organic," Charlie said.

Hinton and Cynthia looked at him.

"It's not part of the creature," Charlie said. "It's just made to look like it is."

"We're dealing with an alien life form here," Hinton said. "We don't know what its normality is."

"It's not part of it," Charlie insisted. "It's... I don't know what it is, but it's not part of the creature."

Hinton gave a thin smile and then turned to Cynthia. "Put the blade beneath a few of those scales and lift them," he said.

93

Cynthia nodded and lifted the edges of a few of the scales with a scalpel.

"Now try the same thing with that patch," Hinton said.

Cynthia nodded and placed the blade at the edge of the patch. She inserted the scalpel and twisted it. The area lifted, and a thin crack line appeared between the patch and the surrounding area. She looked at Hinton for permission. He nodded, and she stuck the scalpel in deeper and lifted further. The patch came loose, floating about an inch above the carcass. It trailed wisps of what could have been sealant or glue or a tendril of some sort.

"No blood vessels," Hinton said. He turned to Charlie. "I think you're right—this is not part of the animal. It's something extra." As he said this, the patch floated higher into the water, revealing what was beneath it. Most of this was another layer of scales, but at its center was a perfect hexagon, darkly metallic and textured with a pattern that looked like layered cross sections of a conch shell.

"Flip the patch over," Hinton said.

Cynthia did, revealing a matching hexagon and a mirror image textured pattern.

Hinton shook his head. "Our visitor was not only a fish, but a cybernetic one at that."

"But what is that?" Charlie asked pointing at the patch.

"Probably the biggest reverse-engineering challenge our species will ever face."

Jupiter

The giant planet loomed large before her, the weather patterns bending the sparkly fabric of the dark sky. They were a month out from Planet Song and now the first intercepted broadcasts from there had arrived, weak signals originating from the planet's surface. Teracia's gills rippled. In less than three weeks they were rebuilding their electronic infrastructure. In the long run this would not be a race to be trifled with.

Another communication had arrived, this one from Centrix, eighty years old because of the time delay and encrypted for her eyes only. Only five fahr could send such messages. Agastin, the Chancellor—now Petar because of Agastin's decision to command this mission, the Chancellor's heir—still an infant in the reproductive labs, the High Priest Barracute, and his heir, Occeane. Occeane used this privilege carefully. While his communications to Teracia would be private, he knew the act of sending one to the Vice Commander would attract attention. She could not hide the source of the message, but it had been known for millennium the two of them were friends, so there was nothing irregular about the communication. Still Occeane was a religious nonconformist and one who had issues with the way Song Corp did its business. Anyone known to be in his sphere of influence was watched. Retiring to her quarters, Teracia received the message.

Occeane was not alone. Derath swam beside him and both displayed gray-green and flattened gills. This was not the encouragement she had hoped for.

"Teracia," Occeane began. "We waited a few years before sending you this update, hoping for some improvement in the local situation. That has not come. Centrix is a city of intoxication. On any given day one in twenty fahr occupies that state, often floating in vast herds above the city, oblivious to all but their own ecstasy. Petar has gifted virgin song, some of the strongest known. And they love him for it. Song Corp and its competitors increased profitability for a while by extending credit and charging high interest rates. This was lucrative but now even the corporations are concerned. An addicted population is not a productive population. They earn less and now, for the first time in modern Fahr history, some citizens are in debt beyond their ability to pay. Projections are for this kind of behavior to increase." Occeane nodded to Derath.

"Greeting Teracia, my first mentor," Derath said. "The Holy Son is allowing me to bring the good news. We have found and sequenced about 60% of the original Fahr genome from before the First Modificate. There are sequences, quite a number that don't exist in the modern genetic libraries. Since those libraries are supposed to contain every known sequence, this discovery hints at suppression. But by whom and for what purpose? We'll probably never know. The important thing is we can now add this information to the libraries."

Teracia watched as Occeane gave Derath a gesture of dismissal and the young fahr left. After his departure, Occeane displayed blue joy. "What Derath did not say, because I wouldn't let him, is that we may be able to restore the original relationships between the sexes. By the time you return that may be possible. Who knows if this is a good idea, but I find it appealing."

"The other major bit of news concerns the religious elements we've been exploring. We've now gone beyond simple petitionary prayers into a form of meditation, distinct from that practiced by the Will of the Giver mystics. The ancient mystics, those whose stories are told on the khards, sought a relationship with their deity, rather than just waiting for instructions and living in fear of transgressing those instructions. It's more of a parent-child relationship where affinity is more important than the religious practice. In this system you are encouraged to draw near to the deity. We're finding this refreshing. There's no fear involved, only wonder."

"Teracia, composing these messages to you involves the disconnect of time. We, much more so than other species we've encountered, are locked in relationships which can take millennia to unfold. I can do nothing to lessen the time it takes our messages to reach one another, but I will wait for you. In the meantime, be assured of my prayers."

For only the third time in Teracia's long life the flush came, far deeper than the previous two times.

"Are you aroused, Vice Commander?" Agastin asked when he saw her.

"How could I be aroused?" Teracia said, flashing purple.

"Something's going on."

"No, it isn't."

Agastin studied her for a moment, then rippled his gills. "It's not important. They've picked up signals from Planet Song?"

"A few faint ones, yes."

"What are they saying?" Agastin asked.

"Mostly calls for help and damage reports. They're repairing what we broke, but it will take a while. Millions, perhaps billions, will die before that happens."

"With a population that large, they will survive at least until their next self-inflicted debacle."

"This was not self-inflicted."

"We have what we came for," Agastin said. "Had we not done this, they would have done something worse. It was only a matter of time. We have disarmed them which will give them some time to mature. At least now they don't have a working means of mass self-destruction at their disposal. And you, who've always wanted contact, now have your own private pet."

"Pet?"

"One with which you can do cultural exchanges. Just remember you are the Vice Commander of this ship and those responsibilities take precedence."

"I know of that," Teracia said, pinking.

"Then I'll leave you to them," Agastin said and swam away.

She watched him leave. They had knocked out all the Homines satellites near Planet Song, but they had left the deeper space missions intact. Their Pioneer 10 mission had lasted well beyond its projected life span, and their newer missions were better. When they restored their tracking capabilities, Homines would have the data to determine the route the Fahr ship had taken out of their stellar system. Unlike the approach, there had been no reason for stealth on their journey home. With an object the size of their ship, Homines would know their direction, and if they found Thryke's

PDM and could interpret its contents, they would know much more. Agastin was taking Homines much too lightly.

Decay

Charlie greeted Cynthia Chen when she walked into the lab that morning. Everyone else in the complex was wearing a surgical mask. His was dangling around his neck.

"What's up?" she asked.

"It's decaying," Charlie said. "Inside the containment area everyone's in full HAZMAT." He fished into his lab coat pocket and pulled out a mask. He handed it to her. "I have a spare," he said.

"When?" she asked.

"Middle of the night," Charlie said. "Just started falling apart, chunks of flesh falling off the bones. Like it had been in a hot oven overnight."

"But we constructed the BSC to class three containment specs," Cynthia said. "How would that happen?"

Charlie shrugged. "Spontaneous. One moment it was intact and inert just as we collected it, in a perfect temperature-controlled environment with no external contamination. A few minutes later it's falling apart."

"And the surgical masks?" Cynthia said putting hers on. "We should be safe this far from it?"

"Hinton," Charlie said rolling his eyes.

"You're hoping to get into his department and you're not listening to him?"

Charlie thought about her question for a moment, grinned, and pulled the mask over face. "I don't like breathing my own air," he said. "Hinton sent me to watch for you and get you in there as soon as you arrived."

Cynthia nodded and adjusted the fit of the mask over her face. Now it neatly severed the orca tattoo, but Charlie had lost interest. Lots of younger possibilities in this place. "You coming?" she said and headed towards the biocontainment unit.

"No decay to rapid decay," Hinton said as he greeted the hazmatted duo. "You can watch it happen in real time." He smacked is gloved hand against the counter top. "At this rate there will be nothing left by nightfall."

In the time between Charlie's leaving to go find Cynthia and their return, the creature had lost its shape and was now little more than a pile of goo. "Whatever this is, it's also digesting the bones," he said.

Hinton pursed his lips.

"Is it some kind of acid?" Cynthia asked.

Hinton growled from deep within the HAZMAT suit. "If it is, it's not affecting non-organic elements within the cabinet." He gestured to the device which lay on its side to the right of the goo. "That looks intact, and there's no evidence this is affecting the surfaces on the cabinet itself. There have been no breech alarms. It's also drying out. Did you notice that? That stuff is becoming increasingly viscous."

"Where's the water going?"

"It has to be through the ventilation system, through the filters as water vapor. There's no other way out."

Three days later it was over. Nothing was left of the creature except a fine-grained powder that had self-arranged into the shape of an ant hill. Its device laid inert in the corner of the cabinet. The hexagonal point that connected the device with the animal was partially submerged in the hill. Charlie watched as Cynthia reached in with a pair of tweezers and extracted it, moving it over and setting it down by the device. As she did so the bits of organic dust still clinging to the connection point fell away and as if attracted by a magnet, the particles found their way back to the hill. Charlie shook his head. He'd seen a lot of animal decomposition sites in the past but nothing like this. All the organic material in the creature's body had coalesced. Far as he could see the rest of the cabinet was free of it. He couldn't trust his eyes, of course, but a normal decay process should have spread the resulting material around the enclosure, not gathered it into one spot.

"Bring the contact point to the glass," Hinton said to Cynthia. "Let's take a closer look at it."

Cynthia picked up the contact with the tweezers and brought it forward. As she did so Charlie saw tiny strands that were almost invisible, like those of a spider web, dangling from it. "What are those?" she wondered aloud.

"I don't know," Hinton said, "but I'm guessing they're non-organic. Everything else has decayed and found its way into that mound."

"Wires?"

"Or the alien equivalent of wires. If this is a cybernetic organism, then the organic and non-organic parts have to communicate. We may be looking at the non-organic part of that interface."

"Something that connects it to the neurological system," Cynthia said.

"Yes."

"So how do we disinfect this?" Cynthia said pointing at the device.

"I'm not sure we'll have to," Hinton said.

"Why?"

"Well, this is a guess, but I think we'll find the device to be sterile. It's not being included in that mound of organic material, and everything else connected to that beast is. I think we've already seen the separation of the biological and non-biological."

"But you don't know for sure," Charlie said

Hinton gave a thin smile. "No, of course not. We'll have to take all the precautions, but there would be a certain logic to what I'm saying. We began with a stable inert carcass apparently set to a timer. When that timer went off, we saw rapid organized decay. And now what has decayed is in that mound, and what hasn't is over there," he said gesturing to the device. "And I'm sure you noticed the organic particles attached to the interface seemed determined to join the mound when you moved the interface."

"There's a lot we don't understand here," Cynthia said.

"Yes, like how a particle of that size would have the will to join the larger mass or is it drawn there by some kind of force? And how and why was the process of decay delayed like it was and then went into overdrive, turning everything into powder over a few days? Anyway, there are two things we must do now. We must find a way of ensuring the device is sterile without damaging it and determine the chemical content of that mound."

"Compost," Charlie said.

"Have you ever seen compost that looked like that?"

"No," Charlie admitted. "The particles are too small and uniform."

Act Seven: The Team

Sniper

The militias had come to an uneasy truce brought on by a common enemy. Maria Alatorre was the worst president in the history of the USA: a woman, a Latino, and a socialist to boot. There was no sense in which she could be called "Commander and Chief". She let the aliens win. Didn't even put up a fight and now much of the country was starving. Even those within her domain were struggling, especially those in the cities, and it would have been worse for them if Alatorre hadn't annexed much of the farm land. Now the farmers were being forced to work the land only to have their crops taken, without payment, and distributed. "Fuckin' urbies," Jake said to himself and spat on the ground. He let himself smile. This would be a huge honor, knocking off Alatorre.

The truck was an old fifth-generation Ford F-Series with an extended box. Thompson had filled the vehicle and two other trucks with potatoes, corn, carrots, onions, sacks of flour, and dried beef and pork, a peace offering to the New England Militia. The closer he got to Boston, the more Jake realized the problem. The entire population looked emaciated. They were fuckin' urbies, all of them! No survival skills! He looked back over his shoulder. What they had in these trucks might feed a few dozen families for a month. Jake slumped down into the seat, not wanting his well-fed self to be seen. If he didn't get Alatorre, they'd roast him on a spit.

The trucks pulled to a stop in a wooded area just east of the I-95. They were met by similar vehicles from the New England Militia. Jake got out of the truck, carrying his Winchester in its case. Two dozen men stood around the truck, each wearing a ball cap from a different team. They were all reed thin and smoking ready-mades. Jake could see the packs in their shirt pockets. Food might be a problem here, but tobacco wasn't. A man with a Patriot's ball cap stepped forward and walked up to Jake.

"You the sniper?" he asked.

"Yeah," Jake said extending his hand. "Name's Jake."

The man shook his hand. "Patriots fan," he said.

Jake grinned.

"He's a fucking kid," another said, this one sporting a Bruin's cap.

Jake reddened and turned to the Bruin's fan. The man was an urbie, clear as day. "You want a demonstration?" he asked.

The man said nothing.

"Tell you what," Jake said. "You walk about two hundred paces into those trees. Then you hold out that cap at arm's length."

The Bruin's fan studied Jake and then looked at the others in his group. Each of them was waiting to see what he would do. The Bruin's fan shrugged and walked off into the woods.

Jake took the Winchester out of the case, attached the scope, and spread himself flat against the ground. Waited.

"Can you see it?" the Bruin's fan called out.

A distant flash of yellow flickered through the trees. "Hold it still now," Jake shouted, looking through the scope. He fired.

"Jesus Christ!" came a distant yell.

Jake stood up, rested the butt of the rifle on the ground and turned to the Patriot's fan. "Got a spare smoke?" he said.

The man studied him for a second and then handed him a cigarette. Jake lit up, and they all waited for the Bruin's fan to return. He appeared a few minutes later with a clean puncture through the center of the cap.

"Any more opinions?" Jake asked. No one responded. He grinned.

"We'd better get this food unloaded," the Patriots fan said, gesturing the other men in his group.

Jake watched as some of them clambered into the trucks and threw the sacks of vegetables down into the waiting arms of those on the ground. He finished the cigarette and turned to the Patriot's fan. "So, what's the plan?" he asked.

"In about two hours Alatorre's little motorcade is going to come down that highway on their way to MIT. It'll be the Brink's truck, a couple of Humvees with turrets, and an armored personnel carrier or two. We're going to disable her vehicle. At that point, she'll have to exit it, and that's when you take her out."

"How are you going to disable it?" Jake said studying the motley collection of rifles the men were carrying.

The Patriots fan pursed his lips. "We will and that's all you have to know about it. Your job is to be ready when it happens."

Jake shook his head. "I have to know what I'm dealing with here. It's me that's doing the shooting."

"You understand anything about chain of command, kid?"

"But it's me who's taking the shot. And, if she's got protection, it's me they'll be coming after. I got a right to know what's going on."

"You're damn arrogant for a kid. Anybody ever tell you that?"

Jake said nothing.

"Your commander tell you to do this?"

Jake fidgeted.

"He order you to do it?"

"Yeah," Jake said.

"He give you any conditions in which it's OK to disobey that order?"

"No."

"He tell you who to report to?"

"No. He just said there'd be the New England Militia waiting for me. I guess he left it up to me to figure out who was in charge."

"And have you figured that out yet?"

104

"Yes, sir."

"Good. We've got a spot for you overlooking the highway. We've dug it out and gathered lots of brush. All you have to do is cover yourself with it, and you'll be pretty much invisible. We're going to launch our attack from about a quarter mile down the road and put that Brink's truck into the ditch on the other side. There's going to be a fire fight, and it's not likely to go well for us. We're going to be seriously over matched. They'll wipe us out or take some of us prisoner. It doesn't matter what happens to us as long as we get her. Most of us are as good as dead anyway. I want you to wait until the fighting is over, no matter what happens and no matter how long it takes, because they won't expose her until they think she's safe. When she appears, you take her out. Understood?"

Jake looked at him. "So, you're all planning to..."

"Most of us haven't had a decent meal in two weeks. We've looted everything we can loot, planted, sown, and harvested. Butchered the livestock, shot every deer we can find. Snared rabbits, porcupines, and dogs, and kept our few boats out on the water twenty-four seven. There's too many of us to feed." He gestured to the highway. "No one around her is suffering. So, we're going to make this little sacrifice. It's intentional. We want it to look incompetent, because if we do, then the guard comes down and they'll stop being careful. And that will give you your shot."

Jake said nothing.

"It's what you do for your country," the Patriots fan said studying Jake. "Then the right people will be in a better position to take over and run things."

"Got it," Jake said, though he had seen little unity in the militias to this point. Most of them were fighting amongst themselves much as they were fighting the government.

"Had much experience with death?"

"I've seen it."

"Been close to it?"

"I've caused it."

"Good. Because it's one thing you must be hard about, especially today."

The New England trucks were soon gone with the food. His own trucks soon followed, leaving him with nothing more than vague directions to a rendezvous point a few miles away. He didn't like this. It felt like he was being included in their sacrifice. Was that Thompson's ultimate solution to the problem he was causing with Tracy? Maybe, but it seemed like an elaborate solution if it was. No. Alatorre was on her way, and if he lost his life taking her out, at least there was some honor. Maybe Thompson was being pragmatic. Get rid of the big problem and the little one at the same time. Jake tried not to think more about it.

The New England Militia disappeared into the trees to his left and right. Making his way to the designated spot on the tree line overlooking the highway, he climbed in and covered himself with the brush. There was a whiff of decay in the air, subtle but there. He had a clear but distant view across the other side of the highway where the Brink's truck was supposed to end up, but there was something odd going on down there. He fixed the Winchester in place, looked through the scope, shook his head, looked again, and gasped. There were corpses everywhere. Some were sitting on chairs, others in and on abandoned cars, and still others lying on the ground. A crow sat on the shoulder of one and pecked at its face. This seemed to shimmer until Jake understood he was looking at maggots. He swallowed the bile rising in his throat, took a swig from his canteen, and tried to compose himself. It didn't work. He dragged himself out from under the cover, vomited into a nearby bush, took another swig from the canteen, swished it around in his mouth, and spat. He looked again, this time realizing each corpse was in a different state of decomposition. Some were skeletons, others freshly dead. Most were somewhere in-between. He took several deep breaths, tasting the air. Now that he knew what the smell was, it seemed to magnify. He lost it again.

Was this what they did with their dead? Jake wiped his mouth with the back of his hand. Was this what the Patriot's fan was referring to when he said death was something he'd have to be hard about? He'd thought this was about could he could pull the trigger,

106

not about rotting corpses. How the hell was he supposed to look through the scope when that was what he'd be seeing? Jake took another deep breath. He'd steel himself. He had no choice. With the Winchester he could hit anything on the other side of the road for two hundred yards in either direction. This would take extreme focus, and he still had no idea how they would stop that truck. Somehow it no longer mattered.

Forty-five minutes later he saw the motorcade in the distance. Two restored Humvees with mounted machine guns, an older armored personnel carrier, and the Brink's truck. Alatorre. Their intel had been good. He'd stopped looking through the scope, but now he'd have to. Jake gritted his teeth, took a quick drink, and spat again. The Patriots fan said it would take a while before he had a clear shot, but who knew how the situation would unfold. Best to be ready, though it meant continually looking through the scope and seeing what was there. Concentrate on the living, he told himself. The motorcade was almost there.

Something bounced off the Brink's truck but didn't explode. He had no idea what that "something" was, but the effect was to rock and slow the vehicle without stopping it. A few moments later another impact, this time higher up. The Brink's truck tipped, wobbled on the driver side wheels, fell over, and did a slow-motion slide into the corpse-infested ditch.

Military personnel scrambled. The machine guns on the Humvees opened fire on locations to the left and right of Jake. He could see nothing and only knew the fighting was over when the shooting stopped a short time later. He suspected that was the last he would see of the Patriots' fan. No one on the government side seemed to be hurting, though a few of them were losing it just as he had. After a couple of minutes, a man in a suit crawled out the back door of the tipped Brinks truck. He picked his way through the corpses and crossed the highway with an escort of soldiers, disappearing.

Jake pulled the barrel of the Winchester back into his cover and waited. No one came. Fifteen minutes later they re-emerged, more relaxed and apparently satisfied the danger was over. No one had checked the trees he was in. Bizarre. Jake looked through the scope again, fighting the bile in the back of his throat.

It was another half an hour before Alatorre emerged, surrounded by an entourage of Special Forces folks that made it difficult for him to get a bead on her. She was shorter than most of them, which meant that when he did see her, it was usually only her head. Jake knew a chest shot was preferable but, to do that, he had to get her chest in the scope's cross hairs. That was proving next to impossible. A head shot it would have to be, and Jake was certain he could do it. One of the Humvees winched the Brink's truck into an upright position, and he saw Alatorre making her way to its front cab. He thought he had her head in the cross hairs and then... There seemed to be two of her, but he knew if she got into the cab he would lose her.

He fired.

Alatorre dropped and was immediately surrounded by her people, half of whom were looking in his direction. Then he noticed the shattered Brink's mirror dangling from the side of the truck.

Jake crawled out of his cover and deeper into the trees. He stood, braced the Winchester across his chest, and ran.

Interstate 95

A small fleet of Brink's trucks survived, stored deep enough in an underground parkade that their armored nature shielded them from the pulse. Now they were hauling diesel for generators, various scrounged parts, food, and water, and one of them had become Ground Force One.

It wasn't labeled as such, there wasn't much in the interior of Ground Force One to remind President Maria Alatorre of its airborne predecessor, and worst of all, it had no windows. Every time she had to go somewhere she traveled blind, sitting in a small rolling room with Garneau and a female special forces agent. At least they had wine. The White House wine cellar was the size of a walk-in closet, and it was well stocked at the time of the attack, her private stash. This became the elixir for her claustrophobia and usually meant she arrived at her destination in less than optimal condition.

Garneau watched her take another drink from the green plastic wine glass. He shook his head. "I never thought I'd see Cabernet Sauvignon consumed from plastic."

"I don't taste the plastic," Alatorre replied, holding up the green goblet. "And this doesn't shatter when we hit a pothole."

"It's wrong."

"It's practical."

Garneau still clung to his pre-attack entitlements, although he had stopped shaving. Her chief of staff had one of those patchy beards that made his face look like a diseased animal, a diseased animal that still wore a suit and tie and polished its shoes. Shoe polish was not a priority item. She wondered when Garneau would run out of it. He was one of those few men who seemed self-contained, needing no one to care for him. Some of his staff had mentioned an ex-wife, but she was so far in the past that Garneau had never talked of her.

Before the attack a few of the tabloids had attempted to link the two of them romantically. Both had a good laugh at that one. Alatorre's three failed marriages produced no children, mostly because of a lack of interest. Pressured by husband number three—she only referred to them by numbers now—Alatorre tried for motherhood at forty-two. Nothing happened. She quickly learned that fertility treatments were for younger women, shrugged her shoulders, and went back to work. Number three departed, and she found her interest in sex left with him. She needed Garneau, and she knew it, but their relationship was platonic.

"What's the state of MIT, anyway?" she asked him.

"Most of it is down, like anywhere else, but we've prioritized the bits that will help us rebuild. I think you'll be pleased by the progress."

Alatorre nodded and took more wine. "Part of me is glad this thing doesn't have windows."

"It's not pretty out there."

Alatorre stared down into her plastic wine glass. One of the local militias had disposed of the dead in the ditches beside the interstate. Corpses lined the road approaching Boston, posed as if they were waiting for a bus or sitting in the seats of the many abandoned vehicles.

"How long can we control the country with a million troops?" she asked.

Garneau grunted. "You call that control?"

"No, I suppose not." She grimaced. The federal government had secured the section of the Interstate 95 stretching from Portland, Maine, in the north to Richmond, Virginia, in the south. They were the dominant presence in those two cities and Boston, New Haven, New York, Philadelphia, Atlantic City, and Washington. Things were less certain in the South and into the interior of the country, and the situation on the West Coast, because of communication problems, was still a question mark. Being the dominant presence on the East Coast, however, only meant they were the biggest and best armed tribe. They had control over about seventy-five percent of the area's military facilities, ports, railroads, and airports, but sometimes these assets where isolated and surrounded by various hostile militia groups. By now, however, the government had control of sixty percent of the productive farm land, so some militias were having trouble feeding their people. In six short months, her presidency had been reduced to about half of the continental USA, but at least her people were eating, though well below the level needed to keep them nourished. And this was only going to get worse.

Ground Force One lurched and tipped before righting itself. The President's wine found its way into Garneau's beard.

110

"That was no bloody pot hole," he sputtered. He pushed the button on the intercom system connecting them to the driver. The vehicle was decelerating.

"What was that?" he demanded.

"A projectile, sir. It didn't explode, just hit us low on the right side."

"See who did it?"

"No, sir. But we were driving near a walkway. Could have come from there. Had to have been fired from something though. Not dropped. Hit us at the wrong angle for something dropped, and with too much force. I've maintained control, and she's handling fine."

"Did we engage?" Alatorre said, but she knew the answer. She'd have heard shots. They were traveling with an escort of two rebuilt Humvees with mounted machine guns and a personnel carrier.

"No, Madam President. It was a one-off, and we didn't get a visual. We know the general direction. That's all."

Alatorre handed Garneau a napkin. "Stop and find them?" she asked.

Garneau took the napkin and dabbed his face to little effect. "Our mission is to get to MIT, not go chasing militia. Could easily be walking into a trap."

Alatorre nodded. "Proceed to destination," she told the driver.

The second impact hit higher, but with more force. The Brink's truck tilted, did a slow-motion fall onto its side and slid into the ditch.

The smell hit Alatorre before the pain. Rotting corpses. It had to be.

Garneau and the secret service man unbuckled and scrambled to their feet.

"Are you all right, Madam President?" the secret service woman said.

"I'm fine," Alatorre said. She felt a tenderness in her shoulder where it had been restrained by the belt. She flexed her arm, and it moved well enough. The olfactory assault was far worse.

Garneau was listening. Then she too heard them. Shots. The Humvees engaging someone.

"Then this is a trap," she said.

They went silent listening to the gunfire until it stopped. Someone tried the rear door. "Madam President, are you all right?"

"Code word!" The secret service woman called out.

"Burnt toast," came the reply. It was the most common description of the alien ship, a giant flying chunk of burnt toast.

Garneau opened the door a crack.

"We got them, sir," the officer said. "Is the president all right?"

"I'm fine," Alatorre said. "Just a bruise on my shoulder, I think."

"Captured or dead?" Garneau asked.

"We cut them down, sir," the officer said, a captain Alatorre realized.

"How are the other vehicles?" she asked.

"They only targeted Ground Force One, Madam President."

Garneau looked at Alatorre and then at the captain. "What did they hit us with?" Garneau asked the soldier.

"Large stones, sir."

"Stones?"

"Yes, sir. They threw large stones at us."

"Threw? With what?"

"By the look of them, I'd say giant slingshots, sir."

"Giant slingshots?" Alatorre's eyes widened.

"Big ones, Madam President."

"Get serious. This is America. Everyone's armed to the teeth. Why would they use slingshots?"

"I don't know, Madam President."

Garneau turned to her. "I'll take a look. You'd better stay here in case there are others about."

Alatorre nodded. She hated the enclosures she was forced to live in, even more now than before, but this was prudent, and she knew it.

***

Garneau climbed out of Ground Force One and gagged. Maggots covered much of the nearest corpse. The one beyond it had fewer insects, a more recent death. It was emaciated, a victim of starvation like most of the others. A dozen infested the ditch near Ground Force One. At least they weren't eating their dead. Not like some other militias. Instead they were propping them up in full view of the highway, reminding anyone who happened by of the government's failure to provide.

The captain was studying his face. "Are you injured, sir?"

"It's wine."

"Wine?"

"Red wine. Cabernet Sauvignon. Want to know the vintage?"

"No, sir."

"Good. Point me toward those slingshots and then see what you can do about getting us on our way."

"I wouldn't go alone, sir. I think we got them all but..."

"All right then. Give me an escort."

The captain called half dozen soldiers over and gave them instructions. "The first one is up there," he said to Garneau, pointing to a small rise on the other side of the interstate just beyond the ditch. "The other one's a couple of hundred yards down the highway."

"Your name?"

"Name, sir? It's Siebold, sir. Captain Siebold."

"Thank you, Captain Siebold," he said gesturing to Ground Force One. "Get some of your people to right that truck."

"Yes, sir."

"And make sure they remove the President before you do that," he said with a grin.

The captain tried to smile but could not. Garneau watched as the young man's eyes found the rotting corpse at his feet. The Chief of Staff turned away in time to avoid seeing the captain vomit, but he still heard it. Instead he focused on the rise on the other side of the interstate.

They looked like football uprights cemented into the ground. From each of these dangled catapults of braided and stitched together inner tubes. The uprights were about a third the way down the rise, and further up were small operator's thrones constructed from old tractor seats. In both seats the operators still sat, strapped in by seat belts and riddled by the Humvee's machine gun fire. Other casualties lay scattered up and down the rise.

Garneau stepped over a small depression containing stones of similar size. He hunched down beside the throne to see the angle they had shot from. The stone that hit Ground Force One had been flung down from about a twenty-five-degree angle.

A soft raspy breath. The man strapped to the throne was looking at Garneau through half closed eyes.

"I have an Eatmore," the man said. "Been saving it. It's in my right pocket. You don't look like you need it, but maybe... You could give it to someone who does." The man slumped forward.

Garneau pulled the chocolate bar out of his pocket and looked at it. The bar itself was intact, but the wrapping was covered in blood from a nearby wound. He dropped it on the ground. "Nothing more to be seen here," he said to the men in his escort. He turned and walked back to Ground Force One. Out of the corner of his eye he saw one soldier reach down, pick up the bar and pocket it. The others watched him and said nothing.

***

President Alatorre crawled out of Ground Force One. The minder pulled the President to her feet. She retched immediately at the sight and smell of the corpses. The minder was ready, passing her a handkerchief and a canteen. She looked at him. The young man was barely keeping it in himself, but he was. Under the circumstances this was commendable.

"We'll want to get you out of the line of fire, Madam President," he said in a thin controlled voice. He gestured to the open front door of the Ground Force One.

"Does it smell better?" she said almost losing it again.

"I don't know, Madam President, but you'll be safer."

Alatorre rotated her sore shoulder, straightened up, and kept her eyes fixed on the goal of the vehicle's front door. Each step felt spongy, as if she were walking on a peat bog, and she dared not look down for fear of what she might be stepping on. The minder offered his arm, but she shook her head.

She was barely aware of the Brinks truck's huge side mirror until it shattered beside her. She fell to the ground, unsure if she had been pushed there or lost her footing. The Humvee's guns were firing, and the soldiers were all scrambling around her. She felt a sudden weight and realized the minder had thrown himself over her. "Get off me!" she shouted but could not compete with the din of machine gun fire. The minder stayed where he was.

After a few minutes the shooting stopped. The minder rolled off her, and she glared at him.

"It's my job to protect you, Madam President," he said. "You're injured," he said pointing at her right hand.

To that point Alatorre had been overwhelmed by the stench and the roar of the gunfire. Now she felt pain, a small triangle of glass embedded in the back of her right hand. She reached over, pulled it out and watched as blood filled the hole and then fanned out across the back of her hand. The minder was there with another handkerchief. He wrapped her hand quickly and guided her free left hand to a point on the bandage.

"Press down here, Madam President. I'll go find the medic."

She nodded and climbed into the front seat of the Brinks truck.

"A lone sniper, Madam President," Captain Siebold later reported. "We found a single shell casing, and that was all."

"So, he got away?"

"We were exposed, Madam President. If we'd stood up and run after him—you must understand at that point, we didn't know how many there were—they could have just picked us off from the trees. So, we kept low and by the time we'd crawled up there..."

"He was gone," Alatorre finished.

"Yes, Madam President," Siebold said. "I think this whole thing was set up to give him that shot, because it came from the tree line and not from where we engaged the other militia. He'd picked a spot for that shot, knowing that if they were successful at stopping the truck, you'd appear at some point. When you did, he fired. I think the Humvee's mirror may have saved your life. It's possible he saw a double image and fired at the wrong one."

Alatorre looked down at her bandaged hand. The medic had applied iodine and done a single stitch without anesthetic. It hurt like hell and now it throbbed. She wasn't sure which was worse.

"Why slingshots?" she asked Garneau.

"They're big enough to fling a forty-pound stone with considerable force," Garneau said. "They probably knew small arms fire would not stop a Brink's truck, so they improvised. It's amazing when you think about it. They had to sling those stones with enough accuracy to hit a moving truck, and they did it twice."

"There's similar sized stones all around the area, sir," said Siebold. "I'd say they've been practicing."

"It confirms that they know," Alatorre said.

"It wasn't going to stay secret for long," Garneau said.

"My life as a target," Alatorre said.

MIT

Professor Donaldson placed the chip in Alatorre's gloved left hand and stepped back. Donaldson was bald, but he wore a hairnet anyway, a fact made more comical by huge bushy eyebrows well below the net's reach. This and a pair of white gloves was his only concession to the standard dress protocol of the high-tech industry. Donaldson had, however, insisted Alatorre wear a glove when receiving the chip.

Alatorre studied the tiny device. It didn't seem like much, but she knew, under the circumstances, that being able to manufacture such an item was huge.

"Giant sling shots, snipers, and now this," she said to Garneau. "It's been quite a day." She turned back to Donaldson. "So, what's the time line here?"

"The progress will be gradual. We're manufacturing chips that will, in turn, speed up the process for making more chips. This will eventually lead to the restoration of mechanized computer-controlled manufacturing. But the entire electronic infrastructure of those industries worldwide has been wiped out. We're probably looking at decades for complete restoration."

"Basic infrastructure?" Alatorre asked.

Donaldson pursed his lips. "If conditions were optimal, and by that I mean no human road blocks put in our way and all the raw materials we need, then we could probably do it within a couple of years. But conditions are not optimal, and so the best we can hope for is basic infrastructure restoration. And it will take longer."

Alatorre nodded. "Because we have human road blocks and limited resources?"

"Exactly," Donaldson said.

Alatorre studied Donaldson. "You were an AI specialist before all this, weren't you?"

Donaldson looked at her with surprise. "Yes, Madam President, but I, like most of the others here, have been well... Re-purposed."

"Do you have paper copies of your research?" Alatorre asked.

"Yes, Madam President. I always have print copies of my work. I'm old-school enough to have a healthy distrust of digital storage."

"And does your work touch on cybernetic organisms?"

"Cybernetic organisms?"

"Yes."

Donaldson's brow crinkled. "My work has been in the soft-ware realm, Madam President, computational systems for space missions that require a certain level of autonomy. But I keep abreast of what others are doing. Most of that concerns prosthetics of various kinds and doesn't involve AI in any meaningful way. Why?"

"One never knows when such knowledge might prove useful, Dr. Donaldson. That's down the road. Now we have much more pressing problems. Tell me, professor, what do you need from us?"

Donaldson shuffled his feet and pulled the hairnet down over his eyebrows. Doing so revealed a badly blocked haircut on the back of his neck. Alatorre wondered if he'd done it himself. "The basics, food, water, clothing, medicines," he said. "Keep the old electronics coming. For now, we can scrounge enough raw materials by recycling." He gave his hairnet another tug.

"And?"

"Security. We need more security."

"Security?"

"The local militia is breaking in and stealing stuff. Not the electronics but food, water, medicine. The stuff they need to survive. The stuff we need to survive. And they're getting a lot more aggressive. What used to be clandestine theft is now turning into armed assault. There may be a shortage of food out there but there's no shortage of guns, thanks to our wonderful Second Amendment. We now have scientists and technicians spending half their time not working on restoring our electronic infrastructure but guarding our store rooms with semi-automatic rifles. You've provided us with security people, but there's not enough of them. We can't do this if we have to protect ourselves at the same time."

Alatorre looked at Garneau. "Get him the troops he needs."

"It will mean pulling them away from..."

"Just do it."

"Yes, Madam President," Garneau said, over enunciating every syllable.

"Do you think we'll survive?" Alatorre asked Garneau as they shared another bottle of Cabernet Sauvignon in the back of the truck.

"Who is we?" Garneau asked.

Alatorre surprised herself by reaching out and touching her chief of staff on his knee. She gave him a wry smile. "Humanity."

Garneau cocked an eyebrow. "I'm more concerned with your specific survival, at the moment."

"Thank you for that, but it is part of the same thing, isn't it? You're trying to protect me, or more broadly my office, because someone has to provide ongoing leadership."

"I thought you didn't like being the Leader of the Free World?"

"I don't but that now seems to be an old scenario."

Garneau nodded. "Is there a free world?"

"Exactly. Which brings me back to my original question. Do you think we will survive?"

Garneau rubbed his beard. "I guess that depends on whether our friends, the Fahr, return. We were over matched before, now..." He raised his hands in a sign of surrender.

Alatorre took a sip from the green plastic cup. "I think if they had further designs on this planet we'd have seen more of them by now. They're gone. They've taken what they wanted and left. Not that they won't return, but for now I think we're safe, at least from them, though perhaps not from ourselves."

Garneau gave a nod of resignation.

"The Fahr did, however, give us a gift before they left."

"A gift?"

"They pointed out one of our deficiencies as a species. We have no unity. We're intensely tribal. We fight about everything."

"How is that a gift? I would think it was self-evident. You're a politician. Tribalism is what you do."

"It is what we as a species do, and we need to get past that. Tribalism nearly cost me my life back there, but the sad thing is there's nothing unusual about that. The Fahr have taught us three things. That we are not alone in the universe, that what's out there may be vastly superior to us, and that we need to be unified as a species to face the challenge. This last bit is the only part we can control, but not in our current state. Our entire history is of tribal conflict. We are hardwired for it, and we need to evolve beyond that."

"Evolve?"

"Yes. As a species, we must do that. The good news is it will not be by random mutation."

"How does Donaldson fit into that?"

"Cybernetic organisms may be part of the solution. But the real advances will need to be in genetic engineering. We need to find a way of getting tribalism out of the species." Alatorre said and downed the rest of her wine. "We must gather the best and the brightest."

"I'm not sure I like where this is going."

"Do you think we can solve this?" Alatorre said with a broad sweeping gesture.

"No," Garneau said drinking from the bottle. "I expect we'll be a small remnant before all is said and done."

"More likely remnants," Alatorre said.

Garneau nodded. "Tribes in the old-fashioned sense of the word."

"I don't think there's anything old-fashioned about it. The tribes may have changed but they're still tribes." She sipped her wine. "So, what if one of those remnants became something else, something better?"

"Do I need to point out we're in survival mode here? You want to build a better species? Fine. But first this species has to survive."

Alatorre studied the bandage on her hand. "It's no longer about the survival of the species. It's about the survival of what we will become, because if we don't become something better, we don't survive. At least, we won't survive well."

"Does this mean I have to stop cheering for the Mets?" He grinned.

Alatorre's eyes glazed over. "Get the word out," she said. "I want everyone we can find who has expertise in genetic manipulation, cybernetics, artificial intelligence, robotics, prosthetics, anything related. Draw up a list. Find as many of those people as you can and bring them in."

"We have people to feed, a country to rebuild."

"We won't succeed."

"At what?"

"At either of those two things."

"What are you saying?"

Alatorre studied Garneau. "The K-T extinction," she said.

"The K-T extinction? You're saying this is a mass extinction event?"

"Exactly."

"We're an adaptable species. We've met every challenge we've ever faced."

"And what was the nature of most of those? Think about it. Most of those challenges were other human beings, other tribes. We have no unity, so when we move forward we do so to get an advantage over each other."

Garneau smiled. "Survival of the fittest," he said with a nod.

"Which is why we need to get beyond tribalism. Everything is competitive. Everything is conflict at some level." Alatorre swished her remaining wine around the plastic. "When the aliens showed up, we were incapable of putting forward a common front. They disarmed us and made off with the whales or whatever it was they came for. The Fahr wanted to negotiate with *us*, but there was no unified *us* to negotiate with."

"They didn't give *us* much time," Garneau said.

"They'd been watching us long enough to know it wouldn't matter, that if we came together, it would be temporary and fragile. Think about it. They'd been monitoring our broadcasts for some time. What would they have heard? What would they have seen? Most of it would have been conflict of one sort or another. Even our sporting events are a form of tribalism, benign but still..."

Garneau nodded. "The betrayals and deceptions would all be there. Plenty of historical precedent for that. The thing is we don't think about it. It's just who we are."

"And now here we are in the aftermath, and what's going on? Nothing has changed. We're in our natural state of hyper-competitive tribal groups warring with each other. We might as well be wandering around the African savanna."

"At least the Internet is gone," Garneau said.

Alatorre grinned. "The great tribalism magnifier. Technology enhancing human weakness. That's why I want folks like Donaldson involved. Because if we can get the genetics right, mechanical enhancements will strengthen not weaken us. If we're going to take our place in this galactic—this interstellar ecosystem—we must evolve. The good news is we can take charge of that."

Wrasse

Wrasse greeted Teracia at his door wearing a fillitong, an ancient form of ceremonial dress worn by elite fahr during the first dynasty. It was a bold shimmering metallic green, with red and yellow accents and medallions of gold and silver sown into the fabric. The medallions had symbols, derived as far as Teracia could tell from the same archaic writing system she had first seen on the khards. The fillitong fit Wrasse loosely, designed for the much more robust pre-modificate fahr.

"Like it?" Wrasse said twirling the garment.

Teracia said nothing.

Wrasse came to a momentary stop and studied the Vice Commander. "The implants seemed like a good idea at the time. And I did enjoy the reactions I got from others, but this is easier."

Teracia purpled. She remembered the huge stir Wrasse had caused by having pulsating multicolored implants in his scales and his resulting distress when these deteriorated on board. She gestured to the fillitong. "It looks nice," she said.

"I brought a few other examples with me. I bring them out every once in a while, put them on, and just gaze at my reflection. They warm me up. Now I can wear them whenever I want." He twirled and Teracia glimpsed the engorged diaphragm beneath the garment. Wrasse's ballow inflated gold and his gills rippled.

Teracia willed her gills to respond in kind, but she kept her ballow beige. She swam deeper into the room. The images projected on Wrasse's walls were of creatures known for their bright radiant colors. Teracia recognized most of them, but one was new to her. She stopped before it. Wrasse joined her.

"A species native to Planet Song," he said. "A reef fish with a name close to my own. How could I not put it on my wall? Especially with those colors."

In the millennium before he received the scale implants, Wrasse had been rumored to be a huey, a fahr not aroused by song but by bright displays of animal color. The implants seemed to confirm this, but Wrasse had never acknowledged his orientation. Any affirmation was too much of a chance for negative backlash. He was, after all, an elected official. But now he was the CEO of Song Corp, a permanent non-elected position.

"You're not worried about the brand?" Teracia asked.

"We're heading back to Centrix with the biggest prize in song-collecting history. No one will care about the CEO's appearance."

"Or his orientation?"

Wrasse studied Teracia as his ballow morphed from gold to a deep kelp green. "I am a huey. I don't think that will come as a surprise to anyone. My being public about it will only mean others of similar orientation will be less vulnerable."

Teracia nodded. Hueys hid their interest in the visual, at least in public. When they gathered together, all manner of bright clothing appeared in imitation of specific creatures. Just loud and bright was often enough.

"It wasn't a choice, was it? Any more than my situation was a choice?" Teracia asked.

"No," Wrasse said, gray smudging on the green. "But we are *not* the same." He removed the fillitong, hung it on his wall, and flattened his gills. "We have work to do," he said pinking.

Teracia nodded and noticed Wrasse's diaphragm was back to its normal state. She had changed his mood. She pulled a long stretch of water through her gills. Bonding with Song Corp's new CEO was unlikely to happen, despite their shared experiences.

*****

Wrasse studied the Vice Commander. Emotional manipulation. Surely, she wasn't so stupid as to think this would work with the CEO of Song Corp.

"Personally," he said to her, "I don't care how much they sing during the voyage as long as we get them to Centrix intact and healthy. At least they're now eating. Once we get them to the menagerie, to the ocean we've prepared for them, then all will be well. In the meantime, however, we have certain expectations on board."

"Taste."

"Exactly. And it doesn't help that Agastin is as ribald as the rest of them."

"More so," Teracia said.

"So, we have a problem. We have to get them to sing, but if they do, it could destroy the mission."

"The containment area is sealed. If they sing no one outside of it will hear."

"Which will be even more frustrating to the crew than the current situation."

Teracia said nothing.

"But we could still collect the Song?"

"Yes, but I would advise against it, Lord Wrasse," Teracia said.

Wrasse felt himself blue, but he restrained it. Much as he loved the idea of the honorific, allowing himself to be flattered by the word "Lord" would leave him vulnerable. But then he'd had the title "Minister" for half a millennium and it hadn't hurt him. He could deal with flattery. Some of it might be deserved. "Why would you advise against collecting the Song?" he asked.

"There are no extant recordings of the Singer's virgin song. Prostallen had them destroyed on the last voyage. There was too much risk of them leaking into circulation on board the ship. If that had happened, they may not have made it back to Centrix."

"And you think we run the same risk here?"

"Perhaps even more so. On that voyage, we collected thousands of singing animals so there was no shortage of virgin song

124

with which to distract the crew. On this voyage, we came for only one animal. The crew still want taste, and if we give it to them, they will die."

Wrasse's gills rippled. "Agastin seems to think he would survive. What do you think?"

Teracia said nothing.

"He thinks his elite level genetic engineering will protect him," Wrasse prodded.

Teracia's gills flattened. "Everything we know is based on an analysis of one incident, and there were no elite level fahr among the thirty victims. The analysis pointed to a combination of frequencies that went beyond the usual song impairment to produce something best understood as a series of extreme muscular seizures. So, the real question is will his elite level resistance to impairment protect him from these seizures? Will his resistance dial back those problematic frequencies? We don't know. But, as you've seen, dial those frequencies back through filters and you... "

"Achieve the ultimate combination of arousal and impairment," Wrasse finished. "But that wasn't what you were going to say was it?" His gills rippled. "If Agastin is willing to experiment with his own life, who am I to say no? But for that to happen we will have to get these animals singing."

"You're not worried about his survival?"

Wrasse flattened his gills and looked at her.

Teracia purpled. "No, I don't suppose you would be," she said.

Wrasse allowed the gold on his ballow to dissipate into green. "Agastin's main task was to extract the Singers from Planet Song. He has done so despite the complications, so I suppose we should be grateful. However, he had little to do with the voyage to Planet Song and will have little to do with the return voyage to Centrix. That will be in your and Chief Navigational Officer Baronth's capable claspers. It makes the Commander expendable and should he expend himself... That would simplify things."

"Simplify?"

"It is my understanding you have a highly placed friend back on Centrix. I doubt if I have to explain myself."

Teracia nodded. With Petar as Chancellor, the population of the Fahr world was spiraling down into mass addiction, exactly where Song Corp wanted them. And when they arrived with The Singer...

Food

The staff at Fort Irvin had put some of Diane's people into two empty barracks. The rest returned to their homes in the civilian part of Fort Irwin, but without air conditioning, these homes where almost unbearable. With all the windows open it still took until past midnight for things to cool down enough for sleep. By 9:00 a.m. the following morning the thermometer began its relentless daily march toward 90 degrees.

Diane chose the barracks over her apartment. At least the rooms were large and open, and the windows were high and wide enough to let the cooling desert wind blow through. This wasn't always a cool wind, but the barracks were still far more comfortable than her third-floor apartment. There was the other small matter of no functioning elevator. The climb to her apartment felt as sweat-inducing as the Mojave sun.

The population of Fort Irwin was formerly fed by trucked-in food, and the trucks were gone. No one knew for how long, so they set about trying to preserve some of the meat by salting and drying it. Fresh veggies were a bigger problem because very few residents knew how to preserve these items and the base had a limited number of suitable containers. Soon they were sending the two functioning military trucks out, but forays into the surrounding communities came back empty. No one had food to give. By the end of the third week meals became monotonous, most of them canned tuna or peanut butter and jam sandwiches made with stale bread. Diane was losing weight, a good thing at the time.

By the fourth week breakfast became a small bowl of oatmeal, lunch a bag of potato chips and a single piece of jerky, and supper a few strings of pasta soaked in canned tomato sauce. *Every. Single. Night.* Roasted rodents and birds of various kinds made an appearance, followed by edible cacti. The kids whimpered, often well into the morning's small hours. Diane restricted herself to the morning bowl of oatmeal, but the kids kept whimpering. Eventually they ran out of powdered milk and rationed water.

She'd got in the habit of rising early to avoid the midmorning bathroom crowd. The tube of toothpaste in her bag was now mostly spent, and she put little on her tooth brush. *What am I doing this for?* she wondered. Diane looked in the mirror. The last time she'd seen that many ribs was during a struggle with bulimia in her late teens. It was not a pleasant memory. She picked up her toiletries and walked out to greet the rising sun.

Her bag yielded a package of cigarettes, the one thing the base had not run out of. She lit up, listening to the sound of the match flaring and her own crackly draw on the smoke. Under a street lamp that hadn't cast a shadow in three months, she found a solitary plastic lawn chair. She settled into it, put on her sunglasses and watched the sun's half ball on the horizon until she was forced to look away. "You will eventually kill me, won't you?" she said to it and drifted into a smoking trance.

She was brought back by an excitement of distant voices. Multiple trucks on the horizon. It took a moment to register what this was. They were coming with supplies! She counted the trucks—eight—and then slumped back down in the lawn chair. She wasn't sure of the base's current population, but it had swollen well beyond the 9,000 plus listed in the last census. Eight trucks would not cut it. She questioned her own mindset. This should be good news even if the amount was small, but everything that had happened in the past six weeks had thrown a pall over her life. She was starving, and she had lost her purpose. Motivation, it seemed to Diane, was an illusory concept. Still she forced herself to get up and walk out to meet the coming convoy, if for no other reason than its value as a distraction, a temporary funk deflector.

The trucks had what she expected. Staples. Flour, rice, potatoes, beans, powdered milk, smaller amounts of fresh fruit and vegetables, canned everything especially protein, basic medical supplies, and wonder of wonders, a shortwave radio and a large water purifier, both with accompanying diesel generators. And mail. There were letters for people on the base including one for her.

She carried her prizes back to the barracks, an apple, a Mars Bar, and the letter. The apple was a Granny Smith with a hard outer skin. Biting into it made her gums bleed. She ate all of it including the inner bits, followed by the Mars Bar which she allowed to dissolve in her mouth, a soothing balm for bleeding gums. The letter she looked at but did not open, certain it would contain bad news about her parents or someone close. There was nothing on the envelope to indicate its source, but it was addressed to Diane in her official capacity as the head of Goldstone. Maybe it isn't personal, she thought. The food had helped clarify her thinking. Finally, she opened it.

Dear Dr. McLean,

I hope this letter finds you well. As I'm sure you're aware, many of your fellow Americans are suffering greatly. President Alatorre and I hope you are not among them. If you are, rest assured we will rectify that situation shortly, not only by means of increased aide to your part of the country but by changing your personal situation. The President is gathering scientists from a wide variety of disciplines and bringing them to MIT in Boston to jump-start the rebuilding process. We will include you and your colleague, Mr. Trent Proctor, in that process. Though I cannot speak to the exact means, we will provide transportation for you and Mr. Proctor.

Gerald Garneau, Presidential Chief of Staff

Diane stared at the letter in disbelief. Of what use could two astrophysicists be in reconstructing the country? There must be better choices. She'd done her PhD. so long ago she couldn't remember the last time someone had addressed her as "Doctor". And Proctor? He'd been a perpetual state of thesis revision for the past ten years, far more of a techie than a scientist. Still, the two of them had been in a forefront of all the discoveries related to the coming of the Fahr. Perhaps that was it. Perhaps the President wanted to reward them.

They had a proper meal that night. Canned corned beef, potatoes, canned peas mixed with fresh cooked carrots, and uber sweet canned pears for dessert. About ten percent of the diners ate so fast they threw up, including a young soldier sitting at the table across from Trent and herself. "Let's go outside," she said to Trent as the young soldier cleaned up his mess. They found a bench outside the mess hall and sat down.

Trent was more emaciated than she was. He did not so much eat his food as suck on it, putting each fork full in his mouth and holding it there for a while before chewing. He said little while eating.

"Did you imagine anything like this?" she asked him.

He shook his head. "An explosion maybe. Some kind of shoot'em-up. Didn't expect starvation." He lapsed into silence again.

"What did you think of the letter?"

"I have to get well before I can think through anything," he said quietly.

"It doesn't look like they're giving us much of an option. But, really, what is the option? Go or stay here and die. This desert can't support us."

Proctor put a carrot in his mouth and sucked on it.

Another young soldier appeared at the door with two backpacks. When he saw them, he walked over. "I believe these are for you, Dr. McLean," he said. "They were in the cab of the lead truck."

Diane and Trent looked at each other. "Thank you," she said.

The young soldier nodded his head and smiled. "You're welcome, ma'am." Then he turned and walked away.

"What's this then?" Trent asked.

Each bag had a tag with their respective names.

"Here's yours," Diane said, passing Trent his bag.

Proctor took the bag and set it on the ground to his right. He took a fork full of corned beef and put it in his mouth.

"Aren't you curious?" she asked.

"I'm eating," he said.

Diane shook her head and reached for her own bag. First, she opened the small zippered pocket in the front. It contained a vile of Advil, two lip balms, a toothbrush, a tube of toothpaste, a Swiss Army knife equipped for personal grooming, a roll of breath mints, a plastic container of dental floss, and an assortment of hair and safety pins. "Looks like they've packed a bag for us," she said.

Proctor grunted but continued to feed himself.

Next Diane opened the main part of the bag. She whistled and held the bag up for Proctor to see. It was full of food, granola bars, beef jerky, various candies, dried fruit, protein bars, wrapped and sealed pastries, peanuts, almonds, gummy bears, and three phials of vitamins. "I'm guessing we're supposed to keep these to ourselves," she said.

"For the trip," he said.

Diane nodded. "Road food. Lots of it, so they're not sending a Lear jet to pick us up."

"Doesn't look like it," Trent said.

"I guess I need to go back to my apartment and pack," Diane said. "Best to be ready."

"Yeah, me too," Trent said.

In her weakened state, Diane found the flight of stairs to her apartment a challenge. She wondered if the trucks had come too late, her body so damaged she would die anyway. The closet yielded a collection of pant suits intended for a woman forty-five pounds heavier. She found coins, rolled bills, and lip stick in the pockets of three of the suits, a testament to her dislike of handbags. The fourth had her Visa and Mastercard, the credit cards waved in the general direction of the cashier whenever she was in a hurry. She must have worn that one the last time she went shopping in town. They were useless now that everything had reverted to the barter system, damaged anyway because of the small burnt-out circuit boards embedded in the plastic. She threw the cards into the trash bucket and lowered herself onto the bed.

Someone knocked on her door. She sat up and looked at her wrist, still expecting a working watch after so long without one. Not a morning person. She stumbled to the door and opened it.

"You get to ride in the Camaro," Billy said to Diane without a greeting. "They'll be around in about an hour to pick up you and Trent. Sent me to tell you."

Billy was the only member of her team that did not look emaciated, but then he'd started this whole adventure packing an extra seventy pounds. And he was back to his old goth self now that the fiancé was out of the picture. She, along with her fellow fundamentalists, were living communally at the church waiting for Jesus' immanent return. Billy wanted no part of that.

"What is this all about anyway?" he asked Diane.

"They're taking us to MIT. Some government scientific consultation."

"You're going to Boston? How the hell are you going to get there?"

"The Camaro, I guess." She smiled grimly. "I really have no idea. We got a letter yesterday from the President's chief of staff saying they wanted Trent and I to come. They didn't say how they planned to get us there. Sending the Camaro to pick us up is all I know. It's the best answer I can give."

"Just the two of you?" Billy said, looking disappointed.

"That's what the letter said. Not my decision. Tell you what though. I'll leave you in charge of Goldstone."

Billy laughed. "That's like being left in charge of an empty parking lot." Then he got serious. "They're bumping you up a tier. You'll get fed."

"If I'm going to be meeting with the President, I'm going to be advocating for Fort Irwin and for Goldstone."

Billy gestured to the sky. "There's probably nothing left out there to track."

"Maybe not, but we won't know until we get it up and running. And if the President thinks we're important enough to bring us out to MIT for a consult, they want Goldstone functional again. Maybe to find the Fahr. Who knows? Whatever the case, they can't do Goldstone without Irwin"

Billy nodded. "Well, I've delivered the message. Camaro in an hour. See you when you get back, I guess. I'm not going to say anything about this. I'm not sure they'd let you leave if I did." He turned around and started back down the stairs.

"See you," Diane said. It was probably a mistake leaving Billy in charge of Goldstone, but she doubted he would go anywhere near the place. Nothing to do there.

The Camaro arrived forty-five minutes later with Trent already squeezed into the back seat. He looked peaked and sounded wheezy. "You going to be all right?" she asked him.

"I have a bag full of food," Trent said. "And you know what else? I didn't have Advil in my bag—they gave me Gravol instead."

"Must know something about you. You sure you want the back seat? I'd be happy to switch."

"It's a short trip, this part of it anyway."

Diane held out her hand to the driver. "I'm Diane," she said.

"Sergeant Feinstein," came the reply.

"Where are you taking us, Sergeant Feinstein?"

"Barstow train station, ma'am."

"The trains are running?"

"A few of them, ma'am. They've restored some older locomotives but the lines are crazy. They'll have to detour around militia

132

hot spots and stretches where the tracks are a mess. It won't be a short trip and you'll be going through some hostile territory. My platoon is coming along in case there are problems."

Diane studied Feinstein. "You don't seem very happy about it."

Feinstein said nothing.

"So, is there a problem?" Diane prompted.

"The train has a functional dining car. We're all going to be fed."

"And you don't think it's fair?"

"No ma'am, I don't. Irwin's full of starving kids."

"And we will do something about that. In the meantime, your platoon will not be effective if it's weakened by hunger."

"I suppose not, ma'am."

"Doesn't anyone else know about what's going on here?" Diane asked.

Feinstein shook his head. "No. We were told not to say anything."

Diane felt Trent looking at her from the back seat. When she caught his gaze, he turned and looked out the window.

Terminal

Kale now knew to expect a visit from the fahr every time the water around the Zodiac frothed. It smelled of sulfur. It was like getting a visit from some ancient relative with flatulence.

He knew the reverse was also true. It had been weeks since he had bathed in anything other than salt water. Swimming in it was his only source of exercise, but the action did little to make him feel clean. Kale had no soap or deodorant, no way of cleaning his teeth, and no change of clothing. His dreads, a difficult hairstyle to keep clean at the best of times, now perched on his head like rancid chunks of matted clay.

The Zodiac was now fixed to the side of the enclosure. The humpbacks' habit of surfacing or breaching anywhere in the enclosure meant sitting in the center of the water was out of the question. Now that they were eating again one never knew when the water would erupt with giant mouths. At least he was perfectly positioned to study this when it happened. The irony was not lost on him. Had he not been trying to get close to feeding humpbacks in the first place, he never would have been sucked into the Fahr ship. Now that he had been, he was free to study them when he wanted, but the knowledge he gained would benefit no one. No other human, anyway.

The silence pushed on him, forcing him back into memories. Honi and the cousins in continual rotation. They were gone from him, gone as in dead. And he to them. But floating in a Zodiac left him with little else to think about.

Sulfur. He looked over the side of boat and found froth breaking the surface. More scratching on turtle shells? For an intelligent species, the Fahr sure picked an odd way to communicate. He watched as the creature ascended from the depths, always spotting the balloon-like cranial projection first. Usually this was green or beige, but he had seen it turn pink, yellow, and on one occasion a deep shade of purple. That had happened after he asked for vegetables and explained he could not just eat fish. Afterwards it had brought him a variety of water plants to try, all of them edible so he wondered if it knew more about the human physiology than it let on.

This time it was not carrying a turtle shell. Instead it had something wrapped in what looked like industrial burlap. The fahr held this out to him. Kale took the package and unwrapped it. Inside, perfectly dry, was something that looked like an old writing slate. The word "Hello" appeared as a holographic projection in the air four inches above the slate. He nearly dropped the device. The word dissolved, and a QWERTY keyboard appeared on the surface of the device. He typed a few letters, and they too appeared in the air in front of him. He grinned.

"Better than a turtle shell," he typed.

The fahr's gill slits did a funny little wave.

Handcar

When first discovered no one thought much about the old railroad handcar. Abandoned in a storage shed near the track, it had probably been there for decades. The scouting party took little interest in it, paying more attention to the various hand tools the shed also contained. These they carried back to the camp.

"Does it work?" Peter asked when he heard about the handcar.

The man shrugged. "Wouldn't matter if it did," he said. "If that track's like the others around here, there's probably abandoned freight cars and wrecks of various kinds all up and down its length. It's not as if we could use the thing to go anywhere."

Still Peter noted the car's location. Checking it out would be difficult. He'd have to find some excuse to be absent from the camp for the better part of a day. They'd been running low on medical supplies for weeks. Everything within fifty miles had been looted, so the focus was now shifting to medicinal plants that grew wild in the forest and fields. Part of the problem was the scouts didn't know what to look for, and so far, Thompson hadn't trusted Peter enough to let him leave the camp.

"I'm going to need more supplies, sir." Peter told him.

"I've asked the men to be on the lookout."

"Sir, they have to know what to look for and most of them don't."

"Medicinal plants, you mean?"

"Yes, sir. Every medicine cabinet and dispensary in the area has been harvested."

135

The commander looked at him, rolling his cigarette to the other side of his mouth and back again. "I'm not convinced you're a good risk. It's taking you a while to buy into what we're doing here."

"You have my wife and daughter, sir," Peter said.

"Yes, I do, don't I?" Thompson grinned and nodded, the fishing lures on his hat doing a soft jangle. "You remember what happened when Jacobs took a powder a while back."

"Two days after he left, you married off his wife and daughters, sir," Peter said, trying to keep the emotion off his face.

"He wasn't going to need them anymore."

"Yes, sir."

"So how long this going to take you?"

Peter shrugged. "Depends on what and how much I find, sir. I haven't surveyed the area. Don't know what's there."

"You find more than you can carry, we'll get you some help."

"Yes, sir."

"And no overnighters. You're back here before dusk."

"Understood, sir."

He'd have to scavenge plants on the way to the railway shack and hope what he brought back would have at least some medicinal properties. A few of the camp's woodsman would have enough survivalist training to identify some plants, so he couldn't do a completely bogus collection.

The journey threw thorns, thistles, swamps, mosquitoes, and dense underbrush in his way. It also yielded American ginseng, hart's-tongue, bearberry, and a few other flowers and leaves. These fit into his shoulder bag but were of limited medical use. They would, however, be recognized as medicinal by the woodsmen and that should reduce suspicion.

The handcar was a Sheffield, but Peter knew nothing of the manufacturer or the quality of the device. It proved intact and functional, but while its wood platform seemed sturdy enough, the metal parts were layered in rust and in need of lubrication. He could scrounge some oil or pork fat, but the biggest problem was the cart's location on a short piece of sidetrack no longer connected to the mains. The gap was not massive—about four feet—but the cart's weight might scuttle the plan. It would take four strong men to lift it, putting that well beyond the capabilities of himself, Sonya, and Tracy. He'd have to find a way of getting it on the track before their escape or the plan wouldn't work.

The scouts had left the heavier tools behind including a sledgehammer, several buckets of railroad spikes, the rusted remains of a two-handled logging saw, a box of signal replacement bulbs brown with age, coils of thick wound wire, and four large crowbars hanging on the wall. The crowbars looked new, preserved by a thin coating of light oil. The bars were about the right length and thickness but would need to be fixed in place and secured before he attempted to roll the cart along them to the main track. Peter looked to the sky. He had five hours before he was expected back in camp, and the journey itself would take ninety percent of that. He had to work fast.

The shed itself was built on ties, some rotting. These received the spikes easily, too easily, but the spikes held. He could lay two of the crowbars across once he had them in place. How well they would hold with the cart weighing them down was another question. Peter was sure he would only get one shot. He tested the jerry-rigged tracks one more time, then leaned on the cart and pushed hard. The metal wheels screamed at it him but gave, and the cart rolled the short distance onto the track. He threw wooden stops behind the rear wheels, whistled a long low note, and wiped his brow with the back of his hand. They had an escape vehicle, but he had no idea how far along the track it would take them.

When Peter got back into camp, he went to Thompson.

"I didn't marry off your wife and daughter," the Commander said. "Should have?"

Peter unloaded the contents of his bag and laid it on the table. "This was all I could find, sir," he said. "I'm a little green at this. Most of these plants I've either only seen in a lab or in situations where they're cultivated. Finding them in the wild is tricky. You have to know where to look. Theoretically I knew, but until you get out there..."

"Not interested in excuses, Doc." Thompson said.

"I got better at it as the day went on, sir."

"Yeah, well, for the next few days you'll be staying here. You being gone for the day just increased your workload for tomorrow. You'll have a few comin' round to see you tonight, some that need stitching, and there's a bone to be set."

"I'll do my best, sir."

"You'd better," Thompson said, "and when you're finished with that, they'll be a camp meeting in the clearing. Come when you're finished patching people up." With that he turned and walked away, leaving Peter to stuff the plants back into his bag.

Peter couldn't believe their luck. Camp meeting attendance was compulsory. No one would be around to see them heading in the opposite direction. And Thompson had handed him a reason not to be there, at least not for the roll call.

He slipped by their tent on the way to the infirmary.

"We're going tonight," he told Sonya and Tracy. "Dress in layers and pack the essentials."

Sonya nodded. Tracy frowned. "But Jake's not back yet," she said.

"Jake?"

Tracy said nothing.

"What did I tell you about hormones? They lie to you," Peter said

"They're not lying," she said quietly.

Peter turned to his wife. "I have to see some patients. I'm not sure how long it will take, but I'll be back as soon as I can. Pack a bag for me too. We'll need a jar of oil or bacon grease, lubrication for the cart. Can you handle that?"

Sonya nodded. Peter nodded in Tracy's direction. Sonya pursed her lips.

"Listen to your mother," Peter told the girl.

Pushing through trees, brambles, and undergrowth on the near dark had numerous disadvantages. The least of these were the scratches all three of them had sustained. The worst was the clear path they had made. A camp overflowing with woodsmen would have no trouble tracking them in the early morning light. That gave them five or six hours, but Tracy was in no mood to move quickly.

"Here's the thing," Peter said to her. "We have left the camp. From their point of view, we're deserters. So, if they catch us, or even if we give up and go back, we're in serious trouble. They might execute all three of us, but at the very least, they string me up and marry the two of you off to men you don't know. They already don't like the attention Jake has been paying to you, so it won't be him. So, now we're on a set path. You can get a move on and live or you can drag your heels and die. Which will it be?"

"We didn't have to leave," Tracy said, but she picked up her pace.

All Sonya had scrounged was a small jar of bacon fat, not much but enough. The next problem was seeing where to apply it in the near pitch dark. They only had a single box of matches but found an old oil rag to set ablaze. This burned quickly, but Peter had smeared most of the fat before it was consumed. Peter pumped the handle twice, feeling it rasp and squeak. A few more pumps and the sounds diminished. Satisfied he nodded to his wife and daughter, and they scrambled aboard.

"I don't want to go too far before we can see," he said. "We don't want to run into something at speed and get thrown, but we need to get far enough down the track, so they can't see us from the shack. If we can do that, we'll have the advantage. They won't know how much of a start we have and may let us go."

"They'll come on horseback and they'll have guns," Sonya reminded him.

"This cart moves easily on rail lines. Horses do not. That's the reason they created these things in the first place. We stay out of sight they can't shoot us."

Sonya frowned then adjusted their packs on the cart. Tracy, who hadn't said a thing for hours, sat down and crossed her legs. She let out a sigh and stared off into the darkness. Peter pumped handles and signaled for Sonya to do the same.

About fifteen miles down the track they heard the baying of dogs. The sun was now well above the horizon, and they had made god progress, so Peter doubted the animals could not be from the camp. They began frantically pumping just as half a dozen dogs rounded the corner in full pursuit. One glance told him this was a wild pack and that the animals were gaining on them. Peter looked around for some kind of weapon but found nothing.

Tracy rummaged through her pack. She pulled out a metal sling shot and a bag of small ball bearings. Peter stared at her in amazement. She loaded one ball into the pocket, pulled it back, and took aim at the lead dog, a shepherd cross with a missing ear, now within a few feet of the cart. She released the ball and struck the dog in the forehead. It fell, tripping up two of the other animals. The remaining three kept coming. Tracy reloaded and fired again, this time hitting a mangy golden lab high in its shoulder. It yelped and tumbled into the undergrowth beside the rails. The other two dogs gave up the chase.

Peter looked at his daughter. Tracy was staring at the sling shot as if the thing had suddenly appeared in her hands. She took a couple of deep breaths before putting it and the bag of bearings back in her pack.

"Where did you get...?"

"Jake," she said. "And he showed me how to use it. But it was just target practice. Knocking cans off a fence. I never thought I would..." She started to shake.

Sonya took her daughter in her arms. "You did well. You did really well."

"Yes," Peter said looking down the track at the retreating dogs and then back at his daughter. He still wasn't sure what he'd just seen.

Peter pumped hard, putting as much distance as he could between them, the dogs, and the militia behind them.

Sonya retrieved couple loaves of bread and cheese curds from her bag. They had a moving breakfast while Peter and occasionally Tracy worked the handles.

"They should be at the shed by now," Peter said. "I'd say we have at least thirty miles on them."

"No obstacles yet," Sonya said.

"No and I expected something by now. Especially since this track was well maintained. It would have seen a lot of use before the..."

"Aliens attacked," Tracy finished as they came around the bend.

There before them was a graveyard of mangled locomotives, passenger, flatbed, grain, and tank cars, and other bits of railway carnage. But nothing was on the track, at least not on the track they were on. It had all been pulled aside, dragged away to make the track accessible.

People emerged from the more intact rail cars. Most looked like they'd stepped out of sepia photographs from the 1930s, dirty ragged clothes and resigned looks on their faces. They were a mixed lot with blacks, Latinos, and Asians dotted among soiled but predominantly white faces. They carried pitchforks, wrenches, hammers, crowbars, and a few rifles. Peter hit the brake, brought the cart to a halt, and raised his hands into the air.

"No weapons", he said to them.

The people stared at them exchanging nervous glances.

"They've got the cart," said a middle-aged tattooed man in overalls and flip flops. He held a pitch fork.

"This?" Peter said gesturing to the cart. "We found it in an old abandoned railway shack about thirty miles down the track."

"Careful what you tell them," Sonya whispered.

"You with the militia?" the man asked.

Peter studied them. They were leery of Thompson and his force. "We were running from them," he said.

Sonya gave him an exasperated look.

141

"Running from them? So, they're following you?" Concern spread over the faces of the crowd.

Peter took a deep breath. "I don't know. We had about a six-hour head start. If they're following us, they never got close enough for us to see them."

"They know you were on the track?" The man who spoke this time wore a pair of loose fitting multi-pocketed cargo pants, a T-shirt emblazoned with the album cover of *Super Session*, and a light brown Tilley hat, the cord ties of which dangled beneath a week old dirty blond beard. He held a rifle but kept the barrel pointed at the ground.

Sonya reached out and shook her husband. "We don't know these people!"

"But we do know the people we left," Peter replied. He gestured back the way they came. "Want to go back to that?"

"No," Sonya said.

"So, we have to pick a side, and we can't pick that side."

Sonya nodded.

"They know you were on the track?" the man repeated.

"If they got to the shack, they'll know," Peter admitted. "They found the cart a couple of days ago when they were scouting the area. They weren't interested in it. Just grabbed the tools in the shed and headed back to camp. That's how I heard about it and thought it was worth checking out. When I saw it, I thought we could use it to get away."

"Why did you want to get away? Weren't you well fed? Safe?"

Sonya spoke up. "Well fed, yes. But they have all these military-fascist rules and stark divides between what men and women can and cannot do. And they cull the men they capture, driving the men they don't want from the camp and enslaving the others. But the women, oh no, they keep the woman. Those of breeding age anyway. They're planning little harems for their senior leadership. They already have designs on my daughter."

Tracy's mouth dropped open. "You never told me that!" she said.

The man with the Tilley hat held up his hand and turned to Peter. "So why did they keep you?"

"Medic," Peter said. "I was a combat medic in Afghanistan. That made me useful."

The Tilley hat nodded. "You know, you might have brought them down on us."

"We were just getting away. We had no idea what we'd find along this track. You're as big a surprise to us as we are to you."

The Tilley hat said nothing. Peter waited.

"Well you've saved us the trouble of going after that cart. We knew it was there from the records at the station," he said. "And if we know the militia is coming, we can be ready. I guess we should thank you for that too, but you're not out of the woods yet. The folks at the government offices will want to talk to you."

"Government?"

"We're scavengers here. Taking stuff apart, trying to recycle what we can. But we get fed by Alatorre. They're doing interviews, trying to track down folks with useful skills. All part of the great rebuilding project, I guess. Have you been interviewed?"

"No," Peter said.

"Well, if you were with a militia, that makes sense. They're trying to find important people who disappeared when the aliens attacked. And they're also trying to weed out folks who are hostile to the government, so be careful what you say. You three don't look dangerous, but one never knows. Anyone they lock up gets poor rations. Anyway, for the time being we will have to do just that." The Tilley hat now pointed his rifle at them. "You'll need to come with me. Name's Clement Price in case you need to call me. I'm kind of in charge here—in charge of keeping the peace, making sure people get fed, and the work gets done."

The lockup was an empty rail car. It contained two beds, a washing bowl with soap and towels, a large bottle of water, and a toilet seat mounted over an aluminum basin.

"That's the biffy bowl," Clement said with a grin. "I'd keep it at the far end of the car. Someone will be around to empty it once a day. In the meantime, I'll need your full names and your previous occupations. Brag. The more useful you make yourself appear, the more likely you'll get a quick interview."

They came and got Peter the following day, three men in suits with holstered side arms. They led him, one in front and two behind, through the rail camp and into the town proper. Brunswick, Maryland, he noted. They entered a three-story office building, a post WWII functional box with a not-in-service elevator. On the third floor was a door marked with the American Government eagle. All three men stood back, waiting for Peter to go in. He did, and they followed, taking positions behind him.

The woman behind the desk wore makeup, too much mascara in Peter's opinion, and dyed blonde hair. He guessed she wore a dark green pant suit, though the bottom half of it was behind the desk. She had a dossier in front of her, and Peter saw his name on it.

"You're Dr. Peter Howard, the geneticist?" she asked.

Peter nodded.

"We've been looking for you. Almost gave up hope. President Alatorre wants to see you."

Camp

Thompson was not talking to Jake. Ignoring him was more like it, like Jake had become something insubstantial. But Thompson was the only person ignoring him. Around the camp, he was now known as the "mirror man". Jake found himself assigned to repairing and setting up tents, or worse, to camp clean up detail. This included digging the holes for the latrines and closing the ones that were full. He was not being punished but his favored status was gone. And so was Tracy. Perhaps this was better, her not seeing him like this, if that were the only problem.

Doc Howard and his family had disappeared one night, leaving most of their belongings behind. No one had noticed until the following morning when Sonya had failed to show for her child-minding duties. The camp sent out a search party and learned that the Howards had escaped using an old railway cart. How they had left unseen was a mystery, but Jake's obsession with Tracy made him guilty by association. Of what, he wasn't sure. He'd been in New England when it happened. And they took his rifle.

The Winchester had been added to the ever-growing pool of camp firearms, no longer his to clean and polish. If he wanted to use it, Jake had to get a slip from the sergeant and check out the rifle. Often it was gone before he arrived at munitions with the paperwork. When he managed to get his hands on it, he had to do a major cleaning every time. No gun could get dirty that fast unless someone was deliberately soiling it, pushing sand, soil, or sometimes even shit into the chamber. After a while it was only shit, and then he saw fellow sniper Luke Hawkins carrying the gun.

"It's not him," a voice said behind him.

Jake turned and found old Robby following him. He waited for the old man to catch up.

"It's not Hawkins," Robby said, catching his breath.

Jake looked at him. The old man was wearing a straw hat. Jake had never seen Robby in a hat.

"He's not the one who's soiling your gun."

Jake thought about denying that was the reason he was following Hawkins, but then Old Robby had been around enough times when Jake was swearing and cleaning his gun to know the young man was really pissed. It was pointless to deny it.

"Who do you think did it?"

"Same person who rammed a cow turd into my horn," Robby said.

Jake laughed. "Somebody rammed a cow turd in your trumpet?"

"Same person," Robby said.

"Who?"

145

"You don't want to know, but it's not Hawkins. Oh, he may not do much of a job of keeping the gun clean, but he's not deliberately soiling it."

"Then who?"

"Like I said, you don't want to know. I'm only telling you this 'cause I wouldn't want you to take it out on Hawkins, 'cause he's innocent."

Jake stared at him. "Don't you want to get the guy who put the turd into your horn?"

Robby shuffled his feet and stared off into the distance. "I'm resisting temptation," he said. "I'm doing just what Jesus would want me to do."

"Jesus!" Jake said.

"Don't do that! Don't take His name in vain."

"Sorry."

"Now, I suggest you take up fishing. That's a good way of putting your mind on easier things."

"Fishing?"

"Yeah, fishing. Calm you right down." Robby took his hat off, stared down into it, and winked at Jake. "Well, I'd better go and practice my horn."

"You never practice."

"Well, I have to go blow a little cow shit out of it. Get it ready for the morning. Thinking of doing an extra-long version of Reveille for you all. Now there might be someone out there who doesn't appreciate it much, but it's his own damn fault for ordering someone to soil my horn." With that Robby turned and walked back down the path.

Jake's face reddened as he watched Old Robby go. *It's Thompson! It's fucking Thompson!*

146

Beet Field

Hunting bows were kept in the armory but didn't have to be signed out. Most militia regarded them as a curiosity, but a certain contingent saw a hunting bow as more of a true survival weapon than a gun. The logic of having something to do with wasting gunpowder. It was true none among the camp knew how to make the powder, something Jake put down to their general distrust of soft college educated urbies. But every scouting party that went out came back with more ammunition. Bullets were more common in abandoned buildings than canned food. A lot more common. They wouldn't be running out soon. The truth was good hunting arrows were less common and more expensive than bullets. Still, they were reusable and that counted for something. So, when Jake was invited to come along and try, he did.

Handling a hunting bow was trickier than Jake thought and required a level of strength he wasn't expecting. Still, after just a few misses, he brought down a buck. This endeared him to the group, and he continued practicing with them until he was as good with a bow as he was with a gun. Within a few weeks, none of his fellow archers could touch him. There was no way he would abandon his Winchester though, but he couldn't check out the rifle again. Someone else had. So, he took a bow and a quiver of arrows.

Thompson would be at his thinking place, a small outcrop over a field of beets. Jake walked up to the edge, letting Thompson know he was there. Thompson spit loose tobacco from the roll-your-own in his mouth and lit it, ignoring the young man. Jake walked back to about a hundred yards behind Thompson, fit the arrow, and put it right into the Commander's heart. The Commander coughed, turned his head and then slumped forward, falling into the field below. Jake climbed down, removed the arrow, and cleaned it.

"Didn't miss that time, did I?" he said. He put the arrow back into the quiver and made for the woods on the far side of the field.

Us

A month had passed on the open Pacific. There'd been days when the ocean had taken the Israel Kamakawiwoʻole on a carnival ride, but the double hulled-canoe remained perched atop each wave. Honi was grateful for the time she'd spent on Kale's boat earning her sea legs, though the metaphor didn't quite work in her case. With each passing day Honi took deeper breaths until she forgot she was doing it, and relaxed.

Ka Pua stood in front of her. "Are you feeling that?" she asked. "What?"

Ka Pua pointed at Honi's right bicep and drew a line down to the thumb in her right hand. Both were twitching. Honi stared at them.

"Oh, my god!" she said.

"Can you feel it?" Ka Pua had a huge grin on her face.

"A little I think... I'm not sure... Oh, my god. Look at that!"

Three days later Honi felt a warm tingling in her right breast. She blushed. Privacy was only a dream on board the Israel. They had her dead center on the lower deck in full view of everyone. The ladies would surround her, holding up bed sheets, when Noelani changed and bathed her. Before such a thing had not bothered her much, the reality of her situation. Everyone gave her as much dignity as possible. Now she felt exposed.

She fought the sensation, not from embarrassment but because she didn't want to get sidetracked. Adolescent sexuality was the last thing Honi needed, though she wasn't sure it was a battle she could win. It was true none of her male cousins on board were paying attention to her, but she couldn't help but notice them. When she did, she lost focus on her real task, the struggle to regain control over the rest of her body. Still she did want back those parts of her body that made her more aware of her sexuality. It was both confusing and frustrating.

The wayfinders knew where San Diego was located and roughly how to get there, but they had never read the waves in that part of the ocean. It was steering from the stars, moon, and horizon. Honi could see they were nervous. One of them noticed a disturbance in the ocean, the kind of thing that suggested a land mass, but far as they knew, there were no islands in this part of the Pacific. What then was causing the waves to move in this fashion?

A few hours later they saw it, a container ship flying a Panamanian flag. It was so large the top of it was visible on the horizon hours before the full ship came into view. Off in the distance they could see men standing on the ship's deck and waving frantically to them.

There were about two dozen, almost all were Asian and emaciated. Honi guessed that they were Filipino, but the captain was Caucasian. He looked better fed, but even he was thin.

"We're dead in the water," he said to them. "Our engines are down as is the communication system. No one knows we're out here. We can't radio for help, can't send out a distress signal. We've been drifting for almost two months. There's no food and little water left. Do you have a radio?"

No one aboard the Israel answered.

Other members of the container crew shouted, mostly in broken English and Tagalog. It was a desperate cacophony that included pleas for food, water, passage, medicine, even sunscreen.

The cousins looked at each other, and without a word, continued sailing the Israel toward their original destination.

"What are you doing?" Honi said to them. "They're starving. Can't you see? They need our help!"

"We have none to give them," Ka Pua said.

"What are you talking about? We have food. We have water." Honi said.

"Enough for ourselves and no more. And we have no room for extra passengers."

"We can't just sail away!"

"They are not us," Ka Pua said.

"Not *us*?"

Ka Pua walked away. Honi looked frantically at everyone else. None would meet her gaze. Even her own parents looked away.

Someone on the container ship fired a flare at them. It landed in the water to their starboard side, fizzling in the waves.

Peni looked at Honi. "They are not us," her father said.

"*Us?*"

Her father gestured to the cousins on board the Israel.

"Most of the population of San Diego will not be *us* when we get there," Honi said. "Will they treat *us* in the same way we just treated these folks?"

Peni studied her before responding. "Perhaps so, if their limited resources allow them only to take care of their own. It's a risk we take."

"So, we could die there?"

"I don't think it's likely. Northern California has massive farms so there should at least be food, and we are American citizens."

Honi gritted her teeth. "But we're not from California and we're not from San Diego. We're not part of their *us.*"

"It's not that simple. Our people must survive. By the time we arrive in San Diego, we may be the only ones left. I don't think you understand how little food is in Hawaii. Anyway, we have no room for those sailors on the Israel, we have limited resources." He gestured again to the cousins. "Those of us in leadership had this discussion before we left Kona. We knew there might be hard decisions. We agreed family takes precedence. Sometimes you make choices, hard choices."

"Like taking a quad on a canoe?"

"Honi..."

Honi shook her head and closed her eyes, her way of leaving.

Magnetic Field

Kale. That was the name the homine had received from its parents. It seemed odd to Teracia that a sapient creature would allow itself to be named by another. Someone else defining who you were and how your life would be lived. The Fahr went nameless until they were old enough to name themselves. Her own name, Teracia, meant planetary, a fahr metaphor for solid and steadfast.

"It means strong and manly, but that's not the reason my mother chose it," Kale typed. "She liked the sound of it, the way it goes together with my other names."

Another odd concept she would have to think about. "What is your occupation?" Her question appeared in the hologram.

Kale gestured to a humpback lingering just beneath the water's surface. "I'm a marine biologist. I study whales," he typed.

"Study them?"

"Yes. I'm a humpback whale researcher."

Teracia felt herself blanch and then blue. *This is not possible,* she thought. She made immediate plans to research Kale in the ship's archived Homines database. "This is why you were collected with them?" she asked.

"Wrong place, wrong time," Kale typed.

Teracia did not understand but decided it wasn't important. *What were the chances we would accidentally capture a Homines Singer expert? Astronomical!* "What do we have to do to get them to sing?" she asked.

Kale looked at her, the skin above his eyes wrinkling. "Is this important?" he typed.

"Yes."

"Why?"

"It is what we do. We collect singers. The songs are highly valued."

"You came to our planet to collect animals?"

"Singers," Teracia corrected.

"Singers." The skin above Kale's eyes wrinkled even further. "How long did it take you to get to the Earth?"

"About three hundred of your years," Teracia said.

"Three hundred years?"

"We have a fast ship."

"Fast?" Kale shook his head.

"How old are you, Kale?"

"Forty-two years."

"I am a thousand times that age. For us three hundred years is nothing."

***

Kale's mouth dropped as he stared at the creature in the water beside the Zodiac. "You are forty thousand years old?" he typed.

"Yes, middle-aged for my species. That's why a three-hundred-year long journey is not significant."

"But how...?" The questions inside him piled up, deepened, widened.

"You will have many things to ask of us, and we of you."

Kale looked at Teracia. *Forty thousand years old?* There was no life scenario he could think of where such a thing was possible. On Earth there were a few trees still living at over a thousand years, fungal colonies had survived longer, some ancient sponges, but for vertebrates the upper limit was two hundred years. He reminded himself he was dealing with alien biology.

"So, what do we have to do to get them to sing?" Teracia persisted.

"If you have been alive forty thousand years," Kale typed, "then you have been alive since our species was in its infancy. How is this possible?"

"There are many things I will explain to you, and it will take a while before you understand. For now, it is enough to know you are on an interstellar ocean, a ship that encloses a marine ecosystem. You and the birds and these whales are the only species on board that are atmospheric breathers, which is why you have stay with them. There is no terrestrial environment on this ship. As for our life spans, we have learned to extend them to make such voyages possible. And we will have to do the same with you. Otherwise you will be dead long before we reach our destination".

***

Teracia watched as Kale digested this last bit of information. He had no ballow, but his skin color did change with his emotions, subtle shifts in his pinkish tan complexion. She wondered to what degree the Homines were attuned to these physical reactions. Kale's blood flow pinked his skin, but she had learned that this was not anger so much as alarm or embarrassment.

"You will extend my life?" he typed.

"Our home planet is eighty light years away. It will take us three hundred years to get there. If we don't extend your life you will die of old age long before that happens. "

Kale shook his head. He typed. "Why would I want that? Three hundred years living in the Zodiac? Without family or friends? Kept in a zoo with whales and seagulls? And why would you care? I was captured by accident. I was not your intended target. What value could I have for you?"

"You would ask that after having just revealed that you're an expert in these singers?"

"But you didn't know until a few minutes ago. What were you planning to do with me before you knew?"

"Keep you alive."

"Why?"

"I want you to survive."

"You personally?"

"Yes. I am your protector."

"Protector from what?"

"Corporate interests," Teracia said and then immediately regretted it.

Kale said nothing.

153

"It will take a while before you have a complete understanding of your current situation. For now, it is enough for you to know your survival and the survival of your species may well depend on how useful you can make yourself."

"Survival of my species?"

"Yes, your survival may be crucial to the survival of your species. And you and I must do everything we can to make sure that happens. That's why I asked you about how to get the whales to sing. Having them do so soon is important, and if you can help with that, things will go better for you. And you should also sing more."

"I should sing?"

"Yes."

"But I'm not a good singer."

"It would still be virgin song."

"Virgin song?"

***

Kale was getting a headache. He grimaced and typed again. "You captured them from their feeding grounds off the northern coast of America. They don't sing much when they're feeding, but until recently, they weren't eating at all. This may explain their silence. They're spooked by the experience of being sucked off the planet."

"In our experience, most animals will succumb to their hunger and eat," Teracia replied.

"These animals go for prolonged periods of time without eating," Kale typed. "They binge, put on a lot of fat and then stop, often for months at a time. It's the nature of their species. When you captured them, they were only about half way through their normal feeding season. They were fattening themselves up for a long migration. Maybe that's part of the problem. They have no place to migrate to here. On Earth they would migrate to the warmer waters off Hawaii for breeding and calving. It's in that environment where most of the singing occurs. Here there is no migration. The need to

154

fatten themselves up may be reduced. It's possible they intuitively understand that. These are intelligent animals."

"We have to get them to sing," Teresa said.

"So, you've said, but it's not as if I have a switch for that," he typed. "It's hard to say when or if that will happen, but on Earth when you force a massive adaptation on a species that has evolved to behave differently, it rarely goes well."

"We've been doing this for a billion years, creating environments for singers to flourish," Teracia said through the hologram.

"Yes, but the natural humpback whale environment is half the size of a planet. This ship and this containment area are large but not that large. It only takes about ten minutes for a humpback to swim from one end of the enclosure to the other. That's not a migration."

Kale watched as the balloon on Teracia's forehead went from green to pink and then back again.

"The whales on Planet Song are unique," Teracia said.

"Planet Song?"

"In all of our pet expeditions we've never come across a situation where terrestrial mammals evolved into large aquatic predators and then became singers. Your planet is the richest trove of song we've ever found. That's why we call it Planet Song. When we were first studying the humpback whales, we could never figure out how they found their way from those islands to the northern coast and back again," she said. "That's a huge journey."

"They may just know the way. They are intelligent animals. But I believe they're sensitive to the Earth's magnetic field," Kale typed. "We've found that in other migrating species and it seems to fit. The problem is we have no idea what part of the humpback anatomy would be sensitive to this field. We have no smoking gun."

"Smoking gun?"

"It's an expression. It means we don't have evidence for this idea."

"So, adding an Earth-like magnetic field into the containment area and manipulating it might have some effect?"

Kale shrugged and then realized the gesture was meaningless. "It might," he typed, "but then again it might not. Hard to say without trying it."

"Then we'll try it."

"You can do that?"

"The engineers on board are always looking for a challenge."

The hologram dissolved, as it always did when the conversation was at an end. Teracia sank beneath the water. Kale wondered if the Fahr had a word for goodbye.

Genetics

Peter Howard had seen introductions to the President play out on TV, always with the prerequisite amount of pomp and glitz. But this was no such event. His family were loaded into the back of an old army truck and driven to the White House, a two-and-a-half-hour journey he guessed, though no one had a watch to confirm. The journey was punctuated by frequent stops and much cursing from the driver. Still Peter had no idea which route they used to the White House because the truck's green canvas flaps had been pulled down tight before they left the rail yard. They'd spent the journey straining to look at each other through pale verdant light while speaking little.

The flaps opened at the White House grounds checkpoint. The guard looked at them, nodded, and waved them forward. No one had papers to be checked. They left the flaps up now, not concerned about the rows of onlookers standing behind razor wire. The truck chugged past and dropped Peter, Sonya, and Tracy at a nondescript door at the back of the building, one he suspected was a servant's entrance. As he got out of the truck, Peter could see the camps beyond the wire. Naked children ran through puddles and played with paper boats as their parents sat in old lawn chairs watching. Nothing in the attitude of these folks suggested there was anything out of the ordinary about the Howard family arrival. The driver of the truck opened the door and ushered them in. A few short hallways later, there they were, standing before Maria Alatorre.

The President wore a dark gray pantsuit with matching pumps and no makeup. Her right hand was bandaged, and graying roots had pushed their way out of her scalp and into her short dyed black hair. She looked at the three of them and turned to the young man standing at ease beside her.

"Who's this?" she asked.

"Dr. Peter Howard and his wife and daughter. I'm sorry, Madam President, I don't know their names."

"The geneticist?"

"Yes, ma'am."

Alatorre extended her hand to Sonya. "I'm sorry, I don't have your name."

"Sonya Howard, Madam President, and this is my daughter, Tracy." Sonya looked pleased and Tracy bashful.

"I'm happy to meet you, Sonya, and you too, Tracy." She shook Tracy's hand and stepped back. "I understand you've spent most of the day in the back of one of those infernal military trucks?"

"Just a couple of hours, ma'am," Tracy said, her voice barely above a whisper.

"Still, you must be tired and hungry."

Tracy looked at her mother who nodded.

Alatorre turned to the young man. "Please show Mrs. Howard and her daughter to the room we have prepared for them, and let the staff know they haven't eaten."

"Yes, Madam President."

The man gestured for Sonya and Tracy to follow him, but when Peter tried to join them, Alatorre put her injured hand on his shoulder.

***

Alatorre could feel the scientist's instinctive flinch and wondered what he had been through since the attack. "Please stay for a few moments, Dr. Howard. You can join your wife and daughter later."

"Yes, Madam President," he said looking at her hand.

"Sniper's mistake," she said with a chuckle, "Caught the vehicle's side mirror instead of me, but I took a chuck of the splintered glass in my hand. The stitch will come out in a couple of days." She held out her good hand. "I'm Maria Alatorre, and I'm so honored to meet such an eminent scientist."

"The honor is all mine, Madam President."

Alatorre nodded, and all the people in the room took their cue and exited. Soon there was no one left except for Dr. Howard, Garneau, and herself. The professor raised an eyebrow.

"Yes," Alatorre said with a grim smile. "This is all hush hush. First, I should introduce you to my Chief of Staff, Gerald Garneau."

Garneau stepped forward and shook Dr. Howard's hand. "A pleasure," he said.

"Did you always have a beard?" Dr. Howard asked. "I seem to remember the President's Chief of Staff being clean shaven."

"No. I decided to do without the luxury of shaving cream. Not much of a sacrifice I admit, but I feel better having done it."

Alatorre looked at her Chief of Staff and rolled her eyes. She turned her attention back to the geneticist. "We're about to make you a job offer, Dr. Howard," Alatorre said.

"A job offer, Madam President?"

Garneau nodded with his best reassuring smile.

"Those are few and far between these days in my line of work," Peter said.

"Well, it will mean permanent employment and state protection, but also a degree of isolation," Garneau said. "You and your family will be well taken care of, but neither you nor they will have much freedom of movement."

"It's in the nature of the research, I'm afraid," Alatorre said.

"Sounds ominous," Howard said. "Where will we be?"

158

"MIT," Garneau said.

Dr. Howard studied them. "That's a large prison."

Garneau grimaced. "Most of MIT is not operational, so it's smaller than you think."

No one said anything for a few moments.

"You will not be imprisoned, Dr. Howard," Alatorre said. "But what you will be doing is sensitive."

"So, what will I be doing?"

"First you need to sign something," Garneau said, leading Howard to a document on the table.

Howard scanned this. "A non-disclosure agreement? Do you need something like this under the current circumstances?"

"Even more so," Alatorre said.

Howard signed the document. Alatorre and Garneau looked at each other. "Most people wrestle with that a bit," she said.

"You have no idea what we've just been through," Howard said. "You're going to house, protect, and feed my family, and you will give me meaningful work to do. That's like winning the lottery out there."

Alatorre gestured to three leather armchairs arranged in a semicircle. They all sat down.

"Most of your work has been in genetic medicine, correct?" She said. "Working on gene splicing and other interventions to help us cure diseases we inherit from our parents?"

"Mendelian disorders. Yes."

"What we have in mind here is a little more ambitious. We're looking at the construction of a new human genome from the ground up, perhaps incorporating technological elements, what the science fiction authors used to call a cyborg."

Howard stared at her, and she returned his gaze. "To what end?" he asked.

"You're a black man, Dr. Howard. How does that feel?"

"I'm sorry?"

"How does that feel?" Alatorre repeated

"Feel?"

"Our records show that, before the attack, you lived in Randallstown, Maryland, a significant distance from your work at John Hopkins but also a black community," Garneau said.

Alatorre continued. "You did this despite an income level that would have allowed you to live closer to the university in a more upscale but predominately white neighborhood. Why did you make that choice?"

"I'm sorry, Madam President, but I don't see what this has to do with..."

"I'm Latino, as I'm sure you're aware. So, my comfort zone is with my fellow Latinos and that's fine as far as it goes. The problem is my natural loyalty to the Latino tribe is stronger than my loyalty to humanity, partially because I've never thought about the latter in those terms, but primarily because I have a natural inclination to be loyal to the tribe I belong to. I believe we evolved to behave like this because early in the history of our species, cooperation between the members of our tribe is how we survived."

"OK..."

"Our conflicts have always been within our species. Our reality, until recently, has been perpetual tribal conflict. We're divided in everything we do. We chose sides, always. Sometimes it's benign as in cheering for our favorite sports teams or being loyal fans of actors or musicians. Other times it's more dangerous, as in the state of American politics in the few years before the attack."

"This is news?" Howard said.

"Of course, it isn't, and that's the point," Garneau said. "As a species, we have a natural inclination to be pitted against each other, and you need to look no further than the visceral hatred that that man exacerbated between the political divides in this country. This kind of human behavior is on a continuum throughout recorded history. It's what we do."

"Most of that was fanned by the media and the Internet," Howard said, standing up. "I'm not sure you can make a blanket assumption about the species based on..."

"So how does it feel to be black?" Alatorre said.

Dr. Howard stared at the president. She held his gaze. He sat down and studied his right hand, rotating it so his white palm contrasted with the dark back of his left hand. "Not good," he whispered. "But it's not because of the skin color, it's because..."

"We are a species in continual conflict within itself. It's not so much a pattern as a state of being," Garneau said. "It's the rule, not the exception."

Alatorre continued. "It's the nature of our beast, so much so that we have trouble conceiving of ourselves in any another way. We define ourselves, not in terms of the species we belong to, but in terms of our tribal loyalties within that species. Sure, there are a few enlightened folks who think otherwise, but even they often take sides against each other. We're trapped by our own biology."

"You think this is genetic?" Howard asked.

"Yes," Garneau said.

"And it took contact with the Fahr to show us that," Alatorre said. "They wanted us to dialogue species to species, and our tribal loyalties would not allow us to do that. And now we know we're not alone in the universe. We no longer have the luxury of tribal behavior. We need to fix ourselves."

***

Dr. Howard looked at them. *What were they playing at?* "If human tribal behavior has a substantive genetic component—and I assure you the jury is way out on that question—you picked a fine time to try to bioengineer a new human race. Every piece of equipment I had in my lab is fried. And from what I'm hearing, that's also true of every other such facility on the planet. How are you going to do this?"

"I've been told that using—now let's see if I can remember this—Clustered Regularly Interspaced Short Palindromic Repeats, CRISPR, or Cas9 for short, is quick and inexpensive. And that you can use a gene drive to spread the genetic changes throughout an entire species?"

Howard stared at her. Before the aliens attacked, the Internet had been saturated with material touting CRISPR as the new genetic engineering super tool. It allowed precise targeted gene editing at a small fraction of the former cost, but far fewer on line sources acknowledged that the tool, however promising it may be, was still years away from practical usage. His own research into Mendelian disorders was a starting point, because those disorders only involved single nucleotide mutations.

"That technology is in its infancy, and to this point our few success stories have been limited to monogenetic disorders. Changing the behavior of a species will be a multi-factorial exercise and will involve many non-genetic elements. Most of those tribal behaviors are learned behaviors. Two generations ago the Germans, under Hitler, tried eliminating the Jewish population of Europe. But if you talk to the average modern German, you'll find a well-educated thoughtful person. It would be hard to argue that genetic change was the author of that transformation. And even if we could isolate and modify the genetic components—something which will probably take decades given our current almost nonexistent understanding of how the various components of the human genome work together— you'll still have to create environments that teach and reinforce non-tribal behavior. Gene drives, by the way, work far better in species that reproduce quickly, like mosquitoes. It would probably take millennia for such changes to work their way through the slowly-reproducing human population."

"That depends on the size of the Human population in question, I suppose," Alatorre said. "There won't be seven billion of us, that's for sure."

Howard said nothing. He didn't like the fatalism he was hearing but acknowledged it was realistic. "So, how are we going to do this?" he asked again.

"Come to MIT and see," Alatorre said.

Howard Recruits

Baltimore had not fared as well as Boston and Washington, and Johns Hopkins University had been looted repeatedly, most of the expensive and now useless electronic equipment gone, gathering dust in multiple old warehouses and garages.

Peter Howard owned several big problems, but data loss was not one of them. The data DVDs were stored in a locked cabinet at the corner of the room, exactly where he'd left them. Looters had broken the lock, but they decided the silvery disks were of no value and left them in place. These discs had everything the MIT team would need, including the schematics for each piece of equipment the lab had contained. They needed only a functioning disk drive, and MIT now had several.

Gathering his team presented a problem of a different magnitude. Howard doubted if any of them had been back since the attack, and those still alive were dispersed. Baltimore had not been kind to its citizens. Garneau had gathered some of country's leading scientists but had given little thought to the minions who would do the grunt work. Each of these scientists was used to functioning with a chosen team of post docs, grad students, and lab techs.

Howard sighed. He had two options. Train new people or find his old team, the reality being a combination of the two. He found sheets of old copy paper and scrawled a message.

Anyone with the expertise to work in a high-tech genetics' lab, please present yourself to the military or civilian authorities referencing Doctor Peter Howard. You will be screened and, if found suitable, will be moved to M.I.T, where you will assist in government research. Good food and safe housing are the primary benefits. Immediate family members can also be accommodated.

"Where's a copier when you need one?" he said to the three soldiers that made up his escort. "I'll need about thirty copies of this," he said pointing to the copy paper and handing each a pen. "Then we'll put them up around the campus and at the government offices."

The screening process turned out to be much more difficult than he imagined. It was astonishing how many people tried to pawn themselves off as lab technicians and grad students. Few had paper accreditation, but those who had such were immediately hired as were the two members of Howard's original team who saw the notice. Those who came without documentation had to be interviewed, but this was a quick process. Howard learned to detect posers with a few well-chosen questions. Most of the interviews lasted less than two minutes, but there were hundreds to do. By the end of the ten-hour day, only seven had passed the grade out of a projected need for thirty. He had one last interview. Then it would be on to Washington, New York, and MIT itself.

Howard was exhausted. He looked at the last name on the list. *Shit!* Simon Jeffries. "Give me a minute!" he shouted through the door. He had to collect himself. Jeffries was the one man on his previous staff who had a clear issue with Howard's skin color, a fundamentalist Christian white racist. He was also a good researcher, methodical and precise in everything he did. Howard needed to find a reason to reject the man. Isn't that what Alatorre was talking about? The elimination of tribalism in the species? The President was sure this had to be done, that the human species was hard wired toward this kind of behavior and had to be fixed, but Howard was less sure. Yet here it was. The problem was staring him right in the face, his own tribalism and that of Jeffries'.

"You may enter," he shouted to the door.

Jeffries shuffled into the room and did a double take when he realized the identity of the interviewer.

"Hello, Simon," Howard said.

Simon took two deep breaths. "So, I'm guessing you'll want an explanation as to why I didn't come back that day," he said. "When I reached the ground floor, the level of destruction was much higher than I expected. I started thinking of my family and..."

Howard shook his head. "There's no need. This project requires a level of commitment beyond what you're capable of. I'm sorry Simon."

Tribal Genome

Peter Howard still wondered about the morality of what they were doing. This had nothing to do with whether they should tinker with the human genome. He had long since rejected the idea that scientific research should be restrained by modern interpretations of ancient religious writings. No. His problem was the people outside were dying in ever increasing numbers, and his team lived in conditions of relative wealth and security while researching a way to hasten the extinction of humanity. Their goal was to push evolution, to replace the human race with a more advanced version of itself. This research was, on at least one level, counterintuitive.

And yet, on another level, it made perfect sense. Tribalism in all its various forms was a tragic flaw in the human species. It would eventually kill them all. He could see that now and had known on an instinctive level for quite some time, even if the genetic component in that tribalism was more speculation than anything else. He'd grown up in the era when one tribalist move could have triggered a nuclear holocaust and almost did on several occasions. But still he could not get over the feeling that if they succeeded, what they created would not be human at all.

Donaldson and his team had built them exact replicas of the John Hopkins lab equipment. So, now the search had begun. But what would a tribalism gene look like, or far more likely, what would the combination of genes that led to tribalist behavior look like? Peter was sure that the answer lay not in the human genome per se but in what the human genome had in common with species that also exhibited this behavior. There was quite a range to pick from.

Everything from African lion prides to baboon troops and wolf packs, and even certain kinds of insects. But they would start with the genomes of great apes: chimpanzees, bonobos, gorillas, and orangutans. The first three species exhibited tribalistic behavior, but the orangutans did not. That comparison should prove interesting.

Peter looked over at Eva Hastings, the post doc working at the monitor closest to him. Eva had come into the Baltimore interview months earlier wearing a lab coat, one she never seemed to take off. "Anything to report?"

"Well," Eva said, "as you predicted, narrowing the search has proved fairly easy. Easy in the sense that, because the species are so closely related, there's a lot of duplication in their genomes. Still, I'm not yet seeing common structures on the target chromosomes shared by the three tribal species that are also not shared by the orangutans."

Howard nodded. Gorillas, chimps, and bonobos were more closely related to each other than they were to orangutans. Orangutans had split from the family tree earlier and evolved independently longer. This might mean that at least as far as the great apes were concerned, the genetics involved in tribal behavior may go back to an ancestor common to all four species. The orangutans may have an additional gene or genes that turned off that expression. If they do, and if the team could find those, then it's possible that that gene or a combination of genes might be part of the solution. If the gene or gene combination in question was only found in orangutans, it might be possible to splice and add the sequence to the human genome.

As they had discovered many times in the past, introduced or selected for genes often changed more than intended. Dimitry Belyaev's experiments with breeding Russian foxes to make them tamer had achieved the goal, while resulting in unexpected changes to the colors in the animals' coats, and the shapes of their ears and tails. Howard suspected that Alatorre did not understand the timelines involved. Working with fruit flies was one thing. Their short life spans allowed for the results of genetic manipulation to be ob-

166

served quickly. But something complex as a change in social behavior among advanced primates could take decades to detect, especially when one couldn't enlist the help of the worldwide scientific community. And it wasn't just finding the right genetic combinations and changing the genome; it was also giving those changes time to manifest and hoping something unintended and detrimental did not also arrive.

Decision

For the first few days on the train Diane feared for Trent's life. He seemed lethargic and slept a great deal, and when Trent woke, he often did so to great hacking spasms of dislodged mucous. Awake he ate constantly, small bits at first until his stomach was capable of larger meals. And as this capacity increased, so did his willingness to engage in conversation.

"Did you eat anything back in Irwin?" she asked him.

"Yeah, I did, at first before the kids started crying then..." He shrugged.

"You'd make a great father."

Trent laughed long and hard. "Yeah, that's what I need to be thinking about just now. Fatherhood."

"Just saying."

"I'm glad there aren't any kids on this train," he said.

Diane knew what he meant. Kids were great when things were going well, but they were like smoke alarms when they weren't. Kids, especially small kids, didn't do "suck it up" well. So, being exposed to constant whimpering and requests for food when you were starving yourself was difficult. Still she felt guilty riding on this train with regular meals and a backpack full of goodies. Kids waited at every station, with or without their parents, often holding ice cream buckets or other plastic containers angled to show their emptiness. Diane and Trent had already lobbed half the contents of their goodie bags out the window. At least they didn't have to hear the whimpering.

The jolt forced Diane to drop her book and toppled Trent into the aisle.

"What the hell was that?" he said, picking himself of the floor.

"Feels like we hit something." Diane opened the blinds on her window. The train screamed to a stop in the middle of a coniferous forest. "Where are we?" she asked.

"Idaho, maybe," Trent said. "I heard a purser mention it this morning."

"That far north?"

"Detours, remember?"

"That's one hell of a detour."

The train shuddered and came to a complete stop. Outside the train their military friends were scrambling.

Trent and Diane looked at each other. "Put on the vests?"

They had bullet proof vests and were advised wear them at all times. Both had ignored the advice. Now they scrambled into the vests. Shots echoed off the forest beyond them. They ducked down below window height. The gunfire continued and quickly escalated from single shots to automatic bursts. One such burst raked the side of the car, a rapid sequence of thuds and pings. Diane gasped and threw herself flat against the floor. Trent was already there, and her ear pushed tight against his chest. His breathing calmed her.

"You all right?" he asked.

"I'm not hit if that's what you mean," she said.

They heard a distant bang, too big for a gunshot, too small for a bomb. Then silence. They remained still for a moment, Trent warming Diane. She pulled away from him and sat up. The soldiers were barking orders in the distance.

"I think that was a grenade," she said.

"Anyway, it sounds like we won," Trent said. He held out his arms, and she crawled into them.

Compared to the other train stations they'd been to; Boston's South Station seemed the most functional. Its open-air design made for decent lighting and a makeshift market stretched across the platform with a combination of open bartering and cash transactions. And food. People were selling food, something Diane had not seen at any other station. She looped her hand through Trent's pocketed arm as they pulled their wheeled suitcases through the station to the MIT micro bus.

"The last piece to the puzzle," the military driver said as they got in.

"Puzzle?" Diane said. "What puzzle?"

The soldier shrugged. "I don't know, ma'am. But that's what they're calling you and Mr. Proctor. They don't tell us much about what's going on inside. It's high security and need to know, and I'm one of those people who doesn't need to know. But they're working on something that will make everything better. I have no idea what that is."

Diane looked at Trent. Further discussion would have to wait.

The office was full of old books and smelled like them, adding a slight mildew tang to the air. Trent was still emaciated enough to look small in the overstuffed and ancient arm chair. She was faring better, occupying hers with more substance. Across from them, sitting in a straight-backed oak office chair was President Maria Alatorre and to her right in an identical chair sat Gerald Garneau, her chief of staff. Both were dressed for a day at the office.

"We want to get Goldstone up and running as soon as possible," Alatorre said. "We know that will take more work, so we'll be assigning some of the best engineers and technicians to help you."

Diane waited for an explanation, but none was forthcoming. "Madam President, as much as I appreciate your willingness to get behind Goldstone, it seems to be a misplaced priority. Why put resources into Goldstone when you have all these other much more pressing problems?"

Alatorre nodded to Gerald Garneau, her chief of staff. Garneau placed two legal-sized sheets of paper in front of them.

Diane quickly scanned the document in front of her. "This is a non-disclosure agreement. Can you even enforce such a thing in this environment? There's not much left in the way of judiciary."

"Read further," Trent said to Diane. "This is permanent rest-of-our life stuff."

"Meaning?"

"Once we're in, we can't get out," Trent said.

"We can't let anything about this project get beyond the designated facilities," Alatorre said. "Which is why we won't tell you anything until you're in. If that seems ominous, I apologize, but there isn't another way we can do this. What I will tell you is, if you sign on, you'll be well-fed, sheltered, and protected—you'll have your needs taken care of for the rest of your life. But you will be on a permanent contract. If you decide not to sign, you may leave now, but if you do your resources will be the same as anyone else outside those gates. Your government is doing its best, but the scale of the problem is massive and many more will starve than live. You've already had a taste of that."

Diane looked at Trent. His mouth was making the same sucking motion she'd seen before he got his health back. She knew what he would choose.

"But we will be helping them, right?" she asked Alatorre.

"A major part of our efforts will be directed toward relieving the sufferings of our fellow citizens, yes. But we also know, given the scale of the problem, we will fall short. When we do, things will not be pretty. They're already not pretty. We can't rebuild the infrastructure in time to save more than a small fraction of the population. We have to think ahead."

"Think ahead? To what?"

Alatorre said nothing, bobbing her head in the direction of the nondisclosure agreement.

Diane watched as Trent signed the document.

"We're talking a two-tier society here," she said to him. "The haves and the have-nots."

"No. We're talking about survival, our own first and then theirs. It's not as if the two of us haven't paid our dues."

He was right. Trent had fed the children, given all his food. And she had given most of hers as well. Both had nearly died. They had accomplished nothing through their sacrifice except, perhaps, for the survival of a few toddlers. And what were the chances those children would continue to survive? *Small,* she thought. Unless many more trucks arrived, and if what Alatorre just said was true, that it seemed unlikely.

She could see the pleading in Trent's eyes. He was a good man, but that in itself wasn't enough. She had made such emotional decisions before and regretted them. Still, she would not accomplish much if she left. Her skill set was not well suited to basic survival. No one outside would care that she was an expert satellite tracker. She looked back at the patiently waiting Alatorre. Here was someone who valued what she could do. What were the chances she would find that again? She signed the paper.

Alatorre looked pleased. She shook their hands and gestured for Garneau to take over.

"I'll take my leave," she said. "I'm sure you understand I have other pressing issues." With that she turned and walked out the room.

"Of course," Diane said to the retreating figure.

"These are your lanyards," Garneau said, handing two each to Diane and Trent.

The lanyards featured their photos on one side and the Great Seal of the United States with the American Government bald eagle logo on the other, but this was placed inside a profile of the human head. These had been produced by something that could print photos and manipulate plastic.

"I've given you a spare in case you lose one, but if you do, you must inform security."

Diane nodded. "I see you prepared these in advance," she said, looking at her photo. The image showed her in the fleshier pre-starvation days. She showed Trent.

171

"Same," Trent said, showing his. He had never been over-weight so there was less contrast.

"We didn't think you'd refuse us," Garneau said. "We've yet to have anyone do that."

"So, now that we're official you can tell us what this is all about," Diane said.

Garneau sighed. "Get comfortable. This will probably take a while."

Alatorre wanted Goldstone restored and reconnected to the satellites. At least that's what she had said, but Diane's memory of that day had the satellites going down before Goldstone was off line, which might point to a problem with the satellites themselves. And even if they were still up there, there'd been no contact with the satellites in a year, and it would be several more months before Goldstone was restored. Depending on how autonomous each was, this might present a problem. How many were left? How many would be functional? And even if they functioned, would it matter to this infrastructure-shattered world? This made little sense.

Diane and Trent's first job was to vet their future team. Letters were sent out to the old team members still living in Fort Irwin. Billy called her on the shortwave.

"Diane?"

"I'm here in Boston, over."

"Might as well dispense with that over shit, Diane. Nobody cares." He sounded raspy, but the set was old and did things to the voice.

"Are you all right?"

"No, but I'm in better shape than most."

"Can you tell me more?"

"Fatima committed suicide. Connors and Ishita lost the will and gave up. So, we're only down three, but most of the rest are seriously messed. I'm not sure what you expect us to do."

"What I want to do is get everybody back to Goldstone. We will send the trucks directly there."

Billy didn't respond to this.

"Billy, you still there?"

"Yeah."

"Did you understand what I just said?"

"Get everybody back out to Goldstone. I heard you. I made that walk just after you left. Nearly didn't make it back, and I was still in good condition at the time. There's no way the others can make that journey. There's no bedding, water, food... Sand has found its way into everything. You've got mice in the wiring. I even found a snake in there. These people just can't cope with that the way things are. I can't cope with it."

"We will send the trucks with supplies. They've been feeding us well here."

"I heard you, but Fort Irwin and Goldstone are only six miles apart. There is no way you can feed Goldstone and not feed Fort Irwin. Even if that was ethically a good idea, it will not happen. Irwin is armed to the teeth. If you don't feed them they'll take what they need. You know that."

"Yeah, OK, Billy. I'll see what I can do."

***

"She's right, you know," Alatorre said to Garneau. "We can't feed Goldstone without feeding Fort Irwin."

"That's a lot of mouths and it means trucking in food from Northern California," the Chief of Staff said. "A convoy of that size will attract attention."

"We have to have Goldstone," Alatorre said.

Garneau shook his head. "All right. I'll do what I can."

***

Alatorre wanted to find the Fahr. Find them? By looking where and with what? The President was sure the Fahr were no longer on the Earth; no one had seen their ship since the day of the attack. It was safe to assume they had left and returned to wherever they'd come from. Given the speed the aliens moved that would put them at least as far out as Saturn, perhaps further. And if they'd used that cloaking device again nothing would have detected them.

Everyone on the rebuilding crew had signed the non-disclosure agreement though most of them, like Diane, had only been given a partial glimpse of the Alatorre vision. What exactly she was trying to accomplish wasn't clear. All Diane knew at this point was that it involved a surprising number of esoteric disciplines, like molecular biology, genetics, robotics, neurology, software and hardware engineering, and prosthetic limbs.

San Diego

Honi sat in the waiting room attempting to squeeze a lemon-sized red balloon. She could now move her fingers, but the muscles had atrophied, and she usually dropped anything she tried to hold. Around her everyone watched, fascinated by this strange wheel-chaired creature. She didn't believe her fame could spread far with the current communication limitations, but it had. The surviving residents of southern California all knew of the quadriplegic Hawaiian girl who'd made the improbable canoe journey across the Pacific. Far fewer knew of the excitement she was generating in the medical community.

Her medical records were now in the hands of Dr. Chopra. The nurse wheeled her into the neurologist's surgery. Chopra was British trained and referred to her office in this way. To Honi the surgery meant pain because Chopra's little interventions hurt. Muscles long unused protested when forced into action, no matter how small those actions might be. Pain had returned fully functional, unlike muscle control, and it fought the latter at every opportunity. Still it was rare that Honi wished to be pain free. Pain was about healing; pain was about restoration.

After a few minutes, Dr. Chopra entered the room along with her merry cadre of fellow neurologists and grad students. They beamed at her.

"Well?" Honi said.

"When removed from your body the cells stop forming connections."

"Which means?"

"We're not sure what that means, to be honest, other than it suggests whatever is causing the connections to be established depends on those cells remaining within you. It's something your body is doing that we, at present at least, can't duplicate in the lab."

"Oh," Honi said, disappointed. She had hoped something in her experience would lead to better outcomes for others with similar problems.

"You spent six years of your life as a quadriplegic," Chopra continued, "not able to control parts of your body below the top few inches of your torso. You depended on a motorized wheelchair, a respirator, and a computer, all of which you lost when the attack happened. Losing the respirator alone should have been fatal. Instead you willed yourself to take control of your lungs and then managed an open-air journey across the Pacific Ocean. Remarkable. Not only that, but you are making slow but steady progress restoring the neurological connections in other parts of your body. We just can't figure out how you're doing it."

"Neuroplasticity," Honi said with a shrug. Shrugging was one of the few new actions she could do without pain.

"Your case is not without precedent, but in all the other cases there was a therapeutic element involved, a lot of intervention. Almost always this was initiated shortly after the injury, when the brain and by extension the spinal column, was seeking to repair itself. I know of no other case where regeneration was initiated that long after the injury with the results you've achieved. And I also know of no other case where such a thing has happened through force of will and without the help of a trained professional therapist. You are unique in my experience."

"But what does that mean?"

"It means we have a lot to learn from you. And we can probably speed up your recovery with the therapies we still have. We could do more if most of our equipment had not been destroyed. As it stands we're low on Alatorre's priority list. There are a lot more crucial infrastructure projects now and will be for some time. Her government won't be restoring our lab soon. We don't, for instance, have the tools to monitor your brain activity and see what's going on. But the good news is your problem is not the regeneration of neural pathways. You're doing that on your own, though we have no idea how, but you are doing it and that means we can use basic physiotherapy to help you along."

"But it means staying here?" Honi asked.

"Yes, you'll need to be here. Think of yourself as a giant neurological experiment. We must do our best to study what's happening here. It's quite unprecedented."

"They want me to stay," Honi said.

"And you don't want to," her father said looking around the room she occupied. It was a hospital room, but it was also private with homey touches like throw carpets and a recliner rocker for the guests.

"I don't like hospitals. It's a visceral thing," Honi said.

Peni nodded.

"But this will be about healing, about getting better." She smiled. "It won't be about being told you won't get better, that the damage is permanent. And there's the possibility that what's happening here might benefit others."

"There is that," Peni agreed.

There was a pensiveness about her father that hadn't been there before San Diego. Their arrival had caused a huge stir and made celebrities out of all of them, but Peni was not comfortable. He was a bookish man who wanted nothing more than to live his life and take care of his family. Peni was also not comfortable when the mayor of San Diego arranged for the cousins to occupy the entire eighth floor of a luxury apartment building, a building without a working elevator. Honi couldn't stay with them. Even if they occupied the second floor, she couldn't stay with them. She wondered if that was intentional.

"Are you getting enough to eat?" she asked him.

"For the moment. Your celebrity status helps. You know all those planes that dropped out of the sky around Hawaii?"

"Yeah?" Honi said.

"They all crashed into the ocean, every one of them. I didn't think about what would have happened if they'd hit one the islands." Peni stood up and gestured out Honi's north-facing window. "But they had eighteen planes go down in Northern California. Eighteen! Started huge fires everywhere. Burned thirty-five percent of the crops, but that's not the worst of it. Irrigation requires power, so now there's no way to water the remaining crops. Most are huge losses. And they couldn't move the food because most of the trucks wouldn't start. They've had to rely on rail, but then again most of the trains were down too. They prioritized them, but it still took quite a while to get the food to the southern part of the state. And here we were blissfully sailing across the Pacific Ocean, thinking about the bounty it would be waiting for us once we got to California."

"People are starving everywhere," Honi said.

Peni nodded. "I went down to the dock the other day. They're restoring the shipping fleet, mostly with older diesel engines but a few with the new chips coming in from out east. I asked about Hawaii, whether food was being sent there. No one would tell me anything."

"So, you're wishing we hadn't made the crossing?"

"All we've done is mitigate the tragedy, when you think about it. But I suppose mitigation is better than nothing. It's not like you can just switch off a lifetime of memories. It's not like the loss is not there."

177

Honi reached out and laid a hand on her father's knee. "It's not as if it wouldn't have happened anyway," she said. "All these people starving. Aliens or no aliens. All of this would eventually collapse. You know that, right? Hawaii was just more vulnerable than most places."

"And we were trying to feed all those stranded tourists."

"One tribe, Dad."

"One tribe?"

"The human race."

Her father stood up. "Well, I'd better get back. We will meet and try to decide how to move forward. It's all we can do at this point."

"Yes," Honi said. "Focus on the future."

Peni bent down, kissed his daughter, and left.

Jail

Andreas had blown up a plane on a runway to make a statement. Thirty-six hours later an alien spacecraft entered the atmosphere and removed that statement. The CBC would never read his letter. Paul Watson would never hear of his heroic deed. No one would care. But they found him and put him in jail, again because of an alien. He must be the unluckiest human in the galaxy.

His cell was exactly as portrayed in the movies, pale green walls that contained a steel toilet, a bed with a thin mattress, a basin, a desk, a chair, and a Gideon Bible. The book was soiled and had a bile-like smell to it, as if someone had puked on it and then cleaned it up. The desk seemed silly to him. There were no pens, pencils, paper, or anything else to write with, just this nice flat Arborite surface, perfect for writing had the tools been available. It didn't matter, the only light in the room came from a barred window above the toilet. This provided enough illumination for navigation but not enough for reading or writing. When he thought about it, Andreas realized pens and pencils were potential weapons. Blowing up the Twin Otter had branded him as a violent man.

So, he had nothing to do. Not for twenty-four, then forty-eight, then sixty-four hours. He lost track of how many hours and days had passed. The only stimulation came in the form of meals, sandwiches made with a meat spread he couldn't identify or peanut butter or humus, and always accompanied by a plastic tumbler of lukewarm cola. When he'd first come to Canada, he'd taken the Pepsi challenge six times, choosing Coke three times and Pepsi three times. The lukewarm cola could have been either or one of the generic brands his new Canadian friends used to refer to as "welfare pop".

The guards who brought his meals said nothing much to him apart from inquiring about how well he'd slept or announcing their arrival with a single word like "breakfast", "lunch", or "dinner". They not only didn't answer his questions, they didn't appear to acknowledge he'd asked them. And they wouldn't identify the cola.

The door to his cell had a small window into the hallway beyond, but this was usually closed by means of an outside sliding trap. On one or two occasions his servers had left this open, but the hallway was so dimly lit he couldn't see anything. He also heard nothing, no audible evidence the other cells were occupied.

Then one day he woke to someone staring at him through this window. At first, he thought it was his father and shook his head at the impossibility. But the man continued to watch him, and after a few moments, Andreas realized this was only someone who looked like his father. "May I help you?" he said to the man.

"You're a pilot," the man said.

"I am or at least I was," Andreas acknowledged. He was no longer sure he could trust his memory.

"And have you spent enough time in this hellhole?"

Andreas looked at him. How does one respond to such a rhetorical question?

179

"My name is Jamie O'Hara, and I'm with Canada Post. While you were wasting away in here, the Feds requisitioned all operational light aircraft in the country and handed them over to us. That includes several old but robust Twin Otters, most of which were servicing communities in the north. With all the phone lines and wireless communication down, regular old-fashioned mail is making a comeback. We've a shortage of pilots who know how to fly those old planes. A surprising number of these pilots just went missing after the attack. So, we have these operational bush planes but not enough pilots to fly them."

"I—I—I can do that," Andreas stuttered.

"We'll have someone riding with you, and that person will have a gun."

Andreas nodded. "OK."

"Good, then I'll do what I can to get you out of here." The man turned to leave.

"Mr. O'Hara?" Andreas said.

"Yes?"

"What kind of cola is it?"

Chopra

Dr. Ahanna Chopra stared at the letter. Overnight she had gone from a person of little consequence to someone who had the attention, and the resources, of someone in Alatorre's inner circle. But it also meant leaving California. She read the letter again.

Dr. Ahanna Chopra,

This letter is to let you know President Alatorre knows of your excellent work. She has reviewed your requests for additional resources and decided to do what we can to restore the complete functionality of your laboratory. However, because the means of this restoration is only at MIT, we will move you, your family, your staff, their families, and Ms. Honi Kalawai'a, and her parents to the Boston area. More details to follow.

Gerald Garneau, Presidential Chief of Staff

So, Honi's fame had reached even President Alatorre. But why, with all the problems the government was facing, were they interested in one Hawaiian teenager?

It was near midnight when the train rolled into Boston. At this time of day there were no crowds, just a few lab coat types smoking cigarettes on the platform.

"I'm guessing they're here for us," Honi said to her father as she looked out the window of their train.

"Probably," Peni said. He had been quiet during the trip, rarely joining in conversation. This was not what he wanted, leaving the cousins behind in San Diego, but he had been forced to choose between his daughter's health and keeping them together.

The purser brought Honi's wheelchair and helped her into it. She now had the use of her arms, but they were not strong enough to support her body weight. Honi could slowly work the wheels on the chair though. And she could now twitch her toes which meant there was potential for a full recovery.

It was weird. They'd brought her on a two-week journey across the country for *genetic* testing. That's what they said. Why didn't they just swab her cheek? Then they could have kept the cousins together. But the President was moving Dr. Chopra and her clinic, which meant Honi would lose her therapy. That's how they sold it to her or tried to. This was not about Dr. Chopra, and she knew it. This was about the Hawaiian miracle girl and what the government hoped they could learn from her.

What didn't fit was the timing. They were in the middle of the worst disaster in human history. The estimate had fifty percent of the world's population starving to death by the end of the year, which included a high percentage right here in America. She'd seen enough evidence on the trip to the East Coast. Every town and city they rolled through was in crisis. So why were they focusing on her little miracle? She was grateful for the attention, but still.

The purser rolled her down the ramp and onto the platform. The lab coats disposed of their cigarettes and strolled over to shake the hands of Dr. Chopra and her parents. Honi was glad that they'd gone to the adults first. She didn't want to be fawned over this late at night, so she closed her eyes. Maybe if they thought she was asleep they'd leave her alone. It worked. No one approached her. She listened to their chatter for a few minutes, and then she did fall asleep.

Twin Otter

Within a couple of hours, the guards arrived to help Andreas from his cell. They understood something he didn't, that spending so much time in a cell without exercise and light would make transitioning to the outside world difficult.

Walking down the hallway alone had him gasping for air, never mind the soft light from the Coleman lamp nearly blinding him. He stumbled into the well-windowed reception area, barely able to function. Everything was much too bright.

"There you go, Mr. Huber," a guard said.

Whatever it was the guard was holding in his hand, Andreas couldn't focus on it.

"That bad, eh?" the guard said. He slipped a pair of dark sunglasses over Andreas's eyes. The room softened, bright but closer to what he was used to. Still, he couldn't get things into focus. Everything was an intense blur.

"Thank you," Andreas said.

"We'd normally have more light in solitary than what you had." The guard shrugged.

"Was I ever going to go to trial?" Andreas asked.

"Nothing works like it used to. You confessed to the crime. They had other fish to fry, so you just got left behind. The way I see it, you're lucky the PM thinks you're valuable."

"The PM?"

The guard nodded. "Pierce O' Malley, himself. We don't get a lot of letters here, especially ones from the Prime Minister's Office. And guess what? I get to go along with you on your great adventure. They still consider you to be in custody, so you'll have a prison guard with you at all times. That'd be me." He laughed. "Joe Pender's the name. You can call me Joe."

Joe did not offer his hand. Andreas stared at him, trying the get the guard into focus. He could tell Joe was bald or had his head shaven, he wasn't sure which. And he was a huge stocky man, but he'd need better visual definition to tell if this was fat or muscle. Joe was tall enough to make sitting in the cockpit of an old Twin Otter uncomfortable, especially over a long flight.

"What kind of cola was it?" he asked Joe.

"Cola?"

"What kind of cola did they serve me in the cell?"

Joe looked at him. "Why is that important?"

"I couldn't tell," Andreas said.

Joe nodded. "One of those been-in-solitary-too-long obsessions."

Then Andreas noticed there were two other men in the room, standing out of the way in the corner. "And what are their names?"

"That you don't need to know. They're my backups, for the time being. You and I will be joined at the hip, but backups will come and go. When we're in the air, it will just be you and I, and whatever we're transporting. On the ground I'll have a backup, arranged in advance. Someone will meet the plane everywhere we land."

Andreas wondered about this. It was not as if they could radio ahead and tell them when to meet the aircraft. He realized wherever they flew, they wouldn't be talking to ground control. It won't matter much if the runways were clear. It's not as if there would be a lot of air traffic. And he wasn't going to make a break for it anyway, far too much uncertainty out there. He was being given a chance to earn forgiveness. He laughed.

"You find this funny?" Joe said.

Andreas shook his head. "Just flexing some muscles I haven't used in a long time." He wasn't about to tell Joe he'd gone from wanting to be a martyr to wanting forgiveness for doing something stupid.

"Yeah, well, here's what will happen. We will let you recover a bit, get your eyesight back, eat some decent meals, take a shower, get you some clothes, that kind of thing. Then we'll be going to the airport where the plane is waiting. We're going to pick up a shitload of mail, some special scientific package and a couple of scientist types and fly them out east. As soon as you can read we're going to go over the route and decide where we're going to put down on the way. Refueling and all that stuff."

Andreas frowned. "I have no idea how long I was in that cell. You lose track of time after a while. How much of the stuff have they fixed?"

Joe laughed. "Not much. That EMP, or whatever it was, not only destroyed everything electronic on the planet, it also destroyed all the spare parts. But I'm guessing the reason for your question has to do with how we're going to let the folks on the ground know we're coming in. You know, so my back up will be waiting for us when we land? The thing you should understand about that is the scientific package we will be carrying is a high priority. That means they'll have backups waiting for us at every airfield between here and Ottawa. Seems like overkill, I know, but that's the plan."

Andreas took off the sunglasses the following day by noon, but his eyes still refused to focus on anything small. Reading was out of the question. Joe sent out a request for generic reading glasses, and later that night they were working on the flight plan. They'd put down in Calgary, Winnipeg, Thunder Bay, and Sudbury on the way to Ottawa, with a possible stop in Regina if it looked like the plane was using too much fuel for the Calgary/Winnipeg flight. It all depended on how much weight they'd be carrying.

"Yep, that's pretty much the route we'd thought you'd take," Joe said. "So, no problem with the backups."

He keeps talking about backups, Andreas thought. Pushing the point. There probably weren't backups, especially if pilots were in short supply. Especially if they needed him to make this flight.

The next day Andreas's eyesight returned to normal. Joe wasted no time getting them to the Vancouver airport, making the trip in a thirty-year-old Volvo with two armed guards sitting in the back seat. Andreas wondered why they weren't concerned about him crashing the plane. He had blown up one in Fort Nelson. Then there was the secret high-priority science package they'd be transporting. Why would they entrust something like that to him? It made no sense, but he wasn't about to argue with them.

The old Twin Otter was parked on the tarmac about two hundred yards from the wreckage of an Airbus A320, the body so badly charred that Andreas couldn't make out the country of origin. Three other planes had fallen out of the sky over the Vancouver International Airport, miraculously missing the terminal. The latter looked abandoned, the huge plate glass windows showing no one inside. An older VW micro bus idled beside the plane, and as they approached, two figures got out, a young Asian woman with a whale tattoo on her face and Charlie. Charlie. Andreas was sure he'd seen the last of the young Haida man in Prince Rupert, but here he was, a big grin plastered across his face.

Andreas reached for the door handle.

"Wait for the rest of us to get out," Joe told him.

The two guards got out first, their handguns ready. Joe got out, walked around the front of the Volvo and opened the door for Andreas.

"Do you want me to hold up my hands?" Andreas asked him.

185

"Just keep them where we can see them."

"Hey, Andreas. I told them you could fly that thing," Charlie said.

"After I skipped out on you in Rupert?"

"I thought it was cool, what you did. Well, cool and stupid at the same time. But I get why you tried to run. Probably would have done the same. Quick confession though, from what I hear. I don't think you're cut out to be a criminal."

"So, why are *you* here?" Andreas asked.

"We're taking a package to Ottawa."

"You're one of the scientists?"

"Well, no. Not technically." He gestured to the Asian woman. "She's the scientist. This is Cynthia Chen, a postdoc from the UBC in the department of biology..."

Cynthia Chen reached out quickly and grabbed Charlie's arm, silencing him.

Andreas looked at Cynthia and then back at Charlie. The young Haida blushed.

"So, this is about the alien, isn't it?" Andreas said.

Cynthia gave Charlie one of those laser beam looks that should have taken his head off.

"He was there. He saw it," Charlie said to Cynthia. "I didn't know he'd be the pilot."

"You recommended him," Cynthia said.

"Yeah but that was more of a joke than anything. I didn't think they'd pull him out of jail to do this."

Joe was wide eyed. "What is this about an alien?"

"Jesus," Cynthia mumbled.

Andreas spoke to Joe. "That package we're going to be taking to Ottawa is probably connected to the alien attack."

"Seriously? In what way?"

Charlie and Cynthia looked at each other but said nothing. Charlie tried indicating to Andreas that he should shut up, but Andreas was having none of it. He recounted the tale of his involve-

186

ment in the shooting down of the alien craft and their subsequent discovery of the alien corpse.

"I was taken into custody long before investigators arrived on the scene, so I don't know what happened after that. But Charlie was one of the first to see the creature, and if Ms. Chen is a biologist, it isn't hard to connect the dots."

"What's in the package?" Joe said to Cynthia.

"That's need-to-know," she said.

Joe frowned at her. "Look," he said. "I've read a lot of science fiction, and I've watched all the TV shows and the movies. It's gross watching those alien germs turn the human body into so much goop. So, I know that getting exposed to alien germs is not a good thing. If what's in that package is an alien body part or something, I deserve to know. I'm going to be spending the next day or so locked in a Twin Otter with that thing."

Charlie and Cynthia looked at each other again.

"The package contains nothing organic," Cynthia said. "There are no alien body parts."

"What then?" Joe asked.

"That's need-to-know, and you don't need to know."

Joe shook his head. "I'm not sure how much urgency is attached to this package, but I will tell you this. My pay grade doesn't commit me to taking unnecessary risks. So, if I don't like this assignment, I can refuse it. Then you'll be on the ground for another day or two waiting for a replacement. Your choice."

"Do the math, Joe," Andreas said. "I told you I was the first person to see the alien, and I got close. So, if there was a germ thing going on I was the first person exposed to it, and you've been exposed for a couple of days. You're already turning into a zombie."

"And you're all right?" Joe asked.

"No, but what's messed me up was all that time spent in solitary, not alien exposure."

"You don't know that."

"Yeah, I do. But if you want further proof, just look at Charlie here. He was exposed to the alien only a day or so after I was. Does he look like he's falling apart to you?"

Charlie gave Joe his biggest grin.

Joe smiled back.

"We can't tell you what's in the package, but it's non-organic." Cynthia said. "And as this gentleman has already explained, if there's an infection risk here, you and everyone else have already been exposed." She turned to Andreas and shook his hand. "Pleased to meet you. Andreas, isn't it?"

"Yes."

She turned back to Joe and held up her hand. "See, I'm the biologist here, and I'm not worried about it. I don't think you should be either."

The trip turned out to be nothing more than a series of take-offs, touchdowns and bathroom breaks. The airports in Thunder Bay and Sudbury did not have the backups that Joe had predicted. When these failed to materialize, Andreas just laughed. He stuck to Joe like glue and eventually the big man relaxed.

"You're not going anywhere, are you?" Joe asked.

"Nope," Andreas said. "This flight is purgatory. I'm working off past sins. Well, at least one past sin."

Joe laughed, patted Andreas on the back, and got serious. "You let me down and I'll come after you. You know that, don't you?"

"Now that sounds like the kind of thing a man not sure of himself might say. But don't worry—I'm not going anywhere. I'm not even sure there's a place worth going to. At least there's not a place much different from anyplace else. I don't think Canada has ever had a dark age, but this might well be it."

Andreas had noticed even at the airports, people were gathering, hoping the few planes still in the air would bring them supplies. But all they had was mail and a mysterious box. He kept hoping that Charlie would eventually weaken and tell him what was in it. He was sure he wouldn't get a satisfying explanation from Cynthia.

At the Macdonald–Cartier International Airport in Ottawa, Andreas saw the first signs of a significant police presence. As he taxied up to the terminal a group of ten uniformed police officers surrounded the plane, their eyes locked in the cockpit. He raised his eyebrows and looked at Joe.

"O'Malley," Joe said. He unsnapped the holster and slowly withdrew his revolver. "We wait until the mail, the box, and everyone else is off the plane," he said.

Andreas shrugged his shoulders. Joe was showing the group on the ground that he was in control.

A man wearing overalls grabbed the box and placed it in the back of a waiting van. Charlie and Cynthia entered the vehicle through a sliding side door, and the van left. The mail was the next thing to go, this time onto a waiting push cart.

"All right, out you get," Joe said.

Andreas stepped onto the tarmac, felt his arms forced behind his back and the click of the cuffs. They pushed him into the back of an old black Ford Crown Victoria. "Where are we going?" he asked the police officer behind the wheel.

"Kingston," he said.

"The Kingston Penitentiary?"

"That's the one."

"I thought it was closed?"

"They're opening a small part of it for you."

"Why?"

"You know that little letter you wrote the CBC?"

"Letter?"

"It was delivered a few weeks back. Talks about the reason you blew up that aircraft. Now, you're also the only person in the world to see a live alien. That makes you quite a celebrity, and the wonderful thing about that is you've also committed a serious crime, confessed to it too. They're planning to put you on display, locked the Kingston penitentiary for everyone to see. You're going to be the most famous prisoner in the country."

Andreas slumped back into his seat. *Maybe Paul Watson will hear about it.*

Boat House

"There is one giant logistical problem," Teracia's words projected as a hologram from the slate.

"And what is that?" Kale responded.

"I am the Vice Commander on this ship. It means I have a lot of responsibilities. Yet I am the only one who can enter this enclosure with you. It's much too dangerous for other members of the crew. That means that whatever habitat we construct for you, I will have to put it in place."

"Why is it dangerous for the others and not for you?" Kale asked. "I was planning to ask you why I've met none of the other fahr."

The ballow on Teracia's forehead purpled. "I am unique among my species in that I'm immune to song. If another member of the crew were to enter this enclosure and one of the whales chose that moment to start singing, it could kill or seriously impair him."

Kale thought about this. "Why are they collecting whales if whale song is so dangerous?"

***

Teracia knew this question would come, so she had tried to find a "human" analogy for the Fahr obsession with songs. "OxyContin," she wrote.

"OxyContin? This is like a drug?"

"Yes, but song also behaves like a sexual stimulant for my species. So, we not only get high, we also get aroused, a pleasure-filled and addictive experience depending on the quality of the song. It's also the reason we go on these long interstellar pet collecting expeditions. Finding new songs to feed that addiction has become the major obsession of my species. Humpback whale song is unique—it's the most powerful song we've ever encountered. On your world

OxyContin is a dangerous drug, but people use it anyway. With song, if we filter certain frequencies we can control the level of intoxication and arousal. Although humpback whale song is lethal when heard without these filters, something we call virgin song. With filters it becomes the ultimate pleasurable high."

"So, you're drug dealers?" Kale wrote.

"Song dealers, pet merchants, but we occupy about the same niche in our respective societies. Yes." She felt herself go an even deeper shade of purple.

***

Kale studied the strange creature before him. "Why do I get the impression that you're not comfortable with this state of affairs?" he typed.

"It's complicated," the words appeared before Kale. "You would have to know much more about our society to understand. In the meantime, we must construct a more suitable habitat for you. Something more permanent that meets your needs. It will have to float on the surface."

"A houseboat," Kale said.

"That's a floating habitat?"

"Yes. One that's built of wood."

"For reasons of buoyancy?"

"Yes." Kale watched as Teracia's ballow shimmered back from purple into its normal light brown.

"As I'm sure you understand," the words appeared, "we don't have a lot of need for buoyancy here. No wood, of course, but I may get special permission to manufacture some buoyant plastic. We can do some research into houseboats and see if we can come up with a design."

"Why do you have to get special permission to make plastic?" he typed.

Kale couldn't read Teracia's facial features but had noticed changes in her gills. Now they were flattened as if she were not breathing.

The words appeared before him wavering a bit. It was hard to focus on them. "Two billion years ago we stopped the manufacture of plastic," she wrote. "The plastics did not biodegrade but instead turned into increasingly smaller particles. These particles were ingested by the micro flora and micro fauna on our planet. They were indigestible, so they clogged their digestive systems and our food chains began a slow collapse. We would have been in serious trouble had not another much more momentous event occurred. The star around which our planet revolved became unstable, and we were forced to flee to a safer stellar system. The move took a thousand years, and by the time we left, plastics had changed the biology of our home world. Only those organisms that could tolerate or digest plastic had survived, far fewer species than were there originally. It was what your scientists call 'a mass extinction event'. A few thousand years later the star swelled into a red giant and made that all irrelevant. We never allowed the manufacture of plastics on our new home planet."

"And we're doing the same with plastics?" Kale wrote.

"Yes, and everything on Planet Song is happening much faster. The speed of technical evolution in your species does not allow time for reflection. Our fault, I'm afraid."

"Your fault?"

"This is not the first time we've visited your planet."

Kale digested this. "Then all those crazies that said we'd been visited before were right?" he typed.

"All those funny little entertainments you made? The speculation about alien-like figures on petroglyphs and temples? No. Nothing like that. There was no contact. We merely made sure you survived the black plague, in higher numbers than you would have at least. And we accidentally allowed the discovery of an advanced monitoring device. We're not sure if that pushed you or not. It was a device unlike anything your species would have seen before, and you would not have understood what it was. You had no technological equivalents at the time, but there were also aspects to it that might have pushed your species had your ancestors recognized them for

192

what they were. Gears and lens, that sort of thing. It's hard to know since there's no reference to the device in the data we've intercepted. It is not mentioned in your histories."

"What do you mean by 'pushed'?" Kale wrote.

"It's a technical and religious concept. Pet expeditions are not supposed to do anything to speed up the evolution of any sapient species we encounter. A high regard for the natural evolutionary process, especially with regard to intelligent species, is a key doctrine in our religion."

"And you did that..."

"I was on that ship. It looked as though that plague would do serious damage to your species. The mortality rate could have been as high as ninety-five percent, and a loss that great would have also destroyed the infrastructure. So, even though this event occurred seven hundred years ago, your species was already far removed from its hunter-gatherer origins. Many of the survivors would not have been well-equipped to survive without the infrastructure they depended on. It didn't look good, so we collected the same insects that were causing the problem and infected them with an antibiotic. The losses were still high but nowhere near ninety percent."

"So, technically you interfered with our evolution, insured our survival?"

"Yes."

"And what would you call what you just did to us, the attack that destroyed our electronic infrastructure?"

Teracia's ballow inflated and turned a deep purple. "Extreme interference." The words were twice the size of the normal holographic projections.

Kale pulled his fingers back from the keyboard and stared at her.

"Song Corp..." The two words were red in the hologram. "The culture of the company is to maximize profits. It's no different from similar organizations you have on Planet Song, except in scale and age. Song Corp is the primary cultural force on our planet and some of us wish it were not so."

Her ballow pinked, something that Kale had come to realize was a sign of irritation. In the few short months he had known her, Teracia had achieved a remarkable mastery of written English. Talking to her now was like texting an old friend.

"I digress," the hologram again appeared a bright red. "We were well into our return journey to your planet—an expensive journey driven by the expectation of huge profits—when we began intercepting radio signals and other broadcasts from you. At that point, we were still about one hundred and fifty years away, and as we drew closer, it became clear that you had been pushed and pushed hard. The speed of your technological advance was far outstripping your capacity to reflect about the consequences of the changes you were making. Part of the reason for that was the lack of unity in your species. You had evolved technologically without also evolving a sense of identity or unity as a species. Instead your technological advances were driven by competition between your various tribes, or nations as you call them, and often came as the result of conflict. We watched from a distance as you nearly used nuclear weapons to blow yourselves—and the whales we had come to collect—up in a war that would have made Planet Song uninhabitable. And we would have been too distant at that point to intervene."

"Would you have intervened?" Kale typed.

"Yes, not because of the damage you were about to do to yourselves, but to save the whales. The consensus on board at that point was that your species had been pushed beyond repair. Regrettable because we likely played a part in that, but true nonetheless. I did not agree with that consensus, but I was the lone voice."

Kale thought about this. "Is this why you called yourself my protector?" he typed.

"You are safe for two reasons. The first is that you have some expertise with the Singers. That makes you valuable for the time being. The second reason is that I want you to survive. While I am not in a true position of power here—despite my rank—I am the only one who can enter this containment area. They need me. I am indispensable. They will humor me by keeping you alive."

"Would the other fahr kill me?" Kale typed.

"They would dispose of you once you were no longer useful, not because of malice towards you, but to save money. Keeping you alive is expensive because nothing on this ship is designed for a terrestrial species. They will have to make expensive modifications, which brings me back to the original reason for our conversation, your habitat." Teracia gestured toward the screen with her tentacle. "I've arranged for you to have access to what was your Internet, at least what was on it until we took out that infrastructure. We've modeled it to work in much the same way as it did before except, of course, you can't send messages to or ask questions of anyone back on Planet Song. No one human will be there, although there are simulations, algorithms designed to carry on conversations. You will also be able to watch and listen to entertainments. It's all there. Anything until..."

"You attacked," Kale typed quickly.

"Technically, it was an act of disarmament not of war. There was a lot of collateral damage, which is why I was against that course of action. I wanted negotiation, but they didn't want to wait for your species to decide on leadership." Teracia purpled again. "We like to think of ourselves as an enlightened species, and maybe we were in our past, but now the power in our culture is in the ballows of those who sell songs, those who profit from addiction. No sapient species will win if pitted against virgin song. Song Corp will make sure of that."

Kale had never seen Teracia's ballow go gray before, but she did now. He knew this was a dark emotion, pain of some sort. Depression? Grief? Sorrow? And if she felt that, then he knew he could trust her.

"Search the Internet database and find a design for your houseboat," the hologram said, "and we will build it for you."

Kale watched as Teracia sank beneath the surface.

Boston

Honi woke up in a standardized high-tech hospital bed. She looked around. Apart from the hospital bed in the center, the room had the feel of somebody's bedroom. A series of watercolors hung on the walls, an oak wardrobe stood to one side of a large bay window, and Turkish throw carpets covered most of a hardwood floor. Two stuffed chairs with matching footstools occupied the far end of the room. Dr. Chopra was on her left side looking down on her. Honi pulled herself into a sitting position. "How...?"

"You were pretty out of it," Chopra said. "I'm not sure you were awake when they put you in bed."

"I don't remember."

"It was a long journey, and we got in late," Chopra said.

"Where are my parents?"

"They're in a room down the hall. Didn't last much longer than you did, I'm afraid. As soon as they knew you were alright, they turned in too."

"Is all this stuff working?" Honi asked, gesturing to the electronic medical equipment beside her bed.

"They've prioritized this facility. There's a coal burning electrical generator at the other end of the campus. They also have a chip manufacturing facility that recycles old electronics and a water purification plant. They're able to fix most things electronic, it just takes time. MIT might well be the first major university to be restored to its former glory. So, yes, it all works."

Honi checked her arms and chest. "I'm not plugged into any of it," she said.

"There's no need for that at present."

"At present?"

"Yes. At present."

"So, what are they planning to do with me?" she asked.

"Help you get better, of course, but you're right. There's more to it. And before you ask, I'll tell you I was not informed of the true scope of this project before we arrived. There are others who would be better at explaining this to you."

Honi said nothing.

Chopra nodded to someone outside the room. A man in a white lab coat entered.

"Honi, this is Professor Donaldson. He's an AI specialist, but he's overseeing the re-manufacture of computer chips."

She shook his hand. "Artificial intelligence?"

"That was before all the trouble. You can't do AI research without computers, so restoring that infrastructure is what I've been doing lately. We're making progress, so it shouldn't be too long before I can get back at it. Are you interested?"

"Yes, of course," Honi said. "But why would somebody with your specialty be interested in me?"

"We're also working on links between the human neurological system and AI. To see if one can enhance the other. It's possible something in your experience could be of use to us. Your neurological system behaves in some unusual ways. Through force of will. To this point, this has only involved the restoration of control over your own body, but if that control could be channeled, then..." He shrugged.

"I might control something outside of my body. I might control an AI?"

"It's an intriguing possibility."

Honi's eyes lit up and then, just as quickly, darkened. "And it might control me?"

"We wouldn't design it that way. The human element would always be in control."

Honi looked at him. "You are talking about intelligence here, right? In the AI, I mean. And aren't intelligences supposed to be adaptable? To solve problems? So, what happens if the AI decides I'm the problem?"

"Told you," Chopra said to Donaldson.

"Told him what?" Honi demanded.

"That a mind that can force her own broken spinal column to regenerate is not a mind to be trifled with," Chopra said.

"That's why I asked you if you'd be interested," Donaldson said to Honi. "We're just starting this research. You'd be along every step of the way, an equal part of the research team. We can bring you up to speed quickly on the technical aspects of the work."

"He is the best," Chopra said.

"But that best wants to hack into my neurological system!"

Professor Donaldson laughed so hard the tears ran down his face. "Oh, she's going to be good, this one. She's going to be very good!"

"Told you," Chopra said. "I will talk to your parents. Dr. Donaldson can introduce you to Dr. Howard when he arrives."

Peni

Honi's father was not pleased. "We agreed to this because we understood that this was the only way her therapy could continue," Peni huffed. "No one said anything about using her mind to control computers. And what happened to the genetic component to this?"

"She'll meet Dr. Howard, the geneticist, soon," Chopra said. "It is the main reason she's here, apart from the therapy, of course. But there's another aspect to this that I think you should consider. Honi's therapy needs to be more than just physical. There's a bright mind in there that should be exercised. She did that herself when she had access to the Internet. We want to exercise that mind and working with Dr. Donaldson is a way of doing that. This will give her a chance for a similar level of involvement."

"How long have you known this Donaldson?" her mother asked.

"Less than a day," Chopra admitted. "But by reputation, most of my professional life. Professor Donaldson is a world authority on artificial intelligence, specifically the stuff they send on space missions. Those missions must be able to function independently because of the communication time lag. And from what I've heard, his team all love working with him. No red flags in that regard. Honi would learn from the best, and of course, we'll all be here to watch over her."

Peni frowned. "I don't like this. It feels like our daughter is being hijacked."

Noelani gave her husband a stern look. "And what would you rather have happen here?" she asked. "Didn't you see what was going on in San Diego? Were your eyes closed when we rolled through those cities and towns on the way here? What chance do you think Honi will have out there?"

"Not much," Peni admitted. "And what will we be doing here? You've brought us all the way out from San Diego."

"I don't know what they will do with you," Chopra said. "I'm guessing you will be Honi's principle caregivers, but I don't know for sure. What I do know is that they see you as vital to any progress Honi will make."

Peni pursed his lips. "Exactly the kind of thing you'd expect them to say if they wanted to keep the parents on board."

Noelani gave her husband a look of exasperation.

Peni caught this. "There's something about this that doesn't feel right," he said.

"And so, you'd have her and us thrown out on the street?" his wife asked.

"No. Of course not."

Howard

They've planned it perfectly, Honi thought. *Chopra leaves. A couple of beats later, there's a knock on the door.*

Donaldson walked over and let a tall black man, also dressed in a white lab coat, into the room. Honi wondered about noticing his color, about letting her mind make a thing about his skin tone. She didn't want it to do that, but it did automatically. In much the same way that others would make a thing about her being native Hawaiian or disabled.

"Honi, this is Professor Howard," Donaldson said.

Professor Howard reached forward and shook her hand. "Geneticist," he said.

"The reason I'm here?" Honi said.

"One of the reasons, yes. By now I'm sure you've figured out there's more to it than that."

"And what do you expect to find in my genome?"

"Adenine, thymine, guanine, and cytosine," Howard said.

This time it was Honi's turn to laugh.

"Only one in a thousand sixteen-year-olds would get that joke," Howard said with a grin. He turned to Donaldson. "Maybe I should steal her away from you."

"First dibs, I'm afraid."

"But it's not fair. You were introduced first."

"Life's not fair."

By now Honi had regained control. She liked both men. "But seriously, what will you be looking for?" she asked Professor Howard.

"I don't know, but if there is a genetic component to what you've been able to do, I hope to find it. Can you imagine what we'd be able to do if we could bioengineer a human species that could repair itself by simple force of will?"

Chopra and Donaldson looked at each other with tightened lips.

"Bioengineer a human species?" Honi said.

"Hypothetically, of course," Howard added quickly.

Non-Disclosure

Honi looked up from the book she was reading toward the fuss at her door.

Doctor Chopra was there along with lab coats and something else. Whatever it was, they couldn't get it through her door.

"I told them this design was too wide," said Chopra.

"It's built from an existing design," the first lab coat said. "They've been making them this way for years. Surely they would have considered..."

"This building is 150 years old, maybe more. Doorways were smaller then. No one was thinking about operating a chair that size through doors this narrow."

"I'm sorry," Honi said. "What is going on here?"

"They've made you a chair, dear. It was to be a surprise but I'm afraid..."

"Why?"

"Why what, dear?"

"Why did they make me a chair?" Honi asked louder this time.

"To help you get around, of course."

"And you have a problem with the way I have been getting around?"

"No, of course not, but this is a big campus, and you need to preserve your strength."

"I need to gain strength, not preserve it. And I won't be doing that if I climb back into a motorized wheelchair. I spent four years of my life in one of those, and I won't be getting in one again."

"We thought it might speed up some transit times between buildings..."

"So, this is about you and not me?"

Chopra turned and addressed the lab coats. "Just take it back. We didn't think this through."

"No, you didn't," Honi agreed.

Dr. Howard had been back to see her only once. A cheek swab and that was it. Dr. Donaldson was the big consumer of her time, giving her books to read, projects to do, and teams to be part of. She saw less and less of her parents.

"I never thought I'd wind up doing something like this," she told Donaldson.

"Why? What were you interested in before?"

"Paleontology, whale evolution."

"You lived in Hawaii, so I'm guessing this has something to do with humpbacks?"

Honi was silent for a moment then nodded. "My cousin— though age-wise he was really more like an uncle—was a humpback whale researcher trying to make sense out of their songs. He had hydrophones in the water constantly, recording every note they sang, looking for patterns and meaning. He used to take me out on his boat all the time. I helped him with whale spotting."

Donaldson nodded. "Past tense. Have you seen him since...?"

"No. We think he's stranded somewhere in Alaska because that's where he was studying the whales at the time, but we have no way of knowing. But that's the thing. It's not just past tense. It's not just then and now. It's two different eras, maybe even two different realities. Then I was impaired, now I'm moving toward... Well, I'm not sure where this is going, to be honest, but that's part of the reason studying with you makes sense now. Before I helped him because that was the opportunity I had. Now I'm helping you because this is what's available. The whole reality has changed, and with it my interests. Cetacean paleontology is what I did as a kid when I was thirteen, fourteen, and fifteen years old. I had access to the Internet and all these scholarly papers. Now all that is gone but, in its place, is this wonderful research facility. So, the stimulation is still there, it's just different."

"You understand our interest in you is far deeper than that wonderful mind," Donaldson said.

"You're going to try to do something with me. I know that."

"And how do you feel about that?"

Honi thought for a minute. "Well, you and Dr. Chopra have been talking about structures that will allow my brain to control machines and AI's. That's kind of scary in a way, but it is about moving forward and trying to solve problems, so I guess I'm OK with that. But I'm less sure about what Doctor Howard is doing."

"Has he talked with you?"

"He just came, took cheek swab and left."

"What he's doing is much further away, much more preliminary than what we're doing here. At this point, it's just exploration without a clear road ahead. There's something we've been discussing amongst ourselves in relation to you."

"What?"

"By the laws of this country and this state, you are under the age of consent. You cannot legally sign documents. What we've been discussing with President Alatorre to see if we can make an exception in your case."

"Why? What do you need me to sign?"

"A non-disclosure agreement. You do understand what those are?"

"It means I would be told secrets and that there would be some kind of severe legal penalty if I told those secrets to anyone outside of a predefined group of people."

"Essentially, yes."

"So, that little comment that Dr. Howard made about re-engineering the human species is true?"

Donaldson said nothing.

The room had natural light from two multi-paned windows to Honi's right as she rolled into the room. Two large armchairs covered in matching but fading orange paisley prints squatted at right angles to each other. Furniture from the sixties, she guessed. In one of these President Alatorre sat and in the other a man she didn't recognize but assumed was Gerald Garneau, the President's Chief of Staff. Neither of them stood as she moved her chair toward them.

They're watching me to see how well I do.

203

Another Turkish carpet, similar to the one in her room, occupied the space opposite the President and her chief of staff. It was clear from its placement that it was where she was to put her chair. She rolled unto it and stopped, facing them.

"And eight months ago, you were a quadriplegic on a ventilator?" President Alatorre asked.

What an odd greeting. "Yes," Honi said.

Alatorre stood up, crossed to Honi, and shook her hand. "I'm sorry," she said. "Most people want the formality, the ritual of being introduced to someone high and mighty. I'm tired of all that. It's such a time waster. And this," she gestured for Garneau to come forward, "is Gerald Garneau, my Chief of Staff."

"Pleased to meet you, Madam President," Honi said. "And you, Mr. Garneau."

Gerald Garneau nodded his acknowledgment. Alatorre frowned at him.

"You must excuse Mr. Garneau. I'm afraid I've been running him ragged."

"It's all right."

Alatorre sat down again and sighed. "I have to be honest here and say I find meeting you intimidating. I know it's supposed to be the other way around, but I assure you, it isn't. I can't tell you why until I'm sure I can trust you."

"Trust me?"

"Yes. You're young. Normally someone in a position of authority would never ask someone your age to take this step. In fact, it wouldn't even be legal, but I am the President of the United States, and I can override that legality if I so choose."

"Dr. Donaldson had to sign something. Is this about that?" Honi said.

"Do you trust him?"

"Of course, but I'm only sixteen. It's up to my parents to sign anything."

"The problem is they won't be of much use to you in this situation. They make decisions that normally require parental authority, like what medical treatments you'll receive or what school you will attend. But what they can't do is control how you will behave or what you will say if you are given access to sensitive information."

"They can't sign a non-disclosure agreement on my behalf because they won't be the ones doing the disclosing," Honi said. "Is that right?"

"Yes. Under normal circumstances a company or government that has secrets—information it doesn't want in public circulation—wouldn't tell that information to someone under the age of consent."

"But I'm to be the subject of whatever it is they're planning to do, and therefore I will have an intimate knowledge of everything." Honi pursed her lips. "Despite my youth."

Garneau nodded and turned to Alatorre. "I see what you mean," he said.

Honi turned to Alatorre for an explanation.

"The examiners have pegged your IQ at around 170, about 30 points higher than my own. That's part of the reason I find you intimidating, but my problem is intelligence and wisdom are not the same thing. The latter is a function of life experience, which is why the age of consent is set where it is. You've put us in an unenviable position here."

"You're worried that, even if you allow an exception to the law, I might not sign."

"Yes."

"You're right, I won't. Because what you're asking me to do is agree to something before I know what it is, and that something involves things that will be done to my body. It would not be wise for me to do that."

"Non-disclosure does not mean we can do things to you that you don't want us to. You can opt out at any time. It does mean, once you've signed the non-disclosure agreement, you cannot talk about what happens here with anyone who has not also signed the agreement. You will still have control over your own body. No one can make modifications you don't want."

"And what is the term of the agreement?"

"It's permanent," Garneau said.

205

"Until I die?"

"Yes."

"And what happens if I want to leave."

"You won't want to."

"But what if I do?"

"In the future it may not matter, but if it does, we won't allow you to leave. And since we don't know how long this research will take, it's easier to say never."

"A prisoner?"

"A guest."

"OK, since you won't tell me what the goal of this research is, I'm going to take a guess. You're hoping to improve the human species in some way. It has something to do with a comprehensive biological and technological integration, producing human minds advanced enough to integrate with the best artificial intelligence and control other less sapient technologies through this integration. You're hoping something in my regenerative abilities will provide a springboard. Am I getting warm?"

Alatorre and Garneau looked at each other but said nothing.

"So, if I'm right about this, then it seems to me the first thing you're going to create is a formalized distinction between classes of human beings, one with and one without. We've always had that, of course, but this will exacerbate it. Because the only way you can achieve what you want to accomplish in our current reality is to hoard most of the remaining resources. Billions will die."

"They will die anyway," Alatorre said. "And many already have. Because the people of this planet, all seven billion of them, highly depended on the existence of the infrastructure the Fahr destroyed. At present we're functioning at less than ten percent of the capacity we had before the Fahr, and that's up from the three or four percent capacity we had immediately afterwards. Starvation cannot be put on hold. We cannot rebuild in time to save more than a small fraction of those lives. You're a bright enough young woman to know that. And I suspect you saw plenty of evidence for what I'm saying on your rail journey across the country. Am I right?"

Honi said nothing.

"And it's also worth remembering the shattered lives you saw were in the United States of America, one of the most powerful and efficient economies on the planet, and a virtual bread basket to the rest of the world before the attack. So, if you saw that level of distress here, you can amplify it many times over to calculate what it looks like elsewhere. Sure, we could pour all our resources into keeping these folks alive a few weeks longer, but those resources would run out, and in the end, only scattered remnants would survive. And these remnants would not survive well. They would be in a constant state of struggle to find the resources they need and to defend themselves from other tribal groups intent on taking those resources from them. It will not be pretty—it is not pretty."

"So, your strategy is to focus on these researchers here? These elites?"

Alatorre pulled a document out of her attaché case and handed it to Honi. "I've already approved the exception. If you want to know more, you must sign the non-disclosure agreement. But I will tell you this. This is not about us. This is not about haves and have-nots."

Honi looked at the non-disclosure agreement before her. She could not survive out there on her own and she knew it, even with her parents' help.

"Not about us?" she said.

"Not about us," Alatorre echoed.

Honi signed the agreement and handed it back to the President. "What is this about then?"

"Starting tomorrow morning, I want you to spend some of your time with Dr. Howard. He already has your DNA, but he's not working on that now. I think you should see what he *is* working on."

***

After Honi had wheeled out the room, Garneau turned to Alatorre. "I'm not sure we should have had her sign before her parents."

"Make sure she understands she can't talk to them about this," Alatorre said.

"So, when will we bring them in?"

"We'll wait a while," Alatorre said.

Letters

"They've found you a working Lear jet," Garneau said reading from a letter.

"A Lear jet?" Alatorre said.

"An old model twenty-three. I don't think they made a lot of those, so this is fortunate."

"How old?"

"Made in sixty-three or sixty-four. It needs a bit of TLC. It's been in storage for twenty years. Some tobacco executive in Virginia had it. The problem is, it has some fried electronics, simple stuff apparently. Donaldson already has his crew working on replacement parts. Doesn't think it will be a problem."

"That's good, I guess," Alatorre said, holding up an envelope. "I admire the Canadians. They have a much more functional post office than we have. Their stuff moves around well within Canada. The problem is what happens once it crosses to our side."

"Bartering food for mail," he nodded toward the envelopes. "So, those are from Canada?"

"From the man himself."

"Prime Minister O'Malley?"

"Yep. I'm not sure how long it took to get here, though." She tore the envelope open and a few photographs fell on the floor. She ignored them and read the letter quickly. "Jesus, they have a dead alien!"

"What!?!"

"You heard me. One of them crash-landed on an island off their west coast."

"Close to where the ship was last seen?"

"I don't know. Where's Haida Gwaii?"

"I think that's it, yeah. Used to be called the Queen Charlotte Islands. Just below the southern tip of the Alaskan panhandle," Garneau said. He picked up the photographs and shared them with Alatorre.

"It looks like a fish," she said.

"Definitely aquatic."

"My God!" she said shaking her head. "This kind of adds credence to the whale theory."

"You don't suppose we could get a hold of it?"

"O'Malley's not likely to give this prize up," she said. "Besides, they've already got it in a biocontainment facility at the University of British Columbia."

"They have a functional biocontainment facility?"

"I suspect they're prioritizing things just like we are." She turned the envelope over. "This letter's already a month old, so they've had this beast for a while."

"There's a second letter from O'Malley here," Garneau said, handing the letter to Alatorre. "This one's more recent. Well, by a couple of weeks anyway."

Alatorre tore the second envelope open and read it quickly. "They want our help," she said. "This thing has a device of some kind patched into its neurological system. They want to know if we'd like to form a team to reverse engineer it. And here's the other thing. The body of the creature is gone. Underwent a sudden and rapid decomposition, turning it into dust in less than three days. The only thing left is this device, and a powder made up of basic organic compounds."

"Somebody fucked up," Garneau said.

"Maybe. But the important thing is we get to be part of this. Who knows what we can discover."

"Agreed. But let's see if we can get a little more."

"More?"

209

"The photos also show the wreckage of some kind of vehicle. Let's see if we can get access to that."

"Yes, of course. Let's make a deal. How soon do you think that Lear jet will be ready? It sure as hell will be faster than mail. This may need a face-to-face."

Immersion

Honi had enough strength to operate the wheelchair at a slow pace and manipulate lighter objects, but things were not improving. There seemed to be a limit to how much long-dormant muscles could be restored. The problem was much greater with her legs. She could move them slowly and painfully, and she could stand but only for a few minutes. Unassisted they would not bear her weight beyond standing. The physiotherapists continued to work on her but were making little progress.

Dr. Chopra assured her this was not a neurological issue. On that front, she had made remarkable progress. As far as Dr. Chopra could tell, Honi had achieved the complete restoration of her neurological system. The problem was her muscles had lay dormant for too long. This was discouraging news.

Dr. Donaldson called her into his office. She could tell from the look on his face their relationship was about to change. Donaldson was manipulating the pencil in his fingers as if practicing a conjuring trick. He studied her for a long time before saying anything. He put the pencil down and stood up. "We've known for a long time that, eventually, you would become the object of our experiments. I wanted to give you as much healing time as possible before we began. Dr. Chopra tells me that you're at an impasse in your physiotherapy. Is she right?"

Honi bit her lip and grimaced. "I think she is, yes. I can't walk." She stood up, attempted a step, and collapsed back into her wheelchair.

"I see pain," he said.

Honi said nothing.

"The interface is ready for testing. Are you ready?"

"It feels like giving up," she said.

"But you know it isn't, right?"

"Yes, of course, but..." She trailed off.

Donaldson waited.

Honi made a small change to her chair so she was facing at a right angle to Dr. Donaldson. "All right. Let's do this."

The interface was a long piece of what looked like transparent tape. It had several layers, all pellucid. Honi could see the electronics embedded within. The tape felt abrasive on her skin, which she supposed meant that it was making connections with her neurological system.

"Are you feeling discomfort?" Donaldson asked.

"There's no pain, but it doesn't feel pleasant. It's nothing I can't live with. I'm sure I'll get used to it. But why are we starting with my arm? My legs are a much bigger problem."

"We are not working on mobility issues now," Donaldson said.

"Then what?"

"We've been working on it."

"The Human-AI connection?"

"Yes."

Honi shrugged. "I just thought we'd start with something more fundamental."

"If this works, everything else will expand out from it. If you can interface with and control the AI, then as things move forward, all its extensions will be there for you. Mobility will not be an issue, but if we focus just on mobility, then it will be just you controlling the extension. I'm sure we can make that work and probably quicker than we can do this, but considering what we hope to accomplish here, focusing on mobility will delay the more important work."

Donaldson gestured to one of the lab coats. A suitcase-sized device rolled in on a cart. Honi had seen the prototype but now it seemed bigger, especially with a large 27-inch monitor attached.

"So, I will finally be attached to this thing?"

"Yes, and then it will greet you with small electronic pulses. About what your brain would expect from its own neurological system."

"It will greet me?"

"More like feel you. It will recognize the connection in the same way a computer recognizes something plugged into it through a USB port."

"And what will I feel?"

"That's what we don't know. We hope you will tell us."

"Boldly go where no woman has gone before."

"Wilma Shatner," Donaldson said with a grin.

"Wilma?"

"My lame attempt at humor."

"Ha, ha."

"Are you ready?"

"Shouldn't I tell my parents about this?"

Donaldson frowned. "*Have* you been telling your parents about this?"

"No," Honi admitted. "They think I've been studying general physics and electrical engineering. The President's chief of staff said that was all I could say. Sometimes I wish I hadn't signed that thing."

"Then you wouldn't be here."

"But I don't understand why my parents haven't been brought into the loop."

"They will be," Donaldson said.

"When?"

"In most cases with things like this, there's vetting process. Yours is the only case I can think of where we went around that, but if we hadn't then we couldn't work with you. I thought it was risky, but it was the President's call. The thing is, your parents are not comfortable here. Being pulled from a rural Hawaiian existence and plopped down in the middle of MIT is quite a change. They're doing it for you, of course, but that doesn't make it easier. We wanted to make sure we had something to show them before letting them in on the larger picture."

"And now it looks like we've stalled on the physical front," Honi said. "So, if we will show them anything, it will have to be..."

"Exactly."

I've trapped them, Honi thought. *I've committed myself to this thing so, no matter what happens, I have to stay here. I know too much.* She shrugged. *What was the alternative? Because of me they have food and lodging. They are safe. But they will be angry.* She was sure of that.

Honi looked down at the cable Donaldson held in his hand. He wasn't kidding about the USB part. She looked to the bottom of the interface and realized that it too had a USB port.

"That's so old school," she said.

"It is USB X," he said reaching for her arm.

"Still..."

Donaldson made the connection. At first nothing happened apart from a mild tingling sensation. Honi felt herself reaching as if she were moving an arm, but she wasn't. She was reaching with something else, but whatever the sensation was, it felt like it had fingers. Like moving in the dark when you couldn't see what you were reaching for expecting some familiar tactile sensation. Like probing for a light switch. But there was no light switch, just the reaching. She waved this phantom appendage but felt nothing.

She looked at Donaldson and found his mouth open in wonder. "What?" she said.

"Your skin is flushing rapidly, as if your whole face is a blinking LED readout."

"I don't feel that."

"What do you feel?"

"As if I'm reaching into the dark with my hand, only it's not my hand. It's a phantom version of it. I'm trying to find something to touch, at least that's what it feels like. I don't know, I'm just

213

reaching. It's the only way I can describe it. No. Wait a minute. I'm feeling warmth... wet warmth. Like tepid bath water."

"Your face has stopped flushing," Donaldson said.

***

Honi acted like she had not heard him. Her eyes glazed over, and she let out a long slow breath, exhaling until she had no more air in her lungs. There was a long pause. Her eyes flickered. This was followed by a long, slow inhale. She began regular breathing again, but it was the slow automatic breathing of an unconscious person.

"Honi, can you hear me?" Donaldson asked.

He got no response. He looked at the lab coat. *What happens if I unplug her?* he wondered.

"We'd better do something, sir," the lab coat said.

It took Donaldson until that moment to realize that the lab coat was female. He'd been so focused on the task at hand, so focused on Honi and what they were about to do, that he'd objectified everything else in the room.

"On my Mac, you must eject the hard drive before you can disconnect it," the lab coat said.

My God, she's worse than I am, thought Donaldson.

"She's not a computer, she's a person," Donaldson said.

"So, we just unplug her?"

Of all the contingencies that Donaldson had contemplated before attempting the connection, this one he hadn't considered. And now it seemed so obvious. What would happen if he unplugged Honi? He had no idea. And if she were damaged, he could never forgive himself.

"I don't know," he said.

***

Honi was submerged, but in what she couldn't tell. She felt the air leaving her lungs and wondered why she didn't feel the need for oxygen. It seemed irrelevant somehow. Feeling she should breathe, she triggered it. And it was that. A trigger, the flipping of a switch. She breathed slow and easy. Now Honi understood that she was inside the AI. Somehow her mind had moved inside the box on the cart. She remembered the monitor connected to the device. *Hello,* she said in her mind.

***

"The monitor!" said the lab coat.

Donaldson looked at the screen. On it the word "hello" had appeared. "I've gone for a swim inside this thing," the words continued on the screen. "Do you know the last time I went for a swim? I think I was twelve. Was I holding my breath?"

"You stopped breathing for a short while," Donaldson said, not at all sure that she could hear him.

More words appeared on the screen. "I realized that, and then I told myself to breathe again. It was like flicking a switch. I had to give myself instructions. Isn't that weird?"

"You weren't responsive for a while."

"I heard you. I was just overwhelmed."

"Can you tell yourself to disconnect?"

"From the device, you mean?"

"Yes. We're worried what might happen if we just unplug you."

"I'll try." The monitor went blank. Her hand had unplugged the USB cable from the interface.

"Wow!" Honi said a moment later.

Decision

"Are you ready for this?" Garneau asked her.

Alatorre looked at the scar on the back of her hand. "I was once almost assassinated, you know," she said.

Garneau grinned. "That wasn't what I asked you," he said.

The President studied her chief of staff. He was her primary advisor and close friend, but he could be pushy. "According to Donaldson, she has integrated with a computer. So, it's likely her parents are going to see changes soon. We have to bring them in."

"Again, that wasn't what I asked you."

"Stop it, Gerald! Of course, I'm not comfortable with this. At the very least it will look like we didn't take their parental rights seriously. At worse it's going to look like we manipulated them into this situation."

"We did."

Alatorre studied Garneau. "You mean I did. It was my decision. It's not something I would have done before... When the rules were different."

"But it was done. We both knew this day was coming."

"You're amazingly unhelpful this morning."

Garneau spread his hands out in a gesture of acceptance. "If you like, I'll handle it."

"No, this is mine."

Four solid raps announced the arrival. Both Alatorre and Garneau stood as Honi's parents were shown into the room. Both were dressed in bright floral Hawaiian shirts, hers yellow and his blue.

"Mr. Peni Kalawai'a and Mrs. Noelani Kalawai'a, Madam President," the guard announced.

Alatorre smiled and stepped forward to shake their hands. Her meeting with Honi had been much less formal, but her parents wouldn't know about that. Part of the teenager's non-disclosure agreement. The President directed Honi's parents into the chairs provided.

"I like the shirts," Alatorre said after the two sat.

"Thank you, Madam President," Honi's father said. "I suspect you won't be seeing a lot more of them, especially on Hawaiian bodies."

Noelani slapped her husband on the arm.

Alatorre gathered herself. "That was a tragedy, one of many worldwide and in the continental United States. Given the complete infrastructure collapse we did what we could with limited resources. But you showed remarkable resourcefulness in escaping from it, and thanks to your efforts, we have met your amazing daughter."

"Do you know the fate of our islands?" Peni asked.

Alatorre sighed. "What I do know is not encouraging. A small remnant has survived by returning to the sea for sustenance."

"And there was nothing you could have done?"

"We had no operational large vessels until several weeks after the attack. Add to that the time the sailings would have taken, and assuming we could have found the supplies to fill the boat in the first place—and by then our resources were falling far short of the demand on the continent—you would not have had a positive outcome. We may have saved a few." Alatorre studied Peni. "But I think you already knew all this."

Peni nodded and went silent.

"And yet you're feeding us and taking care of our handicapped daughter..." Noelani said.

Alatorre nodded. "Which is the primary reason I asked you here today. Your daughter is a lot less handicapped than you think."

"She is certainly engaged with all the computer stuff she's studying, but she doesn't tell us much."

"That's because she can't."

"Can't?"

"She signed a confidentiality agreement shortly after she got here."

Both Honi's parents stared at Alatorre.

217

"A confidentiality agreement?" sputtered Peni. "But she's only sixteen!"

"She's a bright and talkative sixteen-year-old who, because of her abilities, is the subject of some classified research. We had no choice."

"But we're her parents! We should have been asked to sign the same agreement!" Peni struggled not to get out of his chair.

"What we're doing here is not for public knowledge. It requires a different mindset, a different way of thinking about everything that's happening. It's not for public consumption. But you are right. We should have included you. We will give you that opportunity now."

"Why? What's going on here?"

"That's what I can't answer without you signing the non-disclosure agreement," Alatorre said, nodding to Garneau who produced the papers.

"I still don't understand. Why now?" Noelani asked.

"There was a very good chance that Honi's abilities would not have proved useful," Alatorre said. "We were minimizing the risk to the project."

"What project?"

"You will need to sign the non-disclosure agreement to find out. But before you do, I should tell you there is no out clause here. Once you've signed on, it's permanent. You will remain with us for the rest of your lives."

"Is that what Honi signed?" Noelani asked.

"It is."

"So, she's here permanently?"

"She is."

"And if we don't sign?" Peni asked.

"We will continue to take care of you. You are Honi's parents, but you will be removed to another location and will have restricted access to your daughter."

"How restricted?" Noelani asked.

"We don't know. Things are too early for us to make that determination."

"And what happens if we sign and then violate the non-disclosure agreement?" Peni asked.

"You're no longer living in a liberal democracy," Garneau said. Everyone looked at him.

"They need to know that," he explained to Alatorre. "Because it's true."

Interfacing

Data was a flow, Honi realized, just as they said. But she had never considered that in liquid terms before, more like sparks going up and down cables or radio waves across wireless space. The reality was more of a liquid thing, a flow one got used to, and then it became immersion. Controlled immersion because it did what she wanted. Interfacing had an addictive quality. When Honi connected, she also expanded. She thought with more precision and could often solve a problem simply by articulating it. After a while, when not connected, she felt its absence.

Donaldson's research resided in the unit's memory, where she could access it.

"Your work is flawed," she said. "You're trying to mimic human consciousness by giving the machines intensive programming and a large database. The programming mimics human thought processes but does not recreate them. The computer has no overlying consciousness. It does what it's told. If what it's told to do is designed well enough, it can look as though it has consciousness, but it doesn't. When you're connected to it as I am, you quickly realize you are the only consciousness present. So, pursuing this line of research might give you what appears to be artificial intelligence, but it's just advanced programming. My only relationship with this thing is to tell it what to do. It is not my friend, and although we can carry out conversations, these are not familiar conversations. It needs me to think. But it expands me, so I believe this, and similar devices have great potential. It won't be artificial intelligence, rather expanded human intelligence."

Donaldson looked at her. "I, and my colleagues, know of the system's limitations. Are you suggesting pursuing this line of work will lead to failure?"

"If you define the problem in terms of creating true consciousness, then yes. You will fail, but you have expanded human intelligence, or at least, my intelligence. When I am connected, I am far superior to when I'm not connected. To be honest, when I'm connected is when I feel the most complete. Perhaps I can best describe it this way. I was once a quadriplegic. Functionally, all I had was my head and the top of my shoulders. Now I am much more complete. The analogy is similar. When I'm not connected, it feels much like the state I was in when I was a quadriplegic, only in this case the body is my mind. Connected I am whole. Disconnected I am the mental equivalent of a quadriplegic."

"Then we must come up with a more portable version of this machine. And the sooner the better," Donaldson said.

"Yes. I would like to take my whole mind with me wherever I go."

"Interesting," Donaldson said. "You think of it in the possessive—you think of it as yours."

"It is my mind. It does what I want it to do."

Donaldson looked at Honi. She could tell this was not going the way he thought it would. Honi was now his intellectual superior. But she knew, as he did, that hers was still an adolescent mind.

O'Malley

President Maria Alatorre would arrive in a Lear jet, one from the earliest days of executive jets. The old aircraft had seating for six people, a far cry from Air Force One. Perhaps Prime Minister Pierce O' Malley shouldn't be surprised. Things had certainly changed worldwide over the last few months, but he felt a certain satisfaction.

Canada coped so much better than its southern neighbor, mainly because the population was far less inclined toward gun ownership. This had its own issues, considering the American militia groups had an easier time making incursions into Canada. There had not been many raids since these groups seemed content to solidify their holdings on American soil. But he would certainly have to bring up southern Manitoba and Alberta, and the Okanagan region. These had now been under the control of American militias for several weeks. Not that he expected the President to do much. Vast stretches of the American heartland were also controlled by these groups, and her priorities would be there.

The plane from Vancouver had arrived the previous week, and now the scientists and engineers were going over the contents of the package. They couldn't tell him much at this point except it appeared to be a digital/biological interface, its purpose a mystery. Prime Minister O'Malley had heard of the remarkable efforts Alatorre had put forth restoring the research functionality of MIT. They had no equivalent in Canada, but the device had fallen into their laps and not into the American's. This gave him leverage. Canada would maintain ownership of the device and Canadian scientists would be involved in its study. Those two points were nonnegotiable.

O'Malley waited on the tarmac, but with the communications infrastructure years away from restoration, had no certainty of Alatorre's arrival time. Canada Post was oddly comforting though, and the extra time to accomplish things had the nice side effect of slowing everything to a leisurely pace. The Prime Minister was too young to recall a time when life had been like this, but the older members of his cabinet did remember. They had grown up without cell phones, without texting, without the Internet. For them the transition was easier, and they felt less cut off from their devices. Together they were reinventing the art of conversation, the art of making decisions with less information, the art of waiting. Still, O'Malley found it difficult without the tools he was used to using.

Someone pointed at the horizon. An old Lear jet was circling the airport, the pilot trying to determine the best place to land. With no one in the tower, this had to be done visually. The plane made one more circle and before putting down. The noise was deafening to the small crowd, their ears had now readjusted to a machine-free environment. Many of them winced. In the past few months most of them had heard nothing louder than an old automobile.

O'Malley stepped forward as the aircraft arrived at the terminal. It sat there for a good five minutes until O'Malley's security people were in place and the stairs had been rolled up to the cabin door. A scant few months earlier such an arrival would have generated much public interest, but now without a functioning media, no one knew about it. No one except O'Malley's people. He had handpicked a dozen local scientists to attend. These people accompanied Cynthia Chen from UBC and Charlie Dayaang, a young Haida man from Masset on Haida Gwaii.

The door creaked open and a single stilettoed foot appeared. Alatorre emerged in all her finery, but not a single camera clicked. O'Malley stepped forward and took the President's hand as she stepped off the stairway. No flashes went off.

"Welcome, Madam President," he said.

"Thank you, Mr. Prime Minister," she said. She moved closer and whispered to him. "Isn't it wonderful how all the pomp and circumstance has just faded away?"

"Yes," he whispered back. "But we must always be ready."

"Planning on running for office soon, are we?"

O'Malley just stared at her.

"Politics are the least of our concerns now, wouldn't you agree?" Alatorre said.

"It's a hard habit to break," he said.

"It is, but we must break it."

O'Malley smiled at her. "Of course," he said. This is not going well, he thought. "Madam President, let me introduce you to my scientist friends."

Back at the Prime Minister's Office, Alatorre apologized. "I'm sorry if I embarrassed you back there," she said. "Democracy is no longer a reality in the United States. We have no way of conducting meaningful elections. Therefore, what's needed is a strong hand. I intend to provide that. Tell me, how well are your people eating?"

O'Malley leaned back in his chair and studied her. "That would depend on what part of the country you're talking about. Up north and in the major urban centers there are problems as I'm sure there are in the States. We, like you, have distribution issues. Not enough trucks and a dysfunctional railway system. But the rural parts of the country are getting by. We were having a good growing year when the attack happened, so there is food. It's just a question of harvesting it without machinery and getting it to the people who need it."

"And how is that going?"

O'Malley studied the American President. "Should I admit my faults to you?"

Alatorre laughed. "Relax," she said. "I know you're doing better than we are. More of our population is armed and sees little reason to cooperate with the government. But these are small arms, and the militias that wield them are poorly organized. The problem is there are a lot of them. They have their little fiefdoms and they war with each other more than they war with us. That reality has allowed us to establish power bases in all the most important places."

"Like MIT?" O'Malley asked.

"Yes, like MIT," she said. "Which brings me to the reason I am here. You have alien technology that can use the expertise we have in Boston?"

O'Malley nodded. "We believe it's some kind of digital interface, one which was patched into the creature's neurological system. Unfortunately, all we have is the device itself and a few thirty-five-millimeter photographs of how it was connected. As I mentioned in my letter, the creature dissolved a few days after we moved it to the labs at UBC. What we have left of it is nothing more than a powder of simple organic molecules. Nothing even as complicated as an amino acid."

Alatorre stood up and walked to the other end of the room. She turned and looked at O'Malley. "It didn't want to be studied or perhaps, more accurately, the Fahr didn't want it to be studied. This was some kind of failsafe mechanism to prevent us from learning too much about them. It also seems the Fahr do not believe we have the technology to reverse engineer the device. Especially since they had destroyed so much of what we had. But MIT grows daily in its capabilities. We have a coal-fired electrical generating system and can now manufacture chips for most applications. It's a slow process, but it works. And the more we do it the faster it gets. We are on the road to complete technological recovery."

"And this is helping with your food production?" O'Malley asked.

Alatorre said nothing. She sat down again and gave O'Malley an apologetic smile. "Even if that were the focus of what we are doing, it would fail," she said. "The world's food needs are immediate and pressing. By the time we could put in measures to significantly improve food production and distribution, most of the world's population will be dead. Feeding the world was far too dependent on the existing infrastructure, an infrastructure so massive that reconstructing it from scratch will take a lifetime. We are planning for the aftermath and you should be too."

O'Malley's mouth dropped open. "You're giving up?" he said.

Alatorre shook her head. "No, but we know we won't succeed. We'll try to feed our population. To not do so would be ethically problematic. But the task is so massive in scale and the time frames so short that the likelihood of success is small. The Canadian situation may not be as extreme, but I can guarantee you will face the same reality."

The Prime Minister studied his American counterpart. "And how are you planning for this aftermath?"

Alatorre pursed her lips. "Planning for the aftermath has to include our new reality as a species. We have long suspected we were not alone in the universe, and now we know that to be true. What's more we know, at least as far as one other sapient species is concerned, we are over matched. The Fahr tried to negotiate with us. It was half-hearted, from our point of view, but the attempt was made. Keep in mind they had been monitoring our communications for decades. They would have known that we are a deeply divided species. I suspect they knew an attempt to force human unity was likely to fail, and hence their tepid attempt at negotiation. So, we have a problem as a species—a big problem. We need to transcend our tribal natures. And it is my belief we are incapable of choosing to behave differently. John Lennon first sang his famous 'Give Peace a Chance' song in Canada, didn't he?"

"Yes, in Montreal, when I was a small child," O'Malley said.

"That was a plea for us to transcend our tribal natures, to get along. I'm older than you and was a young adult when that event happened. I remember thinking, even then, that his sentiment was naive. We cannot will ourselves to behave in a non-tribal fashion. And as you well know, because you are a politician, it's not enough to have your tribe win. Because as soon as you do, your own tribe splinters into smaller warring sub-tribes."

O'Malley nodded.

"So, now what I'm about to tell you must be kept under wraps. It's not something that can go out for public discussion, and when you hear about it, you'll know the reason. We will help you. We'll put all the resources at MIT at your disposal. We will include Canadian scientists on our team and take you and your government into our confidence. We will share all our progress with you. But only if you agree to silence. You cannot talk about what I'm about to reveal to you. Do you agree?"

"Of course," O'Malley said.

"We are going forward under the assumption the problem is genetic, that we are hardwired to behave in this manner. We believe the only way to change is through genetic engineering. We hope to rebuild the human species."

The Prime Minister's mouth dropped open. He tried the beginnings of several words before closing it.

"We thought we might get that kind of reaction. What we are talking about here is something likely to take generations to achieve. So, humanity, as we know it, is in no immediate danger, even if whatever we create eventually takes over. It's unlikely that either of us will live to see the results. But the work must begin because not doing so will imperil us in the long-term as a species. One more Fahr arrival and we could all be dead."

"If we control our own evolution, we can speed it up. Is that what you're thinking?

"Yes."

"I can see why you wouldn't want that to get out. The religious fanatics would come out in force, not to mention those secular folks who believe any form of genetic engineering is a threat to life on the planet. All those anti-Monsanto crusaders."

"Do you still have those up here? We don't. Our population is happy to get food of any sort regardless of whether or not genetic engineering is involved. But you're right. The general population must not know about what is going on in MIT's more secure labs. Anyone we've recruited to be involved in this project has signed a non-disclosure agreement. And given the current state of the American legal system, the only way we can enforce this is to punish such disclosure in the most capital of ways."

"Tell and you die," O'Malley said.

The President nodded. "That's the threat, anyway. I'm not sure I could do that to anyone, but I am sure there are people within my administration who could. And I'm also sure that there will come a time when they will have to. Statistically the time frame is much too long for such secrecy to be maintained without extreme measures. Not that you or a member of your government should feel threatened by this. But if you revealed what was going on, the relationship between our two countries would deteriorate. And we know we need each other."

"But, as you said, we're dealing with a time frame problem," O'Malley said. "Assuming I can keep my administration in check about this, I can't guarantee what succeeding administrations will do."

"That's why I said democracy is no longer feasible and won't be for the foreseeable future."

"Even if the next administration is not democratically elected, they might still..." O'Malley shook his head. "And I thought I was just soliciting technical help."

"It's easy to be overwhelmed by the problems we are facing here. But we can't forget what caused this. We are facing a new reality here. We're the immature and junior member of a galactic club. To function within that club, we need to make changes. The reality is this is a much bigger issue than feeding our overpopulated planet. I have no doubt that, at some point, I will be portrayed as a traitor to humanity. But I hope, by then, we will have become something much more."

O'Malley looked at Alatorre. He reached for the glass of water on the table and took a long drink. "I'm not in the position to have a say in anything you do. What I will tell you is my priorities must remain with the Canadian people. I was elected to serve them and deal with the current realities on the ground. You have chosen this path and I will not resist you, nor will I tell anyone about what you plan to do. Canadian scientists will be free to join your team if they choose. I can hardly restrict them and then ask for your help in reverse engineering the alien device at the same time. I can see some wisdom in what you want to do, but I'm far from certain I agree with the timing. If the house is on fire, should we make plans for another house or should we fight the fire? I know what my answer is. As for

227

democracy, it got me where I am, so I don't intend to abandon it. However, I will acknowledge that it's another infrastructure that will need to be rebuilt. That could take a long time."

Alatorre nodded. "I understand your position," she said. "Your scientists will be welcome at MIT, providing they sign the non-disclosure agreement, with everything that implies."

O'Malley studied her. "Can I bring up another issue?" he asked.

"Of course."

"As you know, we have a long undefended border. There have been incursions into Canadian territory by the same militias you mentioned earlier. They're in control of the entire Okanagan Valley in BC and parts of southern Manitoba and Alberta. This is not your doing, I know, but to deal with it I will have to take action against American citizens."

Alatorre considered this. "The Okanagan is a prime food growing area, isn't it?"

"All three areas are prime food producing regions, but the Okanagan is the most important. Yes."

"The one area in which we may have an advantage over Canada is in the strength of our remaining military forces. We're still stretched thin—which is why we still have so many problems on our own soil—but we will make a priority to help you out. It is, after all, the American government's fault that these militias are armed to the degree they are. As a side note, you'll be happy to learn that the NRA no longer exists."

"One less problem," O'Malley said.

Alatorre studied him. "One less tribe."

"There's one other thing."

"All right."

"The device was delivered to us by two people. Cynthia Chen is a post doc from the University of British Columbia and has the skill set your research requires. And I'm sure she will want to be part of it. The other person is a special case. Charlie Dayaang is a member of the Haida First Nation and was one of the discoverers of the alien body. He's only eighteen-years-old, but he's driven and bright. We'd like it if he could be of some assistance."

Alatorre pursed her lips. "That will depend on how he wants to be involved. Without at least a graduate-level science education, he cannot be part of the research—at least not initially—though I suppose he could be trained. This is not my area of expertise, so his role will have to be determined by the project managers. But this is a long-term project. There will be plenty of time for him to acquire the skill set, providing he is willing go through the process. We'll take him on, but the extent of his involvement will be up to him. Make sure he understands before he comes."

"I will. Thank you," O'Malley said.

Alatorre stood up. "It's a pity I don't have more time. I'd love to have a chat with Canada's most famous prisoner."

The Canadian Prime Minister got to his feet. "Mr. Andreas Huber, you mean?"

"Yes. I'm sure he has quite a story to tell."

"I think he's sick of telling it. He went from solitary confinement to being on public display. One extreme to the other."

"Well, we each have countries to repair, and I have this added little project. I hope you're successful in restoring the Canadian way of life." Alatorre reached out her hand to the Prime Minister.

O'Malley shook it. "I hope this will be the first of many visits," he said.

"I'm sure we will have occasion to meet again, Prime Minister," and with that she turned and left.

O'Malley watched as she closed the door behind her, then collapsed back into the chair he'd been sitting in. *Did she really say they were planning to genetically re-engineer the human race? Canadian scientists would be staying put.*

ACT EIGHT: THRYKE

Hover Board

As miniaturization went, this was a stopgap measure. The machine was now a backpack, or more precisely, a chair pack. It fit on the back of Honi's wheelchair but could also be a backpack should she ever regain the ability to walk. Donaldson assured her that this was only a matter of time, that his team was working on a prototype set of prosthetics. But when Donaldson gave her the digitized version of the prosthetic design, Honi knew this was not what she wanted. The design of it, a motorized strapped on support system, would be as bulky as the wheelchair. It frustrated her, with all her expanded intelligence, that she still could not will the muscles in her legs to regenerate.

It took less than four days for Honi to come up with an alternative. This was a simple support structure that would keep her upright while mounted on a susboard, her term for an air-suspended hovering skateboard-shaped platform. The device would be controlled by sensors embedded in gloved hands. Because the susboard would not have wheels, it would not be limited to flat surfaces. She could use stairs and even negotiate steep climbs. It was all a matter of precise control, something she could now do easily with the help of her backpack. She gave Donaldson the design.

***

Donaldson looked at Honi in amazement. There were several aspects to the design that had never been attempted before. He wasn't sure they would work, but he had learned not to underestimate Honi. She had already solved many of the problems faced by his design team, including ways to make the manufacturing process much more efficient. There was no reason to think this circumstance was different. He was feeling small.

PDM

The susboard, with its most recent refinements, would keep Honi erect up to twelve feet in the air. She knew that Donaldson did not like when she used the board to hover more than a few inches off the floor. But Honi had spent so much of her life jealous of the mobility of skateboarders. She couldn't resist pushing the susboard to its max. She loved to scoot over people's heads and remind them of what she could now do. This was her adolescence talking, she knew, but she wanted it to talk.

She maneuvered her susboard to get a look at the strange almond-shaped device on the table from every angle, including from several feet above it. Donaldson pursed his lips.

"Do we have a name for this thing?"

"Around here everyone is just calling it 'the device'," Donaldson said.

"That's lame. Should be able to come up with something better than that."

"Maybe, but we don't even know what it does. Naming it will make more sense when we figure that out."

Honi nodded from her susboard perch. The thin threads protruding from the device were best seen from above. These looked like the filaments from a spider's web. Functionally, she thought they were wires, but apart from those used in microscopic chips, she had never seen wires this long that were so thin. And she also doubted if these barely visible strands contained metal. They looked like they might be organic, but according to Cynthia Chen, the Canadian postdoc, everything organic in the original fahr corpse had dissolved. Based on logic alone that would seem to preclude that these strands were organic.

"The idea is to reverse engineer this," Donaldson said. "But our colleague from Canada doesn't like this idea." He smiled in Cynthia Chen's direction. She was technically in charge of the device because of its Canadian origin, but everyone knew her primary function was to be an observer.

Honi looked at Cynthia, smiled then returned her attention to Donaldson. "I agree with Cynthia. This is an alien technology. How would you know where to begin? And if you made a mistake, you could do irreparable damage to it."

"Do you have another idea?" Donaldson asked.

Honi circumnavigated Donaldson on her board. "I know what you're really asking," she said.

"I'm getting used to being transparent."

Honi had now mastered the art of reading human faces, so every emotion, every intention, and every attempt at deception were obvious to her. She liked and disliked the advantage. It gave her more control, but it also allowed her to know how uncomfortable she was making everyone else.

"You'd be risking me or the device. Perhaps both," Honi said.

"I brought you here because..."

"I've interfaced with your computer, and you're thinking I might be able to interface with this thing."

"Not exactly. With your enhanced abilities, you're the best we have. Having you look at this thing..."

"Save it, Professor. We both know the most obvious course of action here."

Donaldson said nothing.

"But you're right. Another one of me might come along." She gestured to the device, "But this is irreplaceable."

"No one is better equipped to assess the dangers involved, and that makes you irreplaceable. I doubt if another one of you is likely to come along."

"Well, it doesn't hurt to look at it, I suppose."

Hacking into the alien device would be risky, Honi knew. She also knew she was the best person for the job. Whatever this thing was, it connected to the creature's neurological system. So, potentially, that was her way in.

She turned her attention to Cynthia Chen. "This device was originally connected to a sapient being, so perhaps our safest route is to first try connecting? No one can really be sure that won't also damage it, but it seems more likely it will either accept or reject the connection. That act, in itself, shouldn't harm it."

Cynthia let out a long noisy breath. "It's been entrusted to me," she said.

"And yet it's been sent here from your government to be investigated," Donaldson said. "At some point, we'll have to do more than just look at it."

Cynthia nodded.

"So, the first problem will be figuring out how to attach these thin strands to my interface. Can I touch it?" Honi asked.

Chen nodded again.

"Bring me my chair," Honi said to Donaldson.

"What are you going to do?" Donaldson asked.

"Get familiar, but I need my faculties to control the susboard. If something unforeseen happens, it's best if I'm not worrying about keeping my balance."

Donaldson pushed the chair over to her. "You're sure you want to do this?"

"Oh, yes," she said. Donaldson did not like it when she showed that level of confidence. But he was misreading her. She was not confident—she was afraid. At least when she had first connected with her computer, her AI, she was dealing with a man-made device. There were traces of human thinking all over it, but this was a different thing altogether. She did not know what would happen, assuming they could make the connection. It was too early for fear. But fear was always a premature emotion, always an advanced warning system.

Honi leaned over the device and touched it with the interface on her arm. Nothing happened. She was about to pull away when the tiny filaments begin to wave side-to-side. Then they brushed up against the upper part of her arm and stiffened.

The water was back, only this time it was more like a cool sea. Honi could taste the salt and feel a gentle surf, but there was nothing threatening here. She felt safe, almost tranquil. She wondered at the source of that emotion. Could the device be doing that to her? And there was still no answer to what the device was.

Sounds came, a long series of pops, drones, rumbles, screams, and squeals. They were tonal octaves of each other sliding somewhere between a B-flat and a B natural. They also extended well beyond the natural human hearing range in both directions. Honi wondered how she knew because she shouldn't be able to hear these sounds but could. She was also sure the sounds were instructions, that she was being asked to choose. She didn't know how she knew this, but she did. However, she had no idea what the options were. It soon became clear that without choosing, she could go no further. It was like knocking on a door, discovering entry required a password, and not knowing the password. After several minutes the filaments pulled away from her arm.

Awareness, foggy dream state awareness. Where was he?

Honi looked at Donaldson and Chen. "It's speaking in a strange single-pitch voice that ranges over about sixteen octaves. I shouldn't be able to hear pitches that low or high, but I can. Somehow, it's equipping me to do it. I'm also sensing it wants me to choose, but since I don't know what the choices are, I can't get beyond this. It waited for me to choose and when I didn't, it disconnected."

"Probably timed to turn itself off if it doesn't get the required input," Donaldson said. "Maybe it's an energy saving protocol."

Honi shook her head and grinned. "To stay connected I'll have to choose. The one thing I sensed during that brief connection was the size of the ocean."

"Ocean?" Chen said.

"When I initially connected with Dr. Donaldson's AI, it felt like being immersed in a warm bath," Honi said. "This is larger. An ocean is the best word I can think of to describe it. Whatever this is has a huge amount of data associated with it." She turned to Dr. Donaldson. "I will need an upgrade. My disk space is now at seventy-eight percent capacity. I'll need more storage and fast, of the Quant drive variety, and not an expansion of my current incredibly slow flash drives."

"Quant drives don't exist, haven't existed. They're a theoretical construct. Before the attack, they were three to five years away."

"I've read the theory. Five to eight times as fast as a flash drive. Sixteen times the storage capacity in a smaller chip. Infinitely connectible high-end electronic synapses. It's what I need."

"Need?"

Honi gestured to the device. "It looks small, I know, but it's enormous."

"Quant drives don't exist, apart from the theory and a few preliminary design ideas, all of which require a facility capable of working with parts much smaller than we can currently handle. We will be looking at a major retooling of our manufacturing process and serious delays."

Honi looked at him. "Explain the problem," she said.

"Problems," he corrected. "Many of them."

"Have your staff prepare documentation explaining the issues. I'll give it my full attention."

Donaldson winced. He was about to be humiliated again and knew it. *I am your creation,* Honi thought. She smiled at him.

Parents

In his younger years Peni had been a competitive surfer. He liked to think genetics was the reason Honi had so easily mastered her susboard, but the two skill sets were different. He had ridden the waves the ocean had thrown at him. She rode a board that generated blasts of air controlled by a computer she wore on her back, a computer she controlled via a link between it and her neurological system. And now she hovered at the door to their apartment. Her wheelchair arrivals were actual visits. Her susboard visits were always brief stops on the way to somewhere else.

"Hi Dad," Honi said, holding a can toward him. "One of the foraging teams found this. I grabbed it for you and Mom."

"Thanks," Peni said, taking the can from his daughter. *Dole Hawaiian Pineapple Chunks.* Back home he would never eat this, not with the fresh fruit so readily available. He wondered if any aspect of the Dole operation was still viable. That was a big operation, but could it function without all the machinery?

Noelani came up behind him and plucked the can out of her husband's hand. "We'll save this for a special treat," she said. "Can you stay for a while?"

"No, sorry, I can't. I have to get back to the lab. We've made a major discovery. I've interfaced with the alien device. No actual communication yet, but it is aware of me!"

Peni went white. "Whose idea was this?"

"Mine."

"No coercion. No attempts to manipulate you? This wasn't Donaldson, was it?"

"No. The decision was completely and totally mine."

"And they let you do it?"

"I chose to."

"Honi, that's alien technology," said Noelani. "You have no idea what you're dealing with..."

"Nor does it have any idea about me, Mom."

"You don't know that. Whoever they were, they knew an awful lot about us when they came. You can't assume..."

"It wasn't designed to interface with a human mind. So, it's an equal playing field in that regard. Mom, I'm well aware of the implications of doing this, but can you imagine the potential? Interfacing with Donaldson's AI expanded my abilities exponentially. This could be infinitely more amazing."

Peni steadied himself. "Honi, you are amazing. In a few short months, you've gone from a quadriplegic to an air-surfing super mind. You intimidate everyone you meet, but we all have a limit. Please be careful."

"I will, Dad. Don't worry." She turned to her mother. "Enjoy the pineapple, Mom," she said. She smiled at them. "See you later, then."

Peni watched his daughter scoot out of sight around a bend in the corridor. He turned to look at his wife.

"I know," she said. "I thought signing those papers would give us some influence, but..."

Peni nodded. He gestured to the can in his wife's hands. "There you have it," he said. "Life as we knew it."

Sea Urchins

It took Honi longer this time, seven weeks to design the quant drive and come up with an efficient manufacturing process. The rest was grunt work, setting up and testing the manufacturing process. It took an additional three months and all that time the device lay inert on the laboratory table. Unless Honi moved closer to it. When she did, the tendrils reached out for her, like a child wanting to be picked up.

Honi sat back into her chair with her new quant drives secured to the backseat. This now had more storage capacity than any known portable computing device before or after the attack. She looked again at the strange almond-shaped thing. Its tendrils waving at her, an invitation hard to resist. This time they had connected a digital analog interface to the signal chain and plugged that into a set of audio speakers, ones designed to play back sound well above and below the normal human hearing range. Donaldson and Chen would hear everything she heard up to a point. Much of it would be beyond their hearing range and hers too if she wasn't connected. Another advantage to these digital connections was the way they often circumnavigated her physical limitations. "Keep the volume low," she said to them. "We don't know what level of amplitude this thing will produce."

Donaldson nodded. Honi could see tiny beads of sweat above his bushy eyebrows. *This is a man who has been in control his entire life, and now he's not.* She wished he was. She felt overwhelmed by responsibility.

Honi moved her arm forward. The tendrils found her bare skin. The ocean cool came and with it the voices. She waited until the sequence was over and pulled away.

"Did you hear it?" she asked them.

"Yes. It's remarkable," Chen said.

"Notice the gaps between the sounds in the second part of the sequence?" Honi asked.

"Yes."

"I believe these are the choices."

"And you will choose one?" Donaldson asked.

Honi nodded. "If I'm lucky, it will let me in, but if I make the wrong choice, well... anything could happen."

"Nothing bad has happened yet," Chen said to Donaldson. "But we still could be putting her in great danger."

"I don't think it will hurt me, at least not intentionally," Honi said. "I survived the first encounter, didn't I?"

"But still..."

"It's either that or dismantle this thing," Donaldson said. He turned to Honi. "You are the only person who has experience with it, and the best person to make this decision."

Honi did her best not to smile. Instead she nodded, communicating to Donaldson and Chen that she understood the responsibility. She held her arm out to the tendrils.

238

One sound, toward the beginning of the second part of the message, had a soft and soothing quality to it. A sound one might make to a fussing baby. Honi chose that sound and played it back to the device. It responded by generating a few more sounds, including repeating the sound Honi had just used. She repeated it again.

Dreams of the nursery, of the first occupation. His childhood.

Everything in the room fled from her, rendering her immediate surroundings irrelevant. She felt a huge data flow. This thing was dumping stuff into her mind at an alarming rate. She rerouted it to the quant drives in her backpack, hoping that the amount of storage would be adequate. The data kept flowing, and as it did, Honi realized she was no longer sensing her body. She tried controlling her fingers. Nothing. She tried licking her lips. Again nothing. The data flow was relentless. At the thirty-two-minute mark, everything stopped. Her fingers flexed, and her tongue moistened her lips. Every bit of storage in the quant drives was in use. They'd run out of space.

She disconnected from the device. Half a dozen other lab coats had now joined Donaldson and Chen in the room. She read concern on all their faces. A couple of deep breaths and a smile.

"I'm fine," she said.

This is not my body! This is not me!

"It started out by trying to dump enormous amounts of data directly into my mind," Honi said to Donaldson. "I rerouted this to the quant drives, but despite all the capacity improvements, we ran out of room. We will need many more terabytes."

Donaldson looked at her. "It was trying to move data into your biological brain?"

"Yes. I rerouted it to protect myself. It was targeting my memories, or at least that part of my brain that stores memories. I

239

felt as if it was trying to replace some of them. That's when I rerouted it."

"Do you feel different? Are you missing memories? Are there new memories there?" Chen asked.

Honi thought about this. Nothing seemed to have changed but memories were odd things. You didn't think about them unless something brought them to mind, especially distant memories. And if some of those were missing and their loss didn't affect her in the present, would she even know they were gone? She did a quick search for her earliest memories and found yellowish water, sea urchins, funny playful fish, and warm feelings of contentment.

"I think I need to talk to Dr. Chopra," she said, climbing onto her hover board.

Cynthia Chen caught her before she left the room.

"We could not do much research on the creature before it dissolved, but we could determine that it's genetic structure was like our own. It had DNA—surprising given its origin—but it was there nonetheless. We had almost no time to study its neurological system, but it might be like what exists in animals on Earth."

"I felt that," Honi said.

"Felt it?"

"I'm sorry, but this is hard to explain. The connections are immediate but alien. If you'll pardon me, it is possible I've just lost my early childhood memories. I want to consult with Dr. Chopra about this before we go further."

Thryke

Dr. Chopra's scans showed nothing, but there were persistent aquatic images replacing Honi's earliest memories. What was even more strange was Honi felt no sense of loss. She understood the absence of her memories intellectually, but emotionally there was

240

nothing. These strange aquatic images seemed like they'd always been there and were part of her past, though she knew this not to be true. She could not risk losing more of her memories. A mechanism needed to be put in place that would channel the device's data dumps directly onto the quant drives.

Honi automated the process, sending the sound back to the device directly from the hardware in her backpack. But when she did this, the device did not respond.

"Now what?" Donaldson asked her.

"It seems to need organic connection, at least initially," Honi said. "Probably because it would've had that with its original host."

"So, we have to put your memories at risk if we want to get further into this thing."

"We have the data on hard drives from the first attempt. Let's see what we can learn from that."

Accessing this felt like watching somebody's home video, one taken in a watery world populated by immature fahr. There were few adults. An automated process took care of the juveniles, and they seemed not to miss interaction with their elders. As Honi watched this, she picked up some of the language, at least the simplified juvenile form of it. And then she got a surprise. Her own memories, those which had been replaced, were also on the quant drives.

"It's a memory management system," she told Donaldson and Chen. "The Fahr supplement their biological memories. My earliest memories are there too, on the quant drives. I've only made one choice, and that one choice maxed out on my storage capacity. We will need a lot more memory."

The new quant drives occupied a suitcase-sized box on a rolling cart, which connected to her backpack via fiber optic cables. Honi sat down in her chair again, extending her arm toward the device. It connected immediately. She now understood some instructions preceding the choices. "The choices are occupations," she told Donaldson.

"Occupations?"

241

"Yes. But the first one I chose is 'childhood'. I chose it because it was the softest and least-threatening sound of all the items."

"How many occupations are there?"

"Sixty-seven."

"Sixty-seven?"

"Yes."

"Then either this species holds down its jobs for short periods of time..."

"Or this is a long-lived species," Honi finished.

She thought about this. "It makes sense. We are talking about a species engaged in interstellar travel."

"And the times involved..."

"Exactly."

The implications of this were enormous. If this was a long-lived species, then each of the sixty-seven occupations would be a goldmine, provided they could interpret what was stored.

"Childhood was first on the list. From that we can assume chronological order. I think I should go directly to the last one," Honi said. "If it was the creature's final occupation, it may give us the reasons the Fahr attacked the Earth."

Donaldson nodded. "That makes sense. Do we know the name of the occupation?"

Honi shook her head. "What vocabulary I have is juvenile. I still don't know the meanings of most of these occupational labels, maybe because they're adult concepts."

Donaldson pursed his lips. "Only one way to find out."

Honi was quicker this time, at deflecting all but the initial burst of the memory data to the quant drives. But her mind still received a taste of the adult mind that created the memories. Its name was Thryke, and the occupation was military, a position of leadership. Honi also got the sense that Thryke was profoundly dissatisfied with his life. This was not a happy fahr. Honi could not ever remember being that unhappy, even in the immediate aftermath of her injury. She had still hung onto hope at that point, but this

Thryke was only clinging to anger and frustration. Honi felt dirtied by her exposure and annoyed that a small part of him had taken up residence in her head.

Can't move. No control. What is this?

The sixty-seventh occupation was far more extensive than the childhood memories. By the time it had downloaded, it depleted half of the extra quant drive's capacity. Honi wondered how long it would take her to review it. And each time she connected a little more of Thryke found its way inside her, but Thryke's memories were those of a dead creature and had no will of their own. Honi was in complete control. They were taking up space within her, but she knew the memories displaced could be called up from the quant drives.

Thryke's ghost did give her an intuitive understanding of some things. She now understood the Fahr communicated nonverbally through a combination of gill movements, color projections from the inflatable bladder on the top of their heads, and touch. Having that small bit of Thryke within her provided this knowledge. It did not, however, help her with vocabulary. The words she had learned, through her interaction with the childhood occupation, were too basic to be of much use in understanding adult fahr communication. So, while she could observe Thryke's memories and could feel them, she still found herself guessing at what they meant.

A few things were clear though. The Fahr spaceship was a giant interstellar ocean where sea creatures roamed at will. These were all Earth-like creatures, most of which would fit into recognizable families and genera. Honi remembered what Dr. Chen had told her about the discovery of the DNA molecule in the fahr corpse. How was it possible, she wondered, that life on a far distant world could be so similar? Perhaps that was how evolution worked, following far more strict rules than scientists realized. Perhaps the absence of the DNA molecule meant the absence of life. She reminded herself this was the only alien life they had ever encountered. It seemed like a huge coincidence, but perhaps that was all it was.

Part of the problem was the Fahr spoke rarely. They kept to themselves, only interacting when it was necessary. Thryke, him-self—and Honi was sure he was male—did not appear to think in words. Sometimes Honi would mentally rehearse things before she spoke to others, especially if it was something important. But Thryke did not do this, or if he did, the archives were not recording this. This only gave Honi the emotional and not the intellectual content of what he was thinking unless he expressed this to others. Even when he did this, what the archive recorded favored his emotional state and many of the words were lost.

There were two other major problems. The first had to do with what, to Honi, seemed a compression of time. The mechanism for storing memories was selective, only choosing to store that which was significant. Most everyday life activities amongst the Fahr had little or no real significance and so were not recorded. This made it harder to get a handle on how the Fahr lived their lives. When she thought about it, Honi realized she did the same thing. Repetitive activities were not remembered, like how she got to and from the lab, brushed her teeth, or what she had for breakfast each day. These things she did so often they were more of a pattern than an active memory. She suspected the same thing was going on in Thryke's memory, the device's algorithm ignored the mundane.

Then there were the blackouts. Thryke would disappear for periods of time, only to reappear later, much more energized. Again, the archive did not record this detail, but Honi knew they were of significant length because of the changes she observed in the ship's coral. The animals laid down their reefs at slow predictable rates, and when the reefs jumped in size, Honi knew a lot of time had passed. She traced back the genesis of these blackouts and realized Thryke was entering a regeneration process. This was the stuff of science fiction that extended space voyages could only be undertak-en if the astronauts were put into hibernation. However, this seemed different in the sense that there was a restorative element. Thryke, before the hibernation, was older and less energetic. After-wards he was restored and had youthful energy, but intellectually, he was the same fahr. Honi realized this process might be the source of his extended lifespan.

She wondered at the length of these blackouts. An incredible amount of data made up Thryke's sixty-seventh occupation. She could fast forward and rewind through this quickly, but the sheer size made anything more than random sampling impossible. Thryke, when he was alive, knew where to go in this archive because he had lived it. Honi could do little more than taste his memories, and when she did, she had no idea whether the memory would contain anything important. To gain targeted access to important memories, she would have to allow more of Thryke into her own mind. She would need that element of his psyche that purposefully went to more important memories.

"This might not work because Thryke is dead, and that would be an intentional act on his part," Dr. Chopra told her.

"It seems to accept my intentions," Honi pointed out. "But it was not my experiences that laid down these memories, that gave them structure. It's like I'm missing the map. I'm wandering around a countryside not knowing where I am or where I should go. I need a map."

"You're talking about a huge risk here. We know nothing of the Fahr mind, nothing of their consciousness. If they can store memories digitally and more importantly transfer those memories in and out of a biological brain, who's to say they can't do the same thing with consciousness. You could be inviting him to take over."

"He's dead," Honi said. "There is no intent. His biological mind is nothing but a fine powder of basic organic chemicals. During my time of connection, I've yet to experience anything that would even hint at another consciousness. In that respect, it's much like my relationship with the backpack. What we're dealing with here is data storage, but the road map is Thryke's intention, an intention that no longer exists. To this point I've allowed so little of him into my head that I have no understanding of his motivations. I think I'll need that understanding before I can more purposefully explore his memories."

"You feel you can do this safely?" Chopra asked.

"I'll be in control, of that I am certain."

I am floating, suspended in another creature's mind. So alien... And it is accessing my PDM. Roaming randomly through my memories. And there is enough of me now that I can feel those ancient memories. It is a violation. But I can do nothing. Nothing.

Intent. Well, at least Honi now understood why Thryke had been so angry. His military ambitions had been thwarted by the Fahr leadership. Just allowing a little more of him into her own head clarified much, and with it came a greater understanding of the Fahr language. Understanding the intent of what he had to say clarified the meanings of the words. And she now knew Thryke was, as she suspected, ancient. The sixty-seventh occupation itself lasted about one thousand years, and if the other occupations were of similar length, his personal lifespan at the time of death was close to 67,000 years.

This was a god, but not the wise all-knowing benevolent Christian god her great uncle, Mikala, had told her about. This was a god of war, an entity intent on destruction. But it was also a god that had every foible known to man, including lust. It was not clear to Honi what Thryke was lusting after, but he seemed desperate to control it, to rise above it. Honi now understood something of what drove Thryke's life, his motivation, his intent. But this was archived intent, memories of intent. Thryke was dead and so intent on his part did not exist. Honi could still only sample his memories, the difference being she now understood much more of what she was sampling. For now, she would work on vocabulary and understanding the Fahr writing system. Afterwards, they would design a search engine specific to this device.

Search Engine

Diane McLean sat before Honi, rubbing each of her fingers and then repeating the action between sips of the concoction that had long since taken the place of coffee. Honi recognized these actions as withdrawal symptoms. The head of NASA's Goldstone facility had addiction issues.

"Tobacco?" she guessed.

Diane nodded. "They hooked me about ten years before all that stuff hit the press about the tobacco companies spiking their products with extra nicotine. You'd think someone with a PhD would have the intelligence to recognize what was being done to her and quit. But it's a think drug, you know, and I work better with that stuff in my system. That's a rationalization, but it's what chemical dependence does to you. So, I've never tried to quit." She shrugged. "Now they're forcing the issue. You can't smoke what you can't get, and they're not supplying the stuff anymore. So, now you and everyone else gets to watch me go through this." She gritted her teeth and sat on her hands. "Anyway, this is my problem, but I thought you should know I'm not normally stressed out like this."

Honi nodded. "I get a visit from the person who discovered the Fahr. What's not to like?"

"Is that how I'm being talked about?" Diane asked. "It was more of a group effort, but I am the head of Goldstone, so I suppose I get the attention."

"You made some shrewd deductions."

"Again, a group effort, but thanks for saying so."

"So, why have you come to see me?"

Diane looked at Honi. "I have some thoughts around the premise of your search engine design. It occurred to me that you may be looking for the wrong thing."

"How's that?"

Diane allowed her fingers to become unfettered. This time they drummed on the tabletop. "Your work at gaining knowledge of the Fahr language is admirable, even astonishing. But, as you yourself have admitted, far from comprehensive. I have no doubt that someone with your enhanced abilities is the best person for this job. My understanding is that you're dealing with an archive of recorded memories that stretch over a thousand years. Is that correct?"

"Yes."

"And the plan is to search for an explanation of why they attacked us?"

"Yes."

"And are your sure you now have that vocabulary, that you know all the words you'll need for the search?"

Honi pursed her lips. "No, of course not, but we're going on the assumption we'll recognize more keywords as we search."

"I think there may be a more efficient way of doing that," Diane said.

"How?"

Diane stopped drumming and laid her hands flat on the tabletop. "We have good reason to suspect they have been monitoring radio and digital signals from the Earth for some time before their arrival. It's clear they had an advanced knowledge of our communication and electronic infrastructure, and they had understood enough of our languages to communicate with us. It seems that the key to understanding why they attacked may be to search for the creature's memories of the English language. We don't know the degree to which this individual fahr was involved in the translation process, but if we could find examples of Fahr translations from English broadcasts, those may be your Rosetta Stone. I'm guessing that finding English words will be a lot easier for two reasons. First, in a one thousand yearlong archive, it's likely that English words will only occur toward the end of it. That reduces the search area. Secondly, they will focus on translation in the areas where they have the most interest. This should tell us why they came."

"Have you ever tried to speak to someone underwater?" Honi asked with a grin. "That's the initial problem with that idea. English is a language spoken in atmospheric conditions. We would have to create a search engine to look for what English words sound like in an aquatic environment, so at least as far as verbal communication is concerned, that will be a tricky exercise. However, I take your point for written or visual communication. That should be easier, and it will also allow us to further restrict the search area. The earliest examples of wireless communication on the planet were forms of Morse Code, and later broadcasts of the human voice and music. It wasn't until television and digital communication that the broadcast of images and text became commonplace. And, of course, ninety-five percent of digital communication would have occurred in the twenty years before the attack, when almost anything was on line."

"I wouldn't focus on the final fifteen to twenty years of the alien's life," Diane said. "By then, they may know English well enough as to not need translation. You might not find the Rosetta Stone."

"When Thryke speaks in his memories, I may not know the meanings of his words, but I do feel his intention," Honi said. "The same is true of his comprehension. I feel his understanding. It gives me an emotional context from which to work. So, if he reads something in English, and I can see the English, I should be able to figure out his understanding of it. The irony of this is that with straight translation one often misses the nuances intended. But if you're coming at this with an understanding of the emotional intention first, it makes the literal meanings of the words less important. I know that seems odd, but to this point I've found it to be true."

Diane had stopped fidgeting and now had her attention on Honi's computer backpack. She sighed. "It's strange looking at what humanity may become. I imagine this is somewhat isolating. Is it?"

"I frighten some people," Honi said. "Maybe even most people. I don't think I've given them reason to fear me, but they do anyway. I should stop zooming around on my susboard the way that I do, but it's such an adrenaline rush. When you've spent much of your life strapped into a wheelchair, it's hard to explain just how amazing that feels. Here's the thing—I have this ability to connect, interact with, and control digital technology. This amplifies me, it makes me more than I was. I'm not sure that qualifies as evolution, but because I'm the first, and at present the only person able to do this, it seems significant. The real test is whether Dr. Howard can find the genetic components to this ability. If he can, then this may be a huge step forward for humanity. If not, then I'm just this one-off, an individual with extraordinary abilities. That is the current situation, and yes, it is isolating."

"And how old are you?" Diane asked

"I'm seventeen, still an adolescent. You try to tell yourself this, that despite all the advantages you have, you're still not mature. You know this intellectually—that you will not be mature until you're in your mid-twenties—but my abilities give me the illusion of maturity. It's an issue, especially when I'm dealing with people not at their intellectual peak. It feels, sometimes, like I'm dealing with children, but I'm barely out of that category myself. So, I often catch myself with this attitude of condescension. It's tricky to navigate, because there's this other part of me that just wants to be liked, even loved, that just wants to fit in. And I see so few people my own age, everyone around me has at least a master's degree." Honi stopped, aware that she may have shared too much.

"I find you charming," Diane said. "And I'm not frightened. You're allowed to take the time you need to mature, you know? It's not something you can push. And you have an intellectual understanding of your own maturation process. Most teenagers don't. Come talk to me anytime."

English

Linguists prepared the English texts in advance. Donaldson then gathered a group of grad students and other individuals to help with the recording. There were eight, seven that Honi recognized and one she did not.

"Who's that?" Honi asked Donaldson, pointing to the dark-haired young man.

"Charlie Dayaang," Donaldson said. "He was part of the Canadian escort for the device. You've already met Cynthia Chen. Charlie was her colleague. The deal with the Canadian Prime Minister was we were to include him on the team, something to do with his being involved in the original discovery of the alien. It's been a challenge, since he lacks formal training in the disciplines we need. A bright kid though and seems eager to learn. So, we've been teaching him basic lab procedures, using him as a gofer, anything we can think of to keep him busy. He's not much older than you, the only other teenager in the facility."

And seriously hot! thought Honi and then corrected herself. *That is not going to happen!* But she couldn't help staring at him.

In the early days of the project, Donaldson had set up a special manufacturing unit specifically to create a technology for the projects they were doing. SMU was what everyone called it, and SMU's latest task was the creation of something akin to a hydrophone. This would be a device that recorded sound in water. The team had made eight, and the devices looked like garden hoses except with wires running out of the back end, and a waterproof mesh at the front end. Each of these now had those front ends immersed in water. The water was in eight sinks, the kind used for washing hair in beauty shops.

Donaldson turned his attention to Charlie and the grad students.

"Here's how this will work," he said to them. "Each of you has been given specific texts we want spoken underwater. For the benefit of those who don't know what we're trying to do here, we will record how the English language sounds in an aquatic environment. Then Honi will use the captured sounds to search the Fahr database. Since the Fahr are an aquatic species, we believe this is how they would've heard the English language. The texts you have been given include the words we're most interested in."

"Don't you need air, in the first place, to produce these sounds?" Charlie asked.

Honi smiled. "You're allowed to breathe before you dunk your head," she said.

"I understand that," Charlie said. "But if you exhale as you speak, you will also create bubbles. And bubbles make noise. On the Fahr ship, however, they will have intercepted the English broadcasts without this extra noise. Those broadcasts wouldn't have been created in a hair washing sink."

Everyone laughed and Honi smiled. "We anticipated that problem," she said. "We will also have you blow bubbles into the water and record that too. Then we'll use noise-canceling software to filter out the bubble sounds from the English words before we do the search."

"Ah," Charlie said and immersed his head in the sink. He blew a long stream of bubbles complete with an oohing sound.

Everyone laughed again.

"Great," Honi said with a grin. "But perhaps you should've waited until we turned the microphone on?"

"Trial run," Charlie said returning the grin.

When the session was over, Honi hovered over to Charlie. He was busy towel drying his hair.

"I don't think we've met," she said, extending her hand.

Charlie waved his hand in the air in front of her. "It's wet at the moment," he said.

"I can wait," Honi said.

He wiped his hand again on the towel. "That should do it," he said extending it.

Honi shook the cold and slightly damp hand.

"Charlie Dayaang," he said.

"Honi Kalawai'a," she said.

"Good solid aboriginal names."

Honi studied him. She wasn't exposed to a lot of continental aboriginal faces in Hawaii. She felt embarrassed for thinking he was Caucasian. "Where are you from?" she asked.

"Haida Gwaii," he said. "It's a big island off Canada's west coast."

"Where they found the alien?"

"Yes. That's kind of why I'm here. It was found on our ancestral lands, and I was one of the first people to see it. And I'm also here, I suppose, as a representative of the Haida First Nation. Though, I'm not sure I'm the best pick for that honor. It's just circumstance, I suppose. And luck. I wanted to get off the island, and this was a good way of doing that. And our current Prime Minister, unlike most of his predecessors, is trying to be more inclusive of First Nations people. Anyway, here I am."

"I've never thought of myself as aboriginal, just native Hawaiian."

"So, here we are, two native kids a long way from where we belong."

Honi said nothing for a moment. "Do we?"

"Do we what?"

"Belong?"

Charlie studied her. "I guess that depends on how you feel about things," he said. "I wanted to get away, so maybe that says something. I don't know. I spent a long time wanting to be something other than Haida. It wasn't so much a rejection of my culture but the restriction I didn't like. I wanted to join the great diversity of ordinary Canadians. But then the alien attack happened, and I realized that what I really wanted was just to be part of humanity, an even bigger tribe than Canadians. So, it wasn't about just being an ordinary Canadian anymore." He shrugged.

"So, you signed the non-disclosure agreement?" Honi asked.

"I'm here aren't I?"

"And you're not concerned about...?"

"The creation of a new human species? I like the idea, in principle, but I also think that's not something I'm likely to see in my lifetime. But, hey, look what they've done with you. That's pretty special."

"Want to do lunch?"

Charlie gestured to her susboard. "Can two people get on that thing?"

"I don't know. I've never tried it with a passenger."

It took several attempts, with a lot of laughter as Charlie kept falling off, but eventually they got the hang of it. Honi took the longest route to the cafeteria, just to keep the warmth of Charlie's body pressed against her.

Gloves

"Do you wear gloves all the time?" Charlie asked.

Honi looked down at her hands and realized anyone who had not known her from before the susboard would never have seen her unconnected to it. "Only when I need mobility or when I need to be connected to the AI." She shrugged. "Which is pretty much all the time when outside of my room."

"So, it's become part of you?"

Honi bit her lower lip. She read the concern on his face. He wanted to get beyond the technology and was even a little turned off by it. *God, I'm not supposed to see that,* she thought. "If I take them off, I lose my mobility and my connection," she said.

"Then what?"

She laughed. "I fall asleep. These days the only time I'm not connected is when I'm in bed."

"Bed?"

Honi blushed. "Sleeping," she said.

"So, if I wanted to take these off of you, we'd need a bed close by?"

"Yeah, I guess we would..."

Mentor

Honi listened again to Thryke's occupations. She'd been so focused on the final occupation she had almost forgotten about the others. By now she had gained enough of the Fahr language she could identify most of them. One stood out. She went to Dr. Howard.

He stared at her in amazement. "He was a genetic engineer? I thought you told me most of his occupations were military?"

"I can only understand about seventy percent of the list, but of that seventy percent almost all of them are military. His time spent working in genetics is one of the few exceptions, and it was his tenth occupation, so early in his life. Genetic engineer is not a literal translation of this occupation's title. In the Fahr language the terminology is more like 'life builder'. When I searched for the terminology in other contexts within Thryke's most recent occupation, I discovered the word was most often used, not to refer to genetic repair or therapy, but to the creation of new genomes, animals, and plants by changing naturally evolved genomes to fit certain niches in the Fahr ecosystem. What's more, there also appears to be a level of disrepute in this occupation in the sense it is often in conflict with Fahr religious beliefs. I think this may be like the way genetic engineering is viewed by certain conservative religious groups on the Earth. The idea that what God has made should not be changed. Anyway, I thought you'd like to know Thryke once held such an occupation."

"And you can access this?"

Thryke was beginning to understand what had happened. He had died, and the Homines had found his body and his PDM. And one of them had the ability to interface with it. But each time it did, it had to pull a little more of him, of Thryke, into itself. And he was growing stronger.

"Yes, I can access it, but I'm not sure how helpful that will be. One thing I've learned by exploring Thryke's final occupation is the degree to which I understand what's going on highly depends on my knowledge of the subject beforehand. Having no military back-ground meant I didn't have the English words for many of the Fahr equivalents. So, even when I gained an understanding of what Thryke was thinking or experiencing, I didn't know how to explain or translate it into English. You can see the problem. I can access his memories of being a genetic engineer, but how much will I under-stand without more in-depth knowledge on this side?"

"You're pretty knowledgeable for someone your age. Didn't you tell me you used to read academic papers about whale evolution including discussions of the genetics involved?"

"I skimmed over that stuff, got the general idea and then moved on. So yes, I understand genetics better than the average per-son my age, but if we assume the Fahr have a more advanced under-standing of this field than we do, then it will take someone of your level of understanding to interact with it. So, we have one of two op-tions here. Either we figure out a way of getting you connected to Thryke's stored memories, or I must be much better educated. How far have you come in your research into the genetics of my ability?"

Dr. Howard frowned. "The President has asked that we focus on finding the genes that give rise to human tribalism. To be honest, that's been a pretty frustrating exercise. There could be as many as several hundred different genes and gene combinations involved.

This is a behavior that evolved over millions of years, in fits and starts, so piecing together the elements of it will take a long time. And if we succeed and can build a better beast, that will also take time with lot more trial and error involved. The new less tribal form of humanity is hundreds of years down the road, perhaps even thousands."

Honi nodded. "I'm going to ask you a question, but before you answer I want to remind you, in my advanced state, I can detect deception or discomfort on your part. Perhaps you should consult with Dr. Donaldson before you answer. The quickest way of overcoming this knowledge barrier may be for you to train me in genetics. In Donaldson's case, he did not understand how quickly, in my enhanced state, I could gain a comprehensive knowledge of his field. Neither did I for that matter, but we all know how that turned out. I can read it in his face how intimidated he is. He even felt obligated to suggest that MIT grant me an honorary PhD, and now he functions as an adviser to me in anything to do with computer and component design and manufacture. I don't care about the degree, except having it gives me a bit more authority to do what I do. Most lab coats don't like being directed by someone my age. And I am aware I'm still an adolescent and have all those annoying hormones raging through my system. So, no matter what happens, I will still need an advisor. The question is how comfortable would you feel in that role?"

Dr. Howard shook his head. "You're intimidating to all of us, not just Dr. Donaldson. Academics has always been a strange amalgam of cooperation and competition, but the competition aspect assumes a level playing field. We cannot compete with you, that much is clear. If we want to accomplish our goals each of us must be prepared to take a lesser role. I would be happy to mentor you in all things genetic."

There was nothing duplicitous in Howard's response. Still Honi felt annoyed for even having to ask the question. "It's lonely," she said.

Howard said nothing, but she saw empathy.

"If I'm right," she said, "Thryke was a geneticist for about a thousand years. That's about twenty times longer than humanity has even known about genetics at the molecular level, and its likely genetics was already a well-established field when Thryke took up that occupation. If you can get me up to snuff on this, we may gain the knowledge we need to make a lot of changes, including what makes me tick on the genetic level and the whole tribalism question."

Most of Dr. Howard's research still existed in digital form thanks to his lab's habit of burning data DVD's at the end of each working day. At John Hopkins, Howard had mainly been involved in research, and toward the end of his tenure, this had been his exclusive preoccupation. However, earlier in his academic life he'd taught introductory courses in genetics, which were also on DVD. Enhanced, Honi got through these sources in three days. Now fortified with a knowledge of vocabulary and procedures, she plowed through all the literature and Howard's existing research in less than three months.

Ears

Charlie Dayaang was on board at the request of the Canadian Government, a political appointment or so they had been led to believe. From what Howard had heard, Canadian Prime Minister O'Malley was not comfortable with what Alatorre wanted to do. But he had, nevertheless, freed up Canadian scientists to join in the research if they chose. So, where were they? Only Cynthia Chen and Charlie Dayaang were here, and they came bearing the device. No other Canadian scientist had arrived and Dayaang was not a scientist. What he was, however, was remarkable. Now Howard had been asked to see if there was a genetic component for what he could do.

"I understand you're capable of eavesdropping on conversations as far as one hundred yards away?" Howard asked.

Charlie blushed. "It's not intentional, and it's also hard to explain. I've had normal hearing for most of my life, but I was making adjustments to some electrical equipment just before the aliens attacked. There was a surge just before the brown out, and I got this tingling sensation. At first it was kind of freaky because I became aware of sounds that I hadn't heard before, and much of it was unfamiliar. Insects, for instance, make all kinds of quiet noises, and if you haven't heard them previously, you're not sure what you're listening to. Various rodents and birds, I was hearing the quieter sounds they make when they moved around. As things progressed, I began hearing their breathing and even freakier, I got to where I could hear their hearts pumping. And the larger the animal, the louder those noises are. I can hear dogs and cats from much further away than insects and mice, maybe three times as far away. And people are the loudest of all. If I'm in the same room as another person, even a large room like a banquet hall, I can hear their hearts pumping, their breathing, and anything they say, even in the quietest of voices. It's not like I can turn it off—it's just there. There's a lot of stuff I'm not intended to hear. Private stuff, but I hear it anyway." He grinned sheepishly. "I always know who farted."

"What else can you hear?"

"When I'm around electrical equipment I can hear humming and buzzing, and depending on what's going on in the system, sometimes crackling and popping."

"And this started when the aliens attacked?"

"Yes. And it's hard to limit it."

"What do you mean, 'hard to limit it'?"

"Well, I've also got really good eyesight, but that's not remarkable because so does almost everyone else. One thing about being human is that most people can see well. But as a little kid you learn to focus your attention on specific things while ignoring the other things you're seeing. You go into the kitchen to get a glass of water and you ignore the tabletop, even though you can see it because it's not important to what you're doing. But when you're a tiny little kid being carried around by your mother, you're looking at everything with equal curiosity because it's all new and amazing. You learn what's important later and how to focus and tune out what isn't. That's kind of where I am, at the moment, with sound. There're all these amazing new things that I can hear, and I'm trying to put the filters in place. But some things are easier to ignore than others. I can tune out electrical white noise or insect sounds, but it's harder to do that when people are talking. There's a kind of voyeurism involved because you can hear things and gain knowledge that you're not supposed to have, that's not intended for you. It's kind of like a superpower that gives you an advantage over other people."

"So, you can hear everything I say, even if it's not intended for you?"

"Not just you, anyone. Sometimes I can even hear voices in the next room or in the hallway if they're close enough to the walls. This place is full of secrets and listening to them is an addiction. I want to tune it out, but it's really hard to do."

Howard pursed his lips. "And do you communicate anything you learn with those outside this complex?"

Charlie looked at him. "Of course not. I signed the same piece of paper that you did."

"Not even to your own Prime Minster?"

Charlie stared at Howard. "I thought I was coming here to give a cheek swab or a blood sample or something like that?"

Howard gave a thin smile. "Yes, of course, that is why you're here."

Ecstasy

"Thryke did not learn English," Honi said. "I'm sure of it."

Donaldson studied her for a moment before replying. "How do you know?"

260

"The few times when English language broadcasts appear in his memories are accompanied either by impatience or dismissiveness. He refers to us by a terminology that's roughly translated as 'small two-legged creature', and when he says it, there's a fair amount of contempt attached to it. But here's the other thing—he often argued with another fahr who has a more positive view of us. I'm getting the impression that whoever this other fahr is, Thryke seems to regard her—and I'm sure this other fahr is female—as his principle nemesis. It's a pity we don't have her memories because I'm getting the impression she understands English. At least she seems to be a lot less dismissive of us than he is, almost protective I'd say, but it's hard to tell because his attitude is so negative that any other fahr might seem positive in comparison."

Donaldson thought about this for a moment. "Maybe this is the fahr who sent us that mysterious Pioneer 10 frequency message just before the attack."

Honi pursed her lips. "It's possible, I suppose, but it's one of those things we'll probably never know. If she sent it, then it's likely she did so without Thryke's knowledge. And if so, it won't be anywhere in his memories. Anyway, the other thing I think I've figured out is why they came. I remember the President saying something about whales that she felt they may have come to collect them. The last time the Fahr ship was seen was off the northwestern coast of Canada, hovering over a spot where humpback whales feed. Anyway, during their conversations, I've often heard the Fahr refer to something they called the Singers. For a while I was confused by this, but then I saw a few intercepted broadcasts they were paying a lot of attention to. These broadcasts featured humpback whales, and they referred to them as the Singers."

"To humpbacks specifically?"

"I think so, yes. At least I never saw specific interest in other species of whale. They think humpbacks are valuable."

"Why?"

"It has something to do with the songs that humpbacks sing. Why else would they refer to them as the Singers? And the emphasis is interesting. When they refer to them, it's almost like they're giving

261

them a title. Like a president, an emperor, a king or a queen. There's an inherent respect in how they say it. It's hard to explain, but I can feel that respect. This is a special animal to them."

Donaldson shook his head. "Humpback whales? They embark on an interstellar journey that, presumably would take hundreds if not thousands of years, and they do this to collect whales?"

"We don't know they specifically came here to collect these whales. Maybe they discovered them after they got here."

Donaldson shook his head again. "No. I disagree. I do think they came here specifically to get those whales, and this reason I think this is the way they first communicated with us. It was that David Crosby/Graham Nash song, remember? You can hear whale song in the background of that recording. It might even be hump-back whale song—I don't know, but it arrived ten years before they revealed themselves orbiting Jupiter. We may be wrong in our as-sumption that that initial message came on that frequency because of the Fahr encountering that mission, but it fits. So does the specu-lation they took ten years to get from the Kuiper Belt to Jupiter. If we assume the choice of that song was intentional, then it means they came for the whales. Their ship was half a light year away at that point. And from that distance, even with the best detection de-vices, it's unlikely they could have heard whales singing in our oceans. They must have known about them in advance."

Honi thought about this. "There's only one way they could've known about the humpbacks existence. They've been here before."

"Use the search engine to search that entire archive for that word. Search for singer and see if that word with that specific em-phasis shows up much earlier on the time line. If it does, then we'll know they knew of the existence about humpback whales much earlier."

Thryke was starting to understand the intentions of the mind he was within. Such a primitive thing. So far, all he'd been able to do was observe its random explorations of his PDM. But this mind was getting more systematic and now it wanted to know when he had first become aware of The Song. This should be interesting. A non-fahr brain would not have the built-in filters that prevented arousal from memories.

It did show up earlier, about 300 years earlier if Honi's sense of the way time unfolded in the device was correct. Thryke and his fahr acquaintances had been referring to the humpback whale as the Singer for about that length of time, but before that, the term was not used. When had Thryke first used the term she wondered? She searched in the archive to see if she could pinpoint his earliest usage.

Thryke was at a social gathering. Honi could not make much sense of what was going on, but she knew Thryke was in the presence of important fahr. And she also sensed a high level of anticipation in the group. At some point, one of the fahr used the term "the Singer", and when he did, Honi felt an instant jolt of enthusiasm in the crowd. Thryke was wary and did not share in the enthusiasm, at least not to the same degree.

What happened next was chaotic, and for the first time since Honi had interfaced with the device, she felt out of control. It began with an increased heart rate, both in Thryke and herself. She knew he was experiencing something so extreme that she couldn't pull back from it. It gathered her in now as it had gathered him in then. She was suddenly and intensely aroused, wet, and she could not turn this off or control it. What's more, she didn't want to. The pleasure was such a rush that she allowed it to carry her wherever it wanted to take her. There was another component to this, and even with her enhanced mind, she was plunged into a state of extreme intoxication. And she could no more control this than she could control her arousal, and just like the arousal, she wanted to abandon herself to it. Never in her life had she felt this good. Soon all conscious thought was gone, replaced by rippling bands of intense pleasure.

When she came to, they were patting her down with wet towels. She had the worst headache she'd ever experienced. She groaned. "Advil! Tylenol! Aspirin! Something! Anything!" she rasped and then blacked out again.

Several hours later she found herself in a hospital bed. Dr. Chopra was standing over her, holding a glass of juice. Honi gratefully took it.

"We thought we would lose you," Chopra said.

Honi finished the juice and held the glass out to Chopra. "Can I have more, please?"

"Yes, of course," she said, handing the glass to a nurse.

"Dr. Donaldson said you were having a seizure," she said.

"Was I? That's not how I remember it."

"What do you remember?"

"Whale song," Honi said. "It does something extreme to them, sexual arousal and a deep intoxication rolled into one. It's the most vivid memory I've yet encountered, and I could not escape it. It did to me in the present what it did to him in the past."

"And what was that?"

Honi blushed. "I was wet, very wet down there."

"What happened?"

Honi explained the experience to the best of her ability. Chopra listened. "Now I'm afraid to interface with it again. I'm worried that if I do, I'll just seek this out. You have no idea how good that felt. Even now, in this weakened state, I want it. I've always wondered what addiction would feel like and now I know. And that's with only one experience. One time and I'm hooked. What does that say to you?"

"Depends on the individual. Heroin, Crystal meth, crack cocaine, fentanyl—even tobacco—but it usually takes more than one instance to create a true addiction. That doesn't mean you won't crave it though, but it won't be a true addiction in the sense of bodily need. You've had a traumatic experience, but you don't seem to be going through withdrawal."

"There was a room full of them, important fahr, and they were all waiting for the Song. I think that's the key here. Humpback whale song, for whatever reason, is acting like an addictive drug to the Fahr. These aliens are—in effect—traffickers, and they've just found the ultimate drug. Depending on how things are done in their society, these animals might have an extremely high value, so much so that they were willing to destroy another sapient species to get it."

"Could you see the impairment coming? Was there an indication that this was about to happen?"

"No, but then I didn't know what to expect in that situation. I'm exploring his memory, but I still don't understand most of what I'm seeing. That's what's scary here. If I knew what to avoid, I could do that. But I had no idea this was about to happen—I'm not sure what triggered it."

"But you were searching for the earliest instance of that word combination, correct?"

"The Singer, yes."

"Then I would start by avoiding that word. We now know what it means, so try to stay away from it."

"I'm worried that I might go there intentionally."

"You won't. You don't have a physical addiction, so going there will be an emotional or intellectual decision. You're stronger than that, Honi. You know you are."

A timid knock on the door. The nurse entered first carrying the requested glass of juice and then Charlie came in, complete with a bouquet.

"Heard you weren't doing well," he said with a grin.

Honi nodded to Dr. Chopra, who nodded back and left the room. Honi took the glass of juice from the nurse and she too left.

Charlie handed her the bouquet.

"You might be the cure," she said to him.

"For what?"

"For that which ails me," she said, patting the bed beside her.

Life Building

The new Cowichan hugged Honi, flexing with her as she moved. At her direction, SMU had manufactured thirty-two terabyte flexible quant drives one-quarter the size of a postage stamp. These were woven together into what the untrained eye would see as a simple cardigan, a sweater with a 163,840-terabyte storage capacity made more efficient by a new thousand-to-one compression algorithm. The Cowichan design was Charlie's idea, borrowed from the neighboring Salish First Nation on Canada's west coast. Still the Cowichan's capacity was minuscule compared to Thryke's personal memory database, a problem Honi hoped to address once they had mined more information from the device. At least now they could deal with more than one searchable occupation at a time. The target, however, remained Thryke's time as a genetic engineer, or as the fahr put it, a life builder.

The other feature of the Cowichan was a massive increase in computation speed, and this was also now at Honi's disposal. She had maximized what a digital computer could do with the current technology, at least one that she could wear. In a matter of three months, and while wearing the sweater, Honi achieved a PhD level understanding of genetics. She now felt ready to tackle Thryke's eleventh occupation.

"I need Dr. Howard now," she said to Donaldson.

Donaldson nodded. "I'm sure you understand you're still an adolescent. The human part of your capacity still has not matured."

"I'll have Dr. Howard."

"Yes, you will."

Honi could tell Donaldson had misgivings about Howard, and she could also tell that there was racism present. Not conscious, but it was there nonetheless. Learned? Environmental? That might account for his relative indifference toward her; there had been no native Hawaiians in his environment. "Can I give you a project?" she asked him.

"I'm listening."

"The biggest limitation we have now is the nature of what we're studying. The mind—ours or theirs—is selective in what it remembers. We need to develop a predictive and interpretive algorithm that will help us fill in the blanks. I'm not even sure at this moment what that would look like, but I have every confidence that you and your staff are more than capable of coming up with the solution."

Donaldson looked at Honi. "You're the only one who can access that data, and when you do your experience is subjective. This is not something we can do without your involvement."

"You're the AI expert. Figure out a way."

Donaldson said nothing for a moment, pursed his lips, and extended his hand. "I'll do my best," he said.

Honi nodded, and the Professor turned and left. The last thing she read on his face was irritation, approaching anger. He didn't like being pushed by her, but she needed more out of him.

Charlie was now the fourth member of Honi's team. He tuned in to the whisperings of her body, and to the interactions between her and the Cowichan and Thryke's memories. Charlie heard everything and could distinguish between those sounds showing normal operating parameters and others which pointed to something being amiss. This was particularly true of Honi's physical body. He was like an early warning system when she was trying to take on too much.

"Are you ready for this?" Charlie asked her.

"I couldn't be readier," she said. It had now been several months since her last interaction with Thryke's memories, the one that nearly killed her. Out of curiosity she had found recordings of humpback song and listened to them, wondering if her experience interacting with Thryke's memories would have left residual emotional scars. What she experienced instead was sadness at the loss of

Kale. Her older cousin had never been found and was presumed lost, in the same way many people had disappeared on that day.

"You're a bit noisy," Charlie said to her, his way of saying her heart rate was up.

"This is a big day. Were you expecting me not to be excited?"

"It's my job to watch over you."

Honi smiled at him. As much as possible, when they were together, she did not wear the Cowichan. Without it she was primal, ordinary, tactile. It was easier to be together. With it there was another deeper layer of analysis that she couldn't shut off. It reduced him to less than what he was. She saw flaws, indecision, everything he was feeling. This was stuff she was never intended to know. The same thing she wanted no one else to know about her. Taking the Cowichan off was the only way to be fair, the only way to be with him. Without it was like being in an intellectual fog as if she were drunk. But her body came alive when she did.

Dr. Howard tolerated Charlie, that was the best one could say about it. He was better than most at keeping a neutral expression— at being professional—but she could still see the distrust. This annoyed her, but there was nothing to be gained by making it an issue. People felt what they felt, and in all other ways he was perfectly fine to work with.

She smiled at him. "This will take about forty-five minutes," she said, holding her arm out to the tendrils. When she heard the choices, she picked the life builder occupation, and guided its download into the Cowichan, while a little more of Thryke took residence in her head.

She had survived, and she was back, allowing just a bit more of him in. Still not enough. And she appeared to be recovered from what she'd gone through. She had no ballow through which he could express his displeasure. But each time she connected, she added to him. Patience had long been a Fahr virtue when he cared to practice it, which wasn't often. Now he had no choice.

Thryke was now a much younger fahr though physically he seemed the same. The anger Honi felt in his final occupation had not yet developed. Instead she found an adolescent cockiness, a much more familiar state to inhabit. And yet when Thryke had laid down these memories, he was more than 10,000 years old. Everything is relative, she decided, even with gods.

The environment in this new occupation alternated between four locations: the first could be described as a laboratory, the second as living accommodations, the third a strange aquatic city, and the fourth an open ocean that extended infinitely in every direction.

The laboratory lacked the sterility of facilities on the Earth. Just like on the ship, marine animals and plants seemed free to come and go. What marked it as a laboratory was the general attitude of the fahr within it, the presence of containment tanks, their equivalent of digital readouts on the walls, and a variety of tools. Most of these were unidentifiable, either neatly hanging on walls or kept in bins. There were larger objects that looked like powered machines, but again, nothing familiar. Except each of these large objects seemed to have a flat surface that displayed characters of a written language projected as holographic images into the space in front of them.

Honi searched the archive from its beginning, knowing that the younger Thryke would have to go through a period of training in his new occupation. She could now speed up and slowdown the playback of the archive. When it appeared that Thryke was receiving instruction, she slowed it down and listened to the conversation. It frustrated her that these conversations were rarely complete. The archiving system was a copy of Thryke's memories, and there were long stretches of these conversations he had forgotten or that the algorithm had ignored. Gradually and with repeated exposure she began to understand.

The Fahr had a large genetic database they continually added to. When Thryke held down this occupation, some 50,000 years ago, the database included not only the genomes of every life form they had encountered to that point, but also each individual gene found within them. There were billions of these and each of them behaved

269

differently depending on the genome, relying on the location within it and in specific combinations with other activated genes. Most of the time these genes seemed to do nothing more than hold down places in the respective genomes or act as switches turning other genes or gene sequences on or off, depending on the species. But even if a gene in a specific genome seemed to serve no purpose, it was often still included, a kind of stasis where it could be awakened by environmental stresses on the species. The database was complete in the sense that every possible action of each gene and its various combinations was known and recorded, including how each would manifest in every known context. The Fahr, over a billion years, had mapped and recorded the behavior of every gene known to exist up to that point. This was fifty thousand years ago, however, and so would not include genes and gene activity specific to Earth.

"Is there a way we can get access to that genetic database?" Howard asked.

"It's a memory," Honi said.

"Meaning?"

"Meaning that we can't access the database. It doesn't physically exist. What we have is Thryke's memory of his interactions with it. But it's amazing to think that something like this existed, and that they were using it to construct new species genomes."

"Were they?"

"Were they what?"

"Constructing new species genomes?"

Honi thought about this. "They were new in the sense that that combination of genes, with those modifications to a specific species, had never existed before, but they were not building genomes from scratch. There's something in their religious beliefs that prohibits that. I'm sensing they have a deep almost religious level respect for the natural evolutionary process. What they appear to be doing in this lab is changing existing species to remove undesirable traits. What's curious is that their primary concern is that the animals—and we're talking animals here—be mute. Most of the genetic engineering that they're doing creates silent animals, animals that communicate by means of visual display rather than by vocalizing. They're trying to eliminate anything in their environment that would create unwanted pitch variations, anything that the Fahr might hear as song. Making the animals mute is the easiest solution."

"That's odd," Howard said. "They go on these long interstellar voyages to collect singers. Yet here they are, changing their genomes so they can't sing."

"They're not changing the animals collected on their interstellar journeys. Thryke is not on the ship during this occupation. He's on their home world. My one experience with song intoxication tells me that while this is an extremely pleasurable experience, it's also one that impairs the listener of the song. Maybe they're trying to keep their population sober by limiting exposure. By that logic only animals that can't vocalize—can't sing—would be welcome in a sober working environment."

Howard nodded. "Makes sense."

"What we know so far is that they have a huge database that includes all the genes known to them, all their various expressions, and that they know how to make specific modifications in the genomes of various animals that changes the way these animals behave. We only have evidence that they're using these modifications to render certain animals mute, but it stands to reason they could make other changes if they wanted to."

The Cowichan had been fitted with HDMI ports that allowed Honi to project the memories onto a screen, but only after she had experienced them. Thryke's memory archive had something that prevented anyone other than the mind linked to the interface from experiencing the memory. Once Honi had accessed the memory, however, she worked out a way for aspects of her experience to be stored on the Cowichan as an MP4 file that could be projected, but this was less than ideal. It meant Dr. Howard was seeing Honi's interpretation of the memory and not the memory itself. The MP4 could not store consciousness or sensory information other than what was visible or audible, and the format also stripped the original emotional content, remembered thought processes, smells, tastes, and tactile sensations. In practice this meant the Doctor Howard was seeing a highly filtered version of the visual and audio aspects of Thryke's memories, a poor substitute for Honi's experience. Still it allowed Howard to experience at least some of what Honi had. This gave them another set of eyes and ears.

***

The MP4 presented Howard with an experience not unlike footage he'd seen from those deep-water subs exploring the Titanic wreck site, except Honi's MP4 files lacked the small drifting particles that always seemed to be part of underwater footage. He suspected that the particles would never have been remembered and therefore were excluded. He soon realized that what he was seeing was what Thryke looked at, what was significant for him. The fahr spent most of this time focused on two machines.

The machines had an organic quality to them, objects one might find in a mangrove swamp or at the bottom of a stagnant jungle pool. Each was coated with organic sludge, a thin layer of micro flora and micro fauna. There were also half-remembered animals, ghostly things that look like they might have been shrimp or crab or tiny fish, creatures that would feed on sludge.

The first machine was the size of a small refrigerator. Its back and sides had the organic sludge, but the part that faced forward was a screen. This didn't display characters and images, rather projecting them holographically into the water in front. The fahr that worked with it made complicated dance-like gestures toward it using their retractable limbs. The machine responded to these gestures verbally or by three dimensional images of what Howard soon recognized were representations of chromosomes and their component parts. Often these parts were highlighted. Howard could see the fahr engaged in conversation, but he could not understand what they were saying.

The second was an odd machine that looked more like the top of a weeping willow tree than anything mechanical or computational. But instead of dangling branches, this machine had strands of something that looked like algae. Behind were flickering lights embedded into the machine's surface. These attracted and repulsed the strands. These were switches, and Howard wondered if they were as organic as they appeared. He took a while to notice four distinct kinds of strands and four different colors given off by the flickering lights. Certain colors accepted compatible strands and rejected incompatible strands. He developed a theory.

The strands and the lights represented cytosine, guanine, adenine, and thymine. This machine was a gene sequencer.

***

Most of Howard's deductions and ideas had already occurred to Honi, but she had missed or failed to notice the different color in the strands and lights. That was the advantage of having two sets of eyes. But if this machine was a gene sequencer, where was the output? Where were the creatures created? She took a renewed interest in the containment tanks, but these items had an indistinct quality that made studying them difficult. Something was in them, but what?

Reverse Engineering

Alatorre found Garneau opening more mail from Canada. "How's it going with the reverse engineering of that spacecraft?"

Garneau looked up and pushed his glasses back up his nose. "Well, it's not a spacecraft. There's nothing about it that shows it would ever have been used outside of atmospheric conditions. It is a curious beast. We now know the Fahr were aquatic. This craft, at least the part of it that contained the pilot, was filled with water. That would've made it heavy. The thing flew like an insect with the aerodynamic capabilities of a bumblebee—a fast bumblebee."

"And there's nothing useful there?"

273

"I wouldn't say that, but if you're looking for technology to aide you in building an interstellar spacecraft, this would not be a good source. And the investigation is in the hands of the Canadians, who as you know, don't share our overall goals." Garneau took a sip of wine. "They're letting us take part, but it landed on their soil, so it's in their hands. It is interesting that they're willing to put the memory database into our hands, but not the alien craft. And they haven't sent anyone to help with our project. I think O'Malley had second thoughts when you told him what we were doing. Anyway, it is what it is. Our people on the ground are telling me that while reverse engineering this thing will give us insights into Fahr technology and lots of other stuff we can use, it's unlikely to be of much use in constructing what you want. Honi still holds the key to that, I'm afraid."

Alatorre grimaced. "We can only push her so hard, and at the moment, she's working with Howard to glean what she can from the creature's genetic engineer occupation."

Garneau set down his wine glass. "Howard should work on what makes her tick. What's holding us back is there's only one of her."

"We don't know that her powers are the result of something genetic. That's just speculation at this point," Alatorre said.

"Wishful thinking, maybe. But we do have a few others who've been enhanced by that same event, so it seems that whatever zapped the planet, zapped them. Random mutation seems far-fetched on one level, but the timing is suspicious. It's either that or they all were attacked by a radioactive spider at the same time. "

Alatorre grinned at him. "The Fahr have the tools to build almost any lifeform from the ground up. The problem is that knowledge is not in an accessible state. Honi told me to think of it this way—if you read a book on genetic engineering and then many years later tried to remember the contents of that book, you will remember the general gist of things but not the specifics. Oh, you might remember one or two specifics, but you won't remember the whole thing. What she's dealing with is the random memories of

274

that creature. There's so much of it, almost 1000 years' worth, finding anything useful is a crapshoot. Besides, it appears even the Fahr have not figured out how to speed up the process. If we understand what we're seeing, the creatures they're changing still mature at the same rate as the original unmodified species. So, if Howard and his staff were to build a modified human, it would still take twenty years for that human to mature. I guess if you lived seventy thousand years, twenty years is nothing. But we have a different perspective on things."

"Yes, but that's about creating a new genome from the ground up," Garneau said. "What I'm talking about is smaller modifications, like figuring out what it is about Honi that gives her the ability to repair her neurological system and use it to interface with digital technology. Can they do that? Because if they can, then we could potentially get a number of Honi's working on the bigger problem."

"Howard thinks they can. He believes that process is integral to what happens when the Fahr go into stasis. Part of what they're doing is replacing and upgrading worn-out body parts. As I understand it, they choose their next occupation right before they go into stasis. Then if that occupation would be better served with upgrades to certain aspects of their physiology, they can do that while the individual is in stasis."

"If we can figure out what they're doing just before one of them goes into stasis, then we steal that technology."

"Honi says they spend an average of one hundred and fifty years in stasis, and she thinks this is tied in to the time it takes the average fahr to mature, that their bodies are rebuilt from the ground up during stasis. So even if we could steal that technology, to find what makes Honi tick, and build another human with her abilities, the fix would not be quick. We'd have to grow the new human being at the same speed they grow up now. Twenty years, give or take."

Garneau nodded. "We, you, and I, may not see the end of this."

275

Goldstone Restored

The restoration of Goldstone was now nearing completion, at least the rebuilding phase, and they had detected a few missions still broadcasting. These were distant, well beyond lunar orbit. As Diane had suspected, no signals were detected from Earth-orbiting satellites. The Fahr had blinded the Earth before they attacked. The complexity of such an operation boggled her mind. There were 1,100 such satellites, all of which had different trajectories, and yet each had ceased to function at the same time. What could do that? Diane considered as she stirred her faux coffee.

"Did you see the photos of that creature before its rapid decomposition?" Diane asked Trent. "They say its brain case was twice the size of a comparably sized cetacean."

"It's not a species to be trifled with," said Trent.

"Yet Alatorre wants their route out of the solar system. She wants to go after them."

"Presumably after a rebuild of the human race," Trent said with a grin. He was still lying in bed. "Which makes you wonder at the urgency of restoring this place."

"If I remember right, she recruited us before she knew of that database's existence," Diane said.

"I've been reflecting on that," Trent said. "At first when we got that letter I was too damaged to think straight about anything. And now that I've been restored and had time to give it some thought, I'm wondering if this was just Alatorre distracting herself from an impossible task. She can't fix the current situation, so she's working toward what she sees as a more achievable goal."

"The aliens are real though, we know that," Diane said. "Which does change the perspective. On one level, we should be planning for a future interaction with what's out there. We know about the Fahr, but based on their brief interaction with us, we can assume that they have had such encounters before. I'm starting to think that Alatorre is a visionary."

"Still, it's a distant future kind of vision and it's sure useful in helping her avoid thinking too much about the brutal reality."

"She's hoping for a jump-start, hoping Honi will find something useful in that alien's memories of its time as a geneticist."

Trent shook his head. "We're a long-lived species. It's not like you're dealing with multiple generations of fruit flies in a single year. With humanity this research will take generations. Even if they discover amazing things in that alien data, even if we learn how to build a better less tribal species, we're still looking at centuries before we can go chasing after them."

"More if we discover the behavior is as much learned as it is genetic." Diane poured Trent a cup of the faux coffee. "Maybe we can learn how to genetically re-engineer this stuff to give it more kick."

Trent accepted the faux coffee with a nod. "Here's what makes that interesting—these will be genetically modified kids, but they will be brought up by old-school human beings, right? That will inject nurturing into it whether or not they like it. Those kids may learn to be tribal even if they're not genetically predisposed to it. Human adaptability is one of the things they want to preserve, right?"

Diane nodded. She couldn't blame the faux coffee for her current headache.

Destination

"We've got mail," Trent said, waving the envelope pushed through the door of their Fort Irwin apartment.

"From who," Diane asked

"*Doctor* Honi Kalawai'a," Trent said.

"She has a doctorate?"

"It appears so."

"In what?"

They both studied the envelope. "It's from the Faculty of Engineering," Diane said.

Trent shook his head. "One year. It took her one year to do that, and she's eighteen. Do they even grant graduate degrees that quickly?"

Diane shrugged. "It's probably a sign of respect more than anything. It's not as if MIT has been focused on the granting of degrees. They're calling her doctor because she's in that role and they know she could pass any set of requirements they put in front of her. Besides, giving her a PhD is also giving her authority, and as we've seen, she wields that authority well."

Trent plucked the envelope out of Diane's fingers. "Let's see what she's sent us." He tore open the side of the envelope, pulled out a single sheet, and handed it to Diane.

She read it quickly. "It's the coordinates for a patch of the night sky," Diane said.

"That's it?"

Diane shrugged. "That's it."

Trent pursed his lips. "A hint."

"She knows where the Fahr home world is," Diane said.

Trent looked at Diane. "Then why doesn't she just tell us?"

"Is that what you want?"

"No," Trent admitted. He sighed and walked to the other end of the room and turned back to Diane. "Aren't you a little bothered by this?"

"How do you mean?"

"She has all the power—that's the problem. She's the only person who can interface with a computer and use its computational power to supplement her own intellectual abilities. And for the same reason she's the only person who can interface with that Fahr memory database. We are totally dependent on her for everything. Before we left, Donaldson was saying she'd made him redundant.

She can solve any problem he and his team are working on in a small fraction of the time it would take the whole team to do it. He almost doesn't want to show her what he's working on."

"She's gifted, that's true. But at least at this point in time, she has done nothing hostile. It's not like she's trying to take over the world or even the work. She's just helping."

"Yes, but at what point does she move from that to something more ominous? Think about it. If you're vastly superior to everyone around you, the temptation has got to be there to assume the position of dominance."

"She also needs us. She's vulnerable"

"At the moment."

Captured

The forest beyond the beet field marked the southern edge of militia territory. It was wide, deep, and dense enough to require several days to get through. The chances of Jake accomplishing this before they caught him were slim. They would have dogs and horses. He was on foot.

He spent the first two days listening for the of baying dogs but heard nothing. During that time, he didn't stop to hunt or gather edibles. By the third day he was hungry. He'd seen only a few deer but realized, in his haste to get away, he'd made a lot of noise. The deer had heard him coming long before they were within visual range. He switched to stealth mode, and a few hours later he saw a doe with a small fawn. Killing the mother would also kill the fawn. Doing the reverse would still leave one animal alive. She could breed again. He brought down the fawn and waited until the bewildered doe accepted her loss and moved on.

It was considered bad form to shoot and eat a fawn, and for that reason, he had never tasted the meat of so young a deer. He lis-

tened again for the baying of the dogs but got nothing but forest silence. Perhaps it would be foolhardy to attract attention by lighting
a fire, but he was hungry and would not eat the meat raw. He found
a small clearing, built a fire, skinned and gutted the animal, and
roasted it on a makeshift spit. It still had the venison taste but was
more tender and less substantial. He thought the fawn would be a
bigger meal than a rabbit, but it was about the same. Still, he was
full and ready to move on when he heard the crackling in the trees.

They were on him before he grabbed the bow, but they weren't
militia. These were Alatorre's men, half a dozen US government soldiers. They all held rifles but did not point them at him.

"A bow hunter," one of them said.

"And he's killed a fawn," said another.

"You're aware that killing a fawn is against the law?" the first
man said.

Jake put the haunch down. He studied the man that had spoken. Connelly his name tag said. He had a Confederate look about
him, despite the modern military dress, and looked like a photo of
an emaciated southern soldier from the Civil War. Scraggly beard,
belt tightened to the final notch and still loose, coat hanging wobbly
from his shoulders. He was a corporal and in charge. The rest of the
soldiers were also malnourished.

"What law is that?" Jake said, gesturing at the spit. "There's
still a bit left. Help yourself."

This time the guns were pointed at him, but each soldier eyed
the others.

"See the doe?" the Connelly asked. "That would have been a
better choice."

"I let her go," Jake said. "You kill the doe, you kill the fawn.
This way I only killed one animal, and the doe can breed again.
Besides it was just me and I'm only passing through. Not planning
to take the meat with me. Killing the doe would've been a waste. I
wasn't expecting dinner guests."

"Where are you heading?" Connelly asked.

"Hoping to find civilization, if such a thing still exists. See, I was held captive by this militia group. A bunch of right-wing assholes that want to bring down the American government. I got away, and so now I'm running from them."

Connelly smiled at him. "Try again," he said studying Jake's well-fed appearance.

Jake gave a grim smile. "I never was a good liar. I was part of them, that's true, but I had a run in with the leader and wound up taking him down. Put an arrow right through his heart. So, they're coming after me. I'm just surprised that you folks found me first, because these woods are one hundred percent militia. We've been pretty good at keeping the Feds out of it."

"Are you talking about Abe Thompson?"

"That's the man," Jake said. "And here's the thing—they are coming after me. Count on it. And the other thing you can count on is that the six of you are no match for what they will be bringing. And they'll take you out just as sure is they'll take me out. I'd get out of here as soon as you can because they are looking for me. You don't want them finding you."

"Is that a threat?" Connelly asked.

"No sir, that's reality. Your only advantage is that you've been warned. I'd get out of here before they show up."

"We'll have to take you in."

"That's fine with me. The chances of survival are better. Not much better, but better."

Connelly spoke to his men. "Grab his bow and quiver," he said to one of them. "And grab what's still on that spit," he said to another. "We'll munch on it on the way back." He gestured to Jake and spoke to a third man. "And you pat him down and make sure he has no other weapons."

He watched as the man extracted hunting and pocket knives from Jake's clothing.

"I'm not going to tie you up," Connelly said to Jake. "You want to run, you'll take that risk. I'm thinking you don't want both us and your militia friends gunning for you. But even if you made that whole militia story up, and you got away from us, you will have a devil of a time surviving in that forest without weapons."

Jake nodded. "I won't be running, but I will walk fast. I suggest you and your men do the same."

They were closer to civilization than Jake thought. A forty-five-minute walk brought them to a truck parked at the end of an old logging road. The truck was an ancient Army vehicle, one that had been in mothballs until recently. It had a cab and a modified flat bed with the metal frame, benches, and a green canvas covering. It was large enough to accommodate three times as many men as the patrol. Connelly had Jake sit in the back against the cab and ordered four men to climb in and guard him.

"We weren't that worried about your militia friends," he said to Jake with his dirty grin.

"So, where are you taking me?" Jake asked.

"I'm sure someone in leadership will want to talk to you. And because you're militia, you'll spend time in custody. None of that should come as a surprise. In the meantime, we all need to eat something, at least my men and I do. There wasn't much left on that spit."

Jake watched as Connelly handed out individual white bread sandwiches. Each one looked about as substantial as a mini donut, and each man got only one. They didn't share with him.

They took Jake's name and left him in a cell for five days, feeding him on those same white bread sandwiches supplemented occasionally by an apple or carrot. They gave him weak tea to drink and books to read, trade paperbacks with science fiction or espionage themes. These he ignored.

The silence seemed to percolate things, especially about his life, what it meant, what it was for. Life within the militia was over, and he was losing the arrogance that came with it. But what was the alternative? Aligning himself with Alatorre and what was left of the corrupt and weak American government? That too seemed like a bad choice, but he was in their clutches now so what to do? He was not at all sure that escaping was an option. Where would he go? What would he do? He would be constantly on the lam, not aligned with anything, not trusting anyone. It wouldn't be much of a life. One look at what was going on in the countryside convinced him that even with his superior survival skills, things would be difficult. Humanity was coming apart at the seams, and Jake realized he didn't care. Not about that, anyway.

The thing he did care about was Tracy. He didn't want to care about her, but no matter how hard he tried to block her out, his mind would find her again. This was even more impossible than all the other scenarios. You couldn't be on the lam while also searching for someone, not without putting yourself at risk. Perhaps checking out of this life was the best option, but there was no obvious way to do that while they held him in a cell. Then it occurred to Jake that there was a way out: he would confess, and they'd have to execute him.

On the fifth day, when they escorted him into an interrogation room, the rage and uncertainty were gone. What was left was a relaxed and sanguine sense of purpose. The room had two chairs and a table. On top of this was a large platter of food, bread, cheeses, olives, and cold cuts. And a plastic tumbler of beer.

"Help yourself," one of his escorts told him. They locked him in the room by himself.

Bribery, Jake thought but didn't care. He was famished and constructed a thick sandwich. The beer was lukewarm, a reminder of lost refrigeration. By the time the door on the other side of the room reopened, he had used it to wash down two sandwiches. Might as well go to his fate on a full stomach.

A young man and a middle-aged woman entered, dressed as civilians in office apparel. The man retreated into the corner, clasped his hands behind his back and puffed out his chest. The woman sat across from Jake. She had a curious 1950s style haircut, which made her look like she'd stepped out of a postwar movie. Even the too red lipstick fit. *Who was she?* he wondered.

283

The woman pulled out a file folder and opened it. "Jacob Punster," she said.

Jake nodded.

"You're an unexpected catch."

Jake looked at her.

"You're one of Abe Thompson's snipers, aren't you?"

Jake said nothing.

"I suppose I should introduce myself before we continue," she said. "Unless, of course, you recognize me."

There was something familiar about her, Jake thought. Maybe he'd seen her on TV at some point. But if he had, he couldn't remember who she was. He shook his head.

"I'm Margaret Mavors, Secretary of Homeland Security with the federal government. I think you've heard of me."

Jake wiped the crumbs from his face. If Margaret Mavors was sitting across from him, there'd be no dramatic unveiling. They already knew.

"The experts tell us, if not for the presence of the Brinks side mirror at the precise moment when you took your shot, President Alatorre would be dead. They're theorizing that you saw two heads and chose the wrong one. Still, that was quite a shot. What were you, one hundred and fifty, two hundred yards away?"

Jake swallowed.

"And now, I'm given to understand, you've made a second assassination attempt. This one on your own commanding officer and more successful. Our sources have confirmed that Abe Thompson is dead, done in by a single arrow from a hunting bow. A marksman with two different and unrelated weapons. I'm impressed. We knew about Thompson, by the way, before you were caught and admitted to killing him. I would say your current situation is untenable. It won't be easy for anyone to determine where your loyalties lie, and both sides want you dead. But because the act against Thompson is the more recent of the assassination attempts, we will assume, for the time being, that you're no longer loyal to that militia. Fair enough?"

"He was an asshole," Jake said.

"Ah, I finally get a few words out of you. What was your reason for trying to kill President Alatorre?"

"The asshole ordered me to do it," Jake said.

Mavors laughed long and hard. "Well, you do have your charms," she said. "As thin as those may be." She studied Jake. "I'm sure I don't need to explain to you the gravity of your situation. Attempting to assassinate the President of the United States is not a forgivable act. However, success at assassinating one of her enemies makes you at least a person of interest. We are not foolish enough to think someone who has attempted two assassinations of major leaders is worthy of our trust. But we do suspect you have something we can use. Let me clearly draw up what's on offer here."

"Just kill me and be done with it," Jake said.

"You haven't heard my offer."

"I don't need to hear it," he said. "I have no loyalties other than to myself. I think you've already figured that out. If I'm supposed to get capital punishment, so be it. Let's get on with it. You won't find me sitting on death row appealing to the President for mercy."

"A proud man, then?"

"A spent man. I got nothing left to give, least wise nothing I want to give you."

Mavors studied Jake. "All right, then," she said and nodded to the young man in the corner. He went through the door behind Mavors and reappeared holding Jake's Winchester. "As I said, I have resources in that camp."

Jake's mouth dropped open.

"Yes, we assumed you'd like that. We've even had it cleaned. This gun nearly killed the President of the United States. It's a historical treasure likely to find its way into the Smithsonian. We won't be giving this back. Even we are not that stupid. But we thought you'd like to know we've given your old Winchester the respect it deserves."

"So, that's not part of your offer?"

Mavors studied him and shook her head. "Surely the return of your firearm is not enough to get your cooperation? My, my, some men do love their guns. I'm afraid not, no. But we'll keep it safe and clean. The offer involves something a bit more esoteric—we'd like to have you tested."

"Tested?"

"Yes."

"For what?"

"Coordination."

"Coordination?"

"And other physical attributes. I'm afraid I can't tell you more than that. Except that you'll remain in custody, though in better conditions than you've just experienced. We want to keep you fit."

"Keep me fit?"

Jake waited for an explanation. Mavors only smiled.

"What's going on here?" he asked.

"As I said, I can't tell you more than that. You don't have, and will never have, the security clearance necessary for such a revelation. While you're in our permanent custody, we will take good care of you. That's all you need to know."

Jake stared at her. "What if I want to die?"

"You don't," Mavors said. "You just need a reason to live. Give this some time and it may provide one."

She nodded to the young man in the corner. He opened the door behind Mavors. Two other men entered, dressed as though they were going to a board meeting. They put Jake in handcuffs and led him through the same door. The three of them walked down a long hall and then straight outside to a waiting police transport vehicle, complete with functioning electronics. They put him in the back, securing him by fastening the cuffs to the wall and putting shackles on his feet. They climbed into the back with him. Jake could hear the door being bolted from the outside.

"Where are we going?" he asked the two men.

Both responded by looking at the watches on their wrists, jabbing at the buttons on them, looking at each other, and nodding.

They were synchronizing, Jake realized. He wondered if he'd be allowed an iPod where he was going. Clearly Alatorre's people had working technology.

Mole

Old Robby Saunders stood before Jake, now clean-shaven and dressed professorial in an emerald green jacket and tan pant combination, while still wearing his hippy sandals. Robby grinned at his old tent mate.

"Hello Jake," old Robby said.

"No one would have picked you to be the mole," Jake said.

"Want to know how I got the messages out?"

Jake did want to know. No one took old Robby seriously, so they'd all cut him slack. Especially with all that over-the-top religious crap he kept doing. Jake gave Old Robby a nod.

"The trumpet," he said.

"Trumpet?"

"You see, we had listeners in the woods from my old band. If I played a certain scale and mode, say the Phrygian for instance, that told them something specific was going on in the camp. Only a fellow jazz musician has an ear that finely tuned. It was the perfect code."

"But all that stuff about people putting shit in your trumpet?"

"You're pretty easy, Jake, you know that? Nobody was putting stuff in my trumpet, but that was the kind of thing that you'd identify with. Pushed you a little further in the direction of trusting me. After that it was pretty easy dropping that hint about Thompson doing the same with your Winchester. I was pretty sure you'd take him out, and quite frankly, we couldn't have recruited a better person for the job. Using a bow, though, that was a nice touch."

"So, it was you who soiled my rifle?"

Robby laughed. "No. You were right the first time about that. Luke Hawkins didn't like you one bit. Saw himself as the resident sharp shooter, but you were so much better, and up to the time when you got the mirror instead of Alatorre, you were getting all the glory. So, when you fell from grace, he was determined to keep you there. Not sure what he thought he would accomplish by ramming dog crap down the barrel of your gun. Just kicking somebody when they're down, I guess. Anyway, it wasn't going help our cause if you went after him, so I redirected you to Thompson." Robby laughed again. "Didn't think you'd be so brazen about it. We had all these plans to smuggle you out of the camp and then you off him in a very public way and do a runner. We thought we'd lost a serious asset."

Jake studied him. "All that religious crap was an act?"

Robby was silent for a moment. "No, it was more of an improvisation," he said.

"Improvisation?"

"I have huge faith in Jesus. With all the crap I pulled as a younger man, he was the only way I could feel good about myself, but I'm normally quieter about it, more private. But in this case, it needed to be bigger, so I made it that. I am a jazz musician. Improvisation is what I do."

"But you tricked me into killing someone. How is that Christian?"

Robby studied him for a moment before replying. "Wow, you really can compartmentalize things, can't you? You belonged to a militia that was offing people and waving the Bible at the same time. I could ask you the same question, but I won't. Because ultimately this isn't about faith—it's about power."

Jake said nothing for a moment. "Yeah, I always thought all that religious stuff was bogus, definitely a control thing. But you just said you have huge faith, so I'm guessing you don't think it's about power. And you haven't answered my question."

"If you'd spend any time in Scripture you'll know one thing, that Heaven will be a place of unity. Everyone will be united under Jesus, under God. One people."

"That's your answer?"

"It will have to do."

Jake shook his head. "Mavors visited me," he said.

"She tell you anything?"

"Something about keeping me alive because of my coordination. Thinks I have exceptional abilities. It was weird shit."

Robby nodded. "Yeah, I had a talk with her about that. They're worried about letting you know too much too early. The rest of us had to sign this non-discloser agreement, so we won't tell anyone about what's really going on, but then we're not going to be incarcerated. You are. And if we control who you talk to, you won't be talking to anyone who hasn't already signed that agreement. She hadn't thought that one through."

"So, you're going to tell me?"

"Well, you won't be given access to weapons. I'm pretty sure you gathered that from your conversation with her. She tell you we recovered your rifle?"

"She showed it to me and told me I'd never get to touch it again."

Robby shook his head. "We're a long way from godly perfection, that's for sure. That was a stupid thing to do. Anyway, they're not interested in your marksmanship. They're interested in your genes."

"Genes?"

"Remember when you told me you couldn't shoot worth shit until the day the aliens attacked?"

"Yeah?"

"Then about the time the aliens attacked, you had this weird interaction with your iPod. Some kind of electrical thing happened and after you were suddenly a better shot, better at throwing things, better at a lot of stuff that required improved coordination?"

"Yeah?"

"Well it turns out you weren't unique in that regard. A few others had similar experiences. There's a young woman who was a quadriplegic at the time of the attack. She was wired up to a respirator to help her breathe and was zapped with the same shock when the aliens attacked. Afterwards she could regenerate her spinal column by just thinking about it and then learned to interface her body with computers and control them. There was another young man who got zapped by his DJ equipment and came out of it able to hear the tiniest of sounds. Nobody's sure what to make of this, but they want to study anyone who's had those experiences, which makes you a person of interest. They think there might have been some kind of change to your genes."

"Seriously?"

"Yeah. It seems pretty far-fetched to me, like something out of a super hero comic book. But I guess they're thinking if can figure out how that happened and if it is genetic, then maybe they can use that to build a better person."

"Build a better...?"

"You know that 'Dr. Howard' guy who was with your militia for a while and then did a runner?"

Jake nodded. "Tracy's dad."

"He's now in charge of this building-a-better-human-being thing. I'm not sure I understand all of what he's up to, but he'll be working with you. I'll let him explain what they're doing."

"Dr. Howard will be working with me?" Jake said. His face flushed.

Old Robby shook his head. "If you weren't such a crack shot, I think Thompson would have slapped you down for all that silliness. But as often happens when you get close to power, things like that get overlooked. You were pushing it though. It wasn't just the fact that she was so damned young, it was also because she was black. Lord knows that militia had its share of white supremacists, so I think Thompson was protecting an asset when he sent you on that mission."

Jake said nothing.

"She seems to still have a thing for you," Robby said. "Talks about you a lot anyways. But if I were you, I'd put her way out of your mind."

But how am I going to do that if I'm working with her father?

Song

Wrasse was not immune to song, at least not to the intoxicating effects of it, but the song had to be strong before it would also arouse him. He was well beyond the stage where he sought out intoxication for its own sake, though this had been useful when he hosted Pet Ministry parties. It allowed the veneer of conformity. He knew, for he had seen the recordings, that his orientation would be no defense against lethal effects of virgin humpback song. It was such an ugly animal, no color at all and prone to vestigial hair follicles. The first song seekers thought these were fungal growths, not surprising given their hideous appearance. Ugly, ugly, ugly. But there was no disputing the power of the Song.

He also had to admit that the animals had a certain grace when swimming. Despite their appearance, they were fun to watch. Especially now that the technicians had tricked them into migratory behavior. Introducing the gradual warming of the water, the generation of something akin to an oceanic current, and a magnetic field that mimicked that found on Planet Song did the trick. Now they swam in endless loops around the containment area. How long this would go on, he had no idea, but Kale had come up with another suggestion. They would gradually introduce a chemical signature into the water that would mimic the volcanic activity of the waters around the Hawaiian Islands on Planet Song.

Now as Wrasse watched, he noticed a slowing. The whales spaced themselves out around the enclosure and came to a stop. The one nearest to him, a male, put his head down and fluke up. The strobe on the wall flashed. *Song! Finally, there was song!*

Finale

Teracia swam the maze of hallways next to the containment area. Checking. Again. There was no bleed, not a single place where even the softest refrain could be heard. The seal was perfect, but that didn't stop them. She swam around the corner and found five crew members, their engorged diaphragms pressed tight against the walls of the containment area.

"Loops of the Song are now in the ship's library," she said to them.

They pulled themselves away from the wall and looked at her, their ballows trying to beige over the contempt orange and then pinking when this failed.

"They're filtered, Mamini," said one. "Might as well be listening to birdsong."

"It's not tasste," said another, this one vaguely familiar.

Teracia could see that all five had varying degrees of song damage, a residual scale slime and some twitching. "This taste will kill you," she said.

"Sso you ssay, Mamini. But there'ss a lot on board who don't believe that."

"Xyros?" Teracia said, suddenly realizing who she was speaking to. The young fahr had deteriorated badly.

Xyros mauved.

"What happened on the last voyage is a matter of public record," she said. "And you were on that ship, were you not? You know what happened."

"Well, here'ss the thing, Mamini. Thosse who died were exposed to all the ssoundss in the Planet Ssong ocean that day. No one knowss for ssure that the Ssong killed them. It could have been ssomething else. I think it wass, becausse they've ssent us on this return voyage to collect them, haven't they? Sso, if the Ssingers were sso dangerouss, why are we even bothering to collect them at all? Why go to all the trouble?"

Xyros had developed tongue palsy, adding sibilance to his speech. This much deterioration meant almost continual exposure to virgin song. He was getting it somewhere. Teracia checked his ballow. She noted that he was now a botanist and vaguely remembered approving the occupational switch.

"And how do you like botany?" Teracia asked.

"Plantss grow sslowly."

"Which leaves plenty of time for other things?"

Xyros said nothing.

"Based on your appearance my guess is that you're scheduled for stasis."

Xyros reddened. "You haven't ansswered my question, Mamini."

Teracia ignored him and swam to the com system. "This is Vice Commander Teracia. When is Botanist Xyros scheduled for stasis?" she asked.

"Botanist Xyros is in the pre-down fast."

Teracia turned to Xyros. "So, you're already in a weakened state and still think you'll survive exposure to the Song when no one else has?"

"Why are we collecting that song?" Xyros demanded.

Teracia inflated gold. "If you want an answer to that question I suggest you ask Minister Wrasse. He is Song Corp's senior representative on this ship. In the meantime, you will confine yourself to your quarters until your fast is completed and you're ready for the down."

"What! You have no right!" Xyros was now rage red.

"I have every right. I am the Vice Commander of this ship, and I am in authority over you and all your companions. If I were you, I would be glad that I hadn't pulled this act of defiance on Commander Agastin. I can guarantee that his reaction would be harsher."

"But..."

"One word from me," Teracia said, "and he will know of this."

Xyros stared at Teracia. His ballow began a slow collapse into his forehead, attempting beige as it did so, but the botanist's attempts still showed streaks of red. Teracia glanced at his companions and found them in various shades of pink. She had made enemies, likely more than were in this little group once the word got out.

"All of you, I don't want to see you again near the containment area. Consider it off limits until I say otherwise. Now leave."

The five of them swam off in single file, waiting until they were almost out of sight before starting.

"Give song, give song, give song..."

They may as well be chanting 'kill us, kill us, kill us', Teracia thought.

There was one room in the ship where it was possible to watch the Singers, an internal observation deck where sound barrier glass had been installed along one wall. Access was restricted to senior officers. When Teracia entered, she found Commander Agastin floating before the wall fully engorged. He acknowledged her arrival with a nod but kept his attention on the Singer suspended in the water a few fahr lengths from the glass. The whale rose to the surface to breath, and with a wave of its mighty fluke, disappeared.

"I'm showing amazing restraint, am I not?" Agastin said.

"Restraint, Commander?"

"Everyone on this ship thought I would throw myself in amongst them the moment they started singing."

"Perhaps you value your life?"

"You were in the middle of the carnage the first time it happened. I've seen the playback. That must have been traumatic." Agastin's gills rippled. "But of course, there were no elite fahr among the victims. Those of us who were engineered to be resistant to the intoxicating effects were not among the victims."

Teracia said nothing.

"I will not be the first," Agastin said. "Do what you must do." The Commander turned and swam out of the room.

He knows. Teracia felt her gills tighten and ballow blanch. *It might just be a deduction on his part.* She turned her attention back to the enclosure. Getting Prostallen into it would be tricky. Doing it without the entire ship finding out would be impossible.

Prostallen's quarters were half the ship's length away from the Singers. He was fading fast, at times barely conscious. If she was going to do this, it would have to be done soon. She triggered the strobe at his entrance, and he bade her enter.

"Are you ready?" she asked the body now fixed to the wall. The ex-commander looked like a bizarre wall-relief sculpture, immobile except for his head. The menders had introduced a small species of shark to control the parasitic fish that fed on him. This clouded the water and littered the floor with fish body parts. These in turn encouraged bottom feeding fish, shrimps, crabs, and snails to the point where the entire floor was a scene of constant motion. Prostallen seemed oblivious to this.

"They're singing?" he asked.

"They are."

"I thought I wouldn't survive," he said, allowing his gills a slight ripple. "How is the crew responding?"

"They want taste."

"They're too young for a death wish."

"As I remember your crew wanted the same."

"Yes, but back then no one knew. Now they do."

"And yet they still want taste which is why we have a problem. How do we get you into the containment area without attracting a lot of attention?"

"I must be towed."

"Hard to do that inconspicuously."

Prostallen thought for a moment. "What if I expressed an interest in meeting the homine? We could spin it that way."

"They will still know you're going into the containment area."

"Are they following you?"

"Me?"

"They know you're meeting with the homine and that means entering the containment area."

"They also know I'm song deaf, and I've been going in there ever since we discovered him. It's old news."

"But now the whales are singing. They weren't before."

Teracia blanched. "I hadn't thought of that." She thought back to Xyros and his friends. That crowd would follow me.

"Let's just do this," Prostallen said.

Teracia nodded. "Agastin knows."

"Does he?"

"He's letting you go first."

Prostallen's gills rippled. "Altruism? Not likely. The quicker we do this, the less likely we'll have an audience."

Stares and muttered comments. That seemed to be the extent of it, but the closer Teracia pulled Prostallen's gurney to the containment area, the more attention she got. It didn't help that a small cloud of parasitic fish, now freed from their predators, were latching on to Prostallen every chance they got. The ex-commander had passed out, lolling his tongue out the side of his mouth and sucking water through his gills in a loud pulsating swoosh. Teracia wished she could wake him and shut him up, but he was unresponsive.

"You're a long way from the stassiss chambers, Mamini."

Xyros and five of his friends were blocking the swimway.

"I seem to remember that you were restricted to your quarters, Xyros, for the duration of your fast," Teracia said, trying to maneuver toward the nearest com button.

One of others placed himself between her and it.

"Well, Mamini, the gardeners sseemed to have need of my sservices for a bit longer, sso I've put off the downing. Not doing the pre-down fast freess me up to have tasste."

"No one may have taste, Xyros. You know that."

"And yet here you are towing the ex-commander toward the containment area. Now, as the Vice Commander on thiss expedition, you'll know that I've already been on a pet collecting expeditions with Commander Prostallen. He'ss never been one to deny his crewss tasste. In fact, he'ss alwayss been a willing partissipant himsself. Sso it doessn't take a brilliant mind to figure out whatss going on here. You're taking him to the containment area sso he can have tasste. If you can do that for him, you can do that for uss."

Teracia inflated her ballow gold and faced the six fahr. "You will all swim away and return to your individual quarters immediately. What is going on with ex-commander Prostallen is of no concern to yours. Further obstruction will result in severe disciplinary measures."

"It will kill him, won't it?" Xyros said. "It'ss the way he wants to go, issn't it? Ssung out in a rush of ecsstassy? We jusst want to honor him by being at hiss sside. What'ss the harm in that?"

"Did I not just give you a direct order?"

"You did, Mamini, you did. But you've got no way of enforssing that, now, and we've all come on this voyage becausse we knew there'd be tasste, powerful tasste, and now we have you, this femfahr, this freak of nature, telling uss we can't have it. We've come too far. We've waited too long for this, and we will have it."

"It will kill you."

"Well, we don't believe that, of coursse. But even if it'ss true, we'd go out in a rush of ecstasy, like the Commander, wouldn't we?"

"She's right. It will kill you."

In all the commotion Prostallen had awoken.

"Not only that, but it will not be a pretty death."

Xyros and his companions stared at Prostallen.

"Oh, I know what you're thinking," Prostallen said. "If it's not a pretty death then why would I want that? But there's a subtle difference, you see. The original event involved thirty able-bodied fahr, who in their extreme ecstasy, threw themselves violently into the bulkhead, windows, and walls of the that ship's observation deck. The key word here is able-bodied. I am not able-bodied. My muscles are atrophied and would not, for that reason, be able to propel me into anything. I have little doubt that in my weakened state, I will not survive the experience, but mine will not be death by self-inflicted dismemberment. Yours would be."

297

Teracia used the distraction provided by Prostallen to slip past the fahr blocking her way to the com button.

"So, you have two choices," Prostallen continued. "You can try to proceed with this misadventure, which if you succeed, will guarantee an ugly death. Or you can turn around and swim away, in which case no one will be the wiser."

"There are two more likely alternatives," Teracia said pushing the com button. "Vice Commander Teracia here! Security team to the containment area!" She turned to Xyros. "You and your friends can give up this foolish idea now, in which case you will know little more than an extended period of confinement. Or you can be difficult, in which case I will turn you over to Commander Agastin, and each of you will risk permanent silence. I don't need to tell you that without diaphragms taste is an impossibility."

"That was risky," Prostallen said as they watched the security team escort Xyros and his friends away from the containment area.

"They were unlikely to see reason, and had they succeeded, we might have had a full-scale revolt on our hands," Teracia said, towing Prostallen again.

"Oh, I doubt that. What we would have had is graphic real time example of the effects of the Song unfiltered. If you remember, that was sobering on the last trip."

Teracia's gills flattened. "Yes, but we also had a ship full of other collected singers on that last trip, so there was no shortage of virgin song to go around. I also remember what it was like getting that ship home short thirty crew members and with the rest impaired. Their commander was incognito as I recall."

"And who's fault was that?" Prostallen said gills rippling.

"You blame me for that? I was following orders."

"A little too well, perhaps?"

"Anyway, in our current situation we're already down six, seven if you count Roont, hopefully the only fahr to ever overdose on Homines singing." Her gills rippled. "Losing another five would not be good, not to mention what would happen if other crew members develop the same death wish. With no other source of virgin song on board that may happen, especially if we don't have a strong deterrent." Teracia stopped before the hatch into the containment area. "Are you sure you want to do this?" she said.

"The damage is done and now I want to finish it," Prostallen said, morphing from green to blue.

Teracia nodded. "Open the hatch, please," she said to the ship's computer. She felt a slight tickle as the security strobe scanned their ballows.

"Only one of you is authorized," the computer said. "Vice Commander Teracia, do you wish to authorize ex-commander Prostallen?"

"Authorize."

The passageway between the swimway and the containment area was just long enough to accommodate the gurney. Teracia pulled Prostallen into it and then stopped. "We have to wait for the water swap," she said. "Flatten your gills."

The ship's water drained from the passageway, and for a moment Teracia floundered on the floor beside Prostallen's gurney. It was always amazing how heavy her body felt when not supported by water. She watched as the water from the containment area flooded into the passageway.

"Feel it?" she said.

"Yes, the oxygen content is higher," Prostallen said. "It's nice."

"After a while you adjust and take smaller breaths." She pulled Prostallen into the containment area. "They're not predictable. I don't know when they'll sing. Would you like to meet Kale while we're waiting?"

"No. I'm here for only one thing."

Teracia nodded. "I'll pull you into the center of the enclosure. They're quite something to see in the flesh, and you'll be exposed to a bit of other virgin song as well. There are other singers here that were captured with whales. Nothing strong enough to give you more than a pleasant buzz, but it's there."

Prostallen said nothing. His ballow became a swirl of yellow, blue and gray; a mix of happiness, fear and regret. The time for conversation was over.

Teracia pulled him forward. A bit of yellow bobbed on the surface in the far corner of the enclosure. Kale in his boat. Nothing of what was about to happen would make sense to him, and she doubted she would have an easy time explaining it. Perhaps she wouldn't have to. Everything would take place below the surface, so there was a good chance he wouldn't see it.

A whale swam up to them. They were used to her by now, but a new fahr being pulled on a gurney was a novelty. Prostallen's ballow went joy blue. Several other whales came, looked them over and left.

"They are magnificent!" Prostallen said.

"Yes, they are"

"There's no way you can get a sense of how large they are unless you're among them!"

"This is true."

Just like her first encounter, Teracia felt it before she heard it, as if the water had suddenly become thicker. She looked at Prostallen. The muscles beneath his scales expanded and contracted in a failed attempt to free themselves from the straps of the gurney. His ballow now inflated and collapsed, a boiling rainbow of shifting hues. The ex-commander's small circular mouth doubled in size, cracked, and bled into the water. The gills were wide open, drawing water through with such force that the organs themselves were pulling apart. By the time she looked at his eyes it was over. It had taken less than thirty seconds for the Song to kill him.

She was numb. Had he even experienced the final ecstasy he so craved? As she looked at Prostallen, the gurney released him, its internal logic sensing that there was nothing left to constrain. She reached for the mortuary bag attached to the gurney, but she lost control and vomited into the space between them. Her ballow went gray as she waited for the water to clear. He was her worst enemy and greatest friend. What she would speak about him at the remembrance?

Teracia dragged what was left of Prostallen into the bag, overrode sensors on the gurney, and strapped him in. The mortuary was half the ship's length away from the containment area. By the time she delivered him, every fahr on board would be reminded of what virgin humpback whale song could do.

Ghost

Honi could feel Thryke now, a small piece of him dangling in her consciousness, ever present but benign. Each time she dived into his memories the size of the piece grew. This bothered her, but there was still no way she could use the data on the quant drives without connecting with the device itself. And it always transferred more of Thryke into her mind before she redirected it to the drives. He was growing inside her, but he was dead. He had no will, no purpose, and yet there was a presence. Non-interactive but irritating nonetheless. There was no sense in which she felt out of control, dirtier perhaps, but that was all. She knew her old memories dispossessed by this process were stored on the quant drives. Diving into the device had now become routine, and she worried that it had become too routine.

Charlie had been playful that morning, stretching out his affections well beyond their usual morning romp. It had been glorious, but she knew Dr. Howard waited for her in the lab. He was the ultimate professional, punctual to a fault. She was a good forty-five minutes late by the time she hovered into his presence.

"Sorry, slept in," she said.

"Both of you?"

"Yeah, both of us," Honi smiled at him.

301

"Where is he?"

"Getting us some breakfast."

"We're behind schedule," Howard said.

Honi read his face. She could see he'd prefer to do this without Charlie, that he felt Charlie was a distraction. He wasn't, at least not in a way Howard had to worry about. When she connected to the Cowichan, she could deal with Charlie and still focus on anything that required her attention. Still it irritated Honi that Howard resented Charlie's presence.

She smiled at him. "Then let's do this. Charlie can monitor me when he gets back." There had been nothing to be concerned about lately, anyway. Blood pressure, heart rate, all within acceptable parameters.

The smaller muscles around the edges of Howard's face relaxed. "Are you sure?" he said.

"It'll be fine," Honi said, reaching and connecting to the device.

Honi felt the connection, felt Thryke.

"Charlie's not good for you, you know," Howard said, his voice having that ambient feel outside voices always had when she connected. It took a moment for Honi to realize what he had said. She flushed. *How dare you say that! Your own daughter has a thing for the man who tried to kill Alatorre.*

She felt the rage surge through her and then realized too late that she had failed to redirect the memory dump. Thryke was there, still dead but now a much larger ghost. She redirected the rest of the memory dump to the quant drives. She sighed, trying to push the anger away. Parameters would have to be set about communication during the initial contact phase.

If this poor creature had gills he would have rippled them! Had she a ballow he would have inflated it the brightest blue! Patience was indeed a virtue. Now there was enough of him that his superior mind could dominate this poor creature. But he wouldn't, at least not yet. He would start by giving her a gift, and then he would then guide her in the use of it.

Honi navigated to the Fahr genetics lab and entered at the spot she had bookmarked on the previous session. Something had changed and took her a few moments before she realized what. There was a precision and depth to everything as if she were experiencing it in real time and not observing memories. And Thryke was there, a much more substantive ghost, not controlling anything, not guiding her, but clarifying everything. There was enough of him now inside her that she could experience the memories the way he had, and these were not the selective and foggy memories of a human being. These were memories the way the Fahr experienced them.

They had perfect recall and all this time she had experienced his memories in the same foggy way she experienced her own. Honi had assumed this was normal, but she had been wrong. And there was now enough of Thryke inside her to experience things his way.

Everywhere she looked, she now understood. The conversations made sense, and she knew what the machines were and their function. It was all clear. Crystal clear.

Genome

Honi looked at the thumb drive in her palm. "It's amazing that this bit of antiquated technology can store the entire human genome, 3.2 billion nucleotides more or less."

"The thing to remember is that the gene data device in Thryke's memory will include nothing from the Earth, because he held that occupation long before they came," Howard said.

She looked up at Howard. "But the information it does contain should jump-start everything we're doing." She held up the thumb drive. "Comparing this to the information in that database will go a long way in helping us to read the instructions."

"And you're sure you can approach this device and use it. I thought it was a memory?"

"Thryke has total recall and spent a millennium working with this machine, so I may not be able to use it, but I will learn from it. Anything he knew I will know. And that includes, if I'm not mistaken, how to construct one. That may be the greatest advantage here. If we can build one that will work in atmospheric conditions. Who knows what we might accomplish?"

Howard smiled and shook his head. "You know, when I became a scientist what excited me the most was how much 'I' might accomplish. I wanted to show the world what 'I' could do. An uppity black man. Oh, I was a good team player, but this was about personal accomplishment. I would show them how hard 'I' could work and how smart 'I' was. Then my—and everyone else's—world came crashing down. We spent time in this dystopian wilderness and then... then I get an offer from the President to work on a dubious project and I take it because there wasn't anywhere else to go. Then I meet you—and I don't have to tell you you're intimidating—and now I'm confronted with an alien technology so advanced that anything I might've accomplished as a scientist is irrelevant. And I'm about to be handed all this knowledge I didn't have to work for."

Honi gave a thin smile and sighed. "Oh, you will have to work for it. Don't fool yourself."

"Just not the work I envisioned."

Honi said nothing, and the silence lengthened as he studied her.

"You alright?"

"I can't contain Thryke, you know, not in here, not without the connection. I'd lose too much of me if I tried because every time I connect I add more of him in. Staying connected is the only way I can limit him. I must sleep connected and that means I can't have Charlie."

"Can't have him?"

"I see all his flaws. He's so transparent when I'm wearing this." She touched the Cowichan. "You all are. I need to take this off properly to respond to him, to all of you really. And now I can't, at least not until I can figure out a way around this."

Howard kept his silence, but she watched the empathy grow. He really had no idea. "I'm sorry, Honi," he said finally.

Honi held up her hand. "We have work to do."

Yes, we do. First, we build the army. Then we fight the battle, bringing down the most advanced civilization in the galaxy. The ancient Fahr might not have appreciated his gifts but these little bipeds certainly would.

Visitor

It took four years of good behavior for Jake to gain some measure of freedom, an ankle bracelet that restricted his movements to a single building and the courtyard it enclosed. There was one exception, the east wing of the building that contained Dr. Howard's Laboratory was still off limits. Too much chance of running into Tracy, he guessed. Dr. Howard agreed to tutor him twice a month on the condition that subject of his daughter never came up. Jake agreed. Howard filled him in on everything that was happening.

In the four years of Jake's imprisonment, his working vocabulary had quadrupled, filled out with technical terms from biology, medicine, and genetics. MIT allowed him to write the exams but wouldn't give him a degree due to an absence of lab time. He hated to admit it, but he now agreed with what Alatorre was doing and was fascinated by everything connected to the goal. A splintered humanity would be no match for the Fahr.

He found his favorite library chair and settled into his latest find *"The Gene: An Intimate History"* by Siddhartha Mukherjee, a book that detailed the history of human genetic research.

Someone took the chair opposite him, but Jake didn't look up.

"Hello, Jake," she said.

Jake peered over the top of his book and dropped it. "Tracy?"

"The same."

Jake picked the book up and stared at her. "You've filled out," he said

"It's called growing up."

"I didn't think they'd ever let me see you again."

"I turned eighteen yesterday, Alatorre's new countrywide age of consent. They dragged me into an office and made me sign that non-disclosure agreement. I already knew everything. Two days ago, I could have told. Now I can't, but I can visit you. Dad can't stop me now."

"You were fourteen, I was eighteen. That was so stupid of me..."

"Did Dad ever tell you about the slingshot?"

"Slingshot?"

"Remember you gave me one and showed me how to use it?"

"Yes. Your dad and I never talked about you. But, yes, I remember that."

"We wouldn't have made it if you hadn't done that. I used it to stop a pack of wild dogs. God, it's amazing how quickly you can do things when you think you're going to die."

Jake nodded. "So, why did you come and see me?"

"It was Alatorre that had me sign the agreement yesterday. She figures you're a waste in here and wants to get you involved in the project. The thing is she thinks you still hate her. You did try to kill her. So, she asked me to..."

"Is that why you came?"

"I came because you were my first love, and I haven't had one since. I came because I wanted to know whether it would still feel the same. She gave me a little push, that's all."

306

Jake slumped back in his chair and took several deep breaths. "I'm almost afraid to ask."

"Yeah, I do," Tracy said.

"You do?"

"Yeah, and here's the thing. If she hadn't prodded me, this would have been so much more difficult. Because I would have been walking in here and finding out I still cared only to have you continue to be shut up in here with me outside. But now..."

"Now?"

"If you agree, I'm supposed to walk you out of here and take you over to sign that same agreement. And once you've done that, you're as free as free gets around this place. Of course, they're going to give you things to do."

"Like what?"

Tracy spread her hands. "I don't know, and I don't know what they're going to do with me either. I only just signed that thing, but they'll find something for us to do. Count on it. This is a tight operation."

Jake took two deep breaths. "I spent four years in here with nothing happening. Then in a single day I get my freedom and you back in my life. It's overwhelming."

"Am I back in your life?"

Jake grinned. "Is there a place where I can buy Twizzlers around here?"

Act Nine: Alpha Tribe

Hockey Night

It was still called the Gardens, home of the Boston Bruins, one of the original six NHL hockey teams from before, but the building had been derelict for years. Now the restoration was complete. Thirty-five years after the last NHL game it shone again, with soya hot dogs, a cola made to the original Coke recipe, popcorn, and real French fries. Tonight, the NHL would begin again, a specter of its former self due to a much smaller pool of players, but it was professional hockey.

Maria Alatorre struggled up the stairs using two canes, refusing the help of her attendants. When she reached the section, she stopped and waited until eight of the crew filed out of the row, clearing the way to her seat. They were perfect, physically indistinguishable from the rest of the fans. She looked down the cleared isle to her seat and found Peter Howard already there. Ten years her junior, the geneticist was one of the few that remained from the secret cabal that started the project. She was ninety-three and he eighty-three she supposed, though she was never sure of even the simplest math these days. They were old in a population where life expectancy had to been rolled back twenty-five years from pre-contact days. She took her seat beside him.

"Do you remember the rules to this game?" she asked him.

"Yes," he replied. "I was a Capitals fan in my youth. Tribal." He winked at her.

They were there to watch but not to watch the game. Around them sat the crew, one hundred and eight individuals in training for the journey to Centrix, the Fahr home world. They were the Continuity, at least that part of it designated to contact life beyond Earth. But that was not how they referred to themselves. They called themselves the "Alpha Tribe". Alatorre hated that. It meant that they saw themselves as separate and distinct, not in natural continuity with humanity at all but a different species. She should not have been surprised by this. *Why be loyal to that which was flawed?* But it wasn't a lack of loyalty, more a realization that they were the future. The whole idea was not that they be loyal to humanity, but that they would not have tribal divisions within themselves. She looked up and down the rows. Half of them wore Boston Bruins jerseys and half the jerseys of the Vancouver Canucks. Each group had studied the team they were supposed to cheer for.

Would they? Alatorre wondered. She was heartened that they sat as a mixed group and not in cheering sections.

Howard nudged her shoulder and pointed to the ice. The referee was about to drop the puck.

***

Honi sat in the section opposite the crew members, also observing. Her twenty-year stasis, the first ever attempted on a human being, made her physically younger than most of them. And she could now move normally, though she still enjoyed zooming about on her susboard. The adrenaline was costly but so much fun. Her down time meant that she had spent most of the past few months catching up, but she had done this with ease. The PDM she had designed ran down her back between her shoulder blades, filling in the spaces between her vertebrae with flexible fourth-generation quant drives. She could now turn this off, an advantage made possible by her stasis enhanced spinal column, a feature she did not share with the Alphas. They also lacked a PDM. Her PDM had four times the memory storage of the Fahr PDM, and contained all of Thryke's memories, all of his military expertise, and an advanced computational engine, something the original Fahr device lacked. She would lead the Alpha Tribe and be more than a match for anything the Fahr might throw at them. She had been waiting 67,000 years for such a battle. Had she, or had he? It no longer mattered. Everything about her was hybrid.

Charlie sat beside her, sixty years old and paunchy. She still liked him, but now saw sexuality as weakness. The attraction was long gone and with it any reason to turn off the PDM. And Charlie didn't ask. While she was in stasis he'd taken up with Cynthia Chen. They had raised two of the Alphas until Cynthia died of a stroke. He had carried on without her, following the non-tribal child rearing protocol until he turned the boy and girl over to Diane and Trent at the NASA training facility. Now the two NASA scientists were gone, both also to cancer, and Jake and Tracy had taken over, focusing on the military side of their training. Charlie's Alphas now sat in the section across from them dressed in Canucks jerseys.

"I'm going back to Haida Gwaii after you and the kids leave," he said to Honi.

"Why?"

"I miss the tribalism."

They both laughed.

He gestured to the Alphas sitting across from them. "Want to know what they're saying?"

"You can still do that?"

"Of course. I'm the best eavesdropper on the planet."

Charlie had trained his ears to the point where he could pick out individual conversations in huge crowds from as far away as several hundred yards.

"No, I don't think so," she said. "I'll be on a ship with them for the next thousand years. Won't be much privacy there. I'll let them have what little they can hold onto here. Did Howard ever figure out if there was a genetic component to your hearing?"

Charlie shook his head. "Nothing he could find. I guess whatever this is, it's not genetic. One of life's little mysteries, I guess."

Honi nodded.

"You want a popcorn, hot dog, or something to drink?"

"No thanks, I fine."

"OK, be right back."

She watched Charlie go. It was genetic, of course. She'd learned that by searching through Thryke's last occupation. The intelligent electromagnetic pulse the Fahr had used to disarm the Earth had a rare side effect. It would occasionally fry a single nucleotide in an organism's genome, simultaneously affecting every instance of it in the entire organism. The changes could be a positive, negative, or neutral. In her case the change had given the ability to regenerate damaged nerve cells and control their linkages. With Charlie, it had unleashed the acute hearing of one of mankind's distant ancestors, an ability that had been switched off for millions of years in the human genome. With Jake, it resulted in early primate level coordination.

Honi kept this knowledge from Howard. She found her own genome in the database and reinserted the original nucleotide, then did the same with Charlie and Jake. Howard would never know, and Honi would be alone in her capabilities. She liked her current advantage and wanted no rivals.

The puck dropped and most of the crowd erupted in enthusiastic cheers. The Alpha Tribe merely watched, talking amongst themselves.

"I take that back," she said to Charlie when he returned with his food. "I do want to know what they're saying."

Charlie listened. "They're talking about the skill levels of the individual players on both teams. There's no favoritism. It's as if they're watching a musical performance and not a hockey game."

Honi smiled. Alatorre had done her bit, now they would do theirs.

311

Swim Through

Kale sat, simulated beer in hand, on his floating porch, for the last time. He was a naked seventy-two-year-old man. Modesty had no meaning in this place. Teracia had arrived earlier in the day and attached yet another leech to his ankle, the Fahr way of taking a blood sample. The beer was laced with a mild intoxicant designed to make mammals placid. All right. He was a mammal, and he did feel mellow.

For thirty years he'd lived on this houseboat studying the whales, learning about the Fahr, and watching an endless stream of what were now quarter of a century old YouTube videos. He now knew how to do every yo-yo and card trick ever invented, could understand the basics of about two dozen languages—which made the watching of foreign films easier—and he had mastered yodeling. This he'd learned in a misguided attempt to make his host's heads explode. It didn't work. They loved it. They inundated him with requests for virgin yodeling.

He was glad for the intoxicant. Kale knew he should feel anxious, but he didn't. What he did feel was a kind of mellow resignation combined with wonder. He would be changed.

Sulfur. Teracia was coming, coming to give him the final swim through. He grinned. She had picked a human idiom and "fahred" it. That's how she put it. Fahred it, like a bad adolescent joke. When all this was over, in 170 years, swim through would make a lot more sense than walk through.

"How is the beer?" she asked.

He reached up behind his right ear to boost the translator, kept low when he wanted to hear normally. "Works," he said. "Close to the real thing."

"Good," she said and plucked the leech off his ankle. "Because I have another drink for you." She extended her tentacle and

312

dropped a small vial into his hand. "Tastes and looks like milk. Wait for my instructions before you drink it."

"OK."

"In about six months I too will enter stasis, but I will come out of it about twenty years before you will. Do you understand why?"

"Because you are merely being rebuilt, but I will be changed."

"Into what?"

Kale frowned. "I don't know. Some kind of fish, I guess."

"No. You will not be a fish. There is no name for what you will be because you will be the first of your kind. You will be unique."

"An aquatic human," Kale said.

"If you wish," Teracia said. "You will have gills, so you can have access to the rest of the ship, and, in time perhaps visit our home world. Your eyes will be changed so they can see in an aquatic environment. Your toes and fingers will be elongated, and you'll find webbing between the digits to aid in swimming. You will never be a good swimmer, but this will make it easier to get around. Your skin will be thicker with a layer of fat beneath to help regulate your temperature. You will look puffy by your current standards, but you will no longer have the thick accumulation of fat around your middle. The ears on the sides of your head will be replaced by diaphragms like our own but smaller. It's unlikely that you will ever meet another like you, so you will have no need for sexual organs."

"Can I keep them anyway?" Kale asked.

Teracia's gills rippled. "They would be vestigial and serve no purpose. In the unlikely event that another like you is created, we should be able to restore your sexuality. In the meantime, because you are male, the diaphragms replacing your ears will be sensitive to song. They will give you a mild form of arousal without the impairment that plagues our species."

"And what about whale song?"

"That you will enjoy, my little gift to you. But your diaphragms will filter out the dangerous frequencies and you will hear it in stereo, something we cannot do. Your work with them should be much more pleasant because of the Song and you can live among them in their environment, if you choose."

313

Kale thought about this. The whales were now family. They came to him for scratches and pets, often carrying him around the enclosure on their backs. Their favorite thing was to breech when he was on the porch, soaking him. They would swim away, making a rapid sucking and blowing sounds with their blowholes, which he realized was an attempt by them to imitate his own laughter. Well, that was one prank they wouldn't play again. He wondered what they would come up with when he was among them.

"You'll have to re-establish relationships, though," she said.

"Because of the changes, you mean?"

"Well, that will be part of it, yes. You'll look and act different."

"And the other part of it?"

Teracia said nothing but purpled a bit. "I want you to drink the milk now and as soon as you do, I want you to get into the water. Then I'll answer your question."

Kale drank the sweetened milk and slipped over the side of the boathouse. Most of the whales had gathered at the surface, something he hadn't seen them do since Mikala's funeral back on Earth. *Am I going to die?* he wondered." Kale felt his consciousness slipping.

"You'll not see these whales again," Teracia said, her voice receding. "By the time you wake only their descendants will be here."

A tinge of sorrow and then...

The End

What's Next?

"Alpha Tribe" is the second book in The Fahr Trilogy. The third book, "The Will of the Giver", is under construction and should make an appearance toward the end of 2019. To learn of its actual publication date and for a change to ensnare a free advanced review copy and other swag, subscribe to my newsletter at tkboomer.com/contact To learn more about T.K. Boomer visit my website at tkboomer.com. Please review "Alpha Tribe" and "Planet Song" online on Amazon.com or on Goodreads. And please recommend the books to others. Thanks.

Appendix A

A Synopsis of Planet Song

This plot synopsis is intended as a reminder for those who have already read "Planet Song". As such it contains almost nothing of the world building and character development that are foundational to the book and the trilogy. Readers who had not read "Planet Song" are strongly encouraged to do so before reading "Alpha Tribe."

To keep this synopsis to a reasonable length I have referenced only major characters and events. In "Planet Song", the first book of "The Fahr Trilogy", I tell the story from the alien point of view. The human characters in this novel appear only in episodic scenes until the final twenty percent of the book, when they become more important players. These earlier episodic scenes illustrate the effects of Fahr activity on Humanity or to show aspects of human development relevant to the overall themes of the trilogy.

The Fahr are an aquatic species with an average life span of seventy millennia, bio-engineered to facilitate long interstellar voyages. Song, in all its various forms, is both arousing and intoxicating to them often resulting in addiction. Their primary motivation for space exploration is the acquisition of new songs and because these songs feed addictions back home, their collection is both a lucrative and an unethical business.

Act One: The Seeking

Teracia, a rare fahr female, deceives Song Corp's CEO, Lord Greyling, into letting her join the crew of its pet collecting expedition to the Earth. The expedition arrives in Earth orbit in the middle of the 14th century AD and discovers a mother lode of singing animals. Prostallen, the ship's commander, is determined to collect these even though this may harm the planets native sapient species, humanity. To do so however he must get the approval of Derath, the ship's sapient species expert, a fahr charged with the responsibility of determining the most ethical course of action. Teracia and Derath work to stop the collection, but Prostallen deceives Derath into giving his approval. When the Fahr dive deep into the Pacific Ocean, they meet a humpback whale. Exposure to the humpback whale song kills thirty members of the crew, but Teracia saves Commander Prostallen's life. Prostallen realizes that, with the most dangerous frequencies filtered out, humpback song will be the ultimate sonic drug. However, the Fahr ship is too small to transport a breeding population of these animals and so they return to their home planet to get a bigger ship, a round trip that will take 650 years

Act Two: The Preparation

Three hundred years later on the Fahr home planet of Centrix. Chancellor Agastin has made himself popular with the common Fahr by feeding their song addictions, but unpopular with his own high counsel due to his ego maniacal behavior. Lord Greyling, Song Corp's CEO, brings Agastin a filtered loop of humpback song. Agastin is so enamored that he decides to head the return expedition himself, abandoning his Chancellorship. An aging and song-damaged Prostallen is asked to go as an advisor, but he refuses to do so unless Teracia is made Vice Commander of the ship. Defense Minister Thryke goes along as military advisor in case there is a conflict with Humanity.

Act Three: Interstellar Space

When the Fahr ship is still over one hundred years from the Earth, communications Officer Roont intercepts radio signals in the form of Morse code. When the Fahr interpret the code, they discover that human technical evolution is proceeding at an alarming rate, including the development of significant weaponry. Teracia argues that this will lead to conflict but Agastin is determined to get the whales. As their journey continues, Agastin discovers the presence of whaling fleets that are killing the humpbacks and later that Humanity has developed atomic weaponry. Concerned that humanity will destroy the planet before they have a chance to collect the whales, Agastin orders a dangerous increase in the ship's speed.

Act Four: Jupiter

The ship enters the solar system at high speed and the ships quantum-computer-controlled debris avoidance system makes several abrupt maneuvers that kill and injure crew members. For safety reasons they force the ship to slow down. By now Humanity has stopped large-scale whaling and managed to avoid nuclear war, but the threat is still there. This reduces the urgency but Agastin is listening to Thryke's military ideas. Teracia and Prostallen still favor diplomacy but mankind has no central government with which to negotiate. Agastin is adamant he will not negotiate with humanity unless such a central government exists. Teracia convinces him to send a message hoping humanity will form a world government and talk. Agastin hijacks the Pioneer 10 radio frequency and sends "Wind on the Water", an old Graham Nash song about the whaling industry he found on Human radio broadcasts. This communicates nothing and only serves to confuse the NASA scientists, who assume that the song on the Pioneer 10 frequency results from terrestrial hacking. In the meantime, Thryke convinces Agastin that putting the ship in orbit around Jupiter will provide them with an ideal military staging location. Teracia again convinces Agastin to negotiate. They send the same song but this time they send it on multiple frequencies and they make sure their ship is detectable from the Earth.

The major human characters make appearances at this point. This includes Diane; a senior NASA administrator who realizes that sending the song is an alien attempt at communication and brings this to the attention of the Maria Alatorre, the American President. Alatorre brings together the leaders of the permanent members of the UN Security Council. They communicate with the Fahr. When they do Agastin demands they form a world government and when they don't he cuts off communication. In meantime news of this becomes public.

This part also introduces several other human characters. Kale is a humpback whale researcher based in Hawaii. Jeff and Reb Saunders are veterans of the Iraq War who have learned how to fly a WW-ll vintage Mitchell B25 bomber. Andreas is a German-Canadian bush pilot and environmentalist who hates the resource extraction companies he serves.

Thryke cloaks the Fahr ship to make it invisible on its journey from Jupiter to the Earth.

Act Five: The Extraction

Thryke shows Agastin and Teracia the weapons he has stored on board the ship. Teracia objects to one weapon in particular, the Xburner, and Agastin forbids its use without prior permission.

Now certain that Humanity faces mortal danger, Teracia tries to warn them by sending a message on the old Pioneer 10 frequency.

Diane believes that the Fahr are on their way to the Earth. When her superior has a nervous breakdown, it forces her into being NASA's primary contact with the media.

Andreas makes his way to Abbottsford to join the crew of the B-25. In the meantime, Reb finds ammunition for the bomber's guns before a scheduled stop at the Abbottsford Airshow.

The leaders of Russia, The US, The UK, China and France attempt a press conference to explain their interaction with the Fahr, but protesters shut them down. They then try to take their concerns to the United Nations but forming a world government to deal with the Fahr is ridiculed and rejected. The evidence for the existence of the Fahr has disappeared.

An amateur astronomer witnesses something pass between the Earth and Mars. A few days later a woman in the Australian Outback takes a video of a dark rectangular object passing in front of the moon.

While giving a press conference Diane is interrupted by two pieces of news. The first is that Teracia's warning about impending war has been noticed on the Pioneer 10 frequency and second is Australian outback video showing the Fahr ship silhouetted against the moon.

Thryke orchestrates the simultaneous destruction of all satellites orbiting the Earth and then detonates intelligent electromagnetic pulses in twelve locations around the planet.

Diane and the rest of the staff at NASA notice that all the satellites they're tracking disappear. Then the power goes out. Soon they also realize that any device with a circuit board or chip is useless.

The leaders of Russia, China, Great Britain, France and the USA are on a conference call to each other discussing the sudden appearance of the Fahr ship when all their lines go dead, and the power goes out. President Alatorre realizes that some kind of EMP device has been deployed.

Commander Agastin orders the ship's descent to the Earth's surface. Thryke, ignoring Agastin's previous instructions, launches the Xburner.

Jeff, Reb and Andreas are at the Abbotsford Air show with the B-25 when the Australian Outback Video appears on the airport monitors. They take off in the B-25. They soon discover that they are the only aircraft flying and that there is mass destruction on the ground. The Fahr ship appears overhead and they give chase.

Kale is in a Zodiac studying humpback whales off the coast of Haida Gwaii. A series of events trap him in the boat without power, paddles or any means of communication. Then he sees a dark form descending over the coastal mountains.

Thryke in the Xburner confronts the B-25. Wanting a challenge, Thryke gives the B-25 a chance. Reb shoots him down.

The Fahr ship goes to the collection point off the coast of Haida Gwaii and begins the process of drawing the whales and several cubic miles of the Pacific Ocean environment into the ship's containment area.

Jeff sees the Fahr ship pulling water into the hold and concludes that attacking the ship at that point of vulnerability is the best course of action. When they try the Fahr ship defends itself by generating powerful sound waves that cause the B-25 to break apart.

Kale and his boat are sucked into the Fahr ships containment area along with the whales.

Appendix B

A brief discussion of Fahr physiology, history and

culture.

Physical Appearance

A Fahr is best described as large fish, about the size of a beluga whale but with scales, fins, and gills. The gill slits are large and flank a small circular mouth in the lower third of the head. This head connects at a right angle to a discernible neck, making the creature's natural posture upright rather than horizontal. The brain is over twice that of any comparably sized cetacean, with an enlarged neocortex making up most of that difference. Fahr eyes resemble those of a predatory mammal, forward facing with a wide field of view. Above these is an inflatable bladder which expands from and contracts into a concave forehead. The Fahr have two retractable limbs, half way in appearance between an elephant trunk and an octopus tentacle, except each ends with four opposable digits. The final obvious feature is a large oval diaphragm on the lower abdomen. This feature functions alternately as an ear, a vibrating surface for creating sound, and when engorged as an organ of pleasurable stimulation. The rest of the body is fish-like, accept that the fins are adapted to keeping the creature upright rather than horizontal. As a result, the Fahr are slow swimmers.

There is one other important feature, an almond-shaped pad a few inches below the neck. Its color and texture blend in with the scales around it but the feature is non-organic, a digital memory archiving device allowing the fahr to store memories externally. The necessity for such a device will become apparent, but for now it is enough to know gaining access to the contents of one of these is the principle reason we know what we do about this alien race.

What follows is from this Fahr digital memory archive.

The Modificates

Sexuality in the epochs before genetic manipulation was an intoxicant, giving rise to violence, destructive competitiveness, social upheaval, and war. To ensure survival of the species, the Fahr genetically engineered their own species away from sexuality and took reproduction into the lab creating an exclusively male population in the process. This became known as the First Modificate.

For a while, Fahr society became more stable and peaceful, and then the leadership noticed productivity and innovation slowing. Soon a great lethargy had set in. A few generations later the suicides began, and within a millennium the Fahr population was less than half the pre-modificate numbers. The geneticists set to work again. They reintroduced arousal not as a response to sexuality but to song. This became known as the Second Modificate. The Fahr had genetically re-engineered themselves to receive intense physical pleasure and intoxication from songs, songs they themselves could not produce. Instead, the songs were sung by carefully regulated pets.

Over time, this gave rise to a third problem. The Aquafar stellar system, where the original Fahr home world was located, had three planets on which life had evolved, but this still limited the number of singers. The Fahr population became bored with these. To find more singers, interstellar travel would be necessary, but this idea was fraught with problems. Chief among them was the length of time necessary for such journeys. The solution was the Third Modificate, a massive increase in Fahr life expectancy. Through a series of genetic changes, timed stasis interventions, and digital memory archiving, they increased the average Fahr lifespan to seventy millennia.

Religion

Early in their history, the Fahr had gone through a series of religious ideas, moving from early animistic tribal beliefs to various forms of monotheism. These too received widespread rejection in the Fahr population as scientific atheism took hold. For much of the middle period of Fahr history, atheism ruled supreme until its own rigidly dogmatic scientific approach encountered a problem: the DNA molecule. Every life-supporting planet they found had it, or the viral RNA form. These were universal and little conclusive evidence existed for their independent evolution on any one planet. These complex molecules seemed to have arrived on each world intact and ready to adapt to whatever environment they found themselves in. The Fahr concluded something or someone was seeding DNA on a galactic scale. They called this entity the Giver of the Double Strand, usually shortened to The Giver. Over time, a succession of mono-occupational mystics developed religious codes around the central idea that DNA driven evolution itself was sacred. These codes became a sacred text called "The Will of the Giver".

The Archiving of Fahr Memories

Keeping a member of their species alive for upwards of seventy millennia involved more than just the artificial lengthening of life spans. No amount of genetic reprogramming and stasis reconstruction could produce a brain capable of storing seventy millennia of worth of memories. They found that four millennia was the upper limit and when this limit was reached, the Fahr brain began an irreversible deterioration leading to dementia and cognitive death.

The solution lay in introducing a personal digital memory (PDM), a hyper-efficient memory archiving system involving a neurological/digital interface and almost unlimited storage. PDMs stored memories in one-millennium chunks, usually referred to as "occupations" because of the Fahr tendency to focus on specific skills sets for that length of time. When Fahr brain capacity approached its limit, a stasis intervention occurred, removing the oldest adult occupation from active memory and placing it in this archive. With an older fahr, this meant up to ninety percent of his accumulated memory was stored in his PDM. Access to these memories involved initiating a digital download through which the older memories, one occupation at a time, transferred back into active memory. For this to happen, however, a quarter of the brain synapses had to lay fallow to allow room for such downloads. This gave rise to a situation where younger fahr, those not yet old enough to need a PDM, had a higher mental capacity than their elders did.

Stasis

Once in every 150 years, each fahr enters stasis, equivalent in time to their active state. During stasis their bodies are rebuilt. The Fahr referred to entering stasis as "going down" and emerging from it as "surfacing." Stasis is used to repair, replace, and rejuvenate bodily structures, all while allowing a natural but slow aging to occur. Older fahr were, therefore, healthy but less robust than their younger counterparts. Eventually, this process becomes less effective, resulting in an average life span of about seventy millennia. As in the human population, life-style choices play a role in individual longevity.

The Display of Emotion

The Fahr have two primary non-verbal means of displaying emotion and these work in tandem. The first is a set of gill slits flanking each side of the mouth. They use these organs for much more than breathing. Each gill slit has individual muscle control, which allows flattening, standing erect, quivering, pulsating, and waving. Each of these elements, when used alone or in combination with the ballow and diaphragm, can communicate an infinite variety of emotions. The simplest of these is gill rippling, the intensity of which can display anything from the human equivalent of a subtle smile to a huge laugh. Continuous gill rippling is usually a sign of intense pleasure. The flattening of gills slits is the Fahr equivalent of a frown.

The ballow, an inflatable bladder in the concave forehead of the Fahr is a much more complex organ. It can display a broad pallet of colors and textures, often several at once and in infinite pattern combinations. Each of these colors and combinations have meanings understood by other Fahr. They can be and often are displays of emotion, but they can also be status displays, allowing their fellow fahr to know their station in life. Red is the color of anger and, depending on its intensity, can mean anything from mild irritation (pink) to rage (deep red with the ballow inflated). Inflation of the ballow is an intensifier of the status or emotion. An inflated gold ballow shows not emotion but high rank. An inflated purple ballow indicates extreme embarrassment or humility and is often interpreted as an apology. A rippling cascade of rainbow colors is a sign the individual fahr has lost control of his ballow and is in a state of extreme intoxication.

Here is a partial list of color meanings in the Fahr ballow. Beige is neutral and most fahr try to maintain this in day-to-day interaction. Green is similar except it adds the element of confidence and self-assurance to the person displaying it. Blue shows a state of well-being or joy. Yellow is fear. Gray is depression or sorrow.

Usually a ballow display will be accompanied by some gill movement to add layers of subtlety to the emotion expressed. Diaphragm vibrations and tentacle movements also contribute. Reaching out and touching a fellow fahr's gill slits is a sign of great affection.

Appendix C

Fahr Trilogy Characters

Within this list, a primary character is one that plays a significant ongoing role in one or more of the books. A secondary character is still important, but it appears less frequently. A tertiary character may be significant in one or two scenes but does not reappear. Incidental characters are not listed here.

These names are arranged alphabetically, using the last name where applicable. As of this writing, "The Will of the Giver" is still under construction so more characters will be added to this list at a later date.

The List

Chancellor Agastin: (Fahr). Agastin is the fahr equivalent of a constitutional monarch on the Fahr home world of Centrix. He is also an elite Fahr, bio-engineered to be resistant to the intoxicating effects of song. Later he takes command of the second expedition to Earth. He is a primary character in "Planet Song" and a secondary character in both "Alpha Tribe" and "The Will of the Giver."

Maria Alatorre: (Human) Alatorre is the first Hispanic president of the United States. She a primary character in "Planet Song" and "Alpha Tribe."

Sadr al-sharia al-Bukhai: (Human) Sadr al-sharia al-Bukhai is a 14th century Persian astrologer notable only because he is the first human to see the Fahr ship in orbit above the Earth. He's a tertiary character in "Planet Song."

Baronth: (Fahr) Baronth is the Chief Navigational Officer on board the Fahr interstellar spacecraft transporting Song Corp's pet collecting expedition to the Earth. He is a primary character in "Planet Song" and has a secondary role in both "Alpha Tribe" and "The Will of the Giver."

High Priest Barracute: (Fahr) Barracute is the conservative leader of the Fahr religion and absolute authority in all matters pertaining to the religious text "The Will of the Giver." When the Chancellor is in stasis, Barracute also assumes the position of head of state. He is the genetic father of Occeane. He is a secondary character in both "Planet Song" and in "The Will of the Giver."

Billy: (Human) Billy is a scientist/technician at NASA's Deep Space Network in Goldstone California. He dresses Goth. He is a secondary character in both "Planet Song" and "Alpha Tribe.

Cynthia Chen: (Human) Chen is a marine biologist doing post doc research at the University of British Columbia. She is a primary character in "Alpha Tribe"

Ahanna Chopra: (Human) Chopra is a neurologist with the practice in San Diego and later at MIT. She is a primary character in "Alpha Tribe."

General Comry: (Human) Comry is in charge of the Presidential Emergency Operation Center beneath the White House. He is a tertiary character in "Alpha Tribe".

Corporal Connelly: (Human) Connelly is the leader of a small band of soldiers that find Jake Punster in the forest. He's a tertiary character in "Alpha Tribe".

Brother Cornelius: (Human) Brother Cornelius is a monk and religious scribe living and working the 14th century Italian monastery. He is the first human to come in contact with Fahr technology. He is a tertiary character in "Planet Song."

Charlie Dayaang: (Human) Charlie is a young man from the Haida First Nation on Haida Gwaii. He is a primary character in "Alpha Tribe."

George Dayaang: (Human) George is Charlie's father and a Haida elder. He is a tertiary character in "Alpha Tribe."

Derath: (Fahr) Derath is the young sapient species expert on board the Fahr ship during the first expedition to the Earth. He later becomes a research assistant to Occeane. He is a primary character in "Planet Song" and a secondary character in both "Alpha Tribe" and "The Will of the Giver."

Professor Donaldson: (Human) Donaldson is an AI and computer specialist at MIT. He is a primary character in "Alpha Tribe".

Albert Einstein: (Human) Einstein appears in a scene where Edwin Hubble shows him the Andromeda galaxy. He is a tertiary character in "Planet Song".

Roderick Evans: (Human) a retired Airforce Major and Korean War vet who accompanies Jeff and Reb when they fly the vintage B-25. He is a tertiary character in "Planet Song".

Patriot's Fan: (Human) Leader of the New England anti-government militia. He is a tertiary character in "Alpha Tribe".

Bruin's Fan: (Human) Second in command the New England anti-government militia. He is a tertiary character in "Alpha Tribe".

Sergeant Feinstein: (Human) Feinstein is part of a contingent of soldiers assigned to guard McLean and Proctor during their train journey across the US. He is a tertiary character in "Alpha Tribe".

Constable Fisk: (Human) Fisk is an RCMP constable stationed in Massett on Haida Gwaii. He is a secondary character in "Alpha Tribe".

Constable Frank: (Human) Frank is the senior constable in the RCMP station in Prince Rupert, BC. He is a secondary character in "Alpha Tribe".

Frederick: (Human) Frederick is 14th century German man whose family falls victim to the black plague. He is a tertiary character from "Planet Song".

Galileo: (Human) The famous scientist appears in one scene where he is exposed to Fahr technology while working on his telescope. He is a tertiary character.

Gerald Garneau: (Human) Garneau is Alatorre's Chief of Staff. He in a tertiary character in "Planet Song" and a primary character in "Alpha Tribe."

Thomas Gardener: (Human) Thomas is a whale prospector. He is a tertiary character in "Planet Song".

Lord Greyling: (Fahr) Graying is the aging CEO of Song Corp, the largest of the Fahr pet collecting corporations. He is a primary character in "Planet Song" and a secondary character in "Alpha Tribe".

Vitaly Gulubev: (Human) Gulubev is the Russian President. He is a secondary character in "Planet Song".

Jeffery Harrison: (Human) Harrison is the British Prime Minister. He is a secondary character in "Planet Song".

Eva Hastings: (Human) Peter Howard's lab assistant at MIT. She is a tertiary character in "Alpha Tribe".

Doctor Hinton: (Human) Hinton is a marine biologist based at the University of British Columbia. He is a secondary character in "Alpha Tribe".

Peter Howard: (Human) Howard is geneticist working out of John Hopkins University. He is a primary character in "Alpha Tribe".

Sonya Howard: (Human) Sonya is Peter Howard's wife. She is a secondary character in "Alpha Tribe".

Tracy Howard: (Human) Tracy is Peter Howard's teenage daughter. She is a secondary character in "Alpha Tribe".

Edwin Hubble: (Human) Hubble appears in a scene where he shows Albert Einstein the Andromeda galaxy. He is a tertiary character in "Planet Song".

Andreas Huber: (Human) Andreas is a German bush pilot and environmentalist working in the Canadian north. He is a primary character in both "Planet Song" and "Alpha Tribe."

Zhao Hui: (Human) Zhao Hui is the Chinese President. He is a secondary character in "Planet Song".

Iekika: (Human) Iekika is a 14th Century Hawaiian shaman, most notable because he is the ancestor of Kale. He is tertiary character in "Planet Song."

Simon Jefferies: (Human) Jefferies in a researcher under Peter Howard at John Hopkins University. He is a tertiary character in "Alpha Tribe".

Ben Johnston: (Human) Johnston is the forestry worker in Fort Nelson who sells Andreas Huber his truck. He is a tertiary character in "Planet Song".

Honi Kalawai'a: (Human) Honi is a cousin of Kale and a quadriplegic who undergoes an amazing transformation. She is a secondary character in "Planet Song" and a primary character in both "Alpha Tribe" and "The Will of the Giver."

Kale Kalawai'a: (Human) Kale is an aboriginal Hawaiian marine biologist, a humpback whale song expert. He is a primary character in all three books of the Fahr trilogy.

Peni Kalawai'a: (Human) Honi's father. He is a secondary character in "Alpha Tribe".

Noelani Kalawai'a: (Human) Honi's mother. She is a secondary character in "Alpha Tribe".

André Lambert: (Human) Lambert is the French President. He is a secondary character in "Planet Song".

Margaret Mavors: (Human) Secretary of Homeland Security in the Alatorre government. She is a tertiary character in "Alpha Tribe".

Diane McLean: (Human) Diane is a senior scientist at NASA's Deep Space Network in Goldstone California. She is later promoted to head of that facility. She is a primary character in both "Planet Song" and "Alpha Tribe."

Mikala: (Human) Mikala in Kale's uncle and Honi's great uncle. He works as a deck hand on Kale's boat. He is a tertiary character in "Planet Song".

Niko: (Human) Niko is part of a Baltimore street gang. He is a tertiary character in "Alpha Tribe".

Daniel Nylander: (Human) Daniel is the head of the Keck Observatory in Hawaii. He is a tertiary character in "Planet Song".

Occeane: (Fahr) Occeane is the heir to the High Priest Barracute and is an elite level Fahr He is Teracia's closest friend and love interest but is hampered by his asexuality. He is a secondary character in both "Planet Song" and "Alpha Tribe", but a primary character in "The Will of the Giver."

Jamie O'Hara: (Human) O'Hara is the Canada Post rep that recruits Andreas. He's a tertiary character in "Alpha Tribe."

Pierce O'Malley: (Human) O'Malley is the Canadian Prime Minister. He is a tertiary character in "Planet Song" and a secondary character in "Alpha Tribe".

Joe Pender: (Human) Pender is the prison guard assigned to Andreas Huber. He's a tertiary character in "Alpha Tribe."

Petar: (Fahr) Petar is the heir to Agastin and is an elite level fahr. He becomes Chancellor when his father steps down. There are mentions of him in both "Planet Song" and "Alpha Tribe" but he does not become a secondary character until "The Will of the Giver."

D.A. Philips: (Human) Philips is Diane McLean's precursor as head of NASA's Deep Space Network in Goldstone California. He is a secondary character in "Planet Song".

Vera Pollock: (Human) Vera is the main support staff person at the RCMP station in Prince Rupert, BC. She is a secondary character in "Alpha Tribe".

Clement Price: (Human) Clement is in charge of a group of workers salvaging parts from ruined rail cars. He's a tertiary character in "Alpha Tribe".

Trent Proctor: (Human) Trent is a scientist/technician at NASA's Deep Space Network in Goldstone California. He is a primary character in both "Planet Song" and "Alpha Tribe."

Prostallen: (Fahr) Prostallen is the Commander of the Song Corp expedition to the Earth. He later becomes an advisor on the second journey to the earth. He is a primary character in "Planet Song" and a secondary character in "Alpha Tribe."

Ka Pua: (Human) Ka Pua is a distant cousin of Kale and Honi, and a nurse. She in a tertiary character in "Planet Song" and a secondary character in "Alpha Tribe".

Jake Punster: (Human) Jake is a sniper and part of an anti-government militia. He is a primary character in "Alpha Tribe".

General Rice: (Human) Rice in the general in charge of Fort Irwin. He is a tertiary character in "Alpha Tribe".

Roont: (Fahr) Roont is a member of the Centrix constabulary, but later becomes a communications officer during the second expedition. He is a primary character in "Planet Song" and a secondary character in "The Will of the Giver."

Robby Saunders: (Human) Saunders appears as a draft dodger in "Planet Song" and later as trumpeter in "Alpha Tribe". He is also the father of Reb and Jeff. He is a tertiary character in "Planet Song" and a secondary character in "Alpha Tribe."

Angela Saunders: (Human) Angela is the wife of Robby Saunders and mother to Reb and Jeff. She is a tertiary character in "Planet Song".

Jeff Saunders: (Human) Jeff is the oldest son of Robby and Angela Saunders. He's a pilot and Iran War veteran. He is a secondary character in "Planet Song".

Reb Saunders: (Human) Reb is the youngest son of Robby and Angela Saunders. He's an Iran War marine veteran with PTSD. He is a secondary character in "Planet Song".

Captain Siebold: (Human) Siebold is the commanding officer of the small military contingent that guards President Alatorre. He's a tertiary character in "Alpha Tribe".

Lord Spargill: (Fahr) Spargill is the ex-CEO of Song Corp. He exists only as a phantom within a quantum computer. He is a tertiary character in "Alpha Tribe".

Benjamin Stofi: (Human) Stofi is the Bernard M. Oliver Chair for SETI. He is a secondary character in "Planet Song".

Teracia: (Fahr) Teracia owns her existence to a mistake in the Fahr reproductivity labs, one of only fourteen females in a population of 25,000,000 males. Her primary motivation is the protection of alien sapient species, those threatened by Fahr pet collecting expeditions. She is a primary character and appears in all three books of The Fahr Trilogy.

Abe Thompson: (Human) Thompson is the commander of an anti-government militia. He is a secondary character in "Alpha Tribe".

Defense Minister Thryke: (Fahr) Thryke is the head of the Fahr military, an aspect of the Fahr government that has little to do.

He is a primary character in "Planet Song" and a secondary character in both "Alpha Tribe" and "The Will of the Giver".

Tommy: (Human) Tommy is part of a Baltimore street gang. He is a tertiary character in "Alpha Tribe".

Leonardo Da Vinci: (Human) The famous artist and inventor appears in a short scene that hints at where he got some of his mechanical ideas. He is a tertiary character in "Planet Song".

Whispering Willy: (Human) Willy is an eighty-year old Airforce vet who accompanies Jeff and Reb when they fly the vintage B-25. He is a tertiary character in "Planet Song".

Wrasse: (Fahr) Wrasse is the Fahr Minister of Pets in Fahr government. He later becomes the CEO of Song Corp. He is a secondary character in all three books of the Fahr Trilogy.

Xyros: (Fahr) Xyros appears first in "Planet Song" as a Junior Navigational Officer and later as a botanist in "Alpha Tribe". He is a secondary character in both "Planet Song" and "Alpha Tribe."

Yarm: (Fahr) Yarm is Agastin's personal assistant during the second expedition. He is a secondary character in "Planet Song".

Acknowledgements

Cover Design: Ben Baldwin. Editors: Adrienne Kerr and Jennifer Laface. Beta Readers: Jacques Spilka, Lou Sytsma, Cheyne Allen, Annie McKitrick, Bill Cook and Nicole Luiken. Formatting consultant: Trish Argell-Smtih. Writers Groups: The Cult of Pain and The Western Word Slingers.

About the Author

T.K. Boomer lives in Sherwood Park Alberta, Canada with his wife. He has a degree in theatre and has had several stage plays produced. In 2014 he published a mainstream fiction novel, "A Walk in the Thai Sun", written under the name G.J.C. McKitrick. Over the years he has been a professional musician, a song writer, a puppet-eer, and a mailman. He has always been a fan of science fiction and, on his retirement in 2012, decided he would devote his remaining days to the writing of it. "Planet Song" was published in 2016, "Alpha Tribe" in 2018 and "The Will of the Giver" should make an appearance in late 2019. Collectively these are known as "The Fahr Trilogy". He has chosen to self-publish, despite the interest of tradi-tional publishers, because of the freedom it affords him.

Visit his website at tkboomer.com.

www.ingramcontent.com/pod-product-compliance
Lightning Source LLC
Chambersburg PA
CBHW030638260626
47157CB00007B/2381